The Dark Side Of Mother Moon

Bob Goddard

Timbuktu Publishing

Copyright:

British Library Cataloguing in Publication Data available.
Originally Published by**: Timbuktu Publishing**
Stables Bungalow, Mill Reach, Buxton, Norwich, NR10 5EJ
www.timbuktu-publishing.co.uk
ISBN 978-0-9563518-4-5 – Amazon Edition
Copyright © Bob Goddard 2018

Design and layout by Zesty Design
www.zestydesign.co.uk
Back cover photograph by Robert Reeves
http://www.robertreeves.com/
Map artwork by J I Rogers
www.mythspinnerstudios.com/

Table of Contents:

Map:

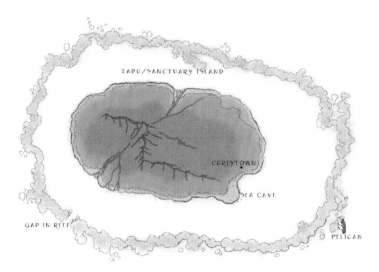

N

TAPU/SANCTUARY ISLAND

CHRISTOWN

SEA CAVE

GAP IN REEF

PELICAN

CRABBING SEA

Dedication:

This book is dedicated to the memory of Robert Hutchings Goddard, who actually knew a thing or two about rocket science

Prologue:

Publisher's note: This book is intended to be a worthy successor to the highly-acclaimed novel 'Mother Moon'. While this sequel can be read and enjoyed as a stand-alone story, we strongly recommend you read Mother Moon first. It can be purchased in paperback direct from the publisher at a discount.

Visit: www.timbuktu-publishing.co.uk/orders.html

Mother Moon can also be found on Ebay, or on Amazon as a paperback or kindle ebook. Search for 'Mother Moon by Bob Goddard.'

"See the Earth below – what magic, what mystery,
what tragedy does she hold?
But... what promise awaits us there?"

Chapter 1
Back From The Dead
Earth 1504

The wave chased a ribbon of foam up the beach to swirl around the boy's bare feet. Sitting with his head between his knees, arms wrapped protectively, he didn't flinch as the water soaked his ragged trousers. Only his chest moved, heaving with the effort of tears that dripped onto the white coral sand.

"Stay here, Mammed." The bedraggled sailor squeezed the lad's shoulder, then picked up a wooden paddle and turned towards the clear blue water. "I'll try to get us something from the boat."

It had been the worst day in Benyamin the Navigator's many years at sea. What had started with such hope in the dead of night had ended in disaster on this bright afternoon. In this idyllic coral lagoon, beneath the sun-sparkled water, his best friend Captain Yonaton – Mammed's father – had been dragged down to his death by a thing out of legend.

"Sea devil!" Benyamin hissed the words through his teeth as he surveyed their heads bobbing in the water, watching his every move. "Who'd have believed it..?" He shook his head and stepped warily into the waves, eyes focussed on the nearest creature, some sort of merman, which was treading water only a boat's length from the shore.

"Back!" He swung the paddle menacingly. "Get back, you demon!" He slapped the paddle on the water with a crack, sending a shower of spray towards the beast. If he could scare it off for a minute or two he might have time to retrieve their supplies from beneath the upturned vessel.

He slapped the water with the paddle again. "Get away, you beast!" But the creature drew closer and made odd gargling noises. It appeared to be pulling another one behind it.

Then the second one turned its head and croaked, "Ben! It's me! I'm alive!"

Mammed was instantly on his feet and screaming. "Papa Yon! Papa Yon! You *are* alive!" He ran down the sandy slope and into the sea, ignoring the strange being in his rush to embrace his father.

"Ess, ess. Nowee sayfee," the creature gurgled, as it retreated to deeper water.

Ben was cautious but followed to help Yonaton to his feet. Apart from a lump on his forehead where he'd hit the mast, the Captain looked healthy enough. Before he left the sea, Yonaton turned and gestured towards the creature who had returned him to the shore. "He saved my life! He saved my life and I don't even know his name."

"His *name!*" Ben stared at the grinning merman. "These things have *names*?"

"Ess, ess. My namee Alexee, chief of Seaple." He raised a webbed hand and indicated the other creatures whose heads bobbed at the surface of the lagoon behind him.

"I'm Yonaton," replied the dripping captain. "This is Ben, and this..." he ruffled the curly hair of the lad whose shoulders he was hugging, "this is my brave son, Mammed."

"I don't believe this," Ben muttered under his breath. "We're talking to monsters!"

"Not monsters, Ben." Yonaton was shaking his head. "They're people, like us, but they live in the sea."

"So..." Mammed looked at his father. "They're sea people, or Seaple for short?"

"Yes – Seaple" Yonaton smiled through his bedraggled beard. "They have some interesting stories too. For one, they believe we all came from the same place on a ship called the Ark."

He turned to Ben and smiled. "And you'll never guess where they think we came from..."

Moon 3660

Ktrina pressed her hot forehead against the cool plass of the sportdome and gazed at the long black shadows streaking the surface outside. Despite the distortion, she could make out the construction team erecting the new solar collector on the crater rim in the distance. The vast disc glistened in the harsh horizontal sunlight in stark contrast to the black sky beyond Sokolova City. The solar collector would be a bone of contention when she returned to the north next week, a reminder her vacation was almost over. The rigours of diplomacy with the Coops shadowed her thoughts like an eclipse.

Shouts and squeals behind her confirmed Ktrina's three children were still chasing the moball while she took a breather from their favourite game. Screeches from the flock of parakeets that swooped through the old recreation hall suggested her sons' shots were improving. They needed to if the ever-hungry boys were to meet her challenge. All five birds had to be downed before they stopped for their picnic lunch, she'd told them, and so far only one lay on the floor, legs twitching comically.

They hadn't hit any of the previous flock and in frustration she'd dispatched them on her own, in a demonstration of agility and deflection targeting. But the exertion had temporarily overwhelmed the thermolibrium of her skinsuit. She was pleased to leave the boys to it while she cooled down by the dome's water-filled plass wall. A squawk followed by a cheer announced the demise of another bird. Maybe they would get lunch after all.

She was turning to congratulate them when a flash outside caught her eye and she swung back in time to witness the distant disc sway and topple. It appeared to fall in slow motion as tiny helmeted figures ran from beneath it. As the dust settled she felt sure that some of the workers had not escaped the crashing tower and its giant array of collecting dishes. Her brain clicked: *Terrorist attack!*

"Comm-call," she said quietly, so as not to alert her sons to the drama unfolding beyond the transparent wall. A two-tone beep in her ear confirmed the channel was open. She named the recipient: "Rescue service, Sok City, Port 19."

Ktrina was answered by the calm, sing-song tones of a voicebot. "Port 19 Rescue. Call logged from Ambassador Ktrina Rozek. What is the problem please?"

"Collapse of collection disc and tower on Nobile Crater. Potential casualties among construction crew. May need urgent medevac. Immediate response required."

"Surface rescue and medevac extraction initiated. Thank you, Ambassador."

"Comm-close," Ktrina said, then turned to face her sons. The youngest two were still scampering noisily after the moball, hoping to hit it towards the remaining three birds, but 12-year-old Paul had stopped and was staring at his mother.

Ktrina smiled reassuringly and clapped her hands twice as she strode to the centre of the sportdome. The three flying parakeets and the two twitching on the floor vanished, as did the moball and the racquets in the hands of the boys chasing it.

"Aww... Mum!" Grig was first to realise who had interrupted their favourite game.

"Mu-uum!" wailed the youngest, Jan. "I had 'em all lined up then. I could have got all three with my next shot."

"Of course you could, darling. And in a moment you will be able to prove it. But I must pop out to attend to something for a few minutes. You three can continue until I get back – perhaps something a little less barbaric when you finish this one, like tennis perhaps? And then we'll stop for lunch."

She turned to the oldest, the gangly, blond-haired Paul. "You are in charge, Paul. No-one is to leave the dome until I return, understand?" He nodded silently, his eyes full of questions.

"Just a few minutes, and I'll be back." She moved towards the exit, clapped her hands and three hologram parakeets swooped into view with a screech.

Earth 1504

"Go on then, surprise me." Ben stopped, waist deep in the sea, and smiled at his miraculously-alive captain. "Seems it's the day for surprises. So where do these, um… sea people, think we came from?"

"From the Moon, Ben. They believe we all came from the Moon."

Ben's lopsided grin vanished. "The *Moon!* Have they gone mad?"

"Ess, ess, vrom Moonee." Alexee, the merman, chief of the Seaple, was now pointing skywards and nodding vigorously.

"Huh!" Ben turned and started wading ashore. "You may be alive, Yonny, my friend. But if you believe this Moon nonsense, you've lost your mind. Come on, let's get you out of these wet clothes before you catch your death." He took hold of Yonaton's elbow. "Help me, Mammed. Your father's had a very bad time. He needs to rest."

Yonaton was too exhausted to argue. Halfway up the beach he sank to his knees then sat on the white sand. Ben and Mammed tugged the sodden calfskin jacket off his shoulders and the late afternoon sun turned the white hairs on his chest golden. All the while he kept his eyes fixed on the lagoon where Alexee was now surrounded by dozens of his fellow sea people. They appeared to be listening intently as their chief's warbling voice carried across the waves.

These were not a few sea-dwelling misfits, he realised, but a whole new species of people, with their own language, culture and history. It was where that history departed from his own that intrigued Yonaton the most. There were so many questions that needed answers.

"I don't understand it, Yonny." Ben interrupted his thoughts. "You cracked your head on the mast, then that... that creature took you. You were under the water for so long – how did you survive?"

"I was inside a cave, Ben." Yonaton pointed at the ridge of rock that ran down into the sea a short distance away. "The entrance is underwater. There's a freshwater stream inside. And what they say is the remains of their ship – our ship – the Ark."

"Are you serious?"

"You can go see for yourself. Alexee will take you."

"You must be kidding! I thought he had dragged you off to drown…"

"I was already drowned, Ben. Funny thing… I was so far gone I thought he was Esther, come to take me to the other side." Yonaton shook his head slowly at the memory. "But he blew into my mouth and somehow got me breathing again. I woke up inside a cave. Took me a while to get my bearings, but I wasn't dreaming, Ben. There really *is* something in there… you'll have to see it."

"Well, nobody's going back in the water today," said Ben, firmly. "You're shaking from the cold. Or shock, maybe. We need to get a fire lit. It will be dark in a couple of hours. And I need to see if there is any food left in the boat." He looked towards the half-submerged hulls of their capsized catamaran, drifting gently in the surf.

"I can light a fire, Ben." Mammed scampered up the beach to collect driftwood.

"Do you think there's anyone still alive out there?" Yonaton was pointing to the reef, where the sea still crashed and thundered. Above the spume was the tip of the Pelican's mast tilted at an unnatural angle.

"Nothing we can do for them if there is, Yonny. You saw what it was like. It's a miracle we weren't *all* drowned… or smashed to pieces on the corals."

Benyamin started back down the beach watching the Seaple chattering excitedly and laughing in the lagoon. Halfway to the water he reached a decision and dropped the paddle. Walking into the waves he tried to lift one bow of the log-canoe catamaran before giving up with a grunt. He took a deep breath and plunged his head under the water instead, but there was no sign of the small barrel that contained the remains of their food. Remembering it had been stowed at the stern, he waded into deeper water and was about to duck below the surface again when a young female face appeared at the end of the boat.

Ben stopped and stared, still not convinced these creatures meant him no harm.

She smiled and said: "Can I help you, sir? You look for something…?"

Her voice unsettled him. It had the same throaty tremble as Alexee, the chief, but her words were clear and distinct. And sweet, just like any young girl from his home town, Loming.

"I… um… thank you. I'm looking for a small barrel. It contains our food."

13

"Baa-rel?" She frowned.

"It's a wooden container…," he held his hands apart, "about this big."

"I will see." She smiled again and slid gracefully under the water.

Ben turned his crooked grin towards the shore to see if Yonaton and Mammed had seen his encounter with this pretty young mermaid. But the captain and his son were deep in conversation and focussed on a plume of smoke rising from sticks piled on the sand. He turned back in time to see the girl's blond hair and freckled forehead emerge, followed by pale blue eyes and a broad white smile.

"Is this baa-rel?" She had a small barrel in her hands.

"Oh, yes!" Ben returned her grin as he took it. "Er… no, actually this is the water barrel, but we need this too."

"I will look again." She disappeared beneath the hull.

Thinking he might direct her, Ben ducked his own head under the water and almost sucked in a lungful of it when he saw her lithe form moving sinuously towards the far canoe.

He emerged spluttering. "My God! She is stark naked!"

Moon 3660

A short corridor connected the Sportdome with the city Ringway buried deep within the towering rim of Amundsen Crater which contained Sokolova City. Ktrina turned left towards Port 19. Commuters flashed past on the belt, but with a little under a kilometre to the port it was quicker to run along the tree-lined boulevard. She leaned forward and put her athletic legs to good use.

Two minutes later, breathless and flushed, Ktrina arrived in the port waiting room which smelled of coffee and freshly-baked croissants. A mining crew, surface suited with helmet visors raised, broke into smiles at the sight of her skinsuit. She ignored their attention and made straight for the port office.

"Ah, Ambassador Rozek." The plump officer looked up from her screen. "I was expecting you. Heard your call to the port rescue service. What a terrible accident out there!"

Ktrina's nod was non-committal. "We will see. What is the status of the rescue… Hana?" she asked, reading her name badge.

The woman shifted in her chair to allow access to her screen. "I'm not sure how many are hurt," she said.

Ktrina's long fingers skimmed the screen to zoom the image out so she could take in the whole scene, then in to focus on the activity beside a bright orange vehicle. She counted three pressure bags, the first being slid inside the ambulance, plus two limping figures being helped on board.

"Looks like five being medevac'd. I need to go find out what happened." She turned to the officer. "Can you log me through the first available airlock. I'll go get suited. Thanks."

She jogged to the row of cubicles on the far side of the waiting room. The miners had gone, the air tunnel entrance door lit red as they boarded the transport waiting outside. Ktrina selected a pair of boots, slipped her feet inside and pressed their buttons. With a pop their linings inflated to lock her feet snugly inside. Then she picked a helmet from the rack, checked it was fully charged and placed it over her head. The attached backpack and front console lay snug over her skinsuit, their weight reassuring. She stepped into the nearest cubicle, placed her feet on the sole-shaped marks and said: "fabricate surface suit."

"Confirm identity." That sing-song voice again.

"Ktrina Rozek."

"Confirmed. Port transit permission granted. Raise arms please, elbows at shoulder height, hands forward, thumbs upward, fingers apart."

Ktrina was scanned from head to toe by a bright band of light.

"Keep very still please."

Mechanical arms extended from the cubicle walls. With a hiss the suit fabricator sprayed a fine gauze over Ktrina's body, leaving the helmet, backpack and front console clear. Then with a buzz the main materials were applied in a series of layers, sprayed on and then set instantly by a bright purple light. In less than a minute Ktrina was encapsulated, the process almost complete.

"Close and seal helmet visor please."

Ktrina clipped the visor down and took a breath of synthetic air.

"Testing integrity, thermal and life support systems. Please remain still."

She felt the newly-formed suit start to cycle through its safety and function analyses. It tightened and expanded and sent shivers of cold up her spine. She was impatient to get out there, check the damaged structure and collect witness statements, but she knew there was no sense in getting twitchy. If she didn't keep still for the systems checks, they would start over and delay her further. Ktrina consoled herself with the knowledge that these latest suit-fab units, installed only last year, were much quicker and more reliable than their predecessors. How people had the patience to struggle into the clumsy old pre-built suits they used in the north, she couldn't imagine.

"Systems check complete. Suit cleared for surface transfer. Thank you, Ktrina Rozek. You may now leave the cubicle."

She was about to thank the voice-bot, a silly habit she'd never been able to shake, when the port officer's rich tones sounded in her ear. "Ambassador Rozek? When you are ready, please use airlock two. There are three sleds and two buggies outside ready to go, so take your pick. And good luck out there."

Ktrina's head-up display, projected on the inside of her visor, showed a faint image of the port officer's face in the top right corner, with her name below. "Thank you, Hana. Can I ask you a favour?"

"Of course. What can I do for you?"

"Could you keep an eye on my three boys? I left them playing moball in the old sportdome. I told them I'd be a few minutes and I'm guessing that was a little optimistic..." Ktrina stepped into the airlock.

"No problem. I've got the sportdome cam up now... Hah! Parakeets! I used to love that game when I was a kid. Want me to speak with them too?"

"Only if they get bored with the birds and start on each other instead."

"Got it. If they get fractious I'll let them know they are being watched and their mother will get a full report."

"Thanks, Hana. I'll be as quick as I can."

That was the boys sorted, but there was something else troubling Ktrina. Something she couldn't quite put her finger on...

Earth 1504

"Well, what did you expect?" Yonaton squinted up at Benyamin who stood dripping in the evening sun, with a barrel under each arm. "I don't suppose they have underwater looms, weaving fabrics out of seaweed. Why would they need clothing? It would hinder their movement through the water."

"I was shocked, that's all." Ben shrugged his shoulders. "Sweet little thing she is. Called Miriam, and she's the daughter of Alexee, the chief."

He set the water barrel down on the sand, then put the other on top and started tugging at its wooden lid with his fingernails.

"You'll like her, Mammed." He turned to the teenager who was poking the fire with a stick, trying to appear disinterested.

"Why?" The word ended in a squeak.

"She's about your age and very pretty. I wish I'd met a mermaid when I was sixteen." He grinned and winked at Yonaton, who didn't respond.

Mammed got to his feet, looking at no-one, and threw his stick into the fire. "Need more wood," he mumbled as he wandered off towards the trees at the top of the beach.

"Go easy on him, Ben," said Yonaton. "He's been through a lot and his emotions are scrambled. Remember what it felt like being sixteen?"

"Yeah, you're right. I'm just jealous. A teenage mermaid and I'm too old even to look!"

"You're too old? I'm fifty-seven, Ben, and I've got more important issues to deal with in the few years I might have left."

"What are you talking about, Yonny? With your ability to come back from the dead you'll outlive us all."

"I was just thinking about what Alexee was telling me. What if he's right, and we did all come from the Moon?"

"Ha! Still not recovered from that bump on the head then?"

"Just wait until you see that ship, Ben. It's not like anything I've seen before. And they have a written record of their history. And... guess how long ago they say we all arrived here?"

"I don't know... two hundred years?" Ben raised his arms in an elaborate shrug.

"One thousand, five hundred and four years ago, Ben."

"But that's—"

"The start of time. Exactly my point. It makes you think, doesn't it? And what – according to our crackpot Cardinal – happened then?"

"We, um... crawled out of the sea?"

"Suppose we all arrived here in a ship called the Ark, and crashed over the reef into this very lagoon, just like we did today, Ben? How would we have arrived on dry land, eh?"

"Makes you think, certainly." Ben tugged at his wispy beard.

"That fat freak has been obliterating our history – we've seen him do it – and writing his own version to suit his religion for as long as we can remember."

"Yes, but *come on,* Yonny my friend. Even *his* ideas didn't include arriving here on a ship from the Moon. That Alexee fella's been chewing on the wrong kind of seaweed."

"Who's been chewing on seaweed?" Mammed dumped an armful of sticks on the sand.

"Your father has a theory, Mammed. We were just discussing it."

"Is this to do with the Seaple?" Mammed was looking towards the lagoon.

"It might be, Mammed," said Yonaton. "Why?"

"Because one of them is trying to get our attention."

The men turned to look. A girl was waving.

"Oh, that's Miriam." Ben waved back. "Looks like she's got something to show us." With her other hand the girl raised some sort of basket from the water. "Go see what she wants, Mammed."

"Why me?"

"Because your father needs to stay here next to the fire and get his strength back. And I'm trying to get the lid off this barrel, so we get something to eat. The wood's swollen with the seawater and jammed tight."

Mammed stood rooted to the spot.

"She won't bite, Mammed." Yonaton spoke softly. "Would you do me a favour and go see what she wants, please?"

The lad started to amble down the sandy slope, then thrust his hands into the pockets of his tattered trousers. He kicked nonchalantly at seashells on the way.

"I remember being a little more *keen* when I was sixteen, Yonny."

"He's shy, Ben. And you always were a randy old goat, even when you were young."

Ben cracked his trademark lopsided grin. "If you say so, Yonny my friend."

Moon 3660

Ktrina was still puzzling over what was bugging her as she detached the sled from the mains supply and checked its complement of spare air. The 10 one-hour packs it carried would provide for her and any overdue construction crew.

That's it! Why **are** *so many crew out there today?* She had counted five at the ambulance and there must have been a dozen more besides…

"Hana. Why were so many crew needed at the construction site today?"

"Oh, didn't you know, Ambassador Rozek? Today is the inauguration ceremony for the new solar collector disc. Only five are construction, the other fifteen are VIPs and dignitaries."

"Ah! Of course. I've been on vacation all week. It slipped my mind." She threw her leg over the sled's seat, plugged her suit in to the sled's supply, and turned the twistgrip. The drive belt bit into the dusty regolith and the handlebars tugged Ktrina's shoulders forwards. She surged away from the port across the lunar surface, swerving to avoid the bigger rocks on the way. She could see that the bright orange ambulance had gone. It would be delivering casualties to the Sokwest emergency centre by now. But there were still three other vehicles parked on the upper slope. One of them, from the green and gold livery, looked like the President's personal hopper.

This high ridge was called Nobile, but was actually where the western rim of the vast, 105-kilometre-wide Amundsen crater overlaid the earlier, slightly smaller one of Nobile. Enormous impacts, billions of years ago, had left a prominent peak. Located so close to the south pole, it was ideal for a solar collector disc to gather energy throughout the lunar day and night. As she powered up the slope, Ktrina could see over her right shoulder the shapes of Sokolova City – a myriad of domes as far as the eye could see – all buried under a blanket of protective regolith. Only communication masts and observation bubbles protruded into the black sky, catching rays from the sun, now dazzling from the southern horizon.

It frustrated and saddened her that humans could build such a sophisticated city of three million souls, but couldn't prevent a terror attack – or the warped ideology that spawned it. She knew better than most the pain and loss it caused. Ethan's smiling face clouded her vision before she fought him back down into memory. These upper slopes of Nobile were littered with big rocks that demanded sharp concentration and a clear eye.

Especially at this speed. She was probably exceeding the recommended 50kph limit, and ought to keep her wits about her, or she'd be joining the casualties at Sokwest. Ktrina stole a glance at the upper left corner of her helmet visor. The head-up display was flashing 87 in red. She rolled off the throttle and took a deep breath in an attempt to calm down. It was difficult to pace herself when she felt so close to catching the vermin who had done this.

Another hopper dropped into view and settled beside the presidential one. Flashing blue lights meant civil defence patrol. She directed a comm-call to the vehicle, which responded instantly.

"Hello? This is Sergeant Malik, Police Response Unit, Sokwest Seven."

She saw two blue suits stepping out of the hopper's door. "Sergeant, this is Ktrina Rozek, approaching your position from Port 19."

"Ah, hello, Ambassador. Yes, I see you – just – the sun's a little bright. What brings you to this accident scene?"

"I saw it happen. I may be able to help, and I want to know the cause."

"We will make a thorough investigation, Ambassa—"

"Time is critical to catching those responsible, officer."

"Well, ma'am, acts of criminal negligence are usually best uncovered through careful—"

"I saw a flash, Sergeant, before the dish fell."

"Oh. Electrical fault, maybe?"

"No, A red flash…"

"Laser? Shit! Oh, excuse me, Ambassador. That would be bad. Very, very bad."

Earth 1504

"Miriam gave us some fish." Mammed held up a woven bag full of wriggling silver shapes.

"Well, that's good news because..." Ben tipped the barrel and a white slurry poured out on to the sand, "the water got in and spoiled the last of our bread and biscuits. The cheese might still be edible though..." He unwrapped a cloth to reveal an unappetising yellow lump.

"She wants her basket back. Says it has to stay in the water or it dries out, or something."

"Here, Mammed, let me see that," said Yonaton, reaching for the soft brown creel. "Looks like it's made from kelp… yes, it is. And with a drawstring too. It's the finest woven basket I've ever seen. Beautiful craftsmanship."

"I can put the fish in the empty barrel," said Benyamin. "Then Mammed can take it back to her. I can see why she wouldn't want it to dry out. It's a work of art."

"She also said she'll bring us more fish for breakfast, but could we take them some fruit in return?"

"Fruit? We don't have any, Mammed." Ben's forehead furrowed.

The frizzy-haired teenager pointed towards the trees. "There's plenty, she says. They find it difficult to get because they don't walk too well."

"Okay, go and see what you can find then." Ben handed the emptied kelp basket back to him. "But be quick and take care not to damage this, it must have taken days to make."

While Mammed was foraging amongst the trees, Benyamin dragged a couple of washed up logs to the fire to act as cooking supports, then went in search of a banana leaf to wrap the fish in.

Left on his own, Yonaton turned his attention back to the Seaple who seemed to be dipping under the water and then showing their backs at the surface in a curious fashion. With a start he realised these weren't the backs of people – they were dolphins, swimming amongst them. He stood up and stared at the spectacle. And then he heard it. Clicks and whistles from the dolphins being answered with grunts and groans from the Seaple…

"What is it, Yonny?" Benyamin tucked the rolled-up banana leaf into the barrel and dropped a couple of coconuts on the sand. He shielded his eyes with his hand. In the low evening sun he couldn't make out what the captain was staring at out in the lagoon.

"Can you see, Ben? There are dolphins swimming among Alexee's people."

"Oh… yeah."

"And can you hear them, Ben? Those whistles and the groaning sounds?"

"Strange noises, that's for sure. What's going on, do you think?"

"I think they're talking to each other, Ben. The dolphins and the Seaple – yeah, I'm sure of it – they're talking to each other!"

"What are you staring at?" Mammed appeared beside them, his shirt held up, bulging with mangoes and pawpaw.

"Sshhh! Listen, Mammed." Yonaton put his arm around the boy's shoulders, and whispered. "Can you hear that? There are dolphins with the Seaple – and they're talking to each other."

The three of them stood in awed silence for a minute, then Yonaton suggested they walk down to the water with the fruit Mammed had collected. Ben followed a few paces behind. As their bare feet touched the sea, Miriam swam towards them with a beaming smile.

Yonaton called to her, "Mammed's brought you some fruit…"

"Thank you! Come and meet our friends… the Dolpheen."

Moon 3660

Ktrina brought her sled to a halt beside the police hopper with a smooth, sideways skid. To her left the top of the slope was covered with shattered remnants of the disc, its multiple collector dishes and tangled support gantry. One of the blue suited figures stepped forward as she unplugged from the machine and introduced himself with a handshake. "I'm Sergeant Malik, Ambassador."

She couldn't see past his visor's gold sunshield, but a handsome brown face appeared on her head up display with the words Jabu Malik, Police Sergeant. "If this was caused by a laser weapon, as you say, ma'am, then we need to find out where it came from."

"And fast, Sergeant, if we are to catch the perpetrators. Have you spoken to the construction team yet?"

"Yes, ma'am. Leif Trons, the chief engineer, is over there, looking for clues to the collapse." He pointed to three yellow suits picking their way through the debris field. "My colleague, Corporal Hersh, is interviewing the VIPs in the two hoppers behind us." He jerked his thumb over his shoulder.

"Was the President hurt?"

"No, ma'am. He hadn't left his vehicle when the disc fell, fortunately. But the head of the Energy Board and two ministers were being shown the powerhouse unit near the base of the tower. Five casualties, one of them critical I understand."

"Let's go see what Mr Trons has found," said Ktrina. Among the wreckage the three construction workers were bent over a part of the fallen tower. "Hop on the sled, Sergeant." She was already astride the machine and plugging in. With the policeman on the pillion, Ktrina drove around the scattered dishes and was approaching the engineers when her comm chimed and Hana appeared.

"Sorry to bother you, Ambassador, but I've just heard on the newsfeed there has been a similar incident in the north. Another solar collector. They're calling it a terrorist attack, possibly."

"Okay, thanks Hana. How are my boys?"

"Oh, they're fine. I spoke to them – made 'em jump," she giggled. "Now they know I'm keeping an eye on them for you, so they're on best behaviour."

"Thank you. I'll return as soon as I can."

Ktrina relayed the news from the north to Sergeant Malik as they stopped and dismounted the sled. The last ten metres were covered on foot, climbing over pieces of fallen gantry and stepping around the dozens of crumpled metre-wide dishes.

"This is it." Leif Trons pointed to a section of bent and twisted metalwork. "You can see where it's been sheared. It's made from steel-titanium alloy, so doesn't give up easily. A powerful laser is the only way to cut it like this."

"Any idea where the laser strike might have come from?" Ktrina was looking along the ridge for signs of movement but could see nothing.

"It came from above, Ambassador. From the melt pattern I'd say around fifty degrees and due north. Either a vehicle flying overhead or a satellite."

"Thank you, Mr Trons. Carry on here, Sergeant. I need to make a call." She stepped aside as she spoke to Sokwest skytraffic control. There had been no passenger vehicles, they said, but a satellite was overhead at the time of the laser strike. Its low polar orbit had taken it past the far side equator already and it would be approaching Cooper City in less than ten minutes.

Ktrina asked them to contact Cooper traffic control immediately with its coordinates, then she called Gunta Krems, Cooper's Foreign Minister. He thanked her, and confirmed they'd also lost a solar collector in a laser attack less than an hour ago. They would intercept the hostile satellite over Cooper skyspace, he assured her.

Chapter 2
Fishing For Clues
Earth 1504

Yonaton was lowering himself into a well, hand over hand down an endless rope, in the darkness. One slip and he'd fall to his death, but his arms were breaking, his grip was weakening, and he was struggling to breathe. Then the rope slithered from his fingers, he dropped like a stone and braced for the sickening crunch of bones.

Now he was running from a wooden monster whose jaws were crashing together right behind him, but his legs wouldn't work and he was struggling to breathe. He was tied to a raft and couldn't escape as the teeth reached over his head and descended with a watery roar.

He was suspended in a blue world of clicks and silence and sinuous shapes, unable to move a muscle, gulping for breath. Esther was coming for him. It was his time and she was close. He gasped for breath. Then a whiskered face said, "Nowee sayfee," and blew into his mouth a choking lungful of fish...

"Oh, God!" He woke, coughing and choking, trying to rid his throat of the fish. The air was full of smoke.

"Sorry, Yonny, my friend." Benyamin smiled through the haze. "I had to relight the fire and the wind blew smoke over you. Are you alright?"

"Yes!" He gasped and coughed again, rolling on to his knees in an attempt to stand up. His head pulsed with pain and when he raised his hand, he found his forehead distended with an egg-sized lump that throbbed at his touch. Beneath him was a tangle of palm leaves that had been their bedding for the night. The fire crackled and another gust of smoke blew into his face.

Yonaton shuffled on hands and knees into clear air, white sand and dazzling sunlight.

"You slept well, Yonny. I thought you would miss breakfast." Ben pointed to a row of small fish laid on a banana leaf beside the fire.

"No. Terrible dreams, Ben." He drew in deep draughts of clean air and tried to remember his nightmare. "Going down a rope, being chased and then drowning..."

"You were just reliving the fun times we had yesterday, Yonny."

"Oh...? Yes, maybe."

"Enough for a month of nightmares. But we are all alive – even you, who spent more time under water than a fish." Ben laughed.

"Oh, God. Don't mention fish."

"But Miriam has brought us more for breakfast. And Mammed has taken her some fruit…" he twisted to look over his shoulder, "and he seems a bit less shy this morning."

Yonaton looked to the lagoon, where Mammed was waist-deep in the sea, talking to the girl they'd met the previous evening. There was something about her… she reminded Yonaton of his daughter, Lucy. Not so much in looks, as her confident way of talking, her certainty of knowing the truth.

"He is lucky she is the one with the language." Ben's lopsided grin was back. "They could have sent one of the old crones to talk to us."

"I'm hoping she can answer a few questions today, Ben." Yonaton was watching the exchange between the two youngsters in the water. "And help us talk to Alexee about raising the Pelican."

"You think we can *rescue* the ship from the reef?" Ben looked surprised.

"We have to." Yonaton looked at their battered log-canoe catamaran, now righted and pulled up on the sand at the water's edge. "There's no way I'm sailing for home in that death-trap."

"I don't fancy our chances back out on the reef, trying to refloat the Pelican in those waves, Yonny." Ben was shaking his head.

"That's why I want to talk to Alexee, see if he has any ideas. You may think he's crazy, Ben, but he knows the sea better than we do. He even talks to dolphins!"

"Here comes Mammed. Looking very pleased with himself…" Ben grinned and winked at Yonaton.

"No teasing, Ben. We should encourage him, not put him off."

The captain raised his voice, "Good morning, Mammed. How are you today?"

"I'm fine, Papa Yon. And Miriam is going to show me the Ark after breakfast."

"Excellent." Yon looked pointedly toward Ben. "Perhaps you can find out where it really came from." He turned back to Mammed and said, "It's great that she can speak our language so well… a lot easier to understand than her father."

"Miriam is taking over as Guardian of Language from her grandmother. That's why she can speak like we do. She says she can show me their writings – the record of their history – too."

"Well, that would be most interesting, Mammed. See what you can learn."

"And perhaps you can fill our water barrel," said Ben, "if there's a fresh water stream inside that cave, like your father says. We've only got a mouthful each left."

"I can get some us green coconuts. We can drink the water from those." Mammed pointed to a nearby tree that curved out and upwards over the water.

"Okay, Mammed," said Yonaton, "but be careful. We don't want any more injuries." He pointed to his own forehead.

The lad, whose climbing abilities had enabled Yonaton and Ben to escape from Loming's harbour tower, scampered to the tree and walked up the first part of the trunk before hitching himself up with hands and feet as its curve steepened. Near the top he stopped and called out: "Hey! Miriam! I'm up here."

From the lagoon came a short shriek, then, "Maa-med! What are you *doing*?"

"Getting green coconuts. Do you want one?"

"What? No! Come down, you will fall."

"No I won't... look!" He gripped the trunk with his knees and waved both hands.

Another shriek.

"Here... catch!" A fat green shape fell into the sea with a splash.

Benyamin, who had been watching this with Yonaton, said, "They've probably never had a green coconut. If they can't walk on land, they won't be able to climb trees. I'd better go and tell her how to cut the top off... if their coral knives are up to the job."

"Let Mammed show her how to do it, Ben. He still has his pocketknife, unlike some people who lost theirs..." Yonaton's salt 'n' pepper beard cracked apart to show white teeth.

"Hey, that's not fair. You're not the only one who fell in the lagoon. It must have dropped out of the sheath."

"Maybe Alexee can find it for you?"

"Huh! Well, I'm not asking him. He gives me the creeps with his, 'ess, ess, vrom Moonee!' nonsense." Ben's imitation of the chief's gargling speech made Yonaton laugh.

"You didn't find it too difficult to talk to his daughter..."

"That's different. I still don't trust them. We were taught they were sea devils for a reason, Yonny."

"Myth and superstition, Ben. I bet nobody's seen them in years."

Moon 3660

Ktrina tucked her long legs beneath her and luxuriated in the slinky feel of her synsilk kimono. The spicy tang of the chocolate chai that Sofi had made was soothing away the stresses of the day.

"I don't see why *you* had to go out there, Ktrina." Sofi was gently chiding her daughter along with the pampering. "Lunatic terrorists on the loose with laser weapons... no place for a single mother of three young boys. Why couldn't you have left the emergency services to deal with it?"

"I told you, Mum. I saw the red flash. There was a chance we might catch them, at last."

"A chance you might have got yourself killed, like that poor mister Brandstock. What are we going to do without a Minister for Industry?" The evening news had been dominated by the attack, the casualties and the minister who had succumbed to his injuries. The Coops had suffered only one casualty, but he was in a critical condition, according to their report. As usual, the blame had been laid squarely on the Freedom League Of Cooper, the rebel band known universally as the FLOC.

"All the more reason to try to catch these people in the act, Mother. Maybe get some justice for Ethan... finally." Ktrina stared into the steam rising from her cup.

"Oh, I know dear... but you mustn't take such risks. Think about the boys. You are away so much as it is. What would they do if they lost their mother too?"

"There was no terrorist within a thousand kilometres, Mum. The cowards skulk in their tunnels and send a satellite to do their dirty work." She frowned. "What I *can't* figure out, is why...?"

"Why do these psychopaths do anything, Ktrina? Their heads are stuffed full of religious nonsense, with nothing but hatred in their hearts. Honest, innocent people aren't safe to go about their lives—"

"But they had to have a reason, Mother. Why attack our solar collectors, here and in the north? What did they stand to gain by it? These new collectors help us extract metals from the regolith, but that doesn't threaten *them*, hidden away in their lava tubes, does it? I really don't get it."

"Could it have been someone other than the FLOC, dear?"

"What... like aliens or something?" Ktrina laughed. "I think we've established there are no little green men here on the Moon, Mum!"

"That's right, *mock* your mother. I'm only here to bring up your children while you go *gallivanting* off to the north. Here to run your bath, make your chai—"

A wail from the playroom cut Sofi short. She hurried off to see what the boys were up to. Ktrina sighed, put down her cup, and followed.

Earth 1504

"Ess, ess… I lookee." The chief of the Seaple turned away, eager to start the search for Ben's missing sheath knife, but Yonaton called him back.

"Before you go, Alexee, can I ask you something?" Yonaton looked over his shoulder at Ben, who was watching from the water's edge. "Before we arrived yesterday, when was the last time you saw landsmen?"

"Thirtee thee years, annee halfee." He smiled and nodded.

"Thirty-three and a half years?"

"Ess, ess. Tuwee laansmaans. Boatee sailee."

"Two landsmen, in a sailing boat? Where did they come from?"

"Crossee Caribeenee…" The merman pointed his webbed hand to the south.

"Caribeenee? You mean, from across the Crabbing Sea?"

"Crabinee… Caribeenee, iss samee."

Yonaton turned and called to Benyamin. "You hear that, Ben? They have the same name for our sea – just sounds a bit different."

Ben reluctantly waded towards them. "But does he know who they were… which town they came from?"

"Ess, ess," nodded Alexee, "tuwee laansmaans fromee Lomee."

"From Loming?" Yonaton felt the hairs on his neck rising. "Are you sure?"

"Ess, ess. Onee oldee – likee Yonee." He reached and tapped Yonaton's chest. "Onee youngee… and fatee!" He blew out his cheeks and held his webbed hand in front of his stomach.

"Do you remember their names?"

"Ess, ess. Writee Histree." He pointed towards the rocky outcrop that contained the cave where Miriam had taken Mammed to see the Ark. The merman smiled and stroked the stiff whiskers protruding sideways from his top lip.

"Oldee namee Frankee Fishermee."

"Fisherman Frank! Are you sure?"

"Ess, ess. Frankee Fishermee. Anee youngee namee Henree."

"Good God!" Yonaton turned and looked Ben in the eye. "Fisherman Frank and a fat young man called Henry. You know who that is, don't you…?"

"Yes, Yonny, my friend. That's our *beloved,* recently-departed, Cardinal. No doubt about it."

Moon 3660

"Grandma, what happened to our daddy?" Jan, the youngest, was in the bath while Sofi soaped his curly blond locks.

"Ethan, your father, was a very brave man. He was in the Rangers, Jan, on border patrol. I'm sure I've told you this before…?"

"Tell me again, Grandma."

"Well, he was on patrol in the Aristarchus region, not too far from the rebel hideout. The terrorists hide in the lava tubes there."

"What happened?"

"He was conducting a routine survey for illegal activity when he saw a flashing light."

"Was it one of the rebels, Grandma?"

"Yes, a young man desperate to escape from the madmen of the FLOC. He was signalling with a mirror, reflecting the sunlight to get attention and send a message."

"How could he send a message that way, Grandma?"

"Your clever father had learned Morse code – a very ancient method of sending words with dots and dashes. He read the signal – 'Help. Need to escape. Have vital intel' – and told his partner he was going to investigate on foot."

"Didn't he think it might be a trap?"

"There was always that risk, Jan. But your father decided he had to try to help this young man to escape, and perhaps gain vital secrets about the FLOC. Ethan's partner stayed in the Ranger's hopper, hidden in a crater, maintaining radio silence while your father went to meet the man.

"Half an hour later they appeared at the lip of the crater, just two hundred metres from the hopper, where they were cut down by fire from the rebel base. Instead of going to rescue them, your father's partner panicked and fled. By the time a military response team returned, your father and the young rebel were dead."

Jan sighed. "I didn't know him, did I Grandma?"

"No, Jan. You were only a baby. Even your older brothers didn't get to know your father properly. Paul was only four—"

"And Grig was two."

"That's right. You *do* know this story, don't you, Jan?"

"I like to hear it again, Grandma. My daddy was very brave, wasn't he?"

"Yes, just like your mother. Now come on, it's past your bedtime young man." She turned on the spray to rinse his head, making him squeal and splutter. "Time to get out and get dried. School in the morning."

Earth 1504

Mammed took one last gulp of air before Miriam pulled him under the water. Yonaton had taught him to swim five years ago. It was one of his first lessons after joining the crew of the Pelican and being adopted into the captain's family. But no swimming lesson had prepared him for this.

The water streamed past them as Miriam's lithe body moved sinuously ahead of him in a seemingly effortless ripple, his wrist gripped firmly in her long webbed fingers. Apart from her webbed feet and hands, there seemed little difference between Miriam and the girls from home, although he'd never seen any without clothes before. She seemed completely unaware of her nakedness and he tried hard not to stare. He'd left his shirt on the beach, but the thought of leaving his ragged trousers there had made his face burn.

Bright rays of sunlight followed them down to the entrance of the cave where they were enveloped by cooler, darker water as they travelled horizontally into the secret world beyond. Just when he thought his lungs would burst, Mammed's head broke the surface and he gasped a shuddering breath in the gloomy air of the cave.

Miriam was laughing at him. "That was short, Maa-med! I teach you to breathe, then we go bottom of lagoon."

"No thanks!" He coughed and smiled as he trod water.

"You climb trees, Maa-med. Much more danger."

"Oh, I'm used to climbing. Trees, walls, cliffs – it's easy."

"For me impossible." Miriam shook her head. "But water is easy."

Mammed tried to make out the cave walls but could see only a shaft of sunlight beaming down from a hole in the cave roof. It was illuminating a large cylindrical green shape protruding from the water at a shallow angle in the distance.

"What's that?" He nodded towards it.

"It is the Ark. Come. I show you." She offered her hand to take his wrist once again and he shivered at her cool, delicate touch.

"It's huge!" Mammed looked up in awe at the smooth rounded side of the Ark as he stood in knee-deep water on a rocky shelf. Close up he could see it was covered in a fine layer of algae. He scraped a little off with his thumbnail to reveal a translucent surface beneath. "What's it made of?"

"Plass. Special material they make on the Moon."

"So… you think this came from the Moon too, do you?"

"Of course! You not believe, Maa-med?" Miriam's eyes widened in surprise.

"Well it seems so… unlikely… don't you think? How could a ship sail from the *Moon*?" He laughed. "And this doesn't look like any ship I've ever seen. It's like some giant round tube."

"This is inside of Ark. For people to travel in. Outside was metal that rotted away. You know it's been here for one thousand, five hundred and four years?"

"What? Since the start of time…?"

"Only since we arrived here. Before here we were on the Moon. Before the Moon, we were here on Earth… before the comet came." Miriam smiled, but Mammed was frowning deeply.

"That's crazy!" Mammed wrinkled his nose. He tapped the Ark. "Do you know what's inside?"

"Remains of pilot, Chris. He was Christakis Niarchos, the man who saved all colonists when the ship crashed in the lagoon."

"Kris? Our Cardinal said he was the Son of God."

"No. He was one of the hundred colonists who came from the Moon. He was very clever pilot and very brave. Released all the pods and saved all the people, but he was trapped when the Ark sank."

"How do you know all this?"

"It is written in our Histree. Stay here Maa-med, I show you." With that she slipped under the water and was gone.

Mammed was left leaning against the great green cylinder Miriam called the Ark. He wondered what he would do if she never returned. Would he be trapped in here for ever? Or might he climb up to the hole in the cave roof where the sunlight streamed in? It would mean hanging by his fingernails as he edged out, high over the water. Judging by the smooth cave wall he could see behind the Ark, it would be an impossible task.

A rippling sound drew his eyes back to the water, where Miriam was approaching. It looked like she'd brought a curved shield with her, but as she drew closer he could see it had the same translucent appearance as the wall of the Ark he'd uncovered beneath the algae.

"Can you take it please, Maa-med?"

He crouched at the edge of the rocky ledge as she pushed the glassy object in his direction.

"Careful," she said. "It is oldest Histree. Must not make scratch."

To Mammed's amazement, more and more of the curved material rose from the water. It appeared to be taller than him. And now, in the sunlight, he could make out lines of squiggles across its surface.

"Can you read it, Maa-med?"

He tilted his head to read down the first column of letters, but could make no sense of the shapes. "I don't understand it, sorry."

"Bring it lower," said Miriam. "I read it for you."

Moon 3660

"Good morning, Ktrina. How was the holiday?" The Foreign Minister's private secretary, Ella, was always pleased to see Ktrina turn up early for briefings.

"Too short, but good fun, thanks. Having the boys to keep entertained means never a dull moment." Ktrina smiled, then inhaled deeply. "Hmm, is that coffee I smell brewing?"

"Yes, a fresh pot." Ella waved at the plass jug of black liquid. "Help yourself. So… did you go anywhere exciting?"

"Oh, let's see… Water World for a whole day. The boys almost turned into fish. The Amazon Rain Forest Park, where we became native Amazonians and slept in a tree house—"

"Wonderful!"

"And best of all, The Armstrong Base Experience."

"Oh, that is *so* good, Ktrina. It's been years since I last went there. How our ancestors ever survived in such primitive conditions, I'll never know."

"They've added some new attractions too. We did the Will and Lian Run, all the way around the perimeter. We toured the original Biosphere tubes and visited a replica of the accommodation block they called the Ghetto – amazing how they slept in those tiny cupboards."

"And did you eat in the Lunar Lunchbox?"

"Yes, we did. I had the Nadia Sokolova breakfast – blini and cold cuts – so I can say I've eaten the same food as our Mother Moon." Ktrina wrinkled her nose. "But I have to say, I didn't think much to it.

"We also had a tour of the Cavern, the old workshops inside Malapert Mountain. They've even got the original plass plant running again, just for five minutes every hour. The incredible blue light from that ancient machine is dazzling, even with the face masks we had to wear. Makes you realise what an easy life we have today—"

"Ah, Ambassador Rozek!" Foreign Minister Jorg Lanimovskiy appeared at his door with a smile. "I thought I heard your voice, Ktrina. Good holiday?"

"Yes, I was just telling Ella about taking the boys to The Armstrong Base Experience."

"Very good. Well, you will have to finish your chat later. There have been some developments I need to brief you about before you head off to Cooper City."

Earth 1504

Miriam gave a little cough, then began reading from the great translucent panel she called their Histree. To Mammed's amazement she had turned the columns of squiggles horizontal, and read them from left to right. "This is the written record of the first people to reach the Earth following the devastation of Comet Santos. It is one year ago that a hundred of us who left the Moon in the Ark landed here, on 11th November 2156. Today's date is therefore 11th November 2157, but we have agreed to celebrate our arrival here by calling this year one."

"What is 'Comet Santos'?" Mammed's brow was furrowed.

"Oh! Don't you know? It was a giant iceball from space, Maamed. It hit Earth twice – in 2087 and 2088 – and it killed everybody. Only the Moon colony survived. Two hundred and ninety-seven people. We all descended from them."

Mammed's frown deepened. "We had a story, when I was little. But I thought it was… just a story."

"Tell me please."

"Umm… Satan changed his name to Santos to fool the people. He threw a great cloud over the Earth so the people wouldn't see his face, then he sprinkled poison-dust in the air and everybody got sick and died. Only the special people who worshipped the Moon survived."

Miriam smiled. "It is fairy story! Some parts are true. Shall I read more Histree?"

"Yes, please."

She cleared her throat. "All except one survived the crash landing in the lagoon of this unnamed island. Our leader and pilot, Christakis Niarchos, bravely freed all the passenger pods from the ship, but was trapped when the Ark sank in the deepest part of the lagoon. His sacrifice is remembered today with a memorial stone erected in the centre of the village we call Christown."

Mammed frowned again – he had seen no sign of a village or memorial stone – but he decided to let Miriam continue reading and ask questions later.

"Because the Ark sank before Chris could release the pods containing our solar panels and transmitting equipment, we have been unable to send any signal to the Moon. We fear that our families back home may be unaware that we landed successfully, far from our intended destination. We must assume that no help or further colonists will follow in the short term and therefore we are on our own on this beautiful but difficult planet.

"Despite extensive training we have all found Earth's gravity to be the biggest hurdle to overcome. Fourteen of us – eight women and six men – elected to stay in the sea to avoid the pain and injuries suffered by the other 85. One of them, Johnny Kapoor, suffered a broken leg after falling on day two and died from septicaemia three weeks later. The lack of any medical supplies has made treating even minor injuries very difficult. The medical and tool pods also sank with the Ark.

"Fortunately, the food, seeds and livestock pods were retrieved and with tools fashioned from stone, wood and coral we have been able to commence farming. The natural flora of the island includes few edible plants, a consequence of the massive tsunamis that swept the Caribbean seventy years ago when the first part of Santos plunged into the North Atlantic near the coast of Spain."

"Miriam, what is flora? And Spain?"

"Flora means all the plants, from grass to trees. Spain was a country far away from here. There is a chart of the world on another piece of Histree. I show you later."

"Okay. Please keep reading. This is amazing."

"The coconut palm grows everywhere along the coast and we are hopeful that our seedlings of papaya, mango and other fruits will provide for us in the future. Our cereals, lentils and legumes have been mostly successful in the small areas we have cleared of forest, but felling trees with stone tools is extremely laborious.

"The lagoon and surrounding seas have been more fruitful, with fish, crustaceans and seaweeds all providing vital foods for our growing community. Our first fish pen shows promise for aqua-farming.

"We have a good source of fresh water which flows through the lava tube terminating in a sea cave. This is convenient for us sea-dwellers who can swim into the cave, but less so for the land-based

35

group, who have to fetch their fresh water from a spring halfway up the mountain. There are plans to build an aqueduct to Christown."

"What's an aqueduct, Miriam?"

"I think… some tube to bring water down. The next part is most interesting, Maa-med…"

"Sorry for the questions. I want to understand everything, that's all…"

Miriam turned back to the Histree. "Before leaving the Moon, all fifty female colonists were implanted with an embryo. This was a plan to maximise the genetic diversity of our community—" Mammed's open mouth stopped her again. "I will answer your questions at the end, Maa-med. Let me finish!"

"Okay, sorry."

"This was a plan to maximise the genetic diversity of our community. What seemed like a good idea on the Moon turned out to be a serious mistake in the difficult conditions here on Earth. Only twenty seven of the fifty foetuses were carried to full term, and those caused great problems for the mothers who are still adapting to Earth gravity on land. Camilla Lim, one of our qualified doctors, died from complications following her long and difficult labour. Her still-born baby boy is buried with her in our graveyard, along with two more babies that did not survive to the end of our first year.

"By contrast, six of our eight sea-dwelling women gave birth to healthy babies and all are thriving in our aquatic domain. Our colony currently stands at 97 adults and 24 infants. We have learned some hard lessons in our first year of terrestrial life, but most of us are content with our wonderful and demanding new home. Contact with our families left behind on the Moon would complete our happiness. Plans to raise the Ark to retrieve our lost pods have been discussed. We currently lack the means to reach the ship.

"Our leader, Nicole Durand, works hard to keep our spirits up and encourages us to solve problems. She was unanimously voted to continue as Governor in an election held yesterday. This concludes my first annual report. Giulia Magrini, of the sea-dwellers of Christown."

Miriam turned to Mammed with shining eyes. "Is it not incredible what our ancestors had to do to survive those first months, Maa-med? No equipment or tools. Longing for a word from their families. Struggling to adapt on land and in the sea. And… if not for them, none of us would be here today."

Moon 3660

Ktrina stepped into the Foreign Minister's office and was met with a smile from General Ndrew Ferreira, Chief of Defence. The old soldier was as immaculately turned out as ever, his dark grey uniform pressed into knife-sharp creases, buttons glinting, and his white hair and moustache precision trimmed.

"Hello, Ambassador Rozek," he said as he delivered a firm handshake. "You are looking well after your vacation. How are the boys? Growing up fast, I imagine?"

"They're fine, thank you. They keep me on my toes, but I have my mother living with me now, so between us we keep them under control... most of the time." She smiled.

"They could join the Ranger Cadets, if discipline is a problem...?"

Ktrina knew he meant well, so fought to subdue the hot surge of anger. In a controlled voice she said, "Losing my husband was bad enough, thank you General. Preparing my sons for the same fate is not an option I'm willing to consider. At least, not until this vicious insurgency is dealt with. There are too many unknowns, too many hidden dangers, to put my boys in harm's way at present."

"Of course! Of course, I quite understand, Ambassador." He raised his hands in submission.

The FM intervened. "It is the insurgency that we want to talk to you about, Ktrina. We have a plan to stop the FLOC launching any more satellites, and to deal them a significant blow at the same time."

She raised her eyebrows. "Can you give me details?"

"We have established that the laser-gun orbital weapon was launched from here..." he gestured towards his office wall, which blinked and became a screen displaying a map of the Moon's nearside. Another gesture zoomed the image towards a flag symbol just above the equator. "... Aristarchus."

Ktrina stiffened. "Where Ethan died," she whispered.

"Yes. I'm sorry to stir up bad memories, Ktrina. We've been monitoring this area for the past year. There's evidence of regular activity around Lava Tube A14. The tunnel has a long straight run and the entrance points due south, so it's a natural launch site for a polar-orbiting satellite."

"Can we see inside?"

"Not since they installed these blast doors earlier this year..." the FM clicked his fingers and an image of a shadowy cave entrance appeared. He clicked again, and a light-enhanced view showed a solid rock-like wall inside.

"Those are *doors*?"

"Yes. We think they open them to make a launch, timed to coincide with our surveillance systems being out of range."

"Really? And how about the Coops?"

"They can't catch them with the doors open either."

"You mean... a bunch of rebels, who are barely scratching an existence in a few tunnels on the equator, know the orbital schedules of both our satellites and the Coops'? And can launch a laser weapon system undetected whenever they wish...?"

"Not too difficult, Ktrina. All our orbital hardware transmits a coded identifier—"

"As does the Coops', presumably?"

"Well, yes. It is essential to avoid... um... misunderstandings."

"So how come we didn't spot the FLOC's weapon and destroy it before it attacked us?"

"It transmitted the identifier of an existing Coop satellite when it overflew our skyspace, and a Sok identifier when it flew over Cooper City."

"The devious devils!"

"Quite. We were querying the presence of two satellites with the same signal when our solar collector was attacked. The Coops had been hit less than thirty minutes previously. Their first reaction was that we'd attacked them. And of course, *we* thought they'd attacked *us* until they said we'd both been suckered by false identity signals, and then hit, one after the other."

Ktrina was aghast. "So... now nobody knows who owns what up there? Or when the next supposedly friendly satellite will open fire on us?"

The General coughed. "Precisely why, Ambassador, we must prevent the FLOC launching any more."

"And that's where you come in, Ktrina," said the FM. "We want you to convey the details of our military response to my opposite number in the north. We understand they are planning some sort of retaliatory action too, so we don't want our forces tripping over each oth—"

"Why don't you brief him yourself, Minister? You must be in touch regularly, surely?"

"The nature of this recent attack has caused us to doubt the security of our communications, Ktrina. You will be meeting with Gunta Krems, Cooper's Foreign Minister, shortly after you arrive this afternoon. You will relay the details by word of mouth so there can be no question of interception. Then you will return here with an outline of their plans committed to memory. The only people who will know in advance are us three, their Foreign Minister and Daval Nakash, their High Priest, of course."

"*That* tattooed creep!"

"As you know, Ktrina, all matters of a military nature must be approved by their religious leader. I share your distaste for the man, but as our senior diplomat you will need to be—"

"Don't worry. I've been doing this job long enough to know how to hide my feelings. And keep well clear of his wandering hands. I shall be a model of tact and diplomacy. But one day, when I leave the service..." She made a sharp downwards motion with the edge of her hand. Both men gave a nervous smile.

Earth 1504

"I always thought that evil old devil, the Cardinal, was a fraud, and this proves it." Yonaton was sitting on a fallen tree trunk while Benyamin poked the remains of their fire.

"Proves it? How?"

"Thirty-three years ago you would have been – what – twelve years old, Ben? Perhaps you wouldn't remember. Our fat friend, Henry, sailed into Loming harbour in Frank's fishing boat... alone.

"He said Frank had taken him fishing, but they'd got caught in a storm and were blown far out to sea. At the height of the storm, old Frank had been swept overboard and Henry thought his time had come too. But then – according to his story – a light had shone out of the clouds and God spoke to him. God's son, Kris, he said, had saved mankind from a watery fate and we had all crawled out of the sea."

"That sounds familiar, Yonny. It's the basis of his religion."

"It all started, Ben, when he returned, after five days at sea, with Frank's boat but no Frank. Nobody in Loming had witnessed the storm, but he said it had been centred on *this* island, which was now taboo. God told him the inhabitants were all sea devils and anyone who approached the forbidden Tapu Island would be thrown to their death on the reefs and eaten by these evil creatures."

"So that's why nobody's been here since then!"

"Yes. A convenient way of preventing anyone finding out he'd actually spent three days here with Frank, talking to the Seaple and learning all their written history."

"But Alexee just told us that fat Henry and old Frank left together, sailing out through a gap in the reef on the far side of the island—"

"Only Frank could have sailed through the reef, Ben. Henry wasn't a sailor – it was his first fishing trip."

"So… if they both left here together, and there was no storm, what happened to Frank? After a lifetime at sea, he was hardly likely to fall overboard."

The two men looked at each other for a long moment.

"That explains," said Ben, "why he was so desperate to stop us reaching Tapu Island. So desperate, he drove the Pelican onto the reef."

"And drowned all his Convertors… and our crew." Yonaton buried his head in his hands. "Maybe we should have let him hang us, Ben. Then they'd all still be alive."

"And so would Henry, the fat old Cardinal, Yonny, my friend." Ben gripped the Captain's forearm. "With his murderous secret safe, he could continue to spread his warped religion and ruin people's lives. Do you think he would have stopped at us? You know he had a grudge against your daughter Lucy for running her free school."

Yonaton sighed and sat up. "You're right. It's good that he's gone. But we've paid a high price to rid ourselves of that evil old bas—"

"Look, Yonny!" Ben was pointing a smouldering stick towards the lagoon. "It looks like Alexee's found something."

Yonaton and Benyamin were back in the water, thanking the chief of the Seaple for finding Ben's knife, when Alexee held up his hand to silence them. He cocked his head, and slid under the water. Then they could hear it too – a faint cascade of buzzing clicks, squeaks and whistles.

"There, Yonny! Look!" Ben was pointing at the end of the rocky ridge that concealed the cave. Dark shapes were breaking the water. "Dolphins! They're swimming this way."

Yonaton counted five barrelling towards them, then a sixth leapt into the air and fell back with a splash. From the squeaks and whistles, it seemed they were excited about something. Alexee surfaced wearing a broad toothy grin.

"Boatee!" he said. "Five laansmaans."

"A boat! Where?" Yonaton scanned the horizon.

Alexee waved vaguely in the direction the dolphins had appeared from. There was no sign of a boat.

"Is it inside the reef?" Ben asked. "Or outside?"

"Insidee. Come soonee." Alexee beamed.

"It's inside the reef, Ben! Who could it be?"

"We'll find out soon enough, Yonny – look, there they are!"

Chapter 3

All Lives Are Precious
Moon 3660

The departure lounge at Sokolova's main skyport was quiet following the early morning rush. Mondays were less frantic than Friday afternoons, when thousands of commuting Coops made their way back home for the weekend. When it was not busy, Ktrina preferred to sit and people-watch in the public area. The VIP lounge was frequented by social climbers and sycophants eager to catch her eye, while the Denmark Diner's coffee and pastries were better and the folk there recognised her but respected her privacy.

Sunday's solar flare meant her flight was delayed, but Ktrina didn't mind too much. It gave her time to think though the details of the upcoming military action she had been briefed about in the FM's office. She reviewed her mixed emotions about the risks involved. She was angry about the recent attack and agreed it could not go unpunished, but Aristarchus had proved a particularly hazardous region for both Sok and Coop forces over the years. For a band of rebels, the FLOC had developed some sophisticated defences. She hoped the new cloaking technology that the General was planning to use for the first time would prove as effective as he claimed.

How had the FLOC managed to attract such talented converts, she wondered? It was only twelve years since the Freedom League Of Cooper had first emerged as an underground resistance to the repressive regime in the north. At first their secret society did little more than poke fun at their religious leaders and expose political corruption. They were an embarrassment to the Coopan government and raised the hackles of the High Priest, but gave no hint of the violence that would follow. Peaceful protest had been their motto until they moved to the Aristarchus Plateau three years later and declared an independent state. From that point on they had become militarised and increasingly aggressive.

The FLOC's stronghold was just north of the equator so the Coops had retaliated, but with limited success. The rebels occupied a maze of lava tubes and tunnels deep underground and had quickly developed high-tech surveillance systems and weaponry. Then they started attacking Sokolovan assets too, which was where Ethan came in. Ktrina took a deep breath and sat up straight as his handsome, smiling face filled her vision, just as it had that first day they'd met at Sokcity Athletics Hall. He was competing for the last time before starting his career in the Rangers, while she would go on to become Heptathlete World Champion for the next three years. Hers had become the famous face, but his smile would be forever etched in her memory.

She thought of the last time she'd seen him, looking relaxed and confident as he ate breakfast while she fed their two toddlers and nursed eight-week-old baby Jan. His routine patrol of the border just south of Aristarchus was tasked to observe, not engage. But when he'd spotted the flashing signal of a rebel trying to desert from the FLOC forces, he'd felt compelled to respond.

Eight years had dulled the pain, but done nothing to quell her rage at the circumstances surrounding his death. Ktrina shook her head as his smile faded and his lips moved. She felt her palms sweating as she imagined her husband's final minutes. According to the voice-log and his partner's report, Ethan was convinced the young man was bringing vital secrets, which was why he set out to meet him. Now they would never know. That knowledge, like the two men's blood, had leaked away leaving nothing more than a red stain on the dusty regolith.

What had happened to 'All Lives Are Precious', the famous motto of their inspirational founding governor, Nadia Sokolova? How had they lost her belief in the sanctity of life and ended up with this bitter struggle for power that left grieving wives and fatherless children? Of one thing she was sure – the Cooper regime of zero tolerance and religious piety was not quelling the insurgency, as they claimed. If anything, the rebels' actions had become more deadly and unpredictable in recent years.

As Ktrina's boarding gate was announced she shouldered her bag and headed once more for her diplomatic duty in the north. She prayed that the Foreign Minister and the General were right. Their new cloaking technology would make the Rangers invisible, they'd said, and no more precious lives needed to be lost.

Earth 1504

Mammed gasped as his head broke the surface. Miriam's breathing drill before they submerged had made the return from the cave to the lagoon less stressful, but his mind was still reeling from the Histree she had read out to him. Could it really be true that people had landed here all those years ago? Was it possible that they came in some kind of ship from the Moon? It seemed ridiculous, but why would anyone carve such a story on that weird sort of glass. And how did that huge tubular thing she called the Ark get there?

"Come, Maa-med," she said, tugging on his arm as she wriggled through the water. "Let's see who has arrived in a boat!"

"What boat?"

"Didn't you hear the Dolpheen? They have found five more landsmen in a boat. They have brought them to your Capteen Yon-ton. Look...!" She pointed across the waves and Mammed spotted the stern of a rowing boat and oars dipping into the water. With a jolt he realised it was their ship's boat – from the Pelican!

He tried to tell Miriam, but swallowed a mouthful of water as she pulled him through the waves, so he concentrated on breathing instead. By the time they reached the boat, it was at the shore and pandemonium had broken out. Dolphins had their smiling faces pushed above the water and were squealing with excitement, their sharp clicks and trilling whistles hurting his ears. There were dozens of Seaple bobbing in the shallows, all chattering in their strange gargling tongue, plus shouts of delight between Ben, Yonaton and the five in the boat.

As they stepped onto the sand the Pelican's four crewmen were greeted with smiles, handshakes and shoulder-slaps. Conor, the bosun, with his right hand heavily bandaged, was treated to a long hug from Yonaton.

"These are our crew," Mammed told Miriam as his feet found the sea bottom, "from the Pelican."

"What is Pelican?"

"Our ship, over there." He turned and pointed to the reef, where the ship's mast tip was still visible above the surf. "They escaped somehow. It's amazing!"

She smiled and let go of his hand. "Go Maa-med. Go speak with them. Tell me later."

As he waded towards the beach Mammed realised there was one left sitting in the boat. Wearing a short purple cape and a troubled expression, was Desmun, the Cardinal's favourite apprentice priest. Nobody was welcoming him.

"Can't believe you all survived," Conor was saying as Mammed reached them at the water's edge. "When that dirty great wave picked up your little boat we was sure you'd all be smashed to bits on the reef."

"Yeah, we thought so too," said Ben. "But it tossed us right over and into the lagoon. Apart from the Captain smacking his head on the mast and drowning..." he looked at Yonaton with a crooked smile, "we had a lucky escape."

"Drownin'?" The bosun looked puzzled.

"Oh, I was well drowned, Conor." Yonaton turned and pointed to Alexee, who was waiting with Miriam in the shallows. "But that fella there – Alexee, the Chief of the Seaple – he saved my life. Blew into my mouth and got me breathing again."

"Well, I'll be jiggered." Conor smiled. "Funny critters, ain't they? 'Elped us too, else we wouldn't be 'ere now."

"What happened to you then?"

"Well, after we 'it that coral 'ead, an' that wicked ol' bastard, the Cardinal, went tits up over the bows, we thought we'd soon be followin' 'im. Couple of his Convertors skittled over the side and went straight down, thanks to them dirty great boots they all wear."

"How many were on the Pelican, Conor?" Yonaton was frowning.

"Lessee now, he 'ad six of his Convertors an' all three bishops on board. Plus 'is fancy boy 'ere," He jerked his thumb at the youth sitting in the boat. "Plus us four, so that's fifteen I reckon."

"And what happened to the others?"

"As she tipped over, they got the Cardinal's long boat over the side and all jumped in it – all that was left of 'em, anyways. Three'd already gone to feed the fishes. But pretty much as soon as they set off, the waves took 'em. Didn't know how to 'andle it in them big seas. Lost an oar or two, then started fillin' wi' water. Next thing they was on the reef. Barely 'eard their screamin' over the roarin' surf. Couple o' minutes... we didn't 'ear 'em no more." He shook his head.

"So, how did you get away?"

"Ship's boat, being 'ung off the stern, was already in the water and bein' tossed around summat terrible. But we managed to get in and was just about to cast off, when that young rascal appeared." He nodded at Desmun. "Been skulkin' in the cabin, or 'e'd a been on the reef with the others. We got 'im in and set off, rowin' like our lives depended on it. Course, I wasn't much use on the oars, thanks to his lordship's partin' gift..." Conor held up his bandaged hand.

"That was for cutting the main halyard, I take it?"

"Yeah, 'e weren't too pleased with me stoppin' the Pelican from runnin' yer down. Could a been worse, though. When 'is Convertors 'ad me pinned down on the main 'atch, I thought 'e was gonna bash me 'ead in with that dirty great stick of 'is. Musta needed me for sailin' the ship, cause 'e smashed me 'and up instead."

"Sorry you had to suffer, but thanks for what you did, Conor. Dropping the mainsail like that definitely saved our lives."

"Yeah, well, anyways, like I said, I wasn't much use rowin' after that, so we set young Desmun on the fourth oar and told 'im to pull for 'is life. I steered between the waves and 'ollared me 'ead off." He laughed.

"Some'ow we managed to get away and around the lee side of the island, where it was a bit calmer. Couldn't see no way through the reef, though, and pretty soon it was gettin' dark. Nothin' for it but to stay where we was 'til dawn.

"When it started gettin' light, we was debatin' settin' off for the Frigate Bird Islands, which was downwind but got no water, or tryin' to 'ead across the waves to Portkaron. That woulda taken a couple o' days and been a tricky ol' passage in the rowin' boat."

"So, how did you get inside the reef, then?"

"Next thing we knows, there was these dolphins all around us, jumpin' an' splashin' and making a right ol' racket, clickin' and squealin' at us. Then, 'avin' got our attention, they all 'ead off towards the reef and we see 'em leapin' over somethin' and gettin' into the lagoon. We figures there must be a way through, so we follows 'em. Turns out there's a narrow gap, but it was blocked off with a barrier made out o' tree trunks.

"Then we sees a fella – one of these mermen critters – wavin' to us from inside the lagoon. Couple of 'em swam up an' moved the barrier so's we could row through. One of 'em told us there was more of us round 'ere, so we came to see… and 'ere we are!" He opened his arms and smiled.

"We're very pleased to see you," said Yonaton. "We thought you'd all gone down with the ship."

"So, 'ow did you and Ben escape from Lomin' Tower? You know 'e was plannin' to 'ang the pair o' you next day, don't you?"

"Yes, that thug, Gorbel, told us. Our escape was a miracle..." Yonaton smiled and put his arm around Mammed's shoulders, "a miracle performed by this young man. He climbed up the outside of the tower—"

"Bloody 'ell!"

"He brought us rope, and saws to cut through the bars."

"Clever lad!" Conor reached out with his good hand to ruffle Mammed's curly hair.

"Once we got out, we made our way to Crayfish Creek," Yonaton pointed to the log-canoe catamaran, "where that was waiting for us."

"'Ow come?"

"Mammed and my other two sons, Ifan and Jack, built it. The Cardinal had seized their fishing boat, the Petrel, and they knew we'd have to get away from Dominion or he'd track us down."

"Bloody 'ell! Settin' out to sea in a couple o' log canoes... in the middle o' the night! That takes some guts."

"We didn't have a choice, Conor. And we couldn't leave Mammed behind. The Cardinal would know it was him who got us out of the tower."

"Don't know 'ow it 'eld together in them seas, Cap'n. Somebody up there..." Conor raised his eyes to the sky, "must 'a been lookin' after you."

"Well, it wasn't *his* God, that's for sure!" Yonaton smiled.

"Nah. Good riddance to the ol' bugger. We'll all be a lot better off without 'im and 'is stupid bloody religion."

"We just have to deal with the rest of his Convertors – and that brute, Gorbel – when we get back to Loming."

"Ah... I don't know if I should tell you this, Cap'n...?" Conor looked at Yonaton with sad eyes and hesitated.

"Go on."

"Well, just before we set off, the Cardinal was givin' that Gorbel a right bollockin' and told 'im to go round up your family, and to 'old 'em 'til we got back. I 'ope they's all right, Cap'n..."

Silence descended on the group. Even the dolphins sensed the tension and were quiet.

Finally Yonaton spoke. "Then it's all the more urgent that we recover the Pelican from the reef and get her repaired so we can sail home."

Moon 3660

The Polar Carrier's ion drives sent a shudder through the passenger compartment as they eased the craft down to the lunar surface. Ktrina could see the red and white lights of Monterey, Cooper's commercial skyport, growing brighter through the cabin window and felt the usual tension in the pit of her stomach. She had made this flight more than a hundred times over the past three years, ever since Jan had been old enough for school and her mum could cope with the boys in her absence.

Despite the familiarity, she still felt uneasy about visiting the north. The people of Cooper were furtive and distrustful. They looked at her shoulder-length curls and southern business-wear as if she came from a different planet. Was it envy or contempt they felt, as they scurried past in their drab browns and greys, their hair clipped to the regulation five centimetres? She pitied them, living forever under the watchful eye of their Xinto monks. It was they, the Xintapo, who really unnerved her, standing menacingly on every street corner in their long black cloaks, stun-guns concealed up their sleeves. The dark, messianic symbols, tattooed all over their scrawny necks, repulsed her every time she saw them.

Ktrina made a point of ignoring the Xintapo as she left the terminal, striding past the huge video billboards, following the crowd heading for the tube. The urban landscape of Cooper was so different to Sokolova City. No commercial advertising was permitted here, but strategic walls were lit up with giant screen images of a beatific figure, the Messiah, who was due to return any day. "I'm Coming!" claimed the screen, as He appeared above the scurrying populace, descending His ladder from heaven. "Are You Ready?" demanded the banner. With his golden halo and billowing white robes, who could doubt that better times would soon be upon them?

Ktrina could. She had seen similar claims ever since her first visit, with no sign of better times or His actual arrival. So how did Daval Nakash maintain the public's belief? Why did the Coopan populace swallow it? She knew he was a powerful and charismatic speaker who fed the people what they craved for – a mixture of fear and hope. And he was an intimidating figure, who used his Xintapo to crush dissent and impose the faith. But she had more immediate matters to attend to, and Ktrina hurried on. She had time – just – to call at the Sok embassy and pick up any messages before heading for the Cooper Government headquarters. The delayed flight had put her on a tight schedule before her meeting at the Foreign Minister's office. And she wasn't looking forward to that at all.

The ambassadorial post had come about as much from her athletic fame as her negotiating skills, she realised. Even in these enlightened times, the Sokolovan government was not above using a little glamour and celebrity to swing arguments and win favours with the Coops. Not that Ktrina felt very glamorous in an old trouser suit and holiday hair, but she didn't regret giving her boys priority on their back-to-school morning. She smiled as she remembered how smart they had looked in their freshly-printed blazers.

Her own jacket bore the creases of previous trips to the north. The Carrier was speedy enough, covering the 11,000 kilometres in under two hours, but it made the journey a wearying bout of acceleration and deceleration with barely twenty minutes in between as they coasted over the equator. Just enough time to sip a pouch of fruit juice and gaze at the craters and plains passing below by day, or the pin-prick lights of mining settlements by night. Her business suit's dark blue trousers didn't look too bad, she knew, thanks to their stirrup straps. The under-foot elastic tapes stopped trouser cuffs riding up in the low gravity, and also pulled creases out when she stood and walked. But the suit had seen better days, it was time to recycle it. She would get a new suit printed at the weekend, and match her sons' freshly-tailored look.

Taking the stairs down to the station in preference to the escalator, Ktrina was still thinking of her three sons, when she sensed someone looking at her. For a fraction of a second she locked eyes with a young man before he looked away and ran past her up the stairway. It was the briefest glimpse, but his pale blue eyes and broken front tooth stayed with her as she boarded the Metro. Had she seen him before? No, she would have remembered that haunted expression. He was just one of a hundred troubled young men she would pass on each visit to Cooper, she decided, as she checked her watch and turned her thoughts back to her meeting with the Foreign Minister and that unnerving letch, the Xinto High Priest, Daval Nakash.

Earth 1504
Mammed stepped away from the huddle of sailors who were engrossed in plans to refloat the Pelican, and looked for Miriam. He'd decided to tell her all about his daring rescue of Ben and Papa Yon from the tower. Then he'd go swimming with her in the lagoon, as she'd promised. But she wasn't with her father now. She was holding the side of the rowing boat and was talking to Desmun, the apprentice priest. Not only that, the upper half of her body was out of the water, for all to see.

Mammed turned and ran up the white sand into the trees, his face burning and his heart hammering. He had carefully averted his eyes every time her breasts had come into view that morning, and now everyone could look at them. All those sailors. And Desmun. Why was she talking to *him,* that officious little prat who thought he could lord it over others because he was the Cardinal's pet? Now the Cardinal was gone – drowned and eaten by sharks, and good riddance – now Desmun would get what was coming to him. And if he spoke to Miriam again... Mammed snatched up a dead branch and smashed it into splinters on the trunk of a tree. Then, with hot, salty rivers running down his face, he ran into the forest and got lost.

It was mid afternoon when Mammed returned to the beach to find Ben blowing their fire back into life. He looked up as the teenager dropped an armload of sticks on the sand with a clatter.

"Ah, so there you are! We were about to send out a search party."

The boy flopped down onto the beach but said nothing.

48

"What have you done to your legs...?"

Mammed looked down and discovered his shins were criss-crossed with scratches and blooded cuts. His left big toe was red and swollen where he'd stumbled over a rock.

"And your chest and arms! You look like you've had a fight with a thorn bush, Mammed. Where've you been?"

"Nowhere."

Benyamin's lopsided grin reached full beam. "Well I wouldn't go *there* again, if I were you."

Silence.

"Miriam was looking for you. Wanted to take you swimming in the lagoon..."

Mammed kicked the sand.

"So I asked her to fetch the barrel of water you forgot this morning." Ben nodded to the barrel sitting on the sand.

"Where's Papa Yon and the others?" Mammed was looking along the beach.

"Gone off in the boat to see something Alexee wanted to show them. Something called pods. He says they might help refloat the Pelican. And I've sent Desmun to collect coconuts. Miriam said she would bring us fish so I'm getting the fire ready to cook a meal. The crew have hardly eaten in two days."

More silence.

"You didn't bring us any fruit back from your escapade in the forest, then...?"

"I brought wood for the fire."

"So I see, thanks. We could do with some fruit, Mammed, so make yourself useful and go fetch as much as you can carry. You can give some to your girlfriend too."

"*Not* my girlfriend." Mammed got to his feet.

"If you say so." Ben smiled. "But before you go, wash yourself off in the lagoon. You look a bloody mess, and the seawater will help heal those scratches."

Moon 3660

Gunta Krems, Cooper's Foreign Minister, was seated behind his polished wooden desk when Ktrina was shown into his office. Standing beside him, looking imperious in all his robed and tattooed glory, was Daval Nakash, the Xinto High Priest. Where the Xintapos' tattoos were restricted to necks and throats and stopped at their earlobes, Nakash wore dark, symbolic artwork over his entire skull, leaving only his eyes, cheeks, nose and lips unadorned. Ktrina swallowed hard.

"Good afternoon, Ambassador. Thank you for coming so promptly." Krems smiled, stood and offered his hand across his desk. The painted priest acknowledged her with the faintest nod.

"Afternoon, Foreign Minister, your Highness." She nodded to both in turn, but shook only the minister's hand. They know my every movement, she thought. "I called at the embassy on the way here, I hope I'm not late?"

"No, not at all. But we have some important business to attend to, and I believe you plan to return south on the 5pm flight?" He raised his bushy eyebrows.

"Yes, if that's possible, Minister...?"

"I'm sure it is. Now, I've had this office swept for surveillance this morning and I'm assured it is clean, so we should now disable our comms, to prevent accidental recording or transmission."

Krems unbuttoned his left shirt sleeve to reveal a slim band encircling his wrist. He reached to the underside and with a twist detached a coin-sized metal disc which he placed on the desk in front of him. Nakash pulled up the sleeve of his black robe to extract his own. Ktrina tugged on the elbow of her jacket sleeve to expose her wrist and quickly placed her comm unit on the desk.

"Thank you. Now please inform us of your government's plans. Then we will tell you ours."

"Very well." Ktrina sat in one of the chairs facing the two men. "The Sokolovan government is planning a limited military incursion into your sovereign territory – with your permission, of course – to disable the FLOC's ability to launch satellite attacks on both our nations. I am authorised to tell you the timing, location and objective of this action."

"Please go on."

"At twelve noon next Sunday, a small Ranger force will attempt to gain entry to Lava Tube A14, at the southern edge of the Aristarchus Plateau. We have identified this as the launch site of the satellite which attacked our solar collector, and yours, Minister, last Friday. Our intention is to gain entry, lay charges in the tube and collapse the south-facing section, so that it cannot again be used to launch a polar-orbiting space vehicle."

"How many of your Rangers will engage in this action?" The High Priest broke his silence.

"I have not been given that information, sorry."

"What equipment will be used to gain entry?" Krems steepled his fingers and stared intently.

"Again, I have not been informed of those operational details, Minister."

"Hmm. Very limited information. Is there nothing else you can tell us about this proposed military action?"

"I'm sorry. That's all I have been given." She lifted her hands and smiled apologetically.

Krems turned and looked up at Nakash, who nodded his tattooed head.

"Very well. It should be enough to ensure our forces don't inadvertently engage one another." He paused and took a deep breath. "We have also established that the satellite which attacked us on Friday was launched from A-Fourteen and plan to degrade the FLOC's ability to launch others. However, they have installed a substantial blast door at the southern end of the lava tube. Are you aware of this?"

"Yes, we are, Minister."

"We believe an easier point of entry will be achieved five kilometres to the north, where a small side tube reaches the surface. We plan to gain entry and destroy the rail-launch system, which will be located around three kilometres to the south, roughly halfway to your Rangers' position. We will coordinate our attacks for twelve noon on Sunday and time the detonation of charges for two pm, to give our respective forces time to withdraw safely. Is that understood?"

"Yes, Minister. I will relay this information to my government immediately upon my retur—"

"And you will ensure the same security?" Nakash barked the question.

"Certainly, your Highness. My government is acutely aware of the need for secrecy."

"Very well, Ambassador." Krems used a softer tone and gave her a brief smile before continuing. "By coordinating our actions in this way and ensuring no leaks of information, we should achieve complete surprise. With luck, both our forces can be in and out quickly, with minimum casualties, leaving the FLOC's launch facility permanently disabled."

"I sincerely hope so, Minister. All lives are precious." Ktrina looked from Krems to Nakash and back again. "If there's nothing else I need to know, I will return south and share this information with Foreign Minister Lanimovskiy and General Ferreira without delay."

"Thank you for coming, Ambassador Rozek. Please speak to no-one on your return journey. We appreciate your absolute discretion." Krems stood and reached across his desk to shake her hand again. Ktrina picked up her comms unit and reinstalled it before pulling her sleeve down.

"Thank you both," she said, without making eye contact. "I should be back at the embassy to resume diplomatic duties by midday tomorrow."

Earth 1504

"Right, here's the plan." Captain Yonaton wiped crumbs of fish and coconut from his beard and addressed the men sitting round the fire. "The wind dies down overnight and picks up again mid-morning, so we need to be on board the Pelican before dawn to stand any chance of getting her off before the wind and waves build up.

"That means leaving here around midnight. We will put five in the boat and three on the catamaran. The boat will tow the catamaran which will be loaded with pods. Alexee has fourteen we can use—"

"What are pods, Papa Yon?" Mammed's brow was furrowed.

"They're big glassy tubes, open at one end, each bigger than a man. When they are filled with air, they should be enough to lift the ship off the reef—"

"Where'd these mermen get the pods from, Cap'n?" Conor went back to sucking the flesh off his fish's bones using his one good hand.

Yonaton smiled at Ben before replying. "Well, that's a long story, Conor. Can we come back to that tomorrow, after we've got the Pelican off the reef?"

"Yeah, okay."

"The idea is to push the pods into the hull through the main hatch – Alexee and his Seaple will help with that – and then the dolphins will blow air into them. We will have to remove most of the ballast stones to lighten the ship, but Alexee reckons the dolphins can bring them out and drop them on the catamaran each time they come up for air."

"That's asking a lot o' the dolphins, Cap'n. And the mermen. Yer sure they're up to it?"

"Only one way to find out, Conor. Unless you have a better plan...?"

"No, no. Sounds a tricky operation, that's all."

"Alexee and his Seaple won't be joining us at the Pelican until after dawn, as the dolphins can't protect them from sharks in the dark. By the time they turn up we need to have both main anchors set as far to seaward as we can – we'll row them out in the boat. That way we can haul the Pelican into deeper water when she lifts off. Then we should be able to tow her away from the reef and around to the leeward side of the island—"

"*Should* be able to...?"

"Nothing's guaranteed, Conor. But if we ever want to go home, we have to rescue the Pelican. Otherwise you'll be eating fish for the rest of your life..."

Moon 3660

The bustling crowds heading for the metro jostled Ktrina as she made her way back towards Monterey, Cooper's main skyport. It was unusual for her to return to the south on the same day she arrived, but Jorg Lanimovskiy, her foreign minister, and General Ndrew Ferreira, the Chief of Defence, had been insistent. They needed to know of the Coop government's plans immediately and, for security, the details could only be conveyed by her in person.

Both nations were determined to prevent any chance of their impending military action being known to the FLOC beforehand. The rebels' spies seemed able to tap into any transmission or recording, so these critical details would be carried in Ktrina's head, in her memory. The weight of responsibility clouded her thoughts as she neared the station and she shook her head to clear her vision.

She was being watched, she knew. The Xintapo's eyes had followed her as she made her way from Cooper's government headquarters to the nearby metro station. The monks' attention told her it wasn't just her hair and clothing that set her apart, they were monitoring her movements on instruction from their boss, the High Priest, Daval Nakash. The tattooed neck of the nearest one twisted to follow her as she passed through the station entrance. The next one locked eyes on her as she approached the stairway leading down to the platforms. It was reassuring and unnerving at the same time.

The stairs were busier now, with folk pushing their way past to avoid the over-crowded escalator. Ktrina was looking down to focus on the steps and avoid tripping when someone bumped into her. Her head snapped up in time to see a young man with blue eyes and broken front tooth.

"For Ethan!" he whispered urgently before hurrying away upwards as the crowd carried her down the stairs.

That haunted face. It was the same one she'd seen earlier, she was sure of it. For a moment she thought she'd been robbed, but her bag was still on her shoulder, securely snapped shut. Then she felt a weight bump against her ribs and gasped. He'd slipped something inside her double-breasted jacket!

Ktrina's first instinct was to pluck it out and hurl it away. She'd heard about bombings on the metro and figured she could be a prime target. But as she reached into her jacket and felt the hard round object inside a soft cover, she decided against it. He'd said, "For Ethan!" hadn't he? She had to know what he meant.

Her mind in turmoil, Ktrina stumbled and almost fell as she neared the bottom of the stairway. She needed somewhere to sit and think, and somewhere private to take a look at whatever it was the young man had thrust inside her jacket. She headed for the toilets.

Privacy was in short supply in Cooper City and she knew the station toilets would be bugged and cammed like everywhere else. She locked herself in the cubicle and made a show of using the facility to convince any watcher her visit was simply a call of nature. Then she fished a tiny penlight out of her bag, gripped it between her teeth and hoisted her jacket over her head. She pretended to be struggling to remove the jacket while she took her first look at the object in her lap.

A grey synsilk bag with a drawstring held what appeared to be a large, dark grey, ceramic egg. She was tugging the bag open when she noticed something written on its side – numbers! They were printed in crumbling black digits and appeared to be fading before her eyes. A brush with her thumb erased the last two instantly, but not before she recognised the sequence. With a start she realised she was staring at Ethan's Ranger ID number. It really *was* for Ethan. Somehow.

There was no time to figure out what it meant, her jacket ploy was wearing a bit thin. She rubbed the remaining numbers away before tucking it inside her bra. Then she pulled her jacket off and vigorously brushed the sleeve. She had fallen against the stairwell wall when she stumbled, so she hoped this would appear plausible. It was her mind that was doing somersaults.

I was given this for a reason. Something to do with Ethan. I have to find out what it is...

Jacket back on, toilet flushed and egg pressing into her ribcage, Ktrina exited the cubicle and washed her hands. She stared at herself in the smeary mirror and wondered what the hell she was doing. A wild-eyed young man had put a strange object in her jacket and she had no idea what it was or what it meant. And yet here she was – the respected Sokolovan Ambassador, on a highly sensitive mission to Cooper for her government – thinking how she could smuggle the mystery egg back home.

If I get caught...

She splashed water on her face and fished a tissue from her bag to wipe herself dry. The face in the mirror looked pale and scared. *I have three young boys. I shouldn't be doing this. I could just leave it here and walk away...*

Ktrina straightened up, pulled her jacket down and checked her profile in the mirror. "For Ethan," she muttered under her breath, snapped her bag shut and walked out the door.

Earth 1504

Mammed dug deep into the black water of the lagoon with his paddle and marvelled at the swirl of tiny lights it produced. He'd seen it before, of course. Great luminous shapes had lit up the water and sparks had followed in their wake on certain nights while sailing the Pelican. It was just one of those things nobody could explain. And on moonless nights like this, it was reassuring to see bright splashes ahead of them. They marked the oar strokes of the boat that was helping tow them out to the wreck of their beloved ship. Further ahead still were glimmers of light where the Dolpheen, as Miriam called them, were guiding them towards the break in the reef and the open sea beyond.

Miriam had been delighted with the fruit he had collected for her that afternoon. He smiled to himself in the darkness. She had noticed the scratches on his chest and made him wait while she fetched a special sponge she said would heal them. He had tingled all over as she stroked his cuts with the soft yellow sea creature. Maybe she *was* his girlfriend, as Ben had suggested. The thought made him feel dizzy and he pulled his mind back to resume steady strokes with the paddle.

After their meal on the beach and the Captain's announcement of his plan to rescue the Pelican, he'd had little time to think about Miriam. He'd been set to work tightening the lashings that held the log-canoe catamaran together. He knew how, as he'd helped build the vessel with Ifan and Jack, his two older brothers since he'd been adopted into the Captain's family. That was before he'd climbed the harbour tower to release Ben and Papa Yon from the clutches of the murderous Cardinal. Now *that* was a climb to be proud of...

"Are you okay, Mammed?" The Captain's voice came over the stack of pods lashed like a pyramid in the centre of the catamaran. His father was at the front, paddling between the canoes' bows, while Mammed paddled from the stern on the right side.

"Yes, I'm okay."

"Concentrate then, I can tell you are missing your strokes. How about you, Desmun?"

"I'm okay." The voice nearby reminded Mammed the apprentice priest was paddling at the stern of the left-hand canoe. He still felt uncomfortable sharing a boat with the Cardinal's underling.

"Then put some effort into it. We need to get to the Pelican before dawn." There was tension in the Captain's voice.

Mammed pulled hard on his paddle once more, determined to show he could outpace Desmun. His steady strokes left whirlpools of light twirling behind them. With nothing to see but the glimmer in the water and the stars above, no sounds but the creak of oarlocks from the boat ahead, Mammed's thoughts drifted like the tide.

He was back at home with his mother in Portkaron. Ma Fatima, everyone called her, and they treated her with respect. He remembered her dark skin and fiery temper, the way she would shout at him one minute and hug him to her bosom the next. And he remembered his father. His first father, Youssef, before Captain Yonaton had let him join the crew of the Pelican, and then adopted him into his own family.

He remembered sitting beside his father's bed, wiping the beads of sweat off his feverish forehead with a damp cloth. His father's skin was much lighter than Mammed's mother, but in those last days it had seemed almost white. And then he was gone. Gone up to heaven, his mother said, pointing at the sky. Mammed had run into the yard to see a pale face peering down at him and knew his father had gone to live with the Man in the Moon.

But what did he think now? On moonless nights like this it was hard to imagine his Papa Youssef sitting up there. And if Miriam's Histree was true, and people *had* come from the Moon in the Ark, would they come again and bring his father back with them? Or was the whole idea of people going to live in heaven when they died just a story to stop children crying? Now that he was six years older and as tall as his Papa Yon, should he forget those childish ideas and think like a man?

A shout from the boat ahead brought him back to the present. Something out there in the darkness was changing. He couldn't see the oar strokes from the rowing boat any more. Then he felt the tow rope tug the catamaran to the left and he resumed paddling in earnest. They had arrived at the gap in the reef. Mammed's stomach lurched. Next they would be outside, in the open sea, in the pitch-black darkness, where the sharks circled silently below.

Chapter 4

This One Loves Her Work

Moon 3660

Ktrina studied her flickering reflection in the window of the metro. She had every reason to look scared. If she was caught smuggling a suspicious artefact she could expect no mercy from the Coopan government, and little help from her own. She pictured the security checks at the skyport, the walk-through metal detector and the stony-faced women who would pat her clothing down.

Her bag had to go through the X-ray machine, so she couldn't hide the egg in there. She prayed it was all-ceramic, or the metal detector would ring an alarm. And it couldn't stay in her bra, or the pat down would find it for sure.

"Shit!" she muttered under her breath, which earned her a disapproving look from the man sitting next to her. "Sorry!" she smiled. "Forgot to get a present for my boys."

"There's a shop in the departure lounge," he offered, looking serious. "Prices are horrendous, but you might find something…"

"Yes, of course," she nodded, "thank you, I'll take a look." She turned back to the window to avoid further conversation. She'd just remembered she wasn't to speak to anyone. Plus she needed time to think.

Ktrina hurried from the metro and headed directly for the toilets. Seated in a cubicle once more, she exaggerated easing off her shoes, lifting her trousers' stirrup straps and rubbing tired feet. Then she stood, hoisted her trousers and turned to flush, keeping her back to the microcam she had spotted above the door. Within seconds she had retrieved the egg from her bra and slipped it into her panties.

"This had better work," she muttered under her breath as she washed her hands, acutely aware of the ovoid lump pressed uncomfortably between her thighs. Ktrina gave one more tug on the waistband of her trousers, which now sat unusually low on her hips, hoisted her bag on her shoulder and headed for the security gate.

She was perspiring already as the queue shuffled towards the X-ray belt, the metal detector arch and the waiting guards. Her bag disappeared into the X-ray machine and she stepped forward for the pat down. The surly female guard took one look at Ktrina's collar-length hair and dark blue business suit, and barked: "Open jacket – arms out!" before probing her arms, pits and shoulders with steely fingers.

This one loves her work

The guard drew her hands firmly through Ktrina's cleavage then used fingers and thumbs to knead her breasts.

She really loves her work!

Ktrina kept her eyes fixed ahead and her face stony as the hands moved down her torso and fingers made a circuit inside her waistband. Then the guard was squatting, feeling around the ankle and sliding her hands inexorably up Ktrina's left leg, past the knee, one hand inside and one on the outside of her thigh, right up to her crotch. Ktrina held her breath.

The guard's fingers dallied between her thighs as her left hand reached around and felt around her buttocks. Then the right leg, slower this time and more intimate, ending with a squeeze of Ktrina's inner thigh and a pat on the butt as the guard rose and smiled at last.

"Okay. Step through here." She pointed to the arch.

Ktrina let out her breath in a long, slow exhale. She'd done it! The trick with her trouser stirrup straps had worked. Wrapping the elastic around her feet had pulled the cuffs down over her shoes... and held the crotch seam a vital inch below the hidden egg.

She stepped through the arch and the machine bleeped.

Shit!

"Step over here," ordered the next guard, a slim woman with a sensor-wand. She waved it over the front of Ktrina's jacket which made it bleep too.

"Empty your pockets." She held out a plastic tray for their contents – a tissue and the penlight torch that Ktrina had forgotten to put back in her bag. The guard passed her wand up and down and around again. Ktrina held herself motionless, numb with fear.

No more bleeps. The guard gave the tissue and torch back and waved Ktrina over to the end of the X-ray belt where her bag was waiting. She felt a rivulet of sweat trickle down between her shoulder blades as she hoisted her bag and headed for the departure lounge.

Earth 1504

Once they'd passed through the gap in the reef, between the thump and hiss of swells breaking on either side, the log canoe catamaran became harder to paddle. There was little wind to speak of, but the long ocean waves lifted and dropped the flimsy vessel, making it creak beneath the stack of pods. The weight of the long, glassy tubes forced the hulls low in the water, and despite the canvas coverings they had fitted to keep the sea out, Mammed could soon feel water sloshing around his feet.

"Papa Yon!" He shouted. "There is water inside. Should I bail it out now?"

"Yes," came the reply from the darkness. "Keep the boat as dry as you can, but don't stop paddling for long. You too, Desmun, bail out any water then get back to paddling quickly."

As the next wave lifted the bow and the water rushed to the stern, Mammed bailed frantically. He could hear a scraping from the stern of the other canoe telling him Desmun was using his hollow gourd too. Perhaps half the water had been removed when the wave dropped the bow again and the Captain called on them both to resume paddling.

As he dug into the sea once more, Mammed groaned at the burning in his arms and the ache in his back and shoulders. Ahead, to the east, he could see the first hint of dawn in the night sky. They ought to be nearing the Pelican by now if they were to beat the rising wind of the day, but there was no sign of the ship. Was it still out there, impaled on a coral head, or had their trusty merchant vessel been so battered by the waves that it had sunk out of sight, like the Ark in Miriam's Histree?

To take his mind off the pain, Mammed thought about the story she'd read to him. The story that his Papa Yon had asked him to repeat to the sailors as they sat around their fire last night. He had remembered it quite well, he thought, although he'd stumbled over some of the words. To his surprise, there were few wisecracks from the mariners, perhaps because the Captain had told them to listen and not comment. Only Conor's, "Well... I'll be jiggered!" at the end, which had made them all laugh.

Then Yonaton had told them all to lie down and get some sleep, as he would be waking them at midnight to set off on their attempt to raise the Pelican.

"And 'ow about *you* gettin' some sleep then, Cap'n?" Conor had asked.

"I shan't sleep while that thug, Gorbel, has my sons and daughter," he replied grimly.

Mammed thought about his adopted brothers, Ifan and Jack. How they'd welcomed him into the family and taken him on their fishing boat, the Petrel. How Lucy had been strict and bossy about the house, patient when teaching him and the other kids in her front parlour schoolroom, and had hugged him each night before he went to bed. He couldn't wait to get back to Loming and free them from the Convertors.

The Captain called on them to bail again as a long wave started to lift the bows and water rushed to the stern. It was a welcome relief from paddling but Mammed struggled to grip the bailing gourd with his stiff fingers. As he resumed the now-agonising dig and pull with the paddle he glanced at the spreading patch of lighter sky ahead and, for a second, fancied he saw something. He focussed on the spot when the next wave lifted them and there was a mast, tipped low in the water.

"I can see the Pelican, Papa Yon!" he yelled. "It's dead ahead."

A second later he heard the Captain calling to the men in the rowing boat and cheers in reply. As he hauled on his paddle with renewed effort, Mammed heard a song start up and felt his exhaustion lift as he joined in –

"Heave-ho and away we go boys, let blow as she may.

Now pull strong and sing this song boys, let's sa-ail away."

The catamaran began to slip through the sea a little faster and with each passing wave the remains of the Pelican began to take shape out of the cold dark shadows of the dawn.

Moon 3660

Ktrina felt elated at clearing the security checks but was acutely aware she was still being watched. Xintapo stood at strategic points around the departure lounge. There would be cams everywhere too. She walked as naturally as she could with the egg rubbing uncomfortably, and her shortened stirrup straps threatening to pull her trousers off her hips. She couldn't visit the toilets again without raising suspicion, so she'd have to tough it out until she boarded her flight. She headed for the open-plan cafeteria and a soothing cup of chai.

As she queued for her drink, Ktrina realised she had eaten nothing since breakfast. She ordered a mozzacado protein wrap, and was reaching to pass her comm over the terminal to make payment, when she noticed someone smiling at her. There, a little further back in the queue, was the man who had sat next to her on the metro. She quickly looked away, collected her tray and made her way to the seating area.

Two minutes later, as she was swallowing her first bite, she realised metro-man was taking the high stool next to her. Krems' words, 'speak to no-one', rang in her ears. She turned her shoulder to make it clear that conversation was not welcome.

"Did you find your presents?" His voice intruded. She shook her head without turning. "I told you they were expensive here," he persisted.

"Can't talk, sorry," she said, sliding from her stool and carrying her food and drink to another table. She sat with her back to him and hoped he would take the hint. A minute passed. Two minutes.

"You're that athlete, aren't you?" He was standing right behind her. She didn't respond.

"Think you're too high and mighty to speak to ordinary people, is that it…?"

She shook her head, but didn't turn round.

"Well you might learn a few manners if—"

"Come with me, sir." He was cut off in mid-sentence by a gruff voice.

"What! Ow! No…"

Ktrina turned in time to see metro-man being hustled away, his arm twisted behind his back, by one of the Xintapo. The tattooed monk appeared to be a solid block of muscle beneath his black robe. He lifted the startled businessman off his feet and out of the departure lounge within seconds. Ktrina put her elbows on the table and sank her face slowly into her hands.

Earth 1504

If sighting the Pelican had lifted their spirits, its appearance when they drew close sank the sailors' mood. Mammed found it hard to believe that this sorry mess of ropes, sails and spars was the same proud ship that had carried them all year round across the Crabbing Sea. Lying almost on her side, with the lazy ocean swells breaking over her gunwale, the Pelican looked like a wreck waiting to slip to a watery grave. With her timbers creaking and groaning from the sea's punishing blows it sounded like a slow and agonising death.

If Captain Yonaton was disheartened, he didn't show it, calling to the rowing boat crew to pull the catamaran alongside Pelican's stern. Making fast the bow line, he clambered aboard the ship and pulled himself up to the starboard side where he could survey the deck.

"Tie the boat up," he shouted to the crew, "then two of you come aboard to get the sails down and lashed to the deck."

He set about rigging a rope along the length of the ship, so they would have something to hold on to while working. With the cargo hatch now missing and water surging in and out of the hold, it would be easy to get washed in and drowned. As the eastern sky turned red to herald sunrise, Mammed resumed bailing. The confused seas around the ship's stern were breaking over the front of their catamaran and water was building up inside once again. He was about to berate Desmun for not doing the same when he heard sobbing and looked up in surprise. The apprentice priest was crouched in the stern of his canoe, face wet with tears.

"You alright, Desmun?"

The lad shook his head miserably. "No. I... I'm scared."

It was the first time they'd spoken to each other since the crew arrived the previous day. Mammed wasn't quite sure how to respond, or even how he felt. Despite his animosity towards Desmun he couldn't help feeling sorry for him. "We'll be alright. Just need to get this water out. You still got a bailer over there?"

Desmun released his white-knuckled grip on the side of the heaving vessel and retrieved his bailing gourd. He sniffled as he looked down and started scooping out the water.

"When we've got all the water out," said Mammed, "we can have a drink. We brought green coconuts with us, remember?"

"Yeah." Desmun sniffed again. "Thanks."

By the time they had emptied the catamaran's two hulls, the boys could see the Pelican's spars and sails had been pulled out of the water and lashed to the ship's rail. The crew were now all back in the boat and had rowed around to the ship's bow, where Conor was being helped to climb out, his bandaged hand proving to be a significant disability.

"Why is Conor getting on to the ship?" Desmun was puzzled.

"They have to put the anchor and chain on the rowing boat. Need to make it lighter, I s'pose."

"That looks really dangerous," said Desmun as they watched Yonaton lowering the bulky main anchor to lie across the boat near the stern. It made the rowing boat sit low in the water and tip to one side until the men shifted their weight.

Mammed passed him the coconut they were sharing. The sweet milk tasted delicious and seemed to be soothing Desmun's frayed nerves.

"Don't worry," said Mammed, "they spend their lives at sea. They know what they're doing."

"I hope so. I don't want anybody else to get drowned."

They were both silent for a minute, then Desmun spoke again, quietly. "I can't stop thinking about all the dead bodies in the water below us." He was staring into the sea. "If I hadn't been hiding in the cabin, I would be down there with them now. You probably wish I *had* drowned with the others… I know you all hate me…"

"Don't be silly, Desm—"

"I never wanted to be a priest. I don't believe any of that religious stuff."

"Why did you become the Cardinal's apprentice, then?"

"My dad died when I was fourteen. I was the oldest. My mum couldn't afford to keep us all."

"Sorry. I didn't know." Mammed frowned. Papa Youssef's fevered face had returned to haunt him.

"My cousin said there was a job with the Cardinal. My mum would get regular money to feed the younger kids. I didn't want to do it, but you don't argue with my cousin. He's a bully." Desmun straightened up and looked Mammed in the eye. "His name's Gorbel."

"Shit!"

"Yeah. So, I didn't have any choice. Three years ago I became apprentice priest and from the very first day that filthy old bastard never let me alone…"

"Oh…"

"I had to share his cabin. Share his quarters back in Loming. Never let me alone…" Desmun stared away into the distance.

Mammed could think of nothing to say, but his imagination painted lurid, disturbing pictures.

"I hope the sharks tore him to bits while he was still alive!" Desmun was looking into the sea again, but now there was the hint of a smile at the corners of his mouth. "He deserved to be—"

"MAMMED!" They both looked up to see Captain Yonaton with his hands cupped to his mouth. "Come here, please. Desmun, stay where you are."

Mammed took one last drink from the coconut and handed it to Desmun. "Here, you can finish this. You'll have to get bailing to keep both hulls empty, and mind you don't fall in. You wouldn't want to join that fat old sod inside a shark, now would you…?" He grinned, pulled the mooring line to bring the catamaran up to the ship's stern, and climbed on board.

Moon 3660

"Well, *I* think they are primitive and vulgar, touching you with their hands like that. It is indecent. Why can't they use modern scanning machines like we do in *our* skyports?" Ktrina's mother, Sofi, was indignant. Ktrina was beginning to wonder if it had been a good idea, telling of her treatment at the Monterey security gate.

63

"And as for those monks – Shindarbo or whatever they call themselves – I think they are hideous with their horrible tattoos all over their necks. If their Messiah really does return one day, he will take one look at them and go straight back to where he came from, I'm sure."

Sofi had never been to the north but had strong feelings about most things Coopan. Some of Ktrina's opinions were not so different to her mother's, but she was grateful for one of the north's archaic customs. If her security inspection today had been by mechanised body scan, instead of being felt-up by a leering female guard, the mystery egg would have been discovered. Instead of being at home tonight with her mother and three sleeping boys, Ktrina would be in a prison cell awaiting interrogation, like that poor man from the metro.

She had called Gunta Krems as soon as her flight landed to ask if the Sokolovan businessman arrested at the airport had been released. She told him the man was entirely innocent, and was only responding to an earlier remark she had made about buying presents for her boys back home.

"But I *told* you to speak to no-one," replied Krems, curtly. "This was a serious breach of security given the nature of your mission today. And judging by the way this man pursued you and attempted to engage you in further conversation, we have every reason to be suspicious. He will be released when we have established he has no connections with the FLOC, and not before."

She was dismayed that one slip of her tongue had resulted in the man's detention, even if he had brought it upon himself by being overly pushy. But she was even more shocked when she arrived at her own Foreign Minister's office minutes later to be told she was banned from returning to the north until next week. Krems had revoked her visa on security grounds. She would be able to resume diplomatic duties at the Sok embassy in Cooper City only after the risk had passed, by which he meant after Sunday's military action.

After a gruelling day of travel, drama and stress, Ktrina had been too tired to argue. She explained what happened, leaving out any mention of the smuggled egg. Then she delivered the military operation details, and headed home to face her mother's forthright opinions.

"Thanks for the chai, Mum." Ktrina gave Sofi a hug. "It's been a long day. If you don't mind I'm going to bed."

"But you haven't had any supper!"

"Oh, I ate something at the skyport. I'll be fine until breakfast." Ktrina kissed her mum on the cheek, shut herself in her bedroom and reached into the bottom of her shoulder bag. Sleep was the last thing on her mind. Finally she would get a proper look at the mystery egg that had caused so much trouble.

As she slid the smooth grey object from its soft drawstring bag she realised why it had caused such discomfort. It was much bigger than a chicken's egg, more like an avocado, yet had gone undetected at the security check. She'd been incredibly lucky. She'd swapped it to her shoulder bag mid-flight, knowing she would be waved through the Sokolovan arrivals gate without inspection. Now, with the light of her bedside lamp, she could see faint lines that ran almost the length of the egg, and in its bulbous base was a tiny electrical socket.

Ktrina rummaged in her drawer looking for the cable she used to connect old-fashioned devices to her screen or comm. She hadn't seen it in years and was relieved to find it hidden beneath the layers of personal knick-knacks and trivia. Its diminutive metal plug slid into the egg. She connected the cable's other end to her portable screen, and switched on.

Nothing. Checked for connected devices. Nothing. She turned her screen off and on, disconnected and reconnected the plugs. Nothing.

Ktrina sighed with frustration. Whatever information the egg contained, it didn't seem willing to give it up easily. She examined its smooth grey surface, searching for a secret switch, tried pressing it in different places, tapping it, twisting it. Nothing.

Was there some clue in its drawstring bag? She examined the silky purse inside and out, looking for a label or some hidden instruction. There was none. The crumbly numbers that she'd seen in the skyport's toilets had disappeared. She held the bag in front of the light, hoping something else might become visible, but there was not even a clue. She threw the bag down and flopped on her bed with a long, exhausted sigh.

Was this what she had risked everything for... *nothing*? Had she carried this damned egg in her underwear and sweated through an agonising security check, for no good reason at all? Was an innocent businessman being held in a Coopan jail, instead of at home with his family... all because of some useless ceramic *ornament*? How could she have been so stupid?

She heard her mother switching off her wall light in the room next door. Her screen told her it was 22.59. She watched the numbers flick to 23.00 and felt a wave of exhaustion wash over her. She switched the screen off, dropped it and the egg in her bedside drawer, and lay down again. It had been a hell of day.

Earth 1504

"Think you can climb up the foremast and thread this rope through the halyard block?" Captain Yonaton held up a coil of rope. He was standing on the side of the main hatch, his back braced against the deck which was nearly vertical behind him.

Mammed looked along the shiny round pole that stuck out at a giddy angle over the water. It was rising and falling as the ship moved with the waves.

"Should be easy."

"It won't be, Mammed. It's wet and slippery. If you fall, the sharks might get you." The Captain was staring at him intently.

Mammed hesitated and looked at the water, now turned an inky blue by the first glint of sun at the horizon. Were those dark shapes the shadows of the waves, or creatures with fearsome teeth? He raised his gaze to the wobbling tip of the thick, unstayed mast. "Why do we need that rope up there?"

"So we can pull the ship upright when she starts to lift. The other end of this is attached halfway down the anchor line. The crew are laying it out now. If we don't get her upright, the reef will rip the side out of the Pelican when we start to winch in the anchor lines."

Mammed thought for a minute. "Yes, I can do it," he said quietly.

"Let me see your hands."

Mammed held them palm upward for inspection. They were bright red and blistered from his night of work with the paddle.

Yonaton reached over and gently stroked the blisters with his thumbs. "Are they painful?"

"No... Yes, a little bit."

"You sure you can grip that mast properly?"

"Yeah, I'll be alright." It was then that Mammed noticed that the Captain had rags wrapped around his own hands. They were stained red across his palms.

"What's happened to *your* hands, Papa Yon?"

"Same as you. My paddle was a bit rougher, that's all."

Mammed remembered then that the Captain was whittling a chunk of wood to create a makeshift paddle while they sat around the fire last night. It must have torn his hands to shreds.

"Here, Mammed." Yonaton seemed oblivious to his injuries as he tied the end of the rope around Mammed's waist. "You'll have to untie it, pass it through the block and then tie it on again, all with one hand. Remember that special knot I taught you?"

He nodded.

"Off you go then. Best get it done before the wind picks up."
Yonaton squeezed the boy's shoulder.

Moon 3660

Ethan was up next, the baseball-sized shot-put cradled against his
chest, covered in chalky fingerprints. But instead of stepping into the
thrower's circle, he walked over to Ktrina. She was limbering up for
her hurdles race and could do without distractions, but his beaming
smile was captivating. Then he was speaking, his lips moving, but no
words were coming out. She strained to listen over the roar of the
stadium crowd but could hear nothing. Nothing at all.

Now he was frowning at her in frustration, the smile had
vanished. What was he trying to tell her? She had no idea. He was
turning to go, preparing for his throw. As he hoisted the shot-put up to
his shoulder she glimpsed a rectangular speck in its rounded side. With
a gasp she recognised the tiny electric socket...

Ktrina woke with a start and found she was still fully clothed and lying
on top of her bedcover. She rolled towards her bedside table and saw
the clock – 03.21. She'd been asleep over four hours. Her mouth felt
dry and stale. After mouthwash and toothbrush she slipped out of her
crumpled business suit, into a nightdress and slipped under the covers.
But now sleep wouldn't come.

She often saw Ethan in her dreams, but couldn't remember
one with him holding a shot-put. What had he been trying to tell her?
And why was there an electric socket...?

In one movement she was out from under the covers, sitting
on her bed, clutching the egg and staring intently at its tiny socket.
Was there something else she could plug in there? She pulled the cable
from her screen, slotted it into the base of the egg and then clipped the
other end into her wrist-mounted comm unit.

With a click the egg sprang to life in her hand, its sides
snapping open to form six spindly legs. Ktrina let out a short,
involuntary shriek and threw it on the bed. The egg had turned into a
mechanical spider and now, in front of her eyes, it picked itself up
from lying on its side and raised its body, just like an angry crab might
do. Then, with another faint click, the top of the egg rose up and
something fell from its base.

Ktrina felt giddy, thought she was falling. Her vision had
become a crazy blur. Her hand rose to rub her eyes and for a second

she saw a clear view of her bedroom. She opened her eyes again and was assaulted by tilting, disorienting double vision.

"Aggh!" She clasped her hands over her eyes and instantly her view was clear. Rumpled bed cover in the foreground and the door to her bathroom, with the light she'd left on shining through it. She was seeing through the spider's eyes!

"Oh. My. God!" She breathed the words as the view panned to the left. She had shifted her focus and the spider's vision followed as intuitively as if she'd turned her own head. It continued to pan slowly until she recognised her nightdress, then she looked up and saw her hands covering her face. Slowly she moved her hands away and there she was, eyes closed, smiling back at herself in amazement.

She tried opening one eye, then the other, but each time her vision clouded in confusion. It was frustrating because she wanted to look at this *thing* that the egg had become, see how it worked, find out what it was supposed to do.

Of course – she could just unplug! Ktrina reached for her wrist, felt for the cable and pulled it from her comm. Her eyes snapped open just in time to see the spider snap shut and become an egg again. She caught it as it rolled over onto its side.

"Damn!"

Lifting it up to her bedside light, she could see a faint circle at the top of the egg, and turning it over, another at its broad base. The spider's eye, or cam, must rise up with the cap at the top, she thought. But what was it that fell from the base? Only one way to find out…

Ktrina rummaged in her top drawer, where she kept her cosmetics and creams. A tube with a large black screw-top looked suitable. She unscrewed the cap, propped the tube upright so that its contents didn't spill, and wiped the cap's inside with a tissue. She offered it up to the egg. *Yes, that should do it.*

She held the cosmetic cap over the top of the egg with her left hand while she fumbled the cable back into her comm socket with her right. The spider sprang to life, hoisting itself up on its six legs. With another click the cosmetic cap rose as the top of the egg extended beneath it. She had blindfolded the spider, and her vision remained clear.

Beneath the spider was a dark grey ceramic disc attached to the end of the cable. If it had fallen out, how did she remain connected? When Ktrina lifted it up for inspection beneath her lamp she saw that a gossamer thread, like a single strand of spider silk, still connected the disc to the mechanical egg. It was so fine she could barely feel it across her finger as she held it closer to the light. It was a graphene nanofilament! It looked so delicate and yet must be strong enough to wind the disc back into the egg when she disconnected. And it must contain multiple strands to receive inputs from her comm, and send live images back. *What a marvel!*

But why? Ktrina lifted the spider by the top joints of its legs and placed it on the floor. Then she lifted off the black cosmetics cap covering its cam and closed her eyes. It took a few seconds to reorient the cam so she could see past her bed towards the light shining from her bathroom door. *Go forward,* she thought and immediately the image started to change as the spider moved. *Stop.* It halted. *Go into the bathroom.* The shaft of light grew wider as the device trotted obediently through the door. *Stop!*

*Hmmm, **clever** little spider. But what are you for? And what have you got to do with Ethan?*

Earth 1504

Of all his challenging climbs, this was Mammed's least favourite. With arms and legs wrapped around the slippery pole, cheek pressed tight against the unyielding wood, he was hitching himself upward agonisingly slowly. His blistered hands were rubbed raw, his legs chafed, his chest bruised.

Every time the Pelican moved with the waves the mast bucked and heaved, threatening to hurl him into the sea. All he could do was hang on and wait for the motion to subside. Then he'd resume his shuffling crawl, a little higher, a little further out over the waves. He imagined the sharks circling below, teeth bared in hungry grimace, waiting for a chance to sink them into him.

The higher he climbed, the more violent the mast's movements became. He knew the crew had returned from setting the main anchor. He'd heard their voices and then their awed hush as they watched him pulling himself along the mast high above them. The Captain had told them to be quiet and not distract him, but their silence was unnerving. It meant he could hear each approaching wave, the ship's tortured creak as the water hit the hull, and his own rasping breath as he clung tightly to the bouncing timber.

As the mast's quivering slowed once more, he pulled himself higher and cracked his skull on the halyard block. He couldn't see it and daren't turn his head, but he knew it well. He had shinned up the mast every day while sailing on the Pelican, delighting in sitting astride the long wooden yard that held up the foresail and gazing out over the ocean. But that was with the mast almost vertical and not trying its best to shake him off.

Mammed reached forward beneath the mast and felt for the iron hoop that clamped the block to its side. With his fingers gripping the cold metal he eased his other hand back to his waist and fumbled for the rope's knot. It took a minute to figure out how to loosen it and before he released the end, Mammed pulled on the heavy rope to bring a loop of it up to his face. He had barely jammed the bristly fibres into his mouth and clamped them with his teeth, when the mast bounced violently and he was again clinging on with hands, feet and knees, eyes closed in silent prayer.

The shaking slowed. He grabbed the rope at his waist and pulled to free it, then raised his head just enough to see the block. It took four attempts to persuade the thick rope to pass through. Groping under the mast Mammed caught the rope end again and could finally spit out the foul-tasting loop in his mouth. As he pulled through enough rope to retie at his waist, the mast gave an almighty lurch, his hand slipped and Mammed felt the world spin beneath him.

Moon 3660

The aroma of fresh coffee assaulted her nose and made her mouth water as Ktrina stepped into the kitchen. Sofi was bustling around, preparing breakfast. Her mother preferred solitude while she ran through her early morning routines and looked none too pleased when Ktrina walked in looking bleary-eyed.

"You're up early. I thought you'd be having a lie in after all that travelling yesterday."

"No. I've been awake for a while, Mum, thinking about things. I'm ready for some of that coffee."

Sofi turned back to the breakfast table, setting out cereal bowls and spoons for the boys in silence. Ktrina ignored her, poured a mug of steaming coffee and sat down to savour it. She had given up puzzling over the egg-spider and had hidden it in a box in her wardrobe. She would return to it later in the day, but right now she needed caffeine and food. She'd barely eaten anything yesterday and her stomach was clamouring for sustenance.

She was munching her way through a second round of Rugbrød toast when Sofi finally chose to speak. "Your brother-in-law's party has been brought forward to Friday."

"I thought Daniel's birthday was Saturday?" Ktrina licked butter from her fingers.

"It is, but he's working at the weekend now, so they've brought it forward."

"Oh, that's a pity – having to work on his birthday."

"Jean has invited us over at five, so the boys can have games before supper. Can you leave work early... now you're not going to the north this week?" Sofi raised her eyebrows as a form of quizzical demand.

"I should think so. I'm owed some time off anyway." Ktrina stood and approached the smartchef. "I'm having eggs. Like some, Mum?"

"No, thank you dear. You *know* I only eat fruisli in the mornings. Anything else upsets my system." Sofi frowned, as if her digestive needs were being ignored deliberately. In truth, Ktrina found it hard to keep up with her mother's food intolerances, which seemed to multiply with every magazine she read.

"So, why does Daniel have to work at the weekend? I thought he was in their R&D department... regular hours and all that?"

"Oh, *I* don't know, Ktrina. His work is all top secret, so he's hardly going to tell *me* what he's doing, is he?" Sofi seemed particularly tetchy this morning. "Besides, it was Jean who called to say the party was moved to Friday. She never talks about his work with the Rangers, does she?"

Ktrina knew why. Jean had always looked up to her big brother Ethan and hadn't coped at all well with his death. Even now, eight years on, she never referred to the Rangers by name. It was simply Daniel's 'work' and she had no interest in what he did there.

Ethan and Daniel had been best buddies since college and had joined the Rangers together. Ethan, the athlete, was a natural for front line patrol duties. Daniel, who was more of a sci-tech geek, went straight into the force's research and development division at Soknorth. Despite their differences Jean had fallen for her brother's best friend. When Ktrina and Ethan got married, Jean and Daniel got engaged. They'd been a perfect foursome. Ethan's passing had left a hole that could not be filled.

The smartchef pinged and Ktrina took her omelette to the table. Sofi was still bustling around the kitchen, making a point of keeping her back to her daughter.

"Have I done something to upset you this morning, Mum?"

Sofi hesitated, her lips pressed tight for a moment, then said, "I don't know why you can't just get a *boyfriend*, Ktrina, instead of using those... those *toys* in the morning!"

"What! What are talking about, Mum?"

"I wasn't born yesterday, you know. Do you think I can't hear you? Your gasps and moans through the bedroom wall? You could at least wait until I've got up..."

Ktrina was silent as her mind ticked backwards. Yes, she had squealed when the egg sprang to life. And maybe she'd groaned when her eyesight went off kilter. But there was no way she could tell her mother about the spider – she would never hear the last of it.

"I'm sorry, Mum." Ktrina smiled to herself. "I'll try to be quiet in future."

Chapter 5
Raising A Wreck
Earth 1504

Mammed scrunched his eyes closed, bracing for the splash. When it didn't come he opened them to find sky and a large wooden pole above him. His legs were still wrapped around the mast, ankles locked together in a painful but tenacious grip, and he was hanging upside down. Amazingly, the rope was still in his white-knuckled fist. He quickly wrapped it around his waist and tied Papa Yon's special knot.

"Hang on, Mammed!" The Captain called from below. "Can you pull yourself back up?"

In answer Mammed swung himself up and grasped the mast, but try as he might, he couldn't haul himself back on top of it. Fearing his legs would tire and he would fall off, he quickly began to slither down the sloping pole amidst shouts of encouragement from the crew below. The problem was, the tapered mast grew thicker as he descended and soon his ankles were forced apart. His aching legs and blistered hands lost their grip and, with an anguished yell, he fell into the sea.

Mammed kicked and fought his way to the surface, expecting to feel the slicing stab of shark teeth any second. But instead he felt hands grabbing his arms, hauling him up and over the side of the rowing boat. For a while he lay on the floorboards, coughing and shivering in shock.

"Well done, lad." Hands patted his shoulder and ruffled his unruly mop of frizzy hair. He felt the rope around his waist and looked up at the crew with a grin. "I did it, didn't I?"

With a bump the boat came alongside the ship and Mammed was being helped to his feet. Then he stepped across onto the tilted deck of the Pelican and into the arms of Captain Yonaton. "I'm sorry I had to ask you to do that, Mammed." He hugged the soggy teenager warmly. "Nobody else could have done it... I'm very proud of you."

The Captain untied the rope from Mammed's waist and made it fast on a mast cleat. He called to Conor, who was using his one good hand to tidy away ropes on the foredeck. "Are you alright there, Conor? Do you need another pair of hands?"

"I'm okay, Cap'n. A bit slow and awk'ard, but I can manage."

"Okay then, Mammed. Come and help me with the stern anchor."

The rowing boat was already at the back of the ship waiting for the second anchor. Between them Yonaton and Mammed loaded the unwieldy hook across the boat's gunwales and fed chain and rope into its stern. Then Ben and the other three crew were pulling their oars to row as far to windward as the anchor line would allow. They dropped the anchor and turned to head back to the ship.

"Here come the dolphins!" shouted one of the crew. They all twisted their necks to see shapes plunging through the waves to the west. The sleek grey bodies of some of the dolphins had brown figures lying along their backs. "And they're bringing the Seaple with them!"

By the time the crew had rowed back to the Pelican, seven dolphins had arrived, four of them with Seaple clinging to their backs. They swam into the ship's hold through the half-submerged hatchway. Alexee had to ask the excited cetaceans to quieten their chirps and squeals so he could hear Yonaton explaining his plan for refloating the Pelican, getting her off the reef and around to the other side of the island.

There was no time to lose, the Captain said. With the sun rising ever higher above the horizon and the morning breeze beginning to blow, they must work fast to get the ship to safety before the waves built up and made the rescue impossible. Already the ship was creaking from the extra weight of water slapping against her broad hull.

The crew began taking up slack in the two anchor lines, and Yonaton tightened the rope that Mammed had heroically fed through the halyard block. From the mast top it stretched out across the water where it met the bow-line, halfway to the anchor. The effect was to pull the Pelican upright, its mast groaning under the strain.

"She's a tough old girl," Yonaton said to Mammed, who was looking worried as the ship was slowly righted. "Her mast has withstood many a squall in its time."

Sliding the pods one at a time from the deck of the log-canoe catamaran, Mammed and Desmun passed them to Alexee and his Seaple who were treading water in the ship's open hold. The mermen allowed the pods to fill nearly full with water, trapping enough air at the closed upper end to keep them just buoyant. Then they pushed them below the surface and secured them with ropes in the corners of Pelican's capacious hold, four each side forward, and three each side aft.

Before they had finished tying them in place, the dolphins were diving repeatedly to blow air into the open lower ends of the pods. Gradually the deck of the Pelican was starting to lift out of the water. Alexee supervised the dolphins to ensure the pods filled equally, spreading the increasing buoyancy, but already the deck was beginning to creak with the pressure. The dolphins also brought up ballast stones in their beaks for the two teenagers to stack on the catamaran's deck until it could safely take no more. Most of the remaining ballast was dropped through the hole in the hull on to the reef, leaving just enough to give the ship some stability.

Little by little the Pelican rose further from the water, but there were fearsome cracks from below, where the broken hull remained impaled on the pinnacle of reef. Mammed, who had been kneeling by the main hatch watching the activity inside the hold, called out to get the Captain's attention.

"How is it going in there, Alexee?" Yonaton appeared at the hold where the water was now well below deck level.

"Ggllgg fillee fullee no watee," came the gargling reply.

"Say again, and slowly please, Alexee."

"Podee, fillee fullee. No watee!" Alexee gestured towards the pods in the nearest corner.

"Are all the pods now full of air? No water at all?" Yonaton wanted to be sure he understood.

"Ess, ess. Fillee fullee." Alexee smiled and nodded enthusiastically.

"And how about the reef? How much higher do we need to lift so the ship will clear it?"

Alexee held his arms out wide and indicated with his webbed fingertips there was still a long way to go.

"I'm going to tip the ship over…" Yonaton made a tipping motion with his hands, "to see if we can break free from the reef. You tell Mammed here…" the Captain turned towards the lad leaning over the main hatch beside him, "when the hull is clear of the reef, then we can pull her off. Okay?"

Moon 3660

The Ringway was full of morning commuters as Ktrina rode the belt to her Sokwest office. She had given her boys an extra long hug before they set off for school, the memory of her close run-in with Coopan security still fresh in her mind. She *had* taken a crazy risk, and she still had no idea why she'd been given the egg, or what she was supposed to do with it.

She guessed it had some sort of surveillance function, but couldn't imagine what she might want to spy on. There must be a clue, she thought, in the words whispered by the wild-eyed man with the broken tooth, and the numbers that promptly vanished from the drawstring bag. It had to do with Ethan… but what, exactly?

Thinking about her husband, the father of her three boys, made Ktrina wish the egg-spider contained some magic… could somehow bring him back to life. But she had got past those desperate years when every day she half expected him to appear around the next corner, to see his handsome, smiling face and feel his arms wrap around her once again. Thankfully that desperate stage of grieving was over, but a dull, background ache remained, along with a sense of injustice and a hunger for answers. She knew it was stupid to hope that this weird little device might provide them, but she couldn't shake the idea. It dangled before her like a fine gossamer thread.

Ktrina was taking her first sip of chai at her office desk, preparing herself for another uncomfortable call to Gunta Krems, when the receptionist stepped in to say she had a visitor. It was a distressed woman, she said, anxious for news of her husband who had been detained in the north yesterday.

"Ah, yes. I know about this. Can you ask her to wait while I make a call, please? I need to get an update on his situation."

"Good morning, Foreign Minister. I'm calling for an update on Adam Khouri, the businessman who was detained at Monterey Skyport yesterday." Ktrina was trying her best to sound calm and impartial.

"Ambassador Rozek." Gunta Krems made no attempt to hide his disdain. "Your Mr Khouri remains in detention and will do so until we determine the security risk has passed."

"What security risk?" Ktrina felt her pulse quicken. "You know he has been supplying medical equipment for the benefit of your hospitals and patients for years. He is an honest businessman who had *no idea* he was not supposed to talk to me. How can you *possibly* imprison him for that?"

"If you would like to make a submission, in person, to the High Priest, he may reconsider—"

"Oh, I see! This is not about Mr Khouri at all, is it? It is about humiliating me." Ktrina realised they could probably hear the anger in her voice outside her office. She continued more quietly. "I hadn't realised Daval Nakash was now in charge of your foreign policy. I won't be asking for a private audience with him. But I will be giving an interview to the media shortly where I will make a statement about Mr Khouri's arrest and unjustified detention—"

"You would *compromise* our joint military operation? Your government would have something to say about that, I'm sure…"

Ktrina smiled. She had caught him out. "You are the only one who has mentioned a military operation, Mr Krems, over a standard encryption transmission. So you can drop the pretence that security is at stake. Release him or by midday the Moon's news media will be aware of the cynical games you are playing. Goodbye."

She sat for a minute, waiting for her blood to stop boiling, thinking what she might do after being dismissed for undiplomatic behaviour. Threatening the Coopan Foreign Minister might just amount to gross misconduct. Appearing on the news without permission definitely would.

Taking a mirror from her bag, Ktrina checked for tell-tale signs that she'd lost her temper. She buttoned her collar to hide her crimson neck, then forced herself to smile before rising and opening the door. "Mrs Khouri? Would you like to come in now?"

"I'm so sorry to trouble you, Ambassador." The man's wife was early forties, but her red eyes made her older. "I'm worried sick about my husband. He didn't come home from the north yesterday and I've been told he's been arrested! I can't imagine what for. He's an honest businessman—"

"Please, Mrs Khouri. Take a seat. Can I get you something to drink?"

"No. No thank you. You hear such terrible things about their prisons and courts. I don't know what to do..." Her voice dissolved into sobs as she searched her bag for a handkerchief.

"Here..." Ktrina handed her a cup of water. "Please, drink it. And I will explain what is going on."

"You know something...?"

"I do. I was there, at Monterey Skyport, when he was arrested yesterday afternoon. Oh, I'm sorry..." Ktrina passed her a tissue. "Please, finish your water so you don't spill any more. Then I'll tell you what happened."

Mrs Khouri nodded, gulped the water and handed Ktrina the cup. "Thank you."

"Your husband is entirely innocent. He was arrested over a silly misunderstanding."

"What happened?" She was wide eyed.

"He, umm... he spoke to someone who was subject to security surveillance. Someone who was not allowed to speak back."

"I don't understand?"

"Neither did he. So he tried again to speak to this person and the Coopan authorities decided there was an attempted breach of security... and arrested him."

"How do you know all this?"

"I was the person he attempted to speak to."

"You!?"

"Yes, and it was my fault, Mrs Khouri. We found ourselves sitting together on the Metro, on the way to the skyport. I spoke to your husband briefly. Then at the departure lounge, when he tried to make polite conversation, I remembered I wasn't supposed to speak to anyone..." Ktrina wanted to avoid the impression that her husband had been flirting.

The woman sat open mouthed and stared at Ktrina.

"The next minute, those Xinto monks had escorted him away. I had no idea your husband would be prevented from catching his flight home. Or that he would still be detained this morning. I have protested his innocence to the Coopan Foreign Minister, both yesterday and again just now. I'm sure they will release him soon. They have absolutely no reason to keep him—"

"It's ridiculous!"

"Yes, it is. But unfortunately, in the north, ridiculous things can happen. Have you been there yourself, Mrs Khouri?"

"No, and I never will. I won't let Adam go back ever again, either."

"Well, let's get him home first. I have told their Foreign Minister that I will go to the media and say the Coopans are holding an innocent man for no reason. I may have overstepped my diplomatic brief somewhat, but I'm hoping the threat might get him released more quickly."

"That's very kind of you."

"Not at all. The least I could do, in the circumstances. Now, why don't you tell me all about your husband, and this medical equipment he has been making?" Ktrina hoped her visitor would be distracted, but before Mrs Khouri could reply, there was a knock at the door and the receptionist reappeared.

"Sorry to interrupt you, Ambassador, but I thought you would want to see this message immediately." She passed the folded note and slipped out of the office.

"Ha! Well *who's* the scaredy-cat now, eh?"

"What's happened, Ambassador?" Mrs Khouri looked worried.

"It's a message from Gunta Krems, Cooper's Foreign Minister. It says your husband has been released and will be on the 11.00 flight home," said Ktrina, with a victorious grin.

Earth 1504

The Pelican heeled precariously as Captain Yonaton heaved on the mast-head line, but its timbers remained impaled on the reef. Then a larger wave lifted the hull and, with a splintering crack, it finally broke free from the grip of the sea bed. Yonaton yelled to the crew to haul in the anchor ropes to pull the ship into deeper water. It was already mid-morning and the wind and waves were building dangerously.

Swaying drunkenly, the ship wallowed low in the water, but she was afloat… just. The crew laboured at the capstan to haul her to windward against the battering waves. Conor, who had slipped and fallen on his broken hand earlier, was now sitting disconsolately in the stern of the rowing boat, trying to avoid further injury. The two teenagers were busy baling water from the catamaran which was threatening to sink under the weight of ballast stones piled on its deck. Boat and catamaran were still tied to the Pelican and were being tossed wildly by the seas.

Mammed looked up from his baling when he heard Desmun whimpering. He understood why the apprentice priest was scared. Between the frantic shouts of the crew, the crash of waves and flying spray they seemed in the midst of chaos. Mammed prayed it would not end as it had two days previously – in catastrophe.

A string of sharp clicks announced the presence of dolphins, one of them with its smiling face just an arm's length from Mammed's position at the stern of the catamaran. They had swum out through the breach in the ship's hull.

"Don't worry, Desmun," he shouted. "See… we've got the dolphins to look after us now."

The Pelican turned her back to the waves as the crew fought to winch in the stern anchor. The change in motion caused the smaller boats to pitch and crash against the ship's side. Mammed was forced to stop baling and hang on. He saw that Conor was now sitting in the bottom of the rowing boat to avoid being thrown out and shouted to Desmun to do the same. The next big wave tipped the catamaran sideways and with a rumble half the ballast stones slipped off the deck. Mammed wasn't sorry to see them go.

A shout from the ship announced that the stern anchor had pulled free and the Pelican began to turn her bows towards the waves. Hauling now on the bow anchor rope, the crew slowly pulled the ship away from the reef and into deeper water.

"Mammed!" Benyamin pulled the catamaran up to the ship's stern. "You and Desmun have to go help at the capstan. We're needed in the boat now."

The two teenagers scrambled onto the ship and made their way across the swaying deck to the big wooden winch. They took over from the crew, pushing on the spokes to turn the drum and wind in the rope. The ratchet at the capstan's base clicked and clacked as it slowly rotated.

"We're about to lift the bow anchor." Yonaton wheezed with the effort. "Then the crew have to tow us south with the rowing boat, so we don't get blown back onto the reef."

Mammed trusted the Captain's judgement, but couldn't imagine how the rowing boat might pull the ship, especially now it was full of water.

"Some of the ballast stones fell off the catamaran, Papa Yon," he said. "We almost got tipped out too. And the dolphins came out of the hold, but I think Alexee and his Seaple are still in there."

"Yes, I know. I asked Alexee to stay there and make sure the pods don't move. If they come adrift, we lose the ship." He grunted as the capstan came to a halt. "Right, hold it there, lads. I'll go check on the anchor."

Yonaton arrived at the bow to find the anchor rope plunging steeply into the sea, and several links of chain visible. A few more turns on the capstan and the anchor would pull free from the seabed. The rowing boat appeared with Ben and three crew at the oars, Conor steering with his one good hand. The Captain threw them the end of a long coil of rope which he hoped would tow them to safety.

"Soon as the anchor lifts, row south for all you're worth," he called, before returning to the capstan.

"Okay, lads. One last heave and we'll get the anchor up." Yonaton looked astern to where the waves were crashing on coral heads just a few ships' lengths away. He gave a tired grin. "Then we'll find out if we can beat the wind and waves and pull the Pelican clear of the reef."

Moon 3660

Ktrina smoothed the freshly-printed combat suit over her long legs and stood up to slip into her body armour. It wasn't always possible to get along to her Tae Kwon Do class during the week, so she was taking full advantage of the visa ban to catch up on her training. She had been stuck at Yook Dan level for two years and was eager to progress higher, so a session in her lunch break would help. Besides, after all the stress and frustration of the past twenty-four hours, she needed to kick the daylights out of something.

Mrs Khouri had thanked her profusely for getting her husband released so promptly, and asked if Ktrina would come to meet him at the skyport. She had declined. It would be better for them to enjoy their reunion alone, she said, while thinking Mr Khouri might be none too pleased to see her, as she had been responsible for getting him arrested in the first place.

Besides, she'd had a week's work to catch up with after her vacation, and before that a call to make to the Foreign Office. She had confessed to Jorg Lanimovskiy the threats she had made to his opposite number in the north to get the businessman released. He was pleased with the outcome, but not impressed with her methods, warning her against such behaviour in future.

It was the reaction she had expected, but it left her feeling deflated as she caught up with her deskwork. By lunchtime her muscles and her mind were clamouring for a workout after all the sitting and travelling of the day before. So she had jogged to the Sokwest Fitness Centre which housed her Tae Kwon Do club and was pleased to find the Grand Master free to give her an unscheduled lesson.

Now, as she strapped on her helmet and stepped out of the changing room into the practice hall, she saw the Saseong – the Grand Master – waiting on the training mat. He greeted her with a courteous bow and shake of the hand, then called, "Jun bi!"

Ktrina brought her fists up to her chin, then thrust them downwards to show she was ready. Both combatants moved their right legs back and brought fists level with cheek bones, leaning forward in the fighting stance. For an older man, the Saseong was surprisingly nimble and dodged her opening move easily. He retaliated with a twirling kick to the ribs that shocked and winded her, despite the armour.

Self control! C'mon, you can do this!

A feint to the side then a jump and her kick grazed his chin with her toes. *That's better.*

He attacked, she spun. He lunged, she parried. She whirled, dropping to one hand and felt her foot connect with the side of his helmet. He shook his head and smiled. She was wide awake now, and felt the Indomitable Spirit coursing through her veins.

Forty minutes later she was showering away the sweat and discovering several new bruises. Awash with endorphins and glowing with satisfaction, she felt no pain, just like the old days on the athletics field. But this was different, and in some ways it was better. *Perseverance, passion and performance, but without the publicity.*

She smiled at her internal wordplay, grabbed her towel and stepped into the drying booth.

Her third pregnancy had drawn her athletics career to a close. She had continued training in order to regain her fitness, but turned down competitions, knowing she would never achieve her former glory. It was hard to find meaning and purpose after Ethan's death. For a long time, nothing seemed worth doing and it was a year before a friend talked her into trying martial arts. Then, like today, she found she had ample reserves of aggression and enjoyed learning how to channel that energy into precise and controlled action.

She slipped her combat suit into the recycling chute, stepped out of the changing room and headed for the exit.

"Ktrina!" the Grand Master's voice caught her before she reached the door. She turned and raised her eyebrows. "Can you come to the awards ceremony on Saturday?" he said as he closed the distance between them.

"Umm... possibly. What time?"

"Fifteen hundred. I'd really like you to be here, if you can. Bring the boys with you."

"Okay," she smiled "We'll be here. And thanks again for today. It was a great workout."

"Indeed it was, Ktrina. You have lost none of your fire."

Earth 1504

Conor roared words of encouragement, some of them fit only for sailors' ears, as the men heaved on the rowing boat's oars. The tow rope twanged taut with every stroke, but it was hard to tell if the ship was responding. Yonaton dashed the length of the Pelican's deck to check on the coral reef. From the stern it appeared to be getting closer. He ran to the ship's side where the catamaran was lashed fore and aft.

"Don't bale, just paddle!" he shouted. The two teenagers looked up in surprise. "Otherwise we won't clear the reef!" He jumped down onto the front of the catamaran, took his paddle in bloodied, rag-wrapped hands, and started paddling furiously. The two teenagers sensed the danger and copied him, digging liquid lumps out of the sea.

After a hundred strokes, Yonaton stopped to take a look behind them. There was no doubt now. Despite their frantic efforts, the Pelican was drifting inexorably towards the crashing white water at the edge of the reef. This time there would be no reprieve. His precious ship would be reduced to splintered wreckage. He felt a bump as the keel touched the first outlying coral head on its way to destruction.

He started to untie the catamaran, to give the boys a chance of survival, but was stopped by a burst of clicks and squeaks. Alongside the Pelican, playing in the waves, were seven dolphins, smiling and nodding their heads, seemingly oblivious to her fate. *What if...?* Yonaton dashed to the main hatch and called to Alexee.

"Ess, ess!" He replied to the Captain's question. The Chief of the Seaple then dived, swam out through the hole in the hull and resurfaced amidst the dolphins. Yonaton ran to the foredeck to prepare ropes. Whistles and squeals greeted him as he flung the first out over the water. It was caught by a grinning dolphin and soon pulled taut as it headed towards the rowing boat. Six more ropes followed and soon the sea ahead of the ship was alive with bucking shapes and splashing tails as the mammals went to work.

He ran to the stern where the pounding surf boomed and crashed. It was close enough to make his ears hurt. Yonaton stood gripping the stern rail, staring into the boiling water, as slowly, gradually, the Pelican began to inch away from the maelstrom.

With the Pelican clear of the reef, the wind became friend instead of enemy, blowing them steadily westwards. He called to Ben and the crew to rest their oars and told Alexee that the dolphins should take a break from their towing duty too. They might be needed again when the ship reached the entrance to the lagoon and he wanted them rested, just in case.

The ship swayed ponderously with her belly full of water, but Yonaton decided she might carry a sail to hasten their progress. He called on the boys to stop baling the catamaran and join him on deck to hoist the smaller stern sail. By the time it was up and trimmed securely, the gentle morning breeze had built into a full blow and the ship strained to push her half-sunk bulk through the sea. He squinted at the sun and judged it to be midday.

For the first time since they set off in the middle of the night, Yonaton felt he could relax a little. He turned to Mammed, who was standing next to him at the wheel, to say something about the way things were going, but the words never came. Mammed and the ship slipped sideways and something dark and heavy sprang up to knock him senseless.

Moon 3660
"Yeeeaaaooow..." The eight-year-old twirled a mini-meatball through the air on his fork and... "SPLAT!" plunged it into the plate of potato and guacamole.

83

"Jan! Don't *play* with your food!" His grandmother Sofi scolded him angrily.

"Oh, Mum... he's just being a comet." Ktrina was enjoying her boys' company at supper, especially as her eldest son, Paul, was sharing his school history lesson from earlier in the day.

"Go on, Paul, what else did you learn?"

"Well, the Earth was very different before Comet Santos hit. There was hardly any ice at all then... only a little cap at each pole. And there were thousands of cities, each full of millions of people... over eleven billion altogether—"

"What's a billion?" Jan asked as he bit into his meatball comet.

"A thousand million – don't you know *that?*" Paul had to get a dig in.

Jan stopped chewing for a moment. "Wow! That's a lot. Where'd they put 'em all?"

"In the cities, *dummy.*"

"Paul! Please be civil to your little brother." Ktrina was determined to keep the peace. "Jan, just listen to what Paul has to say without interrupting. I want to hear the rest of his lesson. Go on, Paul."

"The seas were full of ships carrying cargo and the skies full of airplanes carrying people. Everybody travelled all over for holidays and business. Then Comet Santos came and changed everything."

"Did it all happen at once?" Ktrina wondered how much of his lesson he'd remembered.

"No. They tried to deflect the comet but it just split in two. The first part did the most damage but it was the second part that killed all the people."

Sofi scowled and put her spoon down in protest. "Do we *have* to listen to this *awful* story while we are trying to eat our supper?"

"Yes, Mum. It's important the boys learn these big lessons from history, and I'm interested to see how much they know."

"Well, it's giving me indigestion." Sofi pulled a face to prove it. "I'll eat mine in my room, if you *don't* mind." She took her bowl and wandered off, muttering.

"Go on, Paul."

"The first part was called Santos One and it crashed in the ocean. Then, a year later, Santos Two landed in the desert and filled the atmosphere with deadly toxins."

"Hmmm, I'm betting your lesson included more detail than *that*, Paul." Ktrina frowned and smiled at the same time. "Let's hear about Santos One first – where and when did it land, and what was the result?"

"It was… it was… the Atlantic Ocean… near Spain. I can't remember when. It caused fires and tidal waves and made lots of volcanoes erupt all at once. Lots of people died and the dust in the atmosphere blocked out the sun."

"That's good, Paul. The year was 2087. What was the effect of the dust blocking out the sun?"

"Well… all the plants died, so there was nothing to eat. And it got cold. Very cold. That's why there's so much ice covering the planet now. After the dust cleared there was so much snow everywhere, it reflected the sun's heat back out into space."

"Good. Anything else you remember about Santos One?"

"Umm… It killed nearly half the people. But the other half would've survived – well, mostly – if it hadn't been for Santos Two."

"So, Santos Two was bigger, was it?" Ktrina was fishing for answers.

"No! It was smaller. But it landed in the wrong place. It crashed in the desert where some bad men had buried lots of deadly toxins years before. They went 'PFFFT'…" he demonstrated with hand-gesture explosions, "and spread all around the world and killed everybody that was left."

"Yes. That's about right, Paul. Well remembered. There are more details, but you will learn those in future lessons, I'm sure."

"And the only people left…" Jan was keen to get some praise too, "were the people living here on the Moon. They were our anteaters." He gave a food-smeary grin.

"Ancesters, dear. Not anteaters." Ktrina smiled back.

"Anteaters are animals, dummy!"

"Paul! I asked you to be civil. You used to get names wrong when you were eight years old, now say you're sorry, please."

"Sorry."

"Okay, now let's finish our supper," she looked at her middle son, "and perhaps Grig will tell us what he has been learning?"

Ten-year-old Grig was always the quiet one, but he was a good listener and consistently outperformed his classmates in tests. Getting him to open up and start talking was the tricky part.

"So…" Ktrina smiled at him, "anything to add to our Earth History lesson, Grig…?"

"Um, well, we've been learning all about the Ark Disaster."

"That's good. What can you tell us about it?"

"The Ark was a big spacecraft built to carry 100 people. They were going to recolonise the Earth, but they never got there. The Ark, and all the colonists, burned up in the atmosphere."

"When did this happen, Grig? Can you remember what year?"

"It was 2156, almost 70 years after Comet Santos. The dust clouds had cleared and the middle part of Earth – around the Equator – looked safe for people to land on. So they built this great big ship, the Ark, and loaded it with equipment and sheep and goats, as well as all the people. But something went wrong and it all got burned up."

"Why is Earth's atmosphere so hot?" Jan wanted to know.

"It isn't normally," said Grig. "But the Ark was going so fast it sorta rubbed on the air and got hotter and hotter until the whole thing burned up."

"Not a bad explanation," said Ktrina. "So… what happened after that?"

"The Lunar Parliament changed the constitution. No more attempts to colonise the Earth. And then they destroyed all the plans and tools for the Ark, so nobody could build another one."

"Yes, that's correct," she said. "And how do you all feel about that?"

Jan shot his hand up, as if he was in class. "Yes, Jan?"

"We shouldn't allow all those people to get killed," he said with a pout.

"Okay. Any other thoughts?" Ktrina looked at the older boys.

"I don't think it's right," said Paul, "that we're not allowed to go back to Earth. If some people want to go and know the risk, we should let them."

"I see. And how about you, Grig… what do you think?"

"My teacher said the politicians are scared of getting the blame if more people die. They are afraid of losing the next election. So none of them is willing to change the constitution."

Ktrina smiled at him and nodded. "I think your teacher is probably right."

Earth 1504

"Ben!" Mammed cupped his hands to his mouth as he hailed the rowing boat. "Papa Yon's fallen down. He won't wake up!" Conor heard the alarm in the teenager's voice and pushed the tiller to bring the boat alongside the Pelican. Ben and one of the crew scrambled aboard.

"Help me move him into the shade," said Ben, as he brushed the hair from the Captain's face and prised open an eyelid. "He's pushed himself too hard. When did he last drink something?"

Mammed thought about the two green coconuts that he and Desmun had shared that morning and realised the Captain had had nothing. He had been too busy, rushing about organising everything. "I don't think he's had anything, Ben…"

"I thought so. It's drydration. Is there any coconut milk left?"

"Yes, there's four on the catamaran."

"Fetch one then, Mammed. We'll see if we can bring him round."

The Pelican had sailed around the southern side of Tapu Island, keeping a respectful distance from the encircling reef, and now approached the narrow entrance to the lagoon at its western end. The Captain sat on the steering deck, back against the wheel stand, nursing a coconut in his lap. It had been a while since he came to and they had helped him to sit up, but he showed no sign of moving further.

"How are you feeling now, Papa Yon?" Mammed was holding a spoke of the great wooden wheel, although steering was unnecessary. Ben and the crew had returned to their oars, and the ship was being towed once again by the rowing boat and dolphins.

"Dizzy… throbbing head." Yonaton fingered the fresh lump on the back of his skull, and squinted up at the lad. "Sorry I blacked out on you, Mammed." He lifted the coconut and drained the last of its milk, before setting the green husk down.

"You scared me. Your head banged so hard on the deck…"

"Yeah, I can feel it. Never had that happen before. Must be getting too old for this."

"You hadn't taken a break, Papa Yon. Or had a drink or anything."

"Huh. Silly old fool, eh?" Yonaton grinned, then winced as his head throbbed again.

"I think you were worried we wouldn't get the Pelican off the reef in time."

"It's not just the ship at stake, Mammed. We need it to get back to Loming and rescue your brothers and sister from that brute, Gorbel. And we nearly didn't make it. If it hadn't been for the dolphins—"

"They're pulling us again now, Papa Yon. We're nearly at the gap in the reef."

"I better get up… see what's going on." Yonaton lifted his arm. "Give me a hand, son."

It took a few heaves, and a fair bit of groaning from the Captain, before he was upright and hanging on to the wheel for support. He used his hand to shield his eyes from the sun.

"Mammed…?"

"Yes, Papa Yon?" The teenager was still holding on to his father, afraid he might fall again, but the Captain was looking over Mammed's shoulder, staring intently at the southern horizon.

"Is that a sail?" he said. "Or have my eyes gone funny too?"

Chapter 6
The Egg Spider Mystery
Moon 3660

The egg sat snugly in the palm of her hand and Ktrina, perched on her bed in her nightdress, stared at it intently. After this morning's misunderstanding with Sofi, she'd decided not to plug in. If it wouldn't reveal its purpose through symbols or codes, perhaps she might gain a flash of inspiration and guess what she was meant to do with it.

It was too finely crafted, too beautiful, to be a plaything. She had seen plenty of animated, mind-controlled toys when she was a child. She had longed for a fluffy kitten that would jump onto her lap when she willed it, and purr when stroked. All the other children had simpets and she had pleaded for one. But her mother had been unmoved and said Ktrina would never have one. She was mistrustful of anything that had access to the mind of an adult, let alone a child. And it turned out she was right.

The revelation that unscrupulous operators were able to hack in to the pets' wireless transmissions, and had been routinely messing with the minds of innocent children, sent shock waves through society. All simpets were recalled, leading to the collapse of the manufacturer. Over the months that followed, high profile court cases led to the imprisonment of the worst offenders. New wifi protocols were introduced, but ultimately it was accepted there was no way to shield transmissions from a determined hacker.

Ktrina remembered it well. She had spent her thirteenth birthday sulking in her room, with a boring mechanical cat that would respond only to voice commands. Her geo-chemist father also chose that day to announce he was being posted to a distant mining town, and would be home only once a month. Her mother had been even more irascible than usual and Ktrina sensed that her father's new job was more about escape than promotion. Within a year he stopped coming home at all and she later learned he had a new lady in his life, although her mother used a different word to describe her.

When she was old enough to travel independently, Ktrina would go visit her father, Matt, and his new wife, Leyla, at their home in the mining town of Barringer on the far side of the Aitken Basin. More recently her ambassadorial duties required Ktrina to visit all the major Sok settlements at least twice a year, so it was easy to combine work with pleasure and keep in touch. She had grown to like her step-mum and was pleased to see her father happy at last. Maybe this week off from visiting the north was a good excuse to go see them again.

She made a mental note to plan a trip for Thursday, then turned her attention back to the smooth grey ovoid in her hand.

Signal hacking was clearly the reason that the egg, when it transformed into a spider, was connected to its host via hard link. The graphene nanofilament might be microscopically slender, but it ensured the egg, and its operator, kept their secrets. But why was it so thin? Was it to stop it being spotted by whoever was being surveilled? That seemed unlikely, since the spider itself was hardly inconspicuous. You wouldn't miss the spindly device creeping in to your office, boardroom or bedroom.

Come to think of it, the egg-spider was a rubbish spying tool. It was way too big! She thought of the microcams in Coopan public toilets. Foreign Minister Lanimovskiy had warned her about them before her first official visit to the north. Once you knew what to look for, they were easy to spot, despite being no bigger than a nail-head. Positioned over doors, they were intended to catch drug-dealers and other criminals, rather than some twisted voyeurism, she was told, but that didn't make her any more comfortable in their beady gaze.

So what use was a spy cam mounted on an animated spider as big as a grapefruit? It didn't make any sense. Maybe she would ask her father on Thursday. He was the only person she could trust with such a secret. She slipped the egg back into the box in her wardrobe and resolved not to think about it any more until morning.

Earth 1504

"Where?" asked Mammed, following the Captain's pointing finger. "Oh... yes, a white sail! I can just see the top of it."

"Who would be sailing out here, I wonder?"

"Want me to climb the mast and take a look, Papa Yon?"

"No. We've had enough falls for one day. If they're coming this way we'll find out. If not, it doesn't matter." The Captain turned and looked over the Pelican's bow. The rowing boat was entering the patch of calm water that signalled the gap in the reef. "Besides, we're about to enter the lagoon. We need to keep our wits about us, or we'll be in trouble again. Looks like a narrow passage through the reef."

Yonaton glanced at the catamaran, still tied to the left side of the ship. Desmun had ceased baling now they were in calmer waters in the lee of the island. "We need to tow the catamaran behind the ship now, Mammed. Can you move it for me – tie it back here?" He jerked his thumb over his shoulder to indicate the stern rail.

As Mammed started down the steps to the mid deck, the Captain called after him. "And bring a couple more coconuts, one for us and one for Alexee and his Seaple."

Yonaton was right to be concerned about the width of the gap in the reef. The tips of the rowers' oars grazed the coral as they passed through and the dolphins were swimming closer together as they negotiated the narrow channel, each with a tow rope in its mouth. He turned the wheel to keep the Pelican in the deepest water, but with her hull half sunk, it would be a close thing.

Mammed stood on the side deck, watching the dark shapes slip past, and gripped the rail as the ship's hull bumped and scraped a coral head deep beneath his feet. Slowly the Pelican nudged her way into the lagoon, passing one of the mermen waiting to close the tree-trunk barrier behind them. Below it hung a heavy net and Mammed understood its true purpose for the first time. It was meant to stop sharks from entering the lagoon.

He turned and ran up the steps to the steering deck. "We did it, Papa Yon!"

The Captain gave a tired smile and nodded, but the boy walked past him, as if he'd seen something behind them. "That sailing boat, Papa Yon – it's the Petrel, Jack and Ifan's fishing boat!"

Yonaton left the wheel and joined Mammed at the stern rail. He held his hand over his eyes and squinted at the white and black smudge near the horizon. "Are you sure, Mammed? Can you see who's on board?"

"No, I can't see anybody. But that's their boat, I'd know it anywhere."

"Can it be they've escaped...?" The Captain was scratching at his beard "And what about Lucy...?" He was muttering more to himself than Mammed.

"I don't know, Papa Yon. But whoever it is they're definitely coming this way." He looked down at the catamaran being towed behind them, where Desmun was standing, also staring at the southern horizon. "It's my brothers' fishing boat!" Mammed shouted. "Maybe they've come looking for us!"

Moon 3660
"That's it, Taryn, pull them good and tight." Ktrina smiled at the young woman strapping in to the seat next to her. "These old hoppers get a bit bumpy on the drive shifts. I don't want you falling out." She winked to make sure the nurse knew she was joking.

As the flight deck lighting faded and the vessel ran through its pre-flight checks, Ktrina wriggled to get comfortable before snugging her own straps down. The hopper, one of the ministry's ancient Zenits, was worn and grubby from a thousand similar trips, and still carried a faint acrid odour after last month's electrical fire. The craft had undergone a full refit, and the screen diagnostics all checked out, but it still left her feeling uneasy. She put it out of her mind and called the tower.

"Sokwest control, this is flight SBH27 awaiting clearance for takeoff, outbound to Barringer." The hopper, like all lunar spacecraft, would fly itself. Autopilots were almost faultless these days, with built-in back up systems, so there was little to do. Ktrina need only liaise with traffic control and they would initiate the takeoff, but, as a conscientious pilot, she always kept an eye on the ship's systems.

The screens showed the view outside the windowless craft, plus a superimposed map and dotted line, the projected path to their destination. The mining outpost of Barringer, on the far edge of Apollo, itself on the rim of the vast South Pole Aitken Basin, was a township of just 2,400. Rich mineral deposits left by a cataclysmic impact back in the Moon's early history, sustained a steady population. Ktrina's father Matt had met biosphere manager Leyla twenty years ago, and they had made the quirky little town their home ever since.

"Flight SBH27, stand by. Your flight is cleared. Takeoff will follow in two minutes."

Ktrina took her three boys to visit their granddad and his wife two or three times a year, much to Sofi's disgust. The youngsters loved it, getting to play with rock samples and explore the vast plant rooms of the vertical farm, as well as running wild in the town arboretum.

"Flight SBH27, takeoff in one minute."

She had decided against involving her father in the egg-spider mystery. He worried about her trips to the north anyway. He would be alarmed if he thought she was mixed up in some secret or subversive activity there.

"SBH27, ten seconds..." Ktrina glanced at her fellow passenger, whose eyes had widened in anticipation. "... five, four, three, two, one..." The hopper shook as the primary rocket drives lit up.

"Goodbye, SBH27. Have a good flight."

Ktrina and Taryn sank into their seats as the hopper lifted off from the Sokwest Skyport, the motors lofting them up and away from the bustling city below. At 2000 metres the vibration stopped abruptly and the two passengers were flung against their straps, eliciting a brief yelp from Taryn. Two seconds later they thumped back into their seats as the plasma drives took over.

Ktrina looked across at the pale, startled face and smiled reassuringly. "Told you there'd be a bump. Don't worry, it's smooth and easy now until we get to Barringer."

"Then what?" The nurse had told Ktrina she'd only travelled on commercial flights before. She hadn't realised the posting to Barringer would mean sharing ministry transports, a money-saving ploy reserved for government employees.

"Oh, just another little bump when we switch back before landing. It's fine, really. You'll soon get used to it." Ktrina unclipped her straps and began extricating herself from her cradle-like seat. "We'll be in half a gee for the next hour, so you can get out if you like. Fancy a coffee?"

"Half a gee? What's that?" The nurse's brow furrowed.

"Half of Earth gravity? You know… three times the normal lunar gravity?" Ktrina had levered herself upright and was trying to swing her legs over the side of her seat.

"Is that why my arms feel so heavy?" The girl grunted with the effort as she tried to move her hand toward her strap release.

"Yeah." Ktrina smiled at her. "You weigh three times your normal weight right now. It's fun. I like to get up and walk around, but you have to give your balance time to catch up." She sat, legs dangling, waiting for her head to stop spinning. "It can take a while."

"I think I'll stay in my seat, if you don't mind." Taryn's hands had flopped back to her sides. "I'm not as strong as you. You must still be as fit as when you were athletics champion."

"I wish!" Ktrina slid carefully to the floor and stood hanging on to her seat for support. "No, those days are long gone, sadly. But I do try to keep in shape… running, martial arts, that sort of thing."

"You're amazing, Ktrina. I can't believe you have three children and manage this career as Ambassador too. If I looked as good as you do—"

"Nonsense. You are young, fit and healthy with an amazing career in nursing. There's no way I could do your job." Ktrina took a tentative, leaden step towards the hostess unit. "So… a coffee, or something else?"

"Oh, no thank you. I'm feeling queasy. I can never drink that apple juice they give you on the commercial flights. But you go ahead, please…"

The two women chatted while Ktrina sipped her drink and paced carefully around the cabin, testing her legs against her new-found weight, tripled by the relentless thrust of the flight. It felt like she was carrying two people on her back. The effort made her heart thump and her breathing laboured, but she always enjoyed pushing her body to its limits. Only when the craft rotated in mid-flight to turn the plasma drives' thrust into a sustained braking force, did she lay back in her seat, as demanded by the hopper's polite, but insistent voicebot.

Sixty-three minutes after takeoff they were both strapped in and bracing for the drive change on the final descent into Barringer. At the moment the plasma drive cut and they once again fell against their straps, Ktrina saw the lights dim. It was the briefest of flickers and by the time the rockets had kicked in two seconds later, she thought maybe she'd imagined it.

She turned to Taryn. "Did you see the lights flicker just then?"

The nurse opened her eyes. "What? No... sorry, I had my eyes shut. I don't like that bit." She frowned. "Is there a problem?" Her voice shook with the vibration of the rocket motors.

"No. No, I thought I saw something, but maybe it was just me." She forced a laugh. "I don't like that bit much either, to tell the truth."

"Flight SBH27, five minutes to landing." The voicebot, at least, sounded relaxed.

Earth 1504

The pale blue lagoon was alive with mermen and dolphins. In the shallows between the beach and the deeper water where the Pelican was anchored, tanned bodies of men, women and children swam. It seemed like all the Seaple had gathered to welcome the great ship to their waters. Among them slipped and bobbed the sleek grey shapes of dolphins, raising toothy grins to chatter in bursts of delighted clicks.

Mammed, watching from the Pelican's steering deck, couldn't help but smile at the dolphins' faces. Their excitement matched his relief that the ship had been saved from certain destruction on the reef. The aches in his shoulders and arms, and the dull, hot throb from his blistered hands, felt like a badge of honour. They had come very close to being swept by the wind and the breakers onto the reef. It was a miracle, he knew, that nobody had been seriously injured, or worse.

His joy soared when he saw Miriam waving to him. She was with her father, Alexee, who was also being hugged by an older woman. Maybe it was Miriam's mother? He'd wondered where her mum might be. They would have been worried about Alexee, out there

94

in the shark-infested ocean, and pleased to see him back safe. Without the Seaple, and the dolphins, Yonaton and his crew would have stood no chance of saving the ship.

Mammed was joined by Conor, whose place in the rowing boat had been taken by the Captain. They turned and watched the boat pulling purposefully for the gap in the reef, going to meet Ifan and Jack's fishing boat. It was now close enough to make out one of his older brothers on the Petrel's foredeck, preparing to lower the sail.

"Well, I'll be jiggered," said the bosun. "Who'd'a thought the Cap'n's two sons…" he turned to Mammed, "his two older sons, that is, would be sailin' over 'ere. 'Specially after that nasty so-an'-so, Gorbel, was given instructions to lock 'em up." He shook his head slowly. "Summat must've 'appened, that's fer sure."

Mammed said nothing, and the old seadog clapped his one good arm around the boy's shoulders. "I 'spect we'll find out, soon enough. An' in the meantime, we can be getting' ourselves ashore, young Mammed. If that rascal Desmun 'asn't sunk 'is cat'maran already." He let out a raucous laugh.

"C'mon lad," he steered Mammed towards the log-canoe contraption now tied alongside once more. "You two'll 'ave to do the paddlin' mind, since I ain't got 'nough 'ands fer the job."

Mammed winced as the paddle pulled at his blisters, but forced a smile for the benefit of Miriam, who was swimming alongside.

"You look tired, Maa-med." Her freckled brow was furrowed with concern. "And your hand is bleeding!"

"Yeah." He glanced down at his right hand which wore a smear of crimson, and sighed. "Been paddling since midnight, and I'm worn out." The bows of the catamaran scrunched on the coral sand and he dropped the paddle into the canoe. "Hopefully, that's the last of it."

"Let me see."

"What?"

"Your hands, Maa-med. Let me see them." She raised her webbed fingers towards him.

Mammed leaned over and turned his painful, claw-like hands outwards. She delicately prised his fingers open with her thumbs and saw the burst blisters and swollen palms. "Oh, these are very bad, Maa-med. My mother will help you." She turned and called, causing the woman with Alexee to look round.

"Is that your mum?"

"Yes, my mother, Rachel. She is doctor." Miriam beckoned her to join them.

Up close, Mammed could see the similarity. With her deeply freckled face and long blond locks she looked like an older version of Miriam. When she smiled at him, Mammed felt he already knew her.

"Ah," she said, "so this is Maa-med I heard so much about!" She took his hands in hers and examined the palms and fingers. "How you do this?" She looked up at him with a furrowed brow.

"Paddling."

She looked at Miriam. "What is this... 'paddlin'?"

"Show her, Maa-med."

He withdrew his hands, picked up the paddle and demonstrated how he used it.

"Ah. Too much working!" She dipped his hands into the sea. "First wash."

Mammed rubbed his hands together in the water and tried not stare. It was awkward with two naked women at his fingertips, especially as Miriam's mum's breasts were bobbing at the surface and appeared to be beckoning to him. He coughed and shifted his kneeling position in the stern of the canoe.

Rachel pulled her large grey shoulder bag around to her front, opened its flap and extracted a green kelp bulb with a stopper in it. "Shake off water," she said. Mammed shook his hands, then she leaned forward and squeezed a thick brown goo into one palm. "Rub together, please."

"Oww!" He took in a sharp breath through his teeth.

"Yes, stings a little." She looked up and smiled again. "It is good, strong idine, antisep."

Mammed had no idea what that meant, but he put on a brave face and worked the cream into the raw craters where blisters had rubbed off.

"Okay, now..." she produced a broad brown ribbon of kelp frond from her sharkskin bag, "we keep it clean." Rachel wrapped the kelp around his palms, finishing each bandage off with a tidy knot at the back of his hands. "Keep on for three days. And no more 'paddlin'."

"Can you do mine, please?" Desmun, who had been watching the procedure, offered his bloody hands for inspection.

"Yes," she said, "and then..." she turned to Conor, who was sitting, arm in a sling, on the side of the catamaran, "... then I look at hand of old man." She smiled and winked at him.

"Well, I'll be jiggered!" he said. "Old man, indeed!"

Moon 3660

96

Six hours later Ktrina was on the skyport bus, waiting as the airway locked on to the hopper's flank with the usual clunk and hiss.

"There you are, Miss." The white-haired driver gestured to the airlock. "Ready for boarding, when you are. Have a pleasant flight." It was a novelty having a human bus operator, and Ktrina rather liked the personal service.

"Thank you." She smiled, shouldered her bag and folded the service printout as she walked to the door. The single-sheet report gave the results of a diagnostic test on the craft's electrical systems she'd asked for. It was followed by a short statement that the hopper was functioning normally and a squiggle that she took to be the technician's signature. It was peace of mind, and she was grateful they'd taken seriously a flicker she'd perhaps only imagined.

She stowed her bag in the compartment at the back of the pilot's seat, climbed in and clipped her harness together. In the screen's outdoor view she could see the skyport bus making its way back to the terminal, where its elderly driver would soon be knocking off. Hers would be the last flight of the day from the sleepy outpost. Her old ministry hopper, meanwhile, was running through its autonomous pre-flight checks, and Ktrina was ready to go home. She cleared her throat, then initiated departure.

"Barringer control, this is flight BSH14 awaiting clearance for takeoff, returning to Sokwest." Ktrina was alone for the return trip, which would give her time to think over the representations she'd received from Barringer's citizens. They were the usual mixture of claims for more money and petty squabbles about power and position. She had treated all requests with the same diplomatic courtesy and would relay them to the relevant government departments. They in turn would bury them without trace, unless she made a point of backing a particular project, or promoting an individual she felt deserved it. In her opinion few did, but she felt a great weight of responsibility knowing she could influence their success or failure. Making those decisions was her least favourite part of her job.

"Flight BSH14, stand by. Your flight is cleared. Takeoff will follow in two minutes."

Relief had come from the pleasant hour she'd spent with her father and step-mum over a late lunch. They had been eager to hear about their grandsons' progress and pressed her for a date to bring the boys to Barringer for a holiday visit. She promised to let them know within the next few days.

"Flight BSH14, takeoff in one minute."

They had heard about her involvement in the release of the Sokolovan businessman, whose wife had told the media of her help in gaining his release. They tut-tutted over the capricious nature of Coopan justice and made it clear they were very proud of her. Ktrina was thankful she had not mentioned her secret egg to her father. He would be less than pleased with her over that. Ethan also disapproved, judging by his frowning face that appeared when she closed her eyes.

"BSH14, ten seconds…" Ktrina tugged her straps and wriggled into her seat's padding as the controller counted down to zero and liftoff. Ethan was still there, and was trying to say something to her, his lips moving silently, but it was the controller's voice she heard.

"Goodbye, BSH14. Have a good flight, and come back soon, Ktrina." She smiled as the lights of Barringer dropped away in her screen's window view. She knew whose voice that was – the dishy, dark-skinned one who always wore a blinding grin when they met in the terminal. Come to think of it, she nearly always bumped into him in the terminal! Maybe that was no accident…?

She was still smiling as she watched the altimeter count up to 2000 and braced for the bump of the drive change. It came with the usual lurch which threw her against the straps. But this time, all the lights went out.

Earth 1504

"You won't fix that with a bit o' seaweed." Conor extracted his arm from the sling and proffered his purple, bloated hand. Miriam's mum Rachel, who was also the Seaple's doctor, inspected it carefully. Mammed and Desmun, cradling their bandaged hands in the stern of the catamaran's nearest canoe, leaned forward to get a better view.

"Oh, oh, oh. Bad, bad, bad," she said. "How you do this?"

"Was that ol' Cardinal. Smashed it wiv 'is staff, 'e did."

"Show me…"

Conor picked up the paddle and brought it slowly down to a stop between his thumb and index finger. "Like that, only 'arder. A lot 'arder."

She pressed gently on his knuckle and the old sailor winced. "Ow! That 'urts, missis."

"Broken bones, I think." She looked up into his craggy face. "When this happen?"

"Two days ago, and yeah, broken bones, fer sure. Don't s'pose yer can do much, can yer?"

"We must reset bones, or they cannot heal. But first we look inside."

"Look *inside*!" Conor withdrew his hand in horror. "You ain't gonna open me up are yer, missis?"

"No! Not to open." She turned and called to Alexee, who was talking to others near the Pelican's stern. They exchanged a few gargling words and then she looked back at Conor. "Peetee can look inside for us. Dolpheen... Peetee." She pointed a webbed hand at a silvery shape that was slipping rapidly through the water towards them.

Conor looked worried, his face growing more creased as the dolphin drew close. "Wassee gonna do then...?"

"He can see inside, see broken bones." She smiled. "Don't worry, it won't hurt."

The dolphin raised its head with a toothy smile and greeted them with a burst of clicks. Rachel replied with strange grunting noises, made in the back of her throat. Then she turned back to Conor. "Your hand goes under water for Peetee to see inside... please?" She indicated he should join her where she knelt in the crystal-clear sea.

Conor slipped off the canoe into the waist-deep water and let her take his hand again. "You sure this ain't gonna 'urt?"

"No, no. It is okay. Please, just keep still."

Then the dolphin slipped under the surface... and produced a stream of high-pitched squeals and squeaks that made Conor's hand tingle and his ears buzz. Rachel turned his hand sideways and the squeaks repeated before the dolphin surfaced and proceeded to fire a volley of chirps and trills at her.

She lifted Conor's hand from the water and had an extended grunting-clicking conversation with Peetee while tracing lines on the back of Conor's hand with her finger. Finally she turned to him and said. "You have two broken bones... here and here." She touched his hand lightly.

"Wha'..? 'E can *see inside* my 'and... jus' by *squeakin'* at it?"

"Yes. Peetee is the best." She smiled.

"Well, I'll be jiggered." Conor used his good hand to scratch his head.

"Now we have to set the bones. And first, we get snail to stop the pain."

"A SNAIL!"

"Yes, of course. Magic snail – conus magus. Don't you know this?"

"Never 'eard o' no snail for stoppin' pain. You sure about this...?" Conor did not look convinced.

"You can try without – if you so tough you don't feel any pain...?" She looked at him with raised eyebrows. "We must reset bones, or maybe go bad and have to cut off hand..." She circled his wrist with her finger and thumb.

"I ain't 'avin' that!" He growled. He thought for a few more seconds and then said: "Magic snail it is, then."

Rachel gave a few grunts of instruction to the dolphin, who sped away with a flick of his tail.

"I can't get over 'ow you talks to each other like that." Conor laughed and shook his head. "'Ow did you ever learn to do it?"

"Easy. When we babies, we play with them. Learn to speak Dolpheen as well as Seaple. We learn Inglees, also. My daughter..." she turned and smiled at Miriam who was watching nearby, "is teacher for the new ones."

Rachel heard a noise and glanced over her shoulder. "Ah, good. He has found one." The dolphin reappeared with a white and brown cone shell held delicately in the tip of its beak. Conor was not impressed. "Oh no, not one o' them! Tha's a cone snail, missis. Dangerous li'l devil, 'e is. One sting could kill yer!"

"So, we must be careful. He has two stings. One to catch little fish, one to defend himself. We must be little fish." She opened the flap of her sharkskin bag and withdrew a fist-sized pouch. From it she produced a small dead fish and a razor-sharp flake of obsidian. With one swift movement she sliced the side off the fish and held it out to Conor.

"Hold this on your hand. Keep it in the water and stay very still." She lowered the cone shell into the water nearby and held the remainder of the fish in front of it. Everyone leaned forward to see what would happen next.

Slowly, cautiously, the shellfish extended a tube and appeared to be sniffing the water near the fish. Then an orange-tipped tentacle reached out and Rachel moved the shell closer to Conor's hand. He watched in horrified fascination as the tentacle closed in and...

"Ahhh!" He jumped back and leaned against the catamaran for support. "Ow! Owowow. That stings!" He looked accusingly at the doctor.

"Only for few seconds. Wait, please..."

"Oooo, tha's goin' all numb now."

"Good. Magic cone has done its job. He can have fish for reward..." she let the mollusc draw the fish into its expanding maw, "and Peetee can take him home." The dolphin took the creature tenderly in its beak, and headed back out to the reef.

"Now," she said taking Conor's hand, "when is numb, we can get to work."

Moon 3660

It took a couple of seconds before Ktrina realised the lights weren't coming back on, and the plasma drives hadn't fired up. Why didn't the back-up power kick in? In the eerie silence and utter darkness that followed, she, and the hopper, were in freefall.

"*Oh, shit!* Gotta find a light." She struggled to release her harness buckle and then grabbed the side of her seat to stop herself floating away in the zero gravity. If she lost her grip in the dark she knew she would be as good as dead. Her hip and leg banged something as she groped her way to the back of the seat, which swung on its gimbals with her every movement. Finally she found the compartment on the seat back, reached in and unclipped the flap of her bag. Immediately she felt items floating out and let go of the seat to jam the bag's flap shut again to avoid losing them.

Now she and her bag were floating free in the pitch-black cabin and something hit her head then her back. Fumbling inside her bag she finally located the one useful item – her penlight. She let go of the bag and used both hands to hold the diminutive torch and switch it on. The beam illuminated a crazy, upside down cabin filled with the floating contents of her bag.

Fighting an overwhelming urge to vomit she swept the penlight's beam to locate the cabin door. There, beside it, was the craft's switch panel. Would clicking the main power switch off and on again bring the ship back to life? It was her only hope… if she could reach it. She tried swimming towards it with her arms but nothing happened. A kick from her legs connected with something and she shot across the cabin and crashed into the door. As she bounced off it, she grabbed for the nearby handle… and dropped her torch.

"No!" She made a grab for the spinning beam and missed. Lunged again and… "Got it!"

Ktrina jammed the penlight in her mouth and clamped it with her teeth. Pulling herself to the panel she yanked open the clear plass cover to reach the switches. At the top was the circular isolation control knob. She grabbed and twisted, off and then on. Nothing. Off and on again. Nothing. Her heart sank like a falling rock.

Ktrina could sense the ship was turning, beginning to tumble as it reached the apex of its trajectory. From here it would be an inexorable fall to the surface. There was nothing she could do to stop it. Ethan appeared again, his mouth moving frantically.

"What?" Her shout of desperation was distorted by the torch in her mouth. "Oh, God! Please help me, Ethan…!"

Tears were clouding her eyes, the water pooling between her eyelids in the weightless conditions. She shook her head to clear her vision. Ethan was still there, doing something with his hands, pushing an invisible something from one to the other. *What does that mean?*

She swung her gaze and the torch beam back to the panel. Maybe the answer was behind it? At the corners were four swivel catches. She scrabbled to twist them open, fighting her body's desire to spin in the opposite direction, with only her left hand on the door handle for leverage. The ship was clearly rolling now, falling over itself in its rush to meet the pock-marked lunar crust. Finally the panel fell forward and hung from a forest of cables. Ktrina grabbed both sides of the bulkhead opening and thrust her head forward.

Twisting her face to shine the light around the compartment, she saw something odd – a rectangular black electrical socket with nothing plugged in it. *There!* Waving gently at the end of a thick red cable was a rectangular black plug. She reached in and grabbed it, checked which way up it fitted and thrust it into the socket.

With a crackle the power surged back into the ship's systems, lights flickered on and a cacophony of noises assaulted Ktrina's ears. She daren't let go, in case the plug fell out again, but then saw a wire clamp beside the socket and pulled it across to hold the plug in place. So that was to blame – a simple clamp left undone when the hopper was rewired? But why no backup power?

She pulled her head out of the bulkhead and stuffed the switch panel back in place, just in time to feel the first of a series of jolts hammer through the ship. Ktrina realised the flight systems were trying to stop the hopper from spinning and reorient it ready to fire the thrusters. She'd better be strapped in before that happened, but making her way back to her seat was proving difficult. The cabin was jerking with each corrective pulse and alarms and instructions were blaring at her from all sides.

Among the jumble of noises was one voice she recognised. "Are you there, Ktrina? Come *in* flight BSH14. Can you hear me?" It was the Barringer controller.

"I'm here. But only just." She took aim at her seat and pushed off from the door. Then the cabin tilted and she collided with the ceiling.

"What's happening, Ktrina? You're dropping like a stone!"

"All the lights went out and the engines shut down." She tried to direct her chaotic tumble towards her seat once more. "The electrics fell apart, but I've got them working again now. Trying to get back in my seat before the— *ouff!*" She was winded as she hit the seat's support frame.

Ktrina finally got both hands on her seat when the motors fired and she was thrown to the floor by the first thrust of the rockets. As she hauled herself upright against the induced g-force and pulled her torso over the side of her chair, the controller was shouting at her, "Get in your seat *now!* Get strapped in Ktrina before—"

His voice was drowned out by the engines. The rockets' exhausts were inaudible due to the vacuum outside, but the fierce vibrations set up a noisy resonance in the cabin. Ktrina was thrown into the seat sideways, her body crushed in agony. Gasping with pain, she strained to turn her shoulder and finally was on her back, flattened by a weight she'd never imagined existed.

"Are you still there, Ktrina? Are you in your seat?" She could only just make out his shouts.

"Yes," she rasped hoarsely. "Sort of..." Her right knee was screaming at her in agony and she realised her leg was half outside the cradle. She grasped her trouser leg and, with gritted teeth and a violent twist of her hips, hauled her calf in over the side and her ankles clashed together.

"You're down to eight hundred metres, Ktrina. Still falling too fast. The motors are programmed to—" His voice disappeared as the engines' reverberation increased in pitch and loud cracks echoed through the cabin. She knew what the motors were programmed to do – stop the hopper crashing, even if it meant tearing the ship apart.

There was nothing Ktrina could do now. She was pinned and helpless, gasping against the crushing weight on her chest. Her screen showed a terrifying vision of craters rushing up to meet her and altimeter numbers tumbling towards zero. She dragged in a deep breath and closed her eyes...

Chapter 7
Learning To Breathe
Earth 1504

Mammed lay back in the sun-sparkled water and luxuriated in the silky touch of Miriam's long, cool fingers on his wrist. After the exhausting night and long, fatiguing morning spent rescuing the Pelican and bringing her safely into the lagoon, he'd felt tired and drained. But when Papa Yon told him his duties were over for the day, he'd jumped at Miriam's invitation to revisit the sea cave and learn some more of the Seaple's Histree.

With his hands bound in Rachel's kelp bandages, he'd had to decline the offer of a high-speed ride to the far end of the island, where the cave and the Ark lay. He couldn't hold on to the dolphin's dorsal fin, he'd said, but he would run the length of the white sandy beach as Peetee and Miriam sped through the light blue water alongside him.

It had begun as a race, but the powerful male dolphin, even with Miriam clinging to his back, had much more stamina and quickly forged ahead. Already weary, Mammed slowed to a comfortable jog and the dolphin and mermaid dropped back to match his pace. Now, in the warm sea beside the rocky outcrop that hid the cave, Mammed relaxed and let Miriam take over. This was her domain and he was exhilarated to feel the refreshing water wash over him as she pulled him through the wavelets towards the cave entrance.

"Now, Maa-med. Do you remember breathing method from yesterday?" She had stopped swimming and was supporting him as he floated on his back, her arm across his chest. "Deep breaths, like this: innnn… and outttt..., innnn… and outttt…"

Mammed concentrated on following her instructions, but couldn't ignore the tingly feeling of her hand on his skin, or the softness of her chest against his shoulder blades. He was lightheaded by the time she announced they were ready to dive down to the underwater mouth of the cavern.

"Now, breathe out – so we sink more easy – aaand… hold it." She slipped from beneath him and he felt her fingers close around his wrist once more. Then they were going down, her supple body undulating gracefully as it towed him towards the cool gloom of the cave. He'd found that thinking of something else was a good idea at times like this, and cast his mind back to meeting his brothers earlier that afternoon.

Jack and Ifan had been delighted to see him and each gave Mammed a warm brotherly hug. They showered him with praise for climbing up the sheer side of Loming's harbour tower, carrying rope and saw blades, to free their father and Benyamin from the Cardinal's clutches. They had been filled in on the details of the escape saga while the Captain, Ben and crew were towing them and their fishing boat through the gap in the reef. Both had thanked Alexee for saving their father from drowning and were amazed to hear details of the rescue of the Pelican that was just being completed when they sailed up to Tapu Island.

Yes, they *had* been arrested by Gorbel and his Convertors, but – amazingly – their sister Lucy was now in charge as temporary Mayor of Loming! The full story would be told tonight, they said, over supper, and they'd caught something special to eat...

"UuuuH!" Mammed sucked in a welcome draught of air as his head broke the surface, but no panicky gasping this time.

Miriam was smiling at him. "That was better, Maa-med. I make you into merman!"

It *was* better. Was it only yesterday she had brought him here for the first time? So much had happened, and much of it seemed strangely wonderful, like the medical procedure he had just witnessed.

"I like your mum," he blurted spontaneously. "I mean... she's an amazing doctor and everything." He felt his face heat up in the cool air.

"You must have doctor in your home... Lomee, is it?"

"Loming. Yes, but he doesn't use dolphins or *sea snails* – that's like magic."

"We use everything from sea. You use everything from land. It is different."

"Your mum looks just like you. She's pretty... only... um... older." Mammed felt sure his face must be aglow in the gloom of the cavern.

Miriam smiled at his clumsy attempt at a compliment, then frowned. "Why you not look like your father, Capteen Yon-ton?" She raised his arm above the water. "You have brown skin, and your hair—"

"Oh, Yonaton's not my real father. He adopted me after my first father, Papa Youssef, died when I was ten. He had light skin too, but my mum, Ma Fatima, has dark brown skin. I'm sort of in between."

"I like it," she said, stroking the skin of his wrist with her thumb, making his arm tingle. "Not like my spotty skin."

"You've got freckles."

"What?"

"Freckles. That's what we call those brown spots. And I... I think they look very nice... on you, anyway."

"Hmm... do you?" She pulled his hand towards her as if to inspect it further, but then leaned forward and planted a kiss on his lips. His wide-eyed look of surprise made her laugh, a tinkling giggle that reverberated around the cave.

"Come on, Maa-med," she said, swimming towards the sunlit end of the cave, towing him behind her. "Let's read more Histree. Maybe find out what made us different..."

Moon 3660

Something hard and uncomfortable was pressing into her face. Ktrina willed her eyes to open and slowly a blurry shape appeared. She tried to lift her head but her neck didn't seem to work. Everything hurt and a jangle of noises assaulted her eardrums. *This is the worst dream ever.*

Her left arm reluctantly dragged its hand up to her chin and she was able to push the blurry shape away from her face. It came into focus – a grey metal structure with holes in it. *Where've I seen this before? It's like a... like a... seat bracket! Oh, God... this isn't a dream, is it?*

In a rush it all came back. The stricken hopper, the death dive, screaming motors and the surface hurtling up to meet her. Plus the fact she never managed to strap herself in. No wonder she was wedged underneath the seats. But somehow – incredibly – she was still alive.

Ktrina tried flexing her fingers. They worked. Her arms hurt, her left wrist especially, but she managed to pull both elbows underneath her chest and started wriggling to push herself up and out. It was then she saw blood dripping from her left wrist and realised her comm had been torn off. That would explain why nobody was trying to contact her to check if she was alright. It also meant she couldn't call for help.

As she emerged from beneath the seats, after shuffling uphill on the steeply sloping floor, Ktrina slid down to the bulkhead at the back of the cabin. Another painful thump. She lay there curled in a foetal position, trying to catch her breath with a ribcage that ached with every gasp. And then she heard the reason why.

"Cabin breach. Pressure 71 percent and falling. All occupants to occupy emergency pressure bags immediately."

She had survived the crash but would soon die from asphyxia... unless she could reach one of the life preserving cocoons stowed in the safety locker. Ktrina pushed herself up into a sitting position and eyed the locker. It was up near the door, beneath the switch panel which was still hanging from its cables following her hasty scramble for her seat. *How the hell am I going to reach that?*

"Cabin breach. Pressure 65 percent and falling. All occupants to occupy emergency pressure bags immediately."

She was becoming light headed as the air became thinner and colder by the second. The floor was tilted over 45 degrees. Her attempts to crawl up it produced only pain and slippage. Ktrina stretched out and pushed her hand up as far as it would go – still only half way to the locker. She gasped for breath.

"Cabin breach. Pressure 59 percent and falling. All occupants to occupy emergency pressure bags immediately."

Come on! You can jump up there! She slid back down into a crouch, right knee screaming in protest. After a couple of deep breaths she launched herself at the locker... and missed by half a metre. Another bruising landing was followed by the slide back down and thump against the cabin's back wall. She lay crumpled, rasping on each lungful of rarefied air.

"Cabin breach. Pressure 53 percent and falling. All occupants to occupy emergency pressure bags immediately."

I'm going to die here. Ethan appeared again, mouth open but not speaking. *What?* He was holding a discus, preparing for a throw, chest rising and falling. Breathing. That's what he was trying to tell her. Ktrina dragged in a deep breath and winced at the pain from her ribs. *Again... ouch. Must get oxygen. Ten lungfuls. That's three... oww. Four... mmMM. Five... oh, God. Six—*

"Cabin breach. Pressure 48 percent and falling. All occupants to occupy emergency pressure bags immediately."

No more time. She crouched, coiled every muscle and leapt for her life. She fell just short of the locker handle, grabbed at the dangling switch panel and caught its wires with two fingers. With weary muscles and agony from her ribcage, Ktrina hauled herself upwards, jammed her bloodied left hand into the bulkhead aperture and, finally, reached the safety locker release button with her right.

Dizzy from lack of oxygen, it took three stabs with her finger to force the catch open and when it did, the locker lid flew open and heavy coiled objects spilled out, hitting her head and shoulders on their way past. Emergency pressure bags! She let go and slid back down with a dull thump.

"Cabin breach. Pressure 43 percent and falling. All occupants to occupy emergency pressure bags immediately."

With pins and needles spreading through her hands and up her arms, Ktrina plucked desperately at the release toggle on the nearest bag. It flew undone and, with a hiss, unrolled along the valley between wall and floor. The bright orange bag was turning grey. She knew what that meant – she was about to pass out. Sick with dizziness, Ktrina dragged her injured legs into the opening, grasped the zipper and pulled it up, over her head and down to the latch-lock that initiated inflation.

With a fresh hiss the bag swelled around her and sweet, oxygen-rich air flooded into her lungs, making her see stars. Muffled by the cocoon's skin she heard: "Cabin breach. Pressure 37 percent and falling. All occupants to occupy emergency pressure bags immediately."

She lay still, panting from the effort and the pain in her ribs, unable to move her bruised limbs or tortured muscles. Ktrina closed her eyes and slipped out of this world… and onto a brightly-lit sports field, where Ethan was waiting with open arms and a beaming smile.

Earth 1504
"I wish I knew how to read it too." Mammed was sitting on the rocky ledge in the shaft of sunlight coming from the hole in the cave roof. He held the curved sheet of plass for Miriam to read, and could see now it had once been part of a pod. Like those they had used that morning to lift the Pelican off the reef.

"I will teach you. After I read the next year, Maa-med."

"Okay, thanks."

She cleared her throat and began. "It is the 31st day of December 2158, the end of our second year here on planet Earth. It has been a year of discoveries and challenges, happiness and tragedy. Our colony has grown with seven more live births this past year, two amongst our small band of sea-dwellers and five for those living on the land. Sadly, one of those new babies survived only four months and one of the first year infants also died, both of unidentified diseases.

"The good news is that all 97 adults are alive and mostly well. Two of the men sustained spinal injuries while cutting down a tree and one of them, George Robinson, is now unable to walk. He spends a large part of his days working with us in the lagoon, where he can be mobile and relatively pain-free. We are still learning the lessons of Earth's massive gravity, but there are signs that we are adapting and strengthening our bones and muscles in this heavyweight environment.

"For those of us living in the waters of the lagoon, different adaptations are appearing. We now suffer none of the salt-water sores or wrinkled skin problems that plagued us in the early months. We are now able to spend up to 18 hours a day in salt water without any ill effects and our need to drink six or eight times a day from the fresh water source in the cave has diminished. This has enabled us to venture further from Christown and explore the lagoon and the island's coast.

"We have discovered two more freshwater streams on the west and north sides of the island, which means we can now live and work anywhere in the lagoon. We have also found there is only one gap in the encircling reef, a narrow passage through which dolphins now come regularly to visit us. We were initially very fearful of these large and powerful creatures, but we now know them to be friendly and sociable. They have taken to herding fish into our traps in exchange for some of the catch and it appears we have made our first new friends here on Earth.

"Sharks, however, are not to be trusted. After an attack in year one, which could have proved fatal had the fish been bigger, we have constructed and fitted a large-mesh gate to the lagoon entrance. Our dolphin friends can leap over and smaller fish can swim through, but the blood-thirsty sharks are kept at bay.

"Thanks to the foresight of our training programme before leaving the Moon, we had a good idea of which animals and plants were safe to eat, and how to commence farming, both on land and sea. With an aqueduct now bringing water from the spring above Christown, our crops are flourishing as more of the jungle is cleared. The sheep, goats and chickens we brought with us are also doing well and providing for our growing colony.

"The only limitation will be suitable land to plant and graze. We estimate our island to be three and a half kilometres long and two and a half kilometres wide. With much of the central and western part taken up with mountain, there will be a limit to the number of people who can live here. Already there is talk amongst our land-based colleagues of building a raft out of pods and tree trunks to transport some of them to the islands of Cuba and Hispaniola to the south, or to the coast of Florida further west.

"We have pooled our memories to produce a chart of the lands and seas of the Caribbean to assist us when we do venture forth, plus one of the whole planet, two thirds of which is under ice. We have also agreed on a standard length for a metre, so we can begin to measure our new homeland with some degree of consistency.

"One of the downsides of coming from an advanced society and losing all our tools and technology when we landed here, is the lack of handwriting skills. I am able to record our history only because of my former hobby of calligraphy. I fear that, besides myself, our community's only record of events passing and knowledge gained will be via word of mouth.

"On behalf of the 126 colonists of planet Earth, this concludes my second annual report. Giulia Magrini, of the sea-dwellers of Christown."

Moon 3660

"Hello. How are you feeling? I didn't expect to see you again so soon." The smiling young woman leaning over her seemed very familiar, but Ktrina couldn't recall who she was.

"I'm Taryn, remember? We flew in together this morning... in that rickety old government hopper."

The nurse! But that flight was months ago... or weeks, at least. Wasn't it?

"Nobody will be flying in it any more, Ktrina. You were SO lucky to get out alive. I was in shock when I heard you'd had—"

"Where am I... and what day is it?" Ktrina tried to lift her head.

"Nooo!" Nurse Taryn put her hand on Ktrina's shoulder. "You need to lie still, my lovely. You are in Barringer Hospital, with concussion and minor injuries – not to mention the effects of hypoxia. And it's still Thursday, about eight in the evening."

Ktrina stared at her in disbelief. "So... we flew from Sokwest this morning...?"

"Yes. We got in to Barringer just after half past nine. You went off to the admin centre to do your work, and I came here – my first day as hospital practice nurse."

"That *crappy* old hopper...!" Ktrina's eyes flew wide as she remembered.

"Yes. You said you thought there was something wrong with it. Apparently, after you took off, all the electrics went out and the engines stopped. It's a miracle you got it working again. Everybody's talking about what you did. Amazing...!"

"I need to tell someone—"

"There's no *need*, Ktrina." The nurse restrained her again as she started to rise. "They've retrieved the flight data. And they've got the onboard cam footage. They're going through it now. I expect you'll be able to speak to someone in the morning." She plumped the pillows and took a close look at Ktrina's face. "You're going to have a black eye and some nasty bruising, but no scars, so don't worry."

Ktrina lifted her left wrist, which was heavily bandaged and stung fiercely. "Tell me what I've done… everything, Taryn, please?"

"Well, your comm dock has been pulled out of your wrist, so there'll be some nerve damage to repair before we can refit it. But they found it – still attached to your comm – wedged in the seat buckle, apparently."

"Oh."

"You've cracked two ribs, but there are no organ punctures, so they will just be sore for a while…"

Ktrina pressed her right elbow tentatively against her ribcage and winced.

"And your right knee has suffered some ligament damage—"

"I know how that happened. I couldn't get my leg back into my seat when the motors went to emergency thrust. It hurt like hell."

"They say you were subjected to three gee – whatever that means."

Ktrina smiled up at her weakly. "Oh… just six times what we had on the flight out. Eighteen times our normal gravity."

Taryn raised her hand to her open mouth. "That's ridiculous!"

"Yeah, I don't recommend it – at least, not unless you're safely strapped in your seat."

"No wonder you've got so many bruises. But nothing serious, Ktrina." She smiled. "Now you need to rest. I've given you a sedative patch…" she touched the side of Ktrina's neck, "so you should have a comfortable night. If you need anything, press the buzzer. I'm in the room next door."

"But my family—!"

"Don't worry. Your father came to see you while you were asleep. He is coming back early tomorrow. Your folks back home know you are safe and resting here tonight. You'll be able to talk to them in the morning." She dimmed the lighting. "Now… get some sleep. You've done *more* than enough for one day!"

Earth 1504

"What I don't understand," said Mammed, staring at the rows of unintelligible squiggles, "is why you read them across, from left to right, instead of down, from top to bottom, like we do." His first lesson, attempting to read the Seaple script, was not going well. "And what is calligraphy?"

"Giulia Magrini says calligraphy is beautiful sort of handwriting, painting with letters. It's in the next Histree. She was the only person who knew how to write. So the land-people didn't do writing or reading at that time. They must have made a new way of writing after they left the island."

"And what about those other islands she talks about? I know Couba, it's where I come from – Portkaron is on the south coast of Couba. But she also talked about an island called Hispaniola – and something called Florida. Where are they?"

"I fetch the chart, Maa-med, then you will see where we are." She took the great sheet of plass, the most ancient Histree, and slipped under the water with it. While he waited for her to return, Mammed got to his feet and waded to the side of the Ark, where the beam of sunlight was now reflecting brightly off the green algae that encrusted it. He scraped some of the covering off and pressed his face to the smeary translucent wall, hoping to see inside. If this really was a spaceship, surely there would be some weird and wonderful things to see? But vague shadows were all he could make out. It was most disappointing.

"Maa-med!" Miriam was back. "If you want to see inside Ark, I can show you when we leave. There is a place..." she pointed downwards, "where you can look through a crack, but it is under water."

"Okay." He sloshed back through the knee-deep water to sit on the rocky ledge and look at the new sheet of plass she had brought to show him.

"This is the chart they made in that second year." She turned it so that the shapes scratched on its inner surface caught the light.

"Wow! This looks just like the chart of the Crabbing Sea that Benyamin made. Look – there's Portkaron, where I come from."

She squinted to read the small words carved into the plass. "It says Santiago de Cuba. That was its name before the comet came."

"And there's Loming on the island of Dominion." He pointed to the big island to the east. "That's where I live now, when I'm not sailing with Papa Yon on the Pelican."

She traced her fingernail under the words. "That island is Hispaniola. Or it was. And your Loming used to be called Port-de-Paix." Miriam's finger drifted north, to a tiny speck. "And here we are now... Sanctuary Island."

"Oh! We call this Tapu Island."

"Taboo? That means forbidden!"

"Yes, we were forbidden to come here by the Cardinal." He ignored her raised eyebrows, and asked, "so... where is Florida?"

"It is here, Maa-med..." she slid her finger to the left and up and stopped on a large shape that extended off the edge of the sheet of plass.

"Oh, that's Merika," he said. "Where Chief Masceola and the Dasony people live. We sailed across the Lanteek Ocean to visit them. It's in the north where the ice cliffs start. That's where Papa Yon and Benyamin were making copies of this sort of writing when the Cardinal caught them. The writing was on some big old stones. It was some sort of ancient burial place I think."

"They sound like gravestones, Maa-med. The early colonists made some here in Christown before they left the island. You should be able to find them amongst the trees somewhere."

She looked back at the chart and sighed. "You've been everywhere, Maa-med, and seen so many things. I would like to see them too, but I can never leave Sanctuary Island."

"Why not?"

"Because of sharks, Maa-med. We cannot swim out in the sea or they eat us!"

"But your father, Alexee, came this morning to help with the Pelican—"

"Yes, but only with Dolpheen for protection. He came back inside the ship."

"Maybe you can come with us on the Pelican when we sail back to Loming?"

"Impossible." She closed her eyes and shook her head. "We can't be out of water for long, or our skin dries out and we get sick. We sleep on the beach at night, when is cool, but go back in the water when the sun rises. Also... I teach the little ones. I give class this morning while you were at the ship."

They were both quiet for a while, then Mammed spoke. "This chart is great – Benyamin and Papa Yon would love to see it. Can we take it to show them?"

"I don't know Maa-med. We have to ask my father. The Histree – especially these oldest ones – should never leave the cave."

"Okay. Are you going to show me inside the Ark now? You can give me a reading lesson tomorrow."

"I put this away, then I take you." Miriam slipped under the water with the chart.

Mammed stood up and moved his shoulder blades awkwardly. His back and arms ached from the paddling marathon and, with a yawn, he realised how tired and hungry he was. And cold. The water in the cavern was cooler than in the lagoon and he was feeling chilled now.

"Come," she said, holding out a hand towards him. "We need to breathe."

Miriam held him once again as she talked him through the same deep breathing exercise they had done before diving on the way in. Then she was pulling him down, following the sloping side of the Ark into the cool depths. Finally, near the floor of the cave, she brought him to the side of the great ship and tapped the hull with her fingernail.

Mammed could make out a gap, a finger-wide crack in the plass wall, and pushed his eye close. Inside the water was crystal clear and brighter, illuminated by the sunlight shining on the hull up above. He peered at rounded shapes that looked like more plass pods, covered in silt. And there, lying on top, grinning at him with rows of teeth and hollow eyes, was a white human skull.

Moon 3660

After an early-hours procedure on her knee, followed by a long morning of checks, scans, and consultations with the doctor, Ktrina had finally been given clearance to leave the tiny Barringer hospital and fly home. She was exhausted from the visits of well wishers, accident investigators and especially by the reporter from Selene News who had flown in to cover the story of her miraculous escape. The interview, and the wreckage of the old ministry hopper, had been prime-time viewing while commuters hurried to their Friday jobs.

The only people she was truly pleased to see, as nurse Taryn settled her into a wheelchair and fussed about her comfort, were her father and step-mum, who'd come to take her to the skyport. They waited patiently as the young medic completed her duties.

"Now then, my lovely," Taryn's bedside manner and confidence had blossomed since their flight together the previous day, "all you have to do is rest, relax and let the nanobots do their work. They will be knitting your ribs back together over the next couple of days, so no heavy exercise, please, and be careful getting in and out of bed.

"Your knee is different. The doctor has reattached your torn tendons and ligaments, so remember what he said, small amounts of *very* light exercise to keep the joint moving and lots of rest. You can walk with the stick we've given you, but don't stay on your feet for more than ten minutes at a time." She bent down and kissed her on the cheek. "Have a safe flight home, Ktrina – and stay strapped in your seat this time!"

"Thank you, Taryn." Ktrina squeezed her arm. "You've been a wonderful nurse. Thank goodness I brought you with me! Hope you enjoy your time here. Barringer is lucky to have you."

Then she was being wheeled out of the medical unit and on to the beltway for the five-minute ride to the skyport. Father Matt and step-mum Leyla were quiet for most of the journey. They had been shocked by Ktrina's narrow escape and didn't know how to voice their feelings. Her dad had insisted he should go with her on the flight home to make sure she was properly looked after, but the Foreign Ministry had laid on a fully-staffed medevac transport and had politely refused his request.

She understood there were serious questions being asked about the flight-worthiness of the remaining three aged Zenit hoppers, all of which were now grounded for safety checks. She had been interviewed by the accident investigation team shortly after breakfast. Ktrina voiced her concerns about the drive change system, the loose electrical connector, the faulty back-up power supply and asked how all of this could have been missed by the diagnostic check. The technician who had left a squiggle signature on her report was suspended and undergoing 'a rigorous interview' she was told.

The news broadcast had reminded viewers that only the day before, Ktrina had negotiated with the Coopan government to secure the release of Sokolovan businessman, Alan Khouri. Inevitably, social media was full of conspiracy theories, which made her laugh. Anybody could have been allocated the faulty hopper for that day's transport... couldn't they? And if they had, it was doubtful they would have survived. It was a disturbing thought, either way.

Ktrina pushed all such thoughts aside as the double doors of Barringer Skyport zipped apart and she was wheeled in to the diminutive lobby. Waiting for her, with a blazing smile and a high-viz tabard, was the darkly handsome controller.

"Well hello again! It's the miracle woman, Ambassador Ktrina Rozek!" He swivelled his 100 watt grin up to meet Ktrina's father's non-smiling face. "And you must be Matt, Ktrina's father?"

"I am," came the frosty reply.

"Dad, this is the Barringer skytraffic controller—"

"I know who he is."

"Darryl Kyter, sir..." he held his hand out to Matt, undeterred by the icy response. "I was talkin' to your daughter when she was undergoin' her ordeal yesterday. It was a very scary time. I'm so happy to see her still alive... sir." He kept his smile fixed and hand outstretched until Matt reluctantly shook it.

"Thank you, sir. And this must be...?" He turned his attention to Leyla, who was less reluctant to shake his large brown hand.

"I'm Leyla, Ktrina's step-mother."

"Honoured, ma'am." His deep, velvet tones appeared to melt Leyla's reserve. She gave him a brief smile before looking nervously at her husband.

"I am sorry, sir, ma'am, but you'll have to say your goodbyes to Ktrina here. I'll take her through to the flight, where the medical team are waitin' for her." He glanced up at the skyport clock. "I can give you a coupla minutes before we need to go through." He turned and walked over to the check-in gate, where he chatted amiably to the duty officer.

"Dad...?" Ktrina looked up at her father questioningly.

"I don't like him," he grumbled. "Far too familiar with people he doesn't know."

"Aww, Dad. He's just being friendly. He was helpful to me yesterday... talked me back into my seat before the crunch came."

"Come on, Matt." Leyla was trying to smooth it over. "Ktrina isn't sixteen any more, you know..."

He turned and glowered at her. "She's still my daughter and—"

"And I always will be, Dad. Now be nice and say goodbye with a smile, or I won't come back with the boys. Nobody wants to holiday with a grumpy granddad." She tried to wink at him, but her bruised face wasn't as supple as normal, so she gave a short laugh instead, to let him know she was joking.

"Oh, okay," he said with a resigned sigh. "You scared the hell out of me, Ktrina. I just want to wrap you up in cotton wool, that's all."

"I know, Dad," she said, pulling him down for a kiss. "I know. But I'll soon be all mended. You don't have to worry." She reached out to Leyla who gave her a gentle hug and peck on the cheek. Ktrina saw the smiling Darryl was walking back towards them.

"I'll be fine. Really." She smiled and squeezed their hands.

"Sorry folks, but the bus is waitin' and we have a schedule to keep..." Darryl took the handles of the wheelchair, gave them another few seconds for goodbyes, then wheeled her through the check-in gate and into the small departure lounge.

"Sorry about my dad."

"Hey, that's alright, Ktrina. Now… I've got somethin' for you." He stopped the wheelchair and walked to the front, pulling off his high-viz tabard. Underneath was Ktrina's shoulder bag.

"My bag!" She was delighted. He dropped it into her lap.

"I went back early this mornin'. Couldn't get your things yesterday, 'cos we had a rush to get you out of the wreck and into the hospital. I only found your comm unit 'cos I saw your wrist bleedin'."

"You were there last night?"

"Of course! I am on the emergency lifeship crew. Whenever there is a call – which is pretty rare in Barringer, I gotta tell ya – I'm usually first on the rescue ship 'cos I work right here at the skyport."

"What was it like… the old hopper, I mean."

"Oh, a complete wreck, Ktrina. How anybody survived that crash is a miracle. And if you hadn't got in the pressure bag when you did, we would have been too late. Even with our turnout time – 22 minutes from crash to rescue – you would have been long gone, my girl." He patted her shoulder gently as he resumed wheeling her towards the departure gate.

"Thanks. And thanks for finding my bag." She opened the flap and was amazed to see her things inside. "… and my stuff, wow!"

"Prob'ly didn't get everythin'. I couldn't find your little torch," he said, "and I figured that was fairly special to you?"

"Oh, my penlight. It saved my life, Darryl. If I hadn't had that, I'd never have been able to fix the electrics."

"That's what I thought, so…" he brought his large brown hand around in front of her face, "I got you a replacement." He opened his broad palm to reveal a tiny torch, identical but fluorescent orange instead of red. "This should be easy to find in the dark… next time you have an emergency."

Earth 1504

Mammed burst into the air, coughing and spluttering. Miriam, who had pulled him up from the depths of the cave when she sensed his distress, looked concerned. "What's wrong, Maa-med?"

"It's a… a skeleton." He was wide-eyed with shock. "The skull… of a person… inside there." He shook his finger accusingly at the Ark as he coughed up water.

"Of course! It is Chris – Christakis Niarchos. The Ark is his tomb. I told you yesterday he was in there… remember?

"Yes, but…" He looked away, frowning.

"But you didn't believe me!"

"So he… really *did* come from the Moon? In a *space*ship?"

"*Yes,* Maa-med!" She slapped the water with frustration. "*This* spaceship – the Ark!"

"I'm sorry. It just didn't seem possible…"

"So, you think I make all this *up*?" She was angry now. "You think we Seaple build this… this *Ark* and carve some fairy story onto sheets of plass just to fool you? Why…?"

"Sorry!"

"Oh, Maa-med." She huffed and shook her head. "You landsmen are so *ignorant* of your past. You stay on this island only nine years then sail away to make your home in Cuba and Hispaniola and Florida. And because you don't have writing, you *forget* what happen before. We keep the Histree, we keep the language and the Ark, we keep the *truth* all these years. Then you come back and say you don't *believe* it!"

"Sorry. Look… I'm sorry. We didn't know. Our parents didn't know either. Our school teachers didn't know any of this, so nobody could teach us. Now it's… it's a lot to take in." He looked away from her freckled face and studied the rotund bulk of the Ark. "And it does seem a bit unlikely – a spaceship bringing us here from the Moon! You've got to admit, that does sound like… well, like a fairy story, doesn't it?"

Miriam didn't reply, but her frown said it all.

"I *do* believe you, Miriam. Well, I do now anyway. But we'll have to convince all the others too, or they'll just think I've gone crazy. We'll have to show them the Histree, and you'll have to read it out to them. And we'll have to bring them in here and show them the Ark, so they believe it too."

A faint buzz made them both turn and look towards the far end of the cave, where the entrance lay deep beneath the water.

"It is Peetee!" said Miriam. A few seconds later the dolphin burst out of the water and landed with resounding splash, which echoed around the cavern. Then his grinning beak was surging towards them and a volley of deafening clicks and whistles made Mammed put his hands over his ears.

"He's come to fetch us," she said. "There is food. Everybody is waiting for us."

The mention of food made Mammed's empty stomach growl. "Good! I'm hungry. Let's go."

Chapter 8
I Always Look This Good
Moon 3660

Ktrina twisted the little penlight and thrilled at the bright beam that burst from it. She tried to turn her head to look up at him, but her neck was too stiff. She clicked the light off and slipped the torch into her bag.

"Thank you, Darryl. You didn't have to do that." *What does he want, apart from the obvious?*

"It's nothin'. A thank you for brightnin' up my life."

She was quiet, not sure where this was leading.

"And I ain't hittin' on you, Ktrina, so you can put that outta your mind right now. Pretty dull round here most the time. You come over to see your father three, maybe four times a year. Makes me happy, that's all. Nothin' more to it."

They arrived at the departure gate and a bored middle-aged woman held her hand out for Ktrina's papers. "You the one that crashed yesterday?" She barely glanced at Ktrina's black and blue face, bandaged wrist or walking stick.

"No, I always look this good." Ktrina couldn't help herself. The grin hurt her face.

"Bwahahaha." Darryl doubled over with laughter. When he straightened up he said, "Maisie, I heard you ask some dumb questions, but that one takes the biscuit."

The woman was smiling now. She handed Ktrina's papers back. "Well, I hope you have a better flight today."

"Thanks! I hope so too."

On the skyport bus the same white-haired driver from yesterday was waiting at the wheel. Like everyone else, he had seen Ktrina's interview and the images of the mangled hopper on the news. He expressed his deepest regret for the accident, wished her a speedy recovery, and apologised for the lack of wheelchair access through the bus's airway.

"No problem, I have a stick," said Ktrina as the airway locked on to the medevac hopper. She started to struggle out of the wheelchair, but Darryl stooped and slipped an arm under her knees and another behind her back.

"Allow me," he said then stopped and looked at her questioningly.

She hesitated for a moment. "Okay, but be careful with my right knee and ribcage. They are fairly delicate right now."

121

Darryl lifted her gently and carried her through the airway into the hopper, where two medics were waiting to strap her into a cradle-cot. Darryl lowered her delicately onto the padded bedding, kissed her on the forehead and whispered, "Get well and come back soon, Ktrina."

Earth 1504
Mammed had thoroughly warmed up from his long run along the sand. He now stood, breathing heavily, beside the fire Benyamin was tending. Miriam and Peetee, who arrived well before him, had been swallowed up by a large group of Seaple and dolphins gathered near the shore. They were listening to Captain Yonaton, who appeared to be telling them a story.

"... so the wicked Cardinal took my ship," he turned and pointed to the Pelican, "and gave chase to the three of us – me, Benyamin and Mammed." He paused while Miriam translated, via throaty grunts, for the benefit of the Dolpheen. "Our only hope of escape was to sail through the reefs of this island, where the Pelican couldn't follow."

Mammed sat down next to Ben and asked, "where's everyone else?"

Pointing with a smoking stick towards Jack and Ifan's fishing boat, Ben said, "your brothers have gone with two of the crew to fetch our supper – they caught some tunnyfish earlier today, so we will all get a feast." He threw the stick into the fire and jerked his thumb over his shoulder. "The other three are in the trees, collecting fruit."

The Captain's voice drifted up the beach towards them. "... turned back to see if we could save anyone, but a huge wave picked up the catamaran and threw us over the reef into the lagoon."

Mammed turned and eyed a pile of ropes, canvas and spars that had appeared at the top of the beach, beneath the trees. It appeared to be the contents of the Pelican. "What's that lot up there for?"

"We've been emptying the ship," said Ben. "Removing everything we can to make it lighter so we can haul it up the beach."

"Haul *the Pelican* up the beach...! Why?"

"There is hardly any tide here, Mammed. If we want to repair that hole in the ship's side, we need to tip her over and pull her out of the water. Then we can replace the damaged ribs and planking."

"Oh, I see." In truth, Mammed could not imagine how they would pull a whole ship up the steeply sloping beach. It sounded like a crazy idea.

"I could do with more firewood, Mammed. When you've got your breath back…"

"Yeah, okay." He struggled to his tired feet and headed up into the woodland.

Mammed had loaded his arms with as many fallen branches as he could carry, when he heard voices coming through the trees. It was Desmun, Conor and one of the other crew members, each carrying a bulging sack. Conor was struggling to keep his bag on his back using only his left hand.

"'Ello young Mammed," he called out. "You on sticks duty, are yer?"

"Yes. You look like you've got a lot of fruit."

"Not only fruit my lad, there's loads o' yams and cassava growin' back there." He lifted his chin to indicate the forest behind him. "Gonna be a good feast today, an' I'm well ready for it, I can tell yer."

They walked on together, Conor keeping his jovial banter going, until Ben looked up from the fire and smiled at the size of their stuffed sacks. "That lot should keep us going for a while."

Down at the water's edge, Yonaton appeared to be coming to the end of his story. "So when we have repaired the Pelican, we will sail back to Loming and tell them the news. Tell them there is a thriving community of sea people living here." He waited for the translation to finish, then continued. "We will re-unite our two peoples and bring you the benefits of our land-based civilisation, and trade with you for your products of the sea."

As he concluded his speech, the rowing boat approached the shore and Ifan held up the tail of a huge silvery fish, so large its head remained hidden in the boat. "We have enough fish for everybody," he announced with a grin.

The sailors were sated for the first time in weeks. They had gorged on roast tunny, baked yams and cassava, followed by a variety of fresh fruit. They had cut the tail end of the giant fish into steaks and cooked them wrapped in banana leaves. There was enough left over to feed them tomorrow as well, despite giving the bulk of the tunny to Alexee to share amongst his people and the Dolpheen.

When they could eat no more, Alexee had called to them to come down to the water's edge and hear his daughter tell them the story of the Seaple. The ten landsmen sat in the rowing boat and on the catamaran, waiting to hear what she had to say.

Miriam coughed, then spoke clearly and confidently. "I am Miriam, daughter of Rachel, our doctor, and Alexee, chief of the Seaple. My father has asked me to tell you about our people and how we came to be here, living in the sea. If we seem strange to you landsmen, I can say we find you fantastical! It is very strange to see you walking and running on the shore on two legs, travelling in ships and boats, and burning your food with fire before you eat it!" She pulled a face and stuck out her tongue to show her disgust, which made them all laugh.

"There are now two hundred and twenty-six men, women and children in the Seaple population, spread around Sanctuary Island in three main locations. There are just a few of us here…" she turned and gestured to the heads bobbing in the water behind her, "because we live close to the fresh water streams at the east, west and north of the island.

"I can tell you how we came to be here, living in this lagoon, and why you landsmen now live differently, on other islands, because we have a written Histree which records what has happened every year since we first arrived… one thousand, five hundred and four years ago."

There was a murmur amongst the sailors as they looked at each other and raised their eyebrows.

"Yes, some of what I tell will be hard for you to believe, but we…" she raised her hands and spread her webbed fingers for effect, "are living proof that our Histree is true. And we can show you more things, later. But first, let me tell you the story of how we Seaple, and you landsmen, first came here… from the Moon."

Moon 3660

"Ambassador Roze-ek." The young medic affected an annoying wake-up voice that suggested she was talking to a child. "We've arrived. We're at Sokwest Skyport."

"Okay, thanks. I *am* awake." Ktrina opened one eye. In truth, she had slept for much of the flight, thanks to the sed-patch which nurse Taryn stuck to her neck before she left Barringer hospital. But she had been alert and thinking with her eyes shut for the past half hour. She relished the rare spell of peace and quiet without anyone asking her questions or trying to engage in polite, but meaningless, conversation.

"The skyport bus will be along in a minute, but you don't need to get up. We'll carry you into the terminal in this cradle-cot, and there'll be a wheelchair waiting for you there."

"Okay, thanks." Krina smiled and closed her eyes again. She didn't need more sleep, she wanted to complete her train of thought without interruption. The medic took the hint and shuffled off to whisper with the doctor who had accompanied the trip back to Sok City.

Ktrina had enjoyed the flight, despite her dad's fears she would be traumatised and fearful after the events of the previous day. Ever practical, she had reasoned that the chance of another accident, especially in a latest-model medevac ship, was vanishingly remote. So she'd relaxed and run her mind over recent events.

First there was Darryl, who was undeniably attractive, good-natured and charming. She'd noticed him before, of course. Who wouldn't? But during and after her accident he seemed to have taken on the role of protector. He'd been first on the lifeship, eager to pull her out of the wreckage, then went back next morning to gather up her bag and scattered possessions. And he'd noticed her torch – a key element in the video footage – was missing and bought a replacement. That was a thoughtful touch. Then he'd scooped her up in his arms and kissed her forehead. It had been quite a surprise, and not entirely unpleasant.

So how did his attentions sit with Ethan? She'd become so used to her late husband popping into her mind in recent days, she almost expected to see him frowning at her over folded arms. But if he was upset, he wasn't showing it. She couldn't quite work out why Ethan had appeared whenever she needed help this past week. Was he merely a figment of her imagination, her brain putting a friendly face on solutions from her own subconscious? Or was the spirit of Ethan somehow invading her thoughts in order to guide and protect her? That idea was kinda spooky and reassuring at the same time.

Thinking about Ethan brought her to the joint military action this coming Sunday. She knew they had to do something about the attacks by the FLOC, but felt very uneasy about sending Rangers out to disable the insurgents' launch system. Aristarchus had proved a very dangerous place and the last thing she wanted was for anyone else to lose their life over a bunch of stupid rebels hiding out in lava tubes.

She hoped the Coops would keep their part of the bargain. The north had such a secretive, repressive regime it was hard to know what they were thinking. And with another deadline for their Messiah's return fast approaching, she was nervous. The downtrodden Coopan population were held in thrall to their Xinto religion, which seemed more like mind control to her. Who knew what might happen when the guy with the halo failed to show up once again? Would there be protest and rebellion on the streets? Would the Xintapo use their stun-guns to quell an uprising?

She had seen the effects of their 'crowd control weapons' on one of her early visits to the north. A man had run when challenged by one of the monks. Instead of running after him, the Xintapo had calmly drawn the device from his sleeve, taken aim and fired. The fleeing man fell instantly and was left twitching and screaming on the ground. Ktrina took her cue from the locals who averted their eyes and hurried past the flailing man. It was clearly unwise to show an interest.

Back in the safety of the Sok embassy she was told the Xintapo's stun-guns shot pellets armed with a devastating electric charge. It is intended only to immobilise the victim, but frequently resulted in permanent injury or even death. Once deployed, the power-packed pellets could only be deactivated by the barrel of the gun that fired them. It was a brutal means of instilling fear in the population and ensuring compliance. Clear evidence that the Coopan government, and the religion which directed it, embraced none of the democracy they enjoyed in the south.

Why had humanity ended up like this – two disparate factions that distrusted each other? She knew the history, had read about the recriminations and the loss of hope that followed the failure of the Ark all those years ago. How the two communities had slowly drifted apart, economically, politically and ideologically. Then that idiotic Drone War, and the famine and disease that followed. Fifteen hundred years had passed and they were no nearer returning to Earth, let alone reaching out to the other planets. In many ways they were no more technically advanced than the original colonists, back in Nadia Sokolova's day. How could five and a half million people be so blinkered and stupid?

She thought about the aged hopper that had almost killed her the day before. Recent government cutbacks had extended the service life of antiquated equipment that should have been scrapped years ago. Outsourcing of repair and maintenance had led to complaints of shoddy workmanship before, but nothing as catastrophic as her crash.

Her medevac ship had flown over the remains of her mangled hopper a few minutes after leaving Barringer. She'd kept her eyes open and focussed on her screen long enough to see the lights of the salvage team, mere specks on the dark lunar surface. It brought to mind shipwrecks from a distant time and place, with a verse from one of her favourite poems, penned over 1600 years ago.

I stumble from my unmade bed
To watch the unmade sea
Where mighty swells surge to the beach
And crash and churn, cold fingers reach
To claim the souls of wounded gulls
That limp among the broken hulls
Strewn by the surf-washed quay

She couldn't remember the rest of it and made a mental note to look it up when she got home. There was something about the lyrical lines that evoked tempestuous oceans in her imagination. But then the events of the past 24 hours, plus the effects of her sed-patch, had washed her thoughts away and she'd drifted off again.

"Here we are, Ambassador." She felt her cot move as the two medics pulled handles from either end, and picked her up. "On to the bus now. Then you'll soon be home again." She would be pleased when this irritating nurse, who spoke as if Ktrina was five years old, handed her over to the person waiting for her with a wheelchair. With any luck it would be her sister-in-law, Jean.

Earth 1504

Once the laughter had died down, and Miriam's annoyed frown had faded, she returned to the story of the Seaple. She sounded undaunted as she addressed the sailors. "You will not laugh so much when I show you the remains of the Ark, the ship that brought our ancestors here."

"That'll be a good 'un, young lady!" It was Conor who spoke up. "Any ship'd rot away in one hundred years, let alone fifteen hundred!"

"A ship like your Pelican, yes," she said. "It is made of wood. But this ship is made of plass, like the pods you used to lift your Pelican from the reef this morning. You have all seen these pods, so tell me, how would you make something like that?" She stared at them defiantly, waiting for an answer.

"You landsmen couldn't do it, could you? Nor could we. The skills and materials needed to make such things were lost to us after we arrived here. So what remains of the Ark is the inside part, made of this same plass material. The outside of the ship, which was made of metal, rotted away many years ago. And inside the ship are the remains of its pilot, a man I think you all know as Lord Kris? His real name was Christakis Niarchos—"

"It's true," said Mammed, "I've seen him – well his skull, anyway."

"Chris was the pilot and leader of the one hundred colonists who flew in the Ark from the Moon. Something went wrong, and the ship crashed into the lagoon here instead of landing on the coast of South America—"

"South Merica? Never 'eard of it! Where's that then, missy?" It was Conor again.

Miriam looked exasperated and turned to her father, speaking in the lilting, gargling tongue of her people. Alexee nodded, spoke to one of the Seaple men and then made the odd groaning noise in his throat that passed for language with the dolphins. Peetee, the largest of the Dolpheen, promptly sped away to the east, with the man clinging to his dorsal fin.

Miriam explained. "They have gone to fetch the chart. It is one of the oldest parts of our Histree and very precious to us. It was created by the colonists soon after they arrived here and will show you where is Suriname, South America, and all the islands of the Caribbean Sea."

"Thank you, Miriam," said Yonaton. "Please continue, and if we've got any further questions, we will save them until the end." He turned and stared the bosun in the eye. "Won't we Conor?"

"That we will, Cap'n. An' sorry for the interruption, Miss."

She took a deep breath and continued. "The Ark was damaged when it landed and started to sink. The captain, Chris, and his co-pilot released the pods from inside the ship. Each pod contained a colonist and they floated to the shore inside them. That's why we still have pods today. Some pods contained seeds for vegetables and trees, some had animals for farming.

"But when Chris went to release the most important pods – the ones containing tools, medical things and signalling equipment – he became trapped and was drowned when the Ark sank. For many years the Ark sat at the bottom of the deepest part of the lagoon, where the people were unable to reach it. Only much later, when the Seaple had learned to work with the Dolpheen, were we able to recover the remains of the ship and put it inside the sea cave where we keep our Histree. Anyone who would like to see it can do so.

"When the colonists arrived from the Moon they were very weak and could barely lift themselves from the sea. Most of them crawled ashore, but fourteen decided to remain in the water where their weakness was less of a problem. Life was very difficult for those first people without any tools or medicines. Some of them died from injury or disease. They had babies and many of those died too. Slowly they grew stronger and planted trees and crops. They farmed the animals they had brought with them. They caught fish and supported each other.

"After a few years it became clear the island was too small to support a growing population and the landsmen started making plans to leave for the larger islands to the south and west. They made a boat like your cat-maran using the pods and wood. After nine years living on this island, half of the people left and moved to Cuba. The next year the rest of the landsmen went to Hispaniola, the island you now call Dominion. We Seaple remained here and this island, this lagoon, has been our home ever since.

"Since the first year, we have kept a written record of events here at Sanctuary Island. One of the colonists had a special skill of handwriting, at a time when none of the others did, and over the years that skill has been passed down from generation to generation. I am the latest Guardian of Language and it is now my job to teach the children and write down our Histree each year."

Miriam paused while Alexee whispered something in her ear. "My father has reminded me to tell you... after they left the island, the landsmen returned every few years. They came in ships made of wood, and brought stories of discovery, of making metals and building houses made out of stone. Some of them started a new colony amongst the forests of Florida and spread north to the lands of ice.

"Then there was a long time when no landsmen came to visit us and we thought we had been forgotten. Finally, thirty-three years ago, a boat sailed to the island and brought a fisherman named Frank, and a younger man called Henry. They stayed here three days, learned our Histree and then left. Nobody has come to see us since then... until you arrived."

The Captain cleared his throat. "Can I say something here, Miriam?"

"Yes, I have finished story."

"Alexee told us yesterday about this visit from Fisherman Frank and a fat young man named Henry—"

"That sounds like it could'a bin our Cardinal, don't it, Cap'n."

"Yes, it was. You're probably old enough to remember, Conor, when fat young Henry returned to Loming harbour in Fisherman Frank's boat, but without Frank? He told of a storm, of old Frank being swept overboard and a visitation from God. He used it to justify his religion and begin his reign of terror. But he never mentioned spending three days here, learning the Seaple's Histree. Instead he said this island was forbidden and any boat that approached it would founder on the reefs and its occupants would be eaten by the evil inhabitants of the island."

"What! You think we are *evil?*" Miriam voiced her shock.

"No! Of course not, Miriam. Just the opposite. It was a story he told to stop other landsmen coming here and finding out what he'd done." Yonaton paused and looked at his fellow sailors.

"We think he pushed poor old Frank overboard on the way back to Loming and left him to drown. Then he peddled his story of Lord Kris, dying while saving mankind from the waters, all of it concocted from what he'd heard of the Seaple's Histree. No wonder he would stop at nothing – including wrecking the Pelican and drowning himself and others – to stop us speaking to the Seaple and finding out the truth!"

"Well..." Conor was lost for words, but only for a moment. "I'll be *jiggered*!"

Moon 3660

"Oh! Ktrina! Your poor face!" Jean couldn't disguise her shock as she caught sight of the black eyes, bruised cheeks and swollen lip. Realising it wasn't the most complimentary or encouraging remark, she remained quiet while the two medics helped Ktrina out of the cot and into the wheelchair. Ktrina thanked them, promised to attend her local clinic next morning for a check up, and then Jean wheeled her away.

After a few metres she stopped, threw her arms around Ktrina's neck and hugged her. "I'm so sorry about that stupid remark. You will look beautiful again in a day or two, don't you worry."

"It's okay, Jean. I know what I look like. If you'd seen the state of the hopper, you'd wonder how I look this good." She smiled, despite the stiffness in her face.

Jean resumed pushing the wheelchair. "We all saw it last night on the news. When they said it was former heptathlete champion and ambassador, Ktrina Rozek, I swear my heart stopped beating. They said you'd had an incredibly lucky escape, falling almost two kilometres when the engines and electrics failed. How ever did you get it started again, Ktrina?"

"Well... it's a long story. Let me start by asking you a question, Jean. And please, don't ever repeat any of this to a soul."

"Cross my heart."

"Well, I know this sounds a bit weird, but do you ever see Ethan? You know, in your mind's eye? You and your brother were so close, I wonder... does his face sort of... pop up from time to time?"

"No. Not really. I think about him quite often, and he appears in dreams occasionally. Why?"

Ktrina spoke quietly. "It was Ethan who saved my life yesterday."

The wheelchair jerked to a stop. Then Jean stepped forward and bent down to bring her face close. She stared searchingly into Ktrina's bloodshot eyes.

"Have you got concussion, Ktrina? You've had a helluva shock—"

"No! I'm fine, really! I don't mean he was there, *physically*. He just appeared inside my head and gave me a hint where the electrical fault might be. I never would have found it without him, Jean. Honestly!"

"You're right. That does sound weird." Jean straightened up. "I wouldn't tell anyone else about it, Ktrina, if I were you." She went back to pushing the wheelchair and changed the subject, as if uncomfortable with the idea.

"Daniel was disappointed you won't be coming to his party this evening. He was looking forward to seeing you all. He'd got some games lined up for the boys an—"

"Won't be coming to his *party*! Why not?"

"Your mum phoned to say you wouldn't be up to it. That you'd need to rest... go straight to bed when you got home."

"No, Jean. We will be there at five, as arranged. I'm sure Mum means well, but the boys will be really sad if they miss the party, and so will I. I probably won't be dancing the night away, but I *can* walk. In fact I need to spend ten minutes on my feet every hour or so... doctor's orders."

"That's great! If you're *really* sure you are up to it, Ktrina?"

"Yes, I'm sure. And if you'll stop and let me get up, I need to exercise now. I've been lying down for the past hour and a half."

Jean stopped the wheelchair and helped Ktrina to her feet. With a walking stick for support, she hobbled the fifty metres to the skyport checkout desk and showed her papers. Her knee throbbing from the effort, she was pleased to resume her seat in the wheelchair for the ride home on the beltway. As they slipped along the tree-lined boulevard, past offices and factories heading towards Sokwest centre, something was niggling Ktrina.

"So... how often does Daniel have to work weekends these days, Jean?"

"Oh, almost never. Must be three years since the last. You know he's the head of his lab team now?"

"Yes, I remember his promotion. So why this weekend... on his birthday?"

"He won't say, Ktrina. I did ask him, but it's top secret, apparently. A field trip to test some new invention, I'm guessing. The R&D department is just a bunch of boys with their toys. Any excuse to go out on the surface and play with their gadgets and gizmos." She laughed.

Ktrina felt her neck prickle. She had a bad feeling about Daniel's field trip.

"Here we are then." Jean wheeled the chair to Krina's front door. "Want me to help you in and wait with you until your mum gets home?"

"No thanks, Jean. You've done more than enough. I really appreciate you bringing me home from the skyport. Besides..." she checked the time, "you've got the hordes descending on you in two hours. You might want to scoot home and lock away your valuables." The smile made her face ache again.

Ktrina had another reason for sending Jean on her way. Something she needed to do before Sofi got home.

Earth 1504

Wood smoke drifted through the trees as Mammed was shaken from a deep sleep by the Captain next morning. He was surprised to find everyone else had already gone to start their first tasks of the day. It was high time he joined them, he was told, starting with collecting wood so that Conor could cook their breakfast.

The hammocks they'd retrieved from the ship had been strung between palm trees as the sun went down the night before. Mammed had drifted off to the sound of his father and elder brothers talking quietly nearby about a fire to send a signal to the Moon. It meant nothing, and after all his toils and torments, Mammed slipped into a deliciously deep and restful sleep. He would have gladly laid there until midday, but Yonaton was insistent – there was too much to do for anyone to be lazing around.

As he stumbled about collecting dry palm fronds and yawning, Conor appeared from the forest with a sack on his shoulder. "Mornin' Master Mammed!" he called out, cheerily. "Pleased to see yer gettin' a good pile o' fuel for me fire. Got more yams to roast in 'ere, plus the rest o' that tunnyfish. Even a one-armed bosun can mek a fine breakfast out o' that, I reckon."

Mammed felt too drowsy to reply. He gathered up his pile of sticks and palm leaves and dragged them to the fire at the top of the beach. Conor was down at the water's edge, washing the soil off the large brown tubers. It reminded Mammed of the previous evening, and Miriam showing them the Seaple's ancient chart, her blond hair tinted red by the lowering sun. All the sailors had craned their necks to see, but his Papa Yon and Benyamin the Navigator had been especially fascinated. Ben traced the outlines of islands and coasts with his finger while the young mermaid read out their names, some familiar and others entirely foreign to them.

Then she had turned the short, curved section of plass pod to show them what was carved on the outside. It was the whole world, she said, and on it the vast Crabbing Sea was reduced to a mere sprinkle of tiny islands sandwiched between two huge areas of land. She read out their names, North America and South America. To the right was the Atlantic Ocean, which sounded a bit like their Lanteek, and beyond that a huge land called Africa. The men had gasped at the idea of vast lands that dwarfed their home islands, and even bigger seas that would prevent them ever going to see them.

Ben had asked if he could make a copy of the chart, and Alexee had agreed to return with it next day. But with the sun now touching the sea, the Seaple, he said, had to go to their sleeping place on the beach beside the nearby stream. After thanks and good-nights, the mermen and women had swum away in the fading light. As Mammed watched them go, one had turned and waved to him, and he'd returned the wave with a smile.

"Oy! Don't stand there daydreaming, lad." Conor's voice brought him back with a jolt. "When you're done fetchin' wood, we need some green coconuts. You can do your climbin' trick and go get us some – there's eight of us fer breakfast."

Eight? Mammed looked up and saw his brother's fishing boat nearing the gap in the reef. He remembered them saying they had to leave early, to get back to Loming in daylight. He was sorry he hadn't said goodbye, but they would be returning in three days, loaded with timber, metal fastenings and tools to repair the Pelican. They would also bring a couple of carpenters from the boatyard, if they could.

He pictured them arriving in Loming harbour, and the excitement at their news that the Pelican and its crew were saved, while the Cardinal and his henchmen had drowned, all but one. He imagined the disbelief at their tales of mermaids and mermen and all they'd learned at Tapu or Sanctuary Island.

"Yer a dozy devil this mornin', ain'tcha!" Conor dropped the sack of wet yams beside the fire. "You better go for a dip in the sea and wash yer face, Mammed. Wake yerself up before you go climbin' trees. Don't want yer fallin' an' breakin' yer dopey neck, now do we?"

He gave Mammed a gentle shove in the direction of the lagoon. It was enough momentum to carry him down the coral sand, stumble into the waves and flop into the cool clear water. He emerged rubbing his face and shaking the water from his curly mop of hair, then leaving a trail of wet footprints to the nearest palm tree.

After concentrating on the climb and tossing six fat green nuts to the sand below, his thoughts returned to Jack and Ifan, and the story they had told before they had all slumped into their hammocks for the night. It was every bit as astonishing as Miriam's and Yonaton's.

Four days ago, while he, Papa Yon and Ben were escaping from Loming on the log-canoe catamaran, his two brothers and his sister Lucy were being arrested by that beast Gorbel and six of his armed militia, the Convertors. It sounded awful. The men had burst into their house just after dawn and dragged the three of them into the street at knife point. Lucy's two youngest children, Agnes and Emily, were left screaming in the arms of neighbours as their mum and uncles were marched away to the town centre.

Lucy's oldest, eleven-year-old Peter, had been sent to the hills the day before to fetch Lucy's husband, Sam. As luck would have it, Sam and his flock of sheep and goats had arrived only minutes after his wife and her brothers had been snatched, so they chased them into town and caught up with them on the church steps. At the head of the flock, Sam's spirited old ram, Titan, had charged Gorbel and knocked him off his feet. Before Sam could intervene, the enraged chief of the Convertors had plunged his sword into the animal's neck. Sam had thrown his shepherd's staff, fitted with a wolf-deterrent spike. In just a few seconds, the beloved Titan and the hated Gorbel were lying on the church steps, dying.

The large crowd who had gathered in support of Jack, Ifan and Lucy, were ready to dispatch the rest of the Convertors on the spot, but after some heroic words from Lucy, the militia had thrown down their weapons and surrendered. Mammed had always been in awe of his feisty big sister, so he could imagine that happening. Even more amazing, Lucy, by popular assent, had been elevated to Mayor of Loming and Jack and Ifan had set off, along with two other fishing boats, to find their father, Ben and Mammed and save them from the Cardinal...

"Oy! Don't you nod off up there, you young rascal!" Conor was staring up at him. "That's enough coconuts, lad. You can come down now and help me with the fire." He returned to his breakfast preparations, muttering under his breath.

Earth 3660

"I still think this is *very* foolish." Sofi was grumbling as they boarded the cube. "Rest and recuperation are what's needed after a traumatic accident. Or, at least they were in *my* day. I'm sure your doctor wouldn't approve of you partying with broken ribs and an injured knee. And look at your *face*, Ktrina... how *can* you go out in public like that?"

"We're hardly going to an all-night strut, Mother! And if you're ashamed to be seen with me, you can always ride the belt to Jean and Daniel's." Ktrina gripped the arms of her wheelchair as Paul tipped it to hoist the smaller front wheels into the boxy transport. "We like travelling this way, don't we boys?"

"Yeah! It's brilliant!" cheered Jan. "We should go by cube all the time, Mum!"

"Just for special occasions. Too expensive to use every day, young man."

Paul set the wheelchair brakes, Ktrina hobbled to the nearest seat and strapped in as the door hissed shut. The cube raised itself onto its four wheels, announced its programmed destination in Soknorth, and set off at a gentle pace to the end of the street. Here it raised a hook to lock on to the rail running beneath the beltway ceiling and hoisted itself into the air.

"Yeehaaa!" yelled Jan. "We're flying!"

Her three boys had their noses pressed to the windows, faces shiny with excitement. Ktrina turned to look at Sofi, who sat tight-lipped, gripping her seat arm with white knuckles. *What would she've made of yesterday's wild ride in the hopper?* She smiled to herself and settled back for the ride.

The cube, once it had reached its full elevation of five metres, set off above the heads of the belt-borne people, flying between the tops of the trees. It slowed as it reached the city Ringway, turned to join the perimeter rail and then accelerated rapidly to match the other traffic. A high-pitched hum filled the cabin.

"Ohhh!" moaned Sofi.

"Wheeee!" shouted Jan.

"Estimated time of arrival," said the voicebot, "six minutes."

"So, how are you feeling now?" Jean had taken over wheelchair duty after the three boys raced indoors after their Uncle Daniel. He'd

135

announced there were parakeets waiting for them in the den. Sofi had headed for the bathroom, complaining she felt sick after the 'awful' ride.

"I'm feeling okay, thanks, Jean. I put another patch on before we left home, so I'm chilled and comfortable. I should have stuck one on Mother!"

"She doesn't get any better with age then?"

"Er, no! But she's good with the boys and I wouldn't want her living on her own, bless her."

"You have the patience of a saint, Ktrina."

Ktrina held her hand up. "You can leave the wheelchair here, Jean. It will be out of the way in the hall. I can walk from here." She set off with her stick, heading for the kitchen.

"Hmm, something smells good! Anything I can help with?"

"That's Daniel's favourite. It's a spicy fish stew called bouillabaisse. He doesn't get it very often because the smartchef can't make it properly. So once in a while, for a special treat, I cook it up for him on the hotplate. A lot of work, but it does taste good."

"Wow! You *have* gone to a lot of trouble." Ktrina lifted the lid and breathed in the heady aroma.

"Don't worry, I've got pizza for the boys and a very mild cheese and potato pie that should suit your mum. There's nothing to do now, Ktrina, but you can help serve it up when the time comes. I'm guessing the boys will be hungry after chasing parakeets for an hour."

"What's for supper, Aunty Jean?" Jan appeared in the doorway while the women were engrossed in conversation. He had the flushed cheeks of someone who had been running after holograms.

"Jan! That's not very polite, is it?" Ktrina apologised for her youngest's lack of decorum.

"What's for supper, Aunty Jean?" This time it was Daniel, who towered over Jan, and wore an idiotic grin. "Us boys have killed all the parrots and are ready for our dinosaur burgers!"

"Oh!" Sofi grimaced. "What an awful thought!"

"Let me apologise for my big kid," said Jean with a laugh. "Wash your hands boys, and go sit to the table. Come on, Ktrina, let's get some food on plates."

Jean conveniently left Ktrina ladling the fish stew into a man-sized bowl for Daniel, plus smaller ones for themselves, while she took plates of pizza and pie to the table. A satisfied silence fell over the birthday supper, with ice creams to follow and Daniel's birthday presents opened a day early. When the cube announced it was waiting outside to take them home, the boys and even her mum agreed it had been a lovely party. Only Ktrina was left with the nagging doubt that she might have done something terribly wrong.

Chapter 9

Another Mission
Earth 1504

It was mid-morning by the time Conor announced that breakfast was ready. Ifan and Jack had disappeared from sight in their fishing boat, heading back to Loming as fast as their sails would push them. The Pelican was now grounded and listing in the shallows, with ropes rigged between the ship and trees at the top of the beach, ready to haul her up and out of the water so repairs could begin. It seemed like an impossible task to Mammed, but the Captain assured him it would work. The ship's capstan, together with blocks and pulleys, would drag the ship sideways up the slipway of logs they'd laid.

Yonaton, Benyamin, Desmun and the three crew perched themselves on the logs by the fire and passed around the coconuts Mammed had prepared, drinking the sweet milk thirstily. Each was handed a banana leaf holding a roasted yam and slab of baked tunnyfish. The Captain had ordered a hearty breakfast to sustain them through the busy day ahead.

"The tide is dropping now," said Yonaton, between mouthfuls. "So next job is to remove the pods from the hold and return them on the catamaran to Alexee's sea cave. This is a job for you two, Mammed and Desmun. I've already arranged with Alexee for a couple of dolphins to tow you there and back, so you won't need to do much paddling."

Mammed looked at his hands. The kelp bandages Rachel had wrapped around them yesterday were already in tatters after his climb of the coconut tree, but his blistered palms and fingers felt much better. It must have been the magic brown goo she put on them. He glanced over at his father's hands. They'd had the same treatment from the Seaple's doctor yesterday afternoon, but already his kelp wrappings were gone and red streaks showed they'd started bleeding again. He wondered what drove him to endure such hardship.

"We don't need to rush now, do we Papa Yon?" He stopped with a chunk of fish halfway to his mouth. "Now that we know Jack and Ifan and Lucy are alright, I mean?"

"No, you're right, Mammed. It's a great relief to me. But we have another mission to prepare for now…"

Everyone paused in their chewing and looked at the Captain warily.

"We have to go and tell all the people of Dominion, and Couba, and Merica. Tell them what we've learned here about where we came from, and how the Seaple have kept the secret of our past safe all these years."

"You reckon any of 'em'll believe it, Cap'n?" Conor sounded sceptical. "I ain't entirely convinced meself yet..."

"We have to try, Conor. Otherwise we'll have another madman like the Cardinal peddling a pack of lies. Someone will try to take over and rule with a mixture of fear and faith. We don't want that, now do we?"

"True enough. But 'ow we gonna convince 'em, Cap'n?"

"I don't know yet. But I'm sure we'll think of something."

Moon 3660

"Ktrina!" Sofi's call from the kitchen brought her daughter limping from her bedroom. The smell of coffee and toast met her at the door.

"What is it, Mum?"

"It's Jean. She says Daniel's poorly. Can you take a call on your screen, since your comm is off-line?"

"Yes. I'll take it in the bedroom, Mum. Thanks."

She sat on her bed, fired up her screen and there was Jean, looking flustered.

"Ktrina. Are you feeling okay this morning? I mean, have you got an upset tummy or anything?"

"No. I feel fine, Jean. Why?"

"It's Daniel. He's been up half the night with terrible diarrhoea. He was supposed to report for work in half an hour. He's just called them to say he's too sick to go!"

"Oh no! Poor Daniel."

"He thinks it was the fish stew, but you and I had it and we're both okay. I feel so guilty, Ktrina. He was really looking forward to his field trip."

"I'm sure it wasn't your fault, Jean. Probably some bug he picked up earlier in the day."

"Well, as long as you're okay, it probably wasn't my cooking. I'd better go. He needs a lot of looking after when he's sick."

"Poor Daniel. What a way to spend his birthday. Give him my love, Jean. Hope he soon recovers."

Ktrina ended the call, shut down her screen and sat with her face in her hands for a long minute. Then she opened her bag, retrieved a napkin from a zipped pocket, and unfolded it to reveal three torn and empty sachets of MaxLax. 'For fast relief from constipation. Do not exceed one dose per 24 hours.'

Oh well. What's done is done. She needed to destroy the evidence and replace Sofi's pharmaceutical supplies before she noticed they were missing. This was not her proudest day.

"It seems poor Daniel has caught some sort of bug," she said as she rejoined Sofi in the kitchen. "He can't do his field trip after all."

"Well, I'm not surprised, Ktrina. That fish stew would have finished me off. Just the smell of it turned my stomach. How he ate two great bowls of the stuff I can't imagine." Sofi huffed and tutted self-righteously as she tipped her fruisli into a dish and poured soya milk on top. "It's a wonder you and Jean aren't ill too. Some people have *no* respect for their digestive systems."

"Yeah, whatever." Ktrina couldn't be bothered to rise to the bait. "Look, Mum, I have to pop in to the clinic this morning for a check up. My knee is much better and I'm supposed to be doing twenty minute walks today. So, can I leave the boys with you for an hour?"

"I don't see why not. You leave them with me every other day." She gave a long-suffering sigh.

"Have you been sipping vinegar this morning, Mum?"

"No! Certainly not!"

"Okay. Just checking." Ktrina smiled to herself. "And then this afternoon I'm taking the boys to the awards ceremony at the Tae Kwon Do club. Would you like to come too...?" She already knew the answer, but wanted to hear it from her mother's lips.

"Good Lord! No, I do *not*! You know how I feel about all that fighting and shouting. I don't know what you see in it, Ktrina. *Really* I don't."

"Okay, no problem. You can have a little peace and quiet for a couple of hours while we're out." She reached for the rugbrød and cloudberry preserve. *Maybe the day wouldn't be so bad, after all.*

Earth 1504

The Captain was right. It *was* possible to haul a ship out of the water and up the beach using ropes and pulleys, plus the Pelican's capstan. But it had been hard work, heaving away on ropes under the midday sun. Finally, he announced the ship was clear of the high water mark and they hammered huge wooden stakes into the sand beneath the keel to stop her slipping back down. Then they all flopped into the lagoon to cool off and soothe their aching muscles.

Mammed and Desmun's trip to the sea cave to return the pods had been easy work by comparison. The dolphins seemed to relish the opportunity to tow the catamaran at speed and all the boys had to do was hang on while the long slim hulls sliced through the water. Alexee and four of his mermen met them at the cave, so unloading the pods was quick and simple. They were back in time to add their muscle to the ship-raising task, which was much appreciated by the others, especially as Conor was handicapped with his arm in a sling.

They were enjoying a drink of coconut milk when Peetee arrived with Miriam in tow. She had been to visit the Seaple community on the north side of the island, she said, teaching the children there the rudiments of English. She asked Mammed if he wanted to return to the sea cave for another session with the Histree, followed by a reading and writing lesson. His eyes asked his father the unspoken question.

"Yes, of course you can go, Mammed. It is important you learn how to read and write this old style of English, so that you can translate it for us in the future. Desmun can go too, if he likes."

Mammed's heart sank. He relished the time he spent with Miriam and didn't want Desmun spoiling it. With an odd tightening in his chest, he realised he didn't want to share her with anyone.

But Desmun was shaking his head. "Um, no thanks. I'll stay here, if you don't mind. I don't like being in the water, so going into the sea cave would be really bad for me. I can tell you one thing, though…" They all looked at him. "I've seen that writing – the writing that was on the chart yesterday – in the Cardinal's private rooms at the back of his church. There's this metal trunk with a great big book in it. I've seen him reading it when he didn't know I was watching. The writing is the same as on that chart, I'm sure of it."

They had barely set off towards the sea cave before Mammed had to let go. The mighty dolphin's tail fluke powered them through the water so fast, he could barely hold on, and he couldn't catch a breath without getting a mouth full of water. He was left coughing in their wake, but Peetee and Miriam were soon back, the dolphin clicking loudly and nodding its beak, and Miriam frowning with concern.

"What is wrong, Maa-med?"

"I can't hold on… and I'm drowning – the water goes down my throat when I try to breathe."

She grunted in dolpheen-speak and Peetee squealed in reply.

"I've told him to go slower, Maa-med. But you have to learn how to time your breathing. When Peetee comes to the surface, you have to breathe in. Then breathe out slowly while you are in the water, and you will be ready to get a quick breath when he comes up next time. You will soon get used to it." She smiled a reassurance.

Mammed wasn't so sure, but he didn't want to look like a coward, or end up running along the sand while they swam beside him so effortlessly. "Okay. I'll try again."

The dolphin nodded, dived and reappeared in between them. Miriam grasped Mammed's hand and placed it firmly at the base of its dorsal fin, then put her own on top. She let out a squeaky grunt and they started to move gently through the water. Mammed still found it an effort to hold on, especially when his tattered trousers threatened to slip off his slender hips. He grabbed them with his spare hand and concentrated on timing his breathing with that of the dolphin. Now he understood why, if they regularly hitched a lift with dolphins, the Seaple went clotheless.

Peetee slowed to a standstill and Mammed was surprised to find they were already at the outcrop of rock that hid the sea cave. The dolphin buzzed excitedly and Miriam's smiling face appeared.

"You did it, Maa-med!" She gave him a swift kiss on the cheek, then made a series of squeaking noises in her throat. The dolphin nodded, squealed and promptly disappeared back in the direction they'd come from. "I've asked him to come back for us when the smoke rises from your fire. Then it will be time to eat."

"Clever!" He smiled. "So... are we going to do the breathing thing now?"

"You *know* how to do it, Maa-med!"

"Yes, but I like it best when you show me." It was his favourite part of these visits to the cave. "Please?" he added, hopefully.

Miriam smiled knowingly. "Okay." She slipped behind him and he felt her long cool fingers touch his chest. "Lie back." His head rested on her shoulder and he felt her warm breath in his ear. "Now, breathe innnn.... and outttt..."

Moon 3660

"Thank you, yes, I'm fine, really." Ktrina smiled at the umpteenth well-wisher. And it was true, she did feel remarkably well, considering it was less than 48 hours since her life-threatening crash. The nanobots were working overtime to rebuild her cracked ribs and torn tendons, judging by the warmth that surrounded the injury sites. Even her face was nearly back to normal, thank goodness.

She had been ushered to the front of the seating in the Tae Kwon Do club's main hall, and was flanked by Grig, Jan and Paul, waiting expectantly for the ceremony to begin. The latest sed-patch had kicked in and she was feeling no pain for the first time since the accident. Plus, she had disposed of the incriminating sachets and replaced her mother's laxatives without incident, so the day was looking up.

The chatter echoing around the hall died away as the Grand Master walked on to the small stage and stood in front of the lectern. He bowed to the silent audience and then welcomed club members and their families to the annual awards ceremony.

"It is an honour for me to recognise all the hard work put in by our members over the past year. And for a few of you, your dedication and skill have earned you the reward of a promotion of ranking in the great Tae Kwon Do tradition.

"As you know, the Lunar Tae Kwon Do Congress rewards skill and attitude, not time served, as was once the case. So every recipient of an award here today can feel pleased they have made real progress and marked an important step up in their ability and personal development."

The next fifteen minutes were filled with cheers and applause as he called up members to receive their awards, in the form of scrolls spelling out their achievements. While the ceremony was underway, Paul turned to his mother and whispered, "Now that I'm twelve, can I join the Tae Kwon Do club please, Mum."

Ktrina smiled and nodded. "I will ask about enrolment before we leave, Paul." She was pleased he felt inspired to take up the sport, but shushed him until the ceremony was over. Finally, it appeared the Grand Master had finished and the applause had died away.

"And now I would like to invite to the stage somebody who, just two days ago, had to fight for her life inside a crashing hopper." Ktrina stiffened. She hadn't been expecting this. "Someone who miraculously survived an accident that would have killed most people... somebody who was so badly beaten up, I really didn't expect to see here today. Please, a big hand for one of our bravest and most distinguished members... Ambassador Ktrina Rozek!"

She squeezed the hands of the two boys sitting closest to her and got to her feet. She had no idea why she was being summoned, but she couldn't deny the Grand Master's request. With her stick for support Ktrina limped up the steps and approached the lectern amidst a deafening round of applause. It was obvious that everyone had seen her story on the news. They were delighted to see her in person.

The Grand Master and Ktrina bowed to each other then he leaned towards the microphone. "We are all honoured to have you here amongst us today, Ktrina, when you should perhaps be resting and recovering from your injuries."

She smiled, and said, "You sound just like my mother!" The hall erupted with laughter.

"Actually," she continued, when the noise died down, "I'm feeling pretty good today. The doctors have pumped me full of nanobots which are busy healing my cracked ribs and injured knee. Plus my Tae Kwon Do training is helping my body to recover more rapidly from the injuries. I promised I would be here today, and I wasn't going to let a little hopper crash keep me away."

Another round of applause faded away and the Grand Master cleared his throat. "I am so pleased you could make it, Ktrina, because as well as congratulating you on your miraculous escape..." he reached for one last scroll hidden beneath the lectern, "I want to congratulate you on becoming the Sokwest Tae Kwon Do club's first member in six years to achieve Seventh Dan – the Chil Dan Black Belt – only two steps from Grand Master." He bowed to her and shook her hand. Ktrina stood rooted in surprise as he passed her the scroll and the hall erupted in applause once more.

He turned to the audience. "I have thought for some time that Ktrina had reached the level of skill, attitude and self-control to deserve the Seventh Dan. But earlier this week Ktrina came here during her lunch break for an unscheduled workout and really showed me what she could do. Her explosive speed, precision and her Indomitable Spirit left me in no doubt that she is a very worthy Chil Dan Black Belt." He bowed to her again and the applause continued long after Ktrina had limped back to her seat and the beaming faces of her three sons.

Earth 1504

"We had nine live births this year and one death." Miriam was reading the third of the colonists' annual reports to Mammed, who was sitting in the shallow water beside the Ark. "One of the new babies passed away in its fifth week, which greatly distressed us all. All life is very precious in our small community, which now numbers one hundred and thirty-four, so each loss leaves us with heavy hearts.

"However, the delight we feel when we see our children playing in the sunshine helps lift our spirits. We notice that the youngsters are adapting well to life here on Earth. While our land-living adults are still wary of walking on the soft sand, for fear of turning an ankle or breaking a bone, the infants run along the sand without a care.

"What is also interesting is the way our sea-dwelling children play with the dolphins in the warm waters of the lagoon. Our babies swim from birth and are very confident in the sea, but some of us have noticed they are also mimicking the sounds of the dolphins, which is funny.

"Other developments of note: The first fruits from the tree seeds we planted have been harvested and make a welcome addition to the coconuts that are plentiful here. These, plus root vegetables, chickens' eggs and occasional pieces of lamb are exchanged for fish, crustaceans, molluscs and edible seaweeds. Our farming techniques, both on land and in the lagoon, are improving and we have a rich and varied diet.

"The clothing we arrived in has fallen apart. We have been stitching and patching, but the synthetic fabric proved very susceptible to the sunlight here and has simply rotted away. This is not a problem for the twenty-five of us who live in the sea, as clothing is a hindrance to swimming and has been abandoned. Our land-living neighbours seem more concerned for their modesty and have been covering themselves using grasses and palm leaves.

"This year they have also been spinning and weaving the wool from their sheep and have been able to make some rudimentary clothing. Plus they have been able to incorporate some of the tougher grasses into heavier cloth to make a sail for a small raft they have built using pods and branches. We have also discovered a forest of kelp that grows outside the reef on the north side of the island, where there is a cold water current. We hope to find a way to harvest more of this seaweed which promises to provide many benefits.

"Sadly, our geology surveys have now concluded there are no metal ores on this small island and so we are still limited to stone, coral, wood and bone for tools. A few of the metal hinges and clasps that secure the caps on the plass pods have been removed, but they are difficult to adapt as they are made of titanium. Our leader, Nicole Durand, has ruled out any attempt to sail to neighbouring islands in search of metal ores until our boat building and sailing skills have improved.

"Despite these limitations we are making progress and look forward to sharing our discoveries with the next group of colonists who come from the Moon to join us. Some of the men have drawn huge letters in the sand hoping they might be seen from the Moon, but I fear our little island is too small to be noticed. We all miss our families back home.

"This concludes my third annual report, dated 31st December 2159. Giulia Magrini, of the sea-dwellers of Christown."

Moon 3660

The beltway to Sokwest Centre had quietened after the Monday morning commuter rush and Ktrina was grateful for the relative peace and the opportunity to breathe in the resinous scent of the cedar trees that lined the boulevard. The twelve-minute ride to work was pleasant without the push and shove of the crowd, and it gave her time to think and prepare for the meeting to come.

She'd been advised to take the week off work to fully recover from her injuries, but the check up at her local clinic that morning had confirmed what she already knew. The nanobots had done their work and her ribs and knee were almost healed. There was some residual swelling and stiffness, as expected, but she could breathe and walk without pain. Her wrist comm had also been reinstalled under local anaesthetic, so she felt there was no good reason to stay at home. Besides, she was eager to discover the outcome of the joint military operation, and there had been no mention of it on any news channel so far.

They say that no news is good news, but she had a feeling the media blackout meant something wasn't quite right. As she left the clinic Ktrina called to let her receptionist, Phoebe, know she would be in shortly and was told the Foreign Minister would like to see her, at her earliest convenience. The summons produced the same dread in the pit of her stomach she'd felt the day before.

After Saturday's unexpected promotion and the Grand Master's glowing words, she'd expected to rise feeling euphoric on Sunday morning, but instead woke with a sense of foreboding. A call from Jean while she was sipping her first coffee had done nothing to improve her mood. Daniel was fully recovered from his '24-hour bug' and had contacted the Rangers to see if he could join the field trip. It was too late to reach the location, he'd been told, which was a surprise to Jean because field trials were usually run within a stone's throw of Sok city.

Ktrina had taken the boys to the Lian Song Botanical Park to lighten her mood and get them out of her mother's hair for a few hours. They'd played ball and Frisbee on the impressive lawns, eaten a picnic and explored the avenues of trees and shrubs, marvelling at the flowers and butterflies. Paul had enjoyed pushing his mum's wheelchair when her leg tired. They had shared jokes and laughter. It had been a perfect Sunday. But she'd still felt the same disquiet gnawing away at her, and it had a name...

Aristarchus.

"Come in, Ktrina." Foreign Minister Jorg Lanimovskiy rose from behind his desk. "I'm pleased to see you up and about after that awful accident last week. Please take a seat."

"Thank you, Minister."

"Rest assured that a full and thorough investigation will reveal exactly what went wrong with that vehicle, and those responsible for any negligence will be prosecuted. How are you feeling today?"

"Remarkably well, considering I almost died on Thursday." She smiled. "Fortunately, our healthcare is more up to date than some of the Ministry's hoppers."

"Quite." He didn't smile back. "You will be aware that all the old Zenits are now grounded pending the accident investigation report?"

"Yes, I heard." She decided against suggesting they should stay that way. Something in the FM's manner made her wary.

He tilted his head. "You're not the only one who has been feeling poorly, I understand…?"

"Oh, why's that, Foreign Minister?"

"I gather that your brother-in-law was sick on Saturday?"

Her neck prickled. *Does he suspect me?* "Yes, poor Daniel. He picked up a stomach bug on his birthday."

"Hmmm" He looked thoughtful. "It was a pity he contracted this illness when he was due to attend a field trial of important new technology. Do you know what he was working on, Ktrina?"

He's trying to catch me out. "No. Daniel never discusses his work."

"I understand the Rangers are suspicious of his sudden illness."

"Well, they needn't suspect Daniel. He was really looking forward to his field trial. He tried to join the test on Sunday, when he was feeling better, but was told he couldn't."

"Do you know where the trial was taking place, Ktrina?" He steepled his fingers and looked at her over them.

"No idea. I thought most field tests took place somewhere near Sok city."

"The trial took place near Lava Tube A14, at the southern edge of the Aristarchus Plain, Ktrina. At twelve noon. On Sunday."

"Oh my god!" Ktrina put her hand to her mouth. "So… the trial took place *during* the military operation?"

The Foreign Minister nodded sombrely. "Fortunately, your brother-in-law's absence did not affect the outcome, but it did reduce the number of casualties."

"Dare I ask…?"

"He would have been part of a team of five, Ktrina. There to observe, nothing more. The other four Rangers, I'm sorry to say, were all killed."

Ktrina sank her face into her hands. The anxiety of the past few days burst out from her chest in deep sobs. Four more like Ethan. Four more young lives snuffed out in the cold, stark wastes of Aristarchus. She quaked at the thought that Daniel would have been among them, if not for her.

"Please, don't upset yourself, Ambassador." The FM pushed a box of tissues across his desk towards her.

She raised her tear-streaked face from her hands. "Don't *upset myself?*" Ktrina stared him in the eye and shook her head slowly. "You heartless bastard!"

Earth 1504

"Ah, buh, kuh, duh, eh, fuh…" Mammed was repeating the odd sounds as Miriam pointed to strange squiggles she had drawn in the wet sand with a slim stick of coral. They were lying side by side, propped up on elbows while the waves licked at their legs. "Guh, huh, ih, juh, kuh, luh…" It would have been a boring school lesson were it not for the glistening body of the mermaid stretched out alongside him.

She'd already scolded him for stealing glances at her when he should have been looking at the letters she was drawing. He forced himself to focus on her alphabet, but it was difficult, when her blond hair curled between her shoulder blades and down her spine almost to her—

"Maa-med! Concentrate."

"Sorry."

She scowled at him, but the corners of her mouth were fighting to suppress a smile. She leaned across and blew in his ear. "Finish the lesson, and you get a kiss." Her seductive wink set off little explosions in his brain.

"Muh, nuh, oh, puh…"

After learning how to pronounce the twenty-six letters, she set him to writing them in the sand. This proved much more tricky. His fingers felt awkward trying to force the coral stick to draw the odd shapes from left to right in a row. Finally he had produced a reasonable copy of her symbols and looked at her expectantly.

"Not yet, Maa-med." She smiled. "Now you have to write your name. Start with muh…"

He struggled to form the letters, but it helped that three of them were the same. As he finished the last one he had an idea. "Let me write your name too."

She spelled it out and slowly the word Miriam appeared beneath Mammed. When he had finished, he drew a shape around the outside, a sort of circle with a dip in the top and a point at the bottom.

"What's that?" She frowned at the wet sand.

"It's a heart."

"What does it mean?"

"It means..." he hesitated, his face turning hot, "it means... Mammed loves Miriam."

She turned to him with a broad grin. Then leaned in and planted a long kiss on his lips.

"Ow, my ears hurt!" Mammed was frowning, holding his hands over the sides of his head, after their third deep dive on the reef.

"It is from pressure. When we go deep, you have to blow into your ears, Maa-med."

"What! How can I do that...?" He twisted his lips comically to the side which made her laugh.

"Not with lips! Inside, back of your mouth, like this..." she puffed out her cheeks and put her index fingers at the back of her jaw. "Push air inside ears to balance pressure of water when going deep. It is easy!"

"Easy for you, maybe..." He experimented, blowing out his cheeks and moving his tongue and jaw around.

"Try it next time we dive. You will soon get used to it."

"Are we going again?" He said, hopefully. "What will we see this time?"

"Yes, this time we will try to find octopus. See it change shape and colour, perhaps."

Mammed turned to face away from her and thrilled once more as her arm wrapped around his chest. "We stay for longer this time, so more breathing, Maa-med. You ready?"

He nodded.

"Innnn... and outttt... innnn.... and—"

Mammed turned to her with his eyes wide and chest full of air. "Mmhmm?"

"Oh, breathe out, Maa-med! Sorry. Didn't you hear?"

He exhaled with a grateful wheeze. "No... hear what?"

"It is Peetee. He is looking for us." She slipped her head under the water and made a deep groaning sound before surfacing again. "There. He will find us soon."

"Umm, Miriam...?"

"Yes?"

"Could you teach me how to speak to the dolphins?"

"I don't know, Maa-med. We learn when we are babies, but I can try. Maybe tomorrow...?"

"That would be great! Thanks."

"Here he is now." They turned to see the silvery grey back of Peetee dipping in and out of the water, heading towards them. Mammed could hear his clicks and squeals. Then he was nodding his head and appeared to be laughing at them.

"We can ask Peetee to help us look for an octopus, Maa-med. He will see one for sure."

"Okay."

Miriam made a few squeaky grunts and the dolphin buzzed a whistle in reply.

"Now, let's do breathing, Maa-med and he will take us for last dive. And remember... blow in your ears!"

Moon 3660

It was almost noon when Ktrina reached her office. Phoebe, the receptionist who doubled as secretary for Ktrina and three other government officials, spotted her red eyes, followed her in and shut the door.

"It is *so* good to see you back again, Ktrina, after your awful accident." She studied her face. "I'm guessing you've had a difficult meeting with Mr Lanimovskiy...?"

"You could say that, yes." Ktrina dropped her bag on her desk and slumped in her chair.

"Not what you needed after all you've been through. What can I get you? Coffee?"

"Yes please, Phoebe. I could do with a brandy, to be honest, but coffee will be fine, thanks." She checked the time. "And you might want to tell the others to watch the midday news..."

Ten minutes later Ktrina was clutching her coffee mug, Phoebe standing beside her, as they watched the Selene News report on Ktrina's pop-up desk viewer. A grim-faced presenter stood in front of a wall screen showing an area of the lunar surface. Above her head were the words 'Military Fiasco'.

"A combined military strike on the FLOC rebel base at Aristarchus Plain yesterday has left at least seven dead, four of them Sokolovan Rangers, according to the Ministry of Defence." The image switched to library footage of Rangers bounding across a patch of dusty regolith.

"The action was taken in response to last weekend's sky-borne laser attack, in which the Nobile solar collector disc was destroyed and Ian Brandstock, Minister for Industry, was fatally injured. The same rebel satellite weapon mounted a similar attack in the north." The picture cut to a tangled pylon and scattered debris strewn across the lunar surface.

"Yesterday's joint-forces military strike was intended to degrade the rebels' ability to launch orbital weapons. In addition to the Rangers' tragic losses, three Coopan Commandos are known to have died and there are believed to be a number of casualties amongst the rebels. In addition to the deaths of military personnel, the mission objectives were not met, according to the short statements issued so far.

"Although the military retaliation took place twenty-four hours ago, details have only just been released by the Coopan and Sokolovan governments. It was hoped to destroy the rebels' launch facility, believed to lie within the heavily-fortified Lava Tube A14, using coordinated attacks by Coopan and Sokolovan forces." An image-graphic showed arrows and words overlaid on a featureless piece of plain.

The presenter went on to read brief statements from both defence departments, but it was apparent she had nothing else to add and no video footage from either of the forces engaged in the action. Ktrina clapped her hands and the screen went blank before sliding down into the back of her desk.

"That's just awful!" Phoebe looked shocked. "How could it have gone so wrong?"

"I don't know, Pheebs." Ktrina shook her head sadly. "I can't believe so many of our Rangers have died for nothing, not to mention the Coopan soldiers. Somebody will need to answer—" She stopped as Amed Sheekai, the ministry's senior analyst, appeared in her open doorway. He stood there, not speaking.

"I know," said Ktrina. "We've just watched it too. Doesn't make any sense, does it?"

He wandered into her office, forehead furrowed. "I don't get it," he said. "The combined forces of both north and south... and they get wiped out without making a dent on the FLOC's defences. It's time to rethink our strategy and start dropping bombs."

"You know that's strictly forbidden by the Korolev Treaty. We saw what happened in the Drone War when the missiles started flying. Over a million dead. No bombs or missiles on populated structures – strict arms limitations – it's all wrapped up in that treaty, and has been for centuries."

"Yeah, but this is different. A single missile would collapse that lava tube and then it'd be game over. The FLOC wouldn't be able to launch anything on a polar orbit, would they?" He was clearly warming to his idea.

"The Coops would never agree to it, Amed," she said with a sigh. "We can't know how many people are inside, how many would die from a sudden depressurisation. Rules of engagement protocols and all that."

"So…" Phoebe spread her hands, "what do we do now? Sit and wait for the rebels to launch another attack?"

"Well, what *we* do, Pheebs, is get on with the job we're paid to do and let the politicians sweat over the big stuff. That's why they get the megabucks and we get paid peanuts." She looked at her digi-list of calls to make, reports to file, issues to resolve that had piled up since Wednesday. "It looks like I've got a week's work to catch up on, so I'd better get started." Amed took the hint and wandered back to his office.

"Oh, yes," said Phoebe, pausing on her way to the door, "your visa's been reinstated, Ktrina. Notice came through just before you arrived this morning. So I guess you'll want me to book your flights to Monterey Skyport later in the week…?"

"Oh what joy!" said Ktrina, with a sarcastic sigh. "To be whisked away in the luxury of the Polar Carrier to the destination of my dreams – Cooper City! I can hardly wait!" She looked again at her list. "But I'll need at least a couple of days to clear this lot, so better make it Thursday out, and Friday back. Usual times, please, Pheebs. Thanks."

Earth 1504

The last of the sunshine was painting Loming golden as Jack and Ifan's fishing boat, the Petrel, slipped into the harbour. Their return, three days after setting off on a quest to find Yonaton, Benyamin and Mammed, had not gone unnoticed. The lookout on the harbour tower had spotted them approaching and word soon spread that the Captain's eldest sons were on their way home.

Their sister Lucy was waiting on the quayside with her husband Sam and their three children, eager for news. Two other fishing boat crews had set out with Jack and Ifan in the hope of preventing the Cardinal getting his hands on the three escapees. They had returned the previous day reporting no sightings, increasing concern that the townsfolk's worst fears might have become reality.

Lucy was wringing her hands as her brothers' boat came alongside the quay. "Any sign of them?" she called out forlornly.

"Yes!" Jack shouted back. "They are all fine."

Cheers erupted from the small crowd that had gathered around the Captain's daughter.

"And the Cardinal is dead!"

An even bigger roar greeted this news and Lucy and Sam, each holding one of their young daughters, hugged each other in delight and relief. Willing hands caught ropes and secured the Petrel, while others reached to welcome the two men ashore. Everyone was eager to hear their story.

"The Captain, Benyamin and Mammed are all well and staying on Tapu Island," said Ifan, which brought a gasp from the crowd. "Don't worry. Everything we were told about that place is untrue – a web of lies spun by the Cardinal to keep people away. The inhabitants are friendly and peaceful people. One of them saved Yonaton from drowning when their log-canoe catamaran was tipped over the reef. The islanders are now helping them while they repair their ship.

"The Cardinal had almost run them down with the Pelican when it struck an outcrop of the reef. He was thrown over the bows of the ship and drowned," said Jack.

"Serves 'im right!" someone shouted. "Good riddance!"

"What about the others?" asked one young woman. "My uncle, Conor, was among the crew,"

"Conor is fine," said Jack. "He has an injured hand, but the island's doctor is seeing to that for him. All the other crew members are fine too, plus the young apprentice priest called Desmun. They all escaped in the ship's boat when the Pelican crashed on the reef."

"And what about the rest of 'em?" asked an older man. "There was six o' the Cardinal's Convertors and three bishops who went wiv 'im."

Jack looked at Ifan who shrugged his shoulders. "I'm afraid they all drowned."

There was a scream from a woman at the back. The old man said, in a wavery voice, "one of 'em was my son. I told 'im 'e was wrong, throwin' in wiv the Cardinal. But 'e didn't deserve that." He turned and slowly walked away.

Ifan had a brief whispered conversation with Lucy, then announced: "There's a lot more to tell you, but we'll give the full story tomorrow, mid-morning, on the church steps. Tell everyone to come, please."

"Thanks Lucy." Jack smiled up at his older sister from the kitchen table. The plate of baked potatoes and steaming lamb casserole had his taste buds straining at the leash. "C'mon, Ifan!" he shouted through the door to the children's bedroom. "It's getting cold! And I'm starving!"

Ifan appeared, children's storybook in hand, and closed the door behind him. "I hope that's given them something better than shipwrecks and drowning to dream about," he said as he sat and surveyed the meal. "Mmmm, this smells delicious."

"Then let's eat," said Lucy. "We've been too worried about father – and what might happen if you had to confront the Cardinal – to have any appetite since Sunday."

She looked to the other end of the table where Sam, her gentle-giant husband sat wearing a weary smile. "And poor Sam hasn't slept either," she said as she broke off a chunk of crusty bread and dipped it in her gravy.

"We've got so much to tell you," said Jack, spooning meat into his mouth. "Mmmm, that's so good." He grinned at his sister as he chewed. "Most of it you're going to find hard to believe. Some of it *we're* still struggling to believe ourselves. We'll have to decide how much we're going to tell the people tomorrow."

"Before we get onto that," said Ifan, "tell us what's been happening here. We set off in such a hurry, you were left with Gorbel and Sam's ram lying on the church steps. Not to mention a mob shouting for you to be Mayor, Lucy…"

"Well, Titan was easy. Erik the butcher gave us a good price for him, although Sam shed a tear at the thought of his best ram on people's dinner plates." She looked up at her husband, who had stopped eating. "Oh, I know you loved him, Sam! But what else were you going to do?"

She realised her two brothers had also paused mid-chew. She looked down at her plate. "Oh, this isn't Titan! It's one of our spring lambs." She laughed. "You men… so sentimental!"

"Anyway, Gorbel was buried yesterday. Nobody blamed Sam for what happened. Most said he had it coming and if Sam hadn't done it, somebody else would." She took a bite of potato. "Not a lot of tears for him. Desmun's mother said her family lived in fear of Gorbel – thought he was almost as bad as the Cardinal. She was pleased to see the back of him."

"So what about being Mayor?" asked Jack.

"I told them I would only do it if there was a proper election, but in the meantime I've suggested some changes which seem to be catching on. Free schools for all our children, with no religious nonsense, for a start." She dipped her spoon back into her gravy. "So what's all this news from Tapu Island that we're going to find hard to believe...?

"The dream of yesterday is the hope of today, and the reality of tomorrow."

– Robert Hutchings Goddard

Chapter 10

A Pointed Nose Cone

Moon 3660

The usual shudder reverberated through the Polar Carrier as it descended into Monterey. Ktrina turned her head to peer through the cabin window and see if she could catch a glimpse of the Coops' secret new craft she'd been told about. She whispered: "Comm – record video," and craned her neck to scan the skyport as it rose to meet her. She might not recognise the ship, but later analysis of her recording may pick it out from the jumble of shapes illuminated by the harsh horizontal sunlight. Her comm could store up to an hour of optical footage, so the minute or two while the Carrier dropped towards its stand was nothing.

She'd made her peace with Jorg Lanimovskiy the day after her outburst in his office. They'd both apologised for things they'd said in the heat of the moment, under the stress of news that neither had been ready to deal with. He'd felt partly to blame for the plans that had gone so badly wrong, but it was the Chief of Defence, General Ferreira, who had resigned over the attack fiasco. She was sorry the old soldier's career had ended in disgrace, but felt it was high time he resigned and let some fresh thinking guide the military.

Lanimovskiy had been reluctant to discuss details of the failed Aristarchus operation – a full report would be published in due course, he said – but it was not the fault of their new cloaking technology. That had performed as expected, despite the absence of the chief development engineer. He made no further mention of Daniel's sudden illness and she gathered the matter had been dropped.

Then he'd changed the subject and asked her to keep an eye open for the Coops' secret spaceship. Its existence had been rumoured for some time, but it had only recently been tracked making test flights. And the word was it was being operated from the military part of Monterey Skyport, so it might be possible for Ktrina to spot it and bring back useful footage.

There! A pointed nose cone glinted between two lattice-work towers. Was that the new craft? If so, it seemed highly unusual, more like a missile from a kiddie's cartoon than a modern spaceship. It disappeared from view and she whispered: "Comm – stop recording." Then she turned her face away from the window and closed her eyes. The bump as the Carrier touched down was gentle compared to the drive-change jolts of the old Zenit hoppers, but after her recent experience it was hard not to tense up.

Besides, arriving in Cooper always made her feel uneasy. There was something not quite right about the place and its people. It felt like a community waiting for something to happen, holding its breath, fearful and uncertain. Ktrina was pleased she would only be here for two days. They would be busy ones, with a full schedule of appointments made for her by the Sokolovan Embassy. She guessed it would be the usual – Coops applying for work visas to the south, Soks facing problems trying to work in the north – but thankfully, no meetings with Gunta Krems or that menacing Daval Nakash. She collected her hand luggage and headed for the Carrier's exit.

Inside the skyport there seemed to be more Xintapo than before, the tattooed monks staring menacingly at inbound visitors, plus a new baggage scan that suggested an increased sense of tension and vulnerability. Perhaps not surprising after the events of last weekend, but what they supposed her fellow travellers might be smuggling she couldn't quite imagine. The thought that she had sneaked a mysterious egg past security on the way out last time brought a brief wave of retrospective panic. And she still had no idea what it was for. She wondered if she might see the wild-eyed young man with the broken tooth again.

Finally she was out of the skyport and heading for the metro, passing more poster-screens that promised the imminent return of the Messiah. Ktrina couldn't quite get her head around the logic of it. She knew the Xinto religion was based on a comeback tour from the haloed one, but setting a date was guaranteeing disappointment amongst the faithful, and ridicule from disbelievers, wasn't it? She knew that 3660 had been billed as The Year by some ancient prophet back in the mists of time, but surely by now, with the year two thirds gone, shouldn't they be dreaming up some clever reinterpretation of the sage's prediction, rather than building expectations to fever pitch?

Oh, well. Not her problem. She secretly hoped that Daval Nakash might finally be deposed by disillusioned followers, but didn't relish the instability that would follow. The Xinto High Priest held sway over so many aspects of Coopan life, it was hard to predict how it might all play out.

The crush for the escalator brought her back to the here and now. Hordes of people were shuffling closer together, elbowing their way forwards for a ride on the mechanised stairway. Ktrina didn't feel part of the herd. Despite her right knee still carrying some stiffness from last week's accident, she decided to take the stairs down to the metro platforms.

Halfway down she met him, the blue-eyed young man with the broken tooth and haunted face, heading upwards. Their eyes met for the briefest moment, his wide and full of questions, it seemed to her. And then he was gone, jogging away up the steps. It was no coincidence, obviously, but how did he know she would be there at that moment? How did he time it so they passed exactly in the middle of the stairwell? She knew why, that part was easy. It was the one spot where the Xintapo standing guard at top and bottom couldn't see them.

The important question was… would she meet him again on the way home tomorrow? And if she did, how could she ask him what the egg-spider was for, without attracting attention?

Earth 1504

"Thank you all for coming." Lucy's voice rang loud and clear over the heads of the citizens of Loming. She and her two brothers stood at the top of the broad flight of stone steps leading up to the church's front door. A chill wind made her hair dance and low clouds scudded overhead. The crowd hushed and all eyes turned towards her.

"You will have heard by now that Captain Yonaton, Benyamin and Mammed are all alive and well. And the Cardinal, who was hell-bent on killing them last Sunday, has drowned."

Shouts of "Good riddance!" and other, rather less savoury cries, came from the crowd.

"Sadly, the Cardinal was not content with killing himself. Several men from our community and others from far away have also lost their lives. So I will now let my two brothers, Jack and Ifan, tell you what happened and what they have discovered at what we were told was the forbidden island."

Jack stepped forward first and addressed the crowd. He described the events leading to the wreck of the Pelican, the drowning of the Cardinal, bishops and Convertors and the survival of Yonaton and his crew. Ifan had drawn the short straw. He had agreed to tell the people of Loming about the Seaple of Tapu Island.

"You have heard how the log-canoe catamaran was lifted by a huge wave and thrown over the reef encircling the island. What my brother hasn't told you is that Captain Yonaton was knocked unconscious and sank deep below the waters of the lagoon." A collective gasp came from the worried faces peering up at him.

"Benyamin and Mammed were convinced that our father had drowned, but amazingly he was rescued and brought back to life by one of the residents of Tapu Island. We have both met this man, whose name is Alexee. He is the chief amongst his people and is a wise and kindly leader. He lives, like all the two hundred and twenty-six inhabitants of Tapu Island, in the lagoon—"

"What! In the *water?*" someone asked.

"Yes, that's right. They are ordinary people just like you and me, who have taken to living in the warm and sheltered waters inside the reef at Tapu Island. We have been told for years that this island was inhabited by Sea Devils who would devour anyone who dared to approach, but that was just a lie concocted by the Cardinal to stop us from meeting these innocent sea people, or Seaple as they call themselves, and discovering his wicked secret—"

"What secret's that?" There was always one vocal person in every crowd.

"Thirty-three years ago a fat young man called Henry and an old man called Fisherman Frank spent three days living with the Seaple of Tapu Island, learning all about a history that we have long forgotten. They left the island in good weather to return to Loming, but only Henry was aboard Fisherman Frank's boat when it arrived here. He told a fantastical story of old Frank being washed off his boat in a storm and a visitation from God—"

"Tha's right! 'E became the Cardinal, din't 'e?"

"He did. And for all these years many have believed his story and followed his teaching – how in the beginning Lord Kris saved the people from the waters, forbade us from returning to Tapu island, and instructed him to destroy all the 'Signs of Satan'… does this sound familiar?"

"Yeah!"

"Well, there is a much simpler explanation. What fat Henry learned from the Seaple gave him an idea for his warped religion, a mixture of ancient myths and new lies designed to subdue us and give him power. The only problem he had was this… if we worked out how to read the ancient writing, or if we ever spoke to the kind and gentle sea people of his 'forbidden island' we would find out the truth. Only one other person knew where he'd been and what he'd learned—"

"Fisherman Frank!"

"That's right. And Henry had a solution for Fisherman Frank…"

"What? He pushed him off his boat!?"

"What do you think? After a lifetime at sea on his own, poor old Frank mysteriously falls off his boat when there's another person on board. That person doesn't stop to pull him out of the sea. Instead he sails home to Loming with tales of a storm when all we'd seen was calm weather."

A wave of muttering and oaths rippled through the crowd.

"So now you know what sort of person the Cardinal really was. An evil, murderous, manipulative monster who planned and plotted to deceive us all. He would stop at nothing to keep his secret and hold on to his power – including hanging Captain Yonaton and Benyamin when they tried to learn the old writing. And when they escaped from the tower, thanks to Mammed, he set out to run all three of them down, to sink their little boat and drown them all."

"'E got what 'e deserved then, din't 'e?"

"Fortunately, Alexee, the chief of the Seaple, knew a way to bring Yonaton back to life after he had drowned in the lagoon. He blew into his mouth to get him breathing again—"

Another round of surprised gasps and comments coursed through the throng.

"It's something that these people have learned over the years they've spent living in water. They've also learned how to keep and farm fish and shellfish, how to harvest and use all types of seaweeds – for food, for medicine and lots more besides. And they've learned how to work with a family of dolphins who have become their friends and neighbours.

"There is a great deal we can learn from the Seaple and it's a shame we have been denied contact with them all these years. Even before the Cardinal scared us off, the deadly reef that surrounds their island and encloses the lagoon has proved an almost impenetrable barrier. Ships and boats are likely to founder on the reef in the rough seas, and the Seaple themselves are unable to leave their safe haven due to sharks in the seas outside the lagoon. It is no wonder, then, that *they* call it Sanctuary Island and I suggest we use this name from now on and consider the island forbidden no more."

"'Ow we gonna go there if there's a deadly reef all around it...?" someone shouted.

"There is one small gap in the reef, where a boat can gain access to the lagoon, but you would never find it without help from the Seaple... and without them opening a gate they have fitted to keep the sharks out."

Ifan deliberately didn't mention the Seaple's ability to talk to the dolphins, or their written history which gave a fantastic explanation for mankind's origins on Earth. Over Lucy's delicious supper the night before they had decided that these revelations should be saved for another day, when they had a way to provide proof or, failing that, some persuasive evidence.

"With help from the Seaple and the dolphins, Captain Yonaton and his crew have been able to raise the Pelican from the reef and move her into the lagoon. Now they need to repair a huge hole in the ship's side and we will be taking timber, planks and rivet-nails with us when we leave to go back to Sanctuary Island at dawn tomorrow. We hope to persuade a couple of our town's shipwrights to go with us to help with the work."

"Yes. I'll go!" shouted one man. "An' I reckon my mate'll go too. I'll ask 'im when I get back to the boatyard."

Moon 3660

Friday, 4pm and Ktrina was looking forward to heading home from the Sokolovan Embassy, eager to escape the claustrophobic atmosphere of Coopan society. She knew she shouldn't complain, having spent only two days in the north this week, but it was more than enough. Even her bid to reconcile her differences with Gunta Krems had led nowhere.

After the state-owned news channel had belatedly shown footage of their dead Coopan Commandos, three surface-suited bodies wearing full regimental insignia, being removed from the battlefield of south Aristarchus, she had been moved to contact the north's Foreign Minister. Could she, on behalf of the Sokolovan government, send wreaths with condolences to the three families, she'd asked, as a tribute to their sacrifice in the common fight against the FLOC?

Impossible, he'd replied. It was strict government policy never to reveal the names of fallen soldiers, in order to prevent FLOC attacks on the families of Commandos. She realised with dismay this meant there would be no funerals, no recognition and therefore no proper closure for any family of these brave northern lads who had died in a futile attempt to deal with the rebels.

Krems had thanked her for the offer then abruptly ended the call. Was he embarrassed by his government's policy which seemed at odds with human dignity? Or was he unwilling to engage in conversation with her after their face-off over the Khouri affair? She couldn't guess which, and felt tired of all the political manoeuvring that her job entailed.

Maybe her last appointment of the week would be a change from the usual tedium of visa application appeals and petty grievances. It wasn't uncommon for Sokolovan citizens to complain their rights had been infringed in the north. In reality they had very few rights under Coopan law, and Ktrina's job mostly consisted of explaining this fact and the two available options – suck it up or ship out. But Klif

Watanabe's story was unusual. So different she had decided to take him to the embassy's Quiet Room to discuss his case.

"Whoa, this is weird!" he said, as he sank into the soft upholstery of a lavish armchair and looked around at the thousands of pyramids lining the walls. "It sounds really strange in here."

Ktrina settled into the chair facing him. "It's an anechoic chamber. Nothing we say in here can be detected by any known bugging technology. But, please, remove your comm for me while we talk."

"So…" his eyebrows shot up as he reached for his wrist and twisted the unit from its dock, "you think the Coops have bugs *inside* the Sok embassy?"

"What do *you* think?" She smiled at him. "Is there anywhere in the north where your every movement isn't recorded, every word analysed, every contact scrutinised?"

"Well, yeah, I suppose. I knew they were paranoid." He frowned as a thought struck him. "Does that mean they suspect me of something…?"

"They suspect everyone, Doctor Watanabe—"

"Please, call me Klif."

"But they don't suspect you of spying, Klif."

"How can you know that?"

"You wouldn't be here, talking to *me*. You'd be having an interview with the Xintapo instead."

"Shit! *Really?* Those guys freak me out." He ran a finger nervously around his collar.

"That's their intention. But we're safe in here. You can speak without fear of anything getting back to the Coops and their menacing monks." She smiled. "You were saying you had a six-month contract to work on guidance systems…?"

"Yes, that's right. A bit strange really, as all our hoppers and carriers rely on four or six drive units – plasma drives mostly – and adjust the thrust to each in order to orient and change the ship's direction. For some reason they wanted to develop gimballed nozzles, something we haven't used for… well forever, practically."

"And that's your field, I gather?"

"Well, no. Not the nozzles themselves. *Nobody* has any expertise with them. All that we have is in the old Earth archives. My specialty is in the guidance side, getting the control systems to talk to the directional hardware."

"And you hadn't completed your contract…?"

"No. Two months still to go. They seemed pleased with my work, and then suddenly, wham, I was terminated for no reason. We'd got the servos responding perfectly to all the input signals. The rocket nozzles should be able to steer their craft in response to autopilot or manual guidance—"

"Any idea what craft this was for?"

"No. That was top secret, and I was warned not to ask questions about it, right at the start."

"Or the fuel they would be using?"

"Oh, that was easy to work out. Good old liquid hydrogen and oxygen. Obvious from the de Laval shape—"

"I'm sorry, I'm not a rocket scientist…" Ktrina frowned at him.

"Ah, that's the hourglass shape inside the nozzles. It tells you what they are burning. These are old fashioned rockets, fuelled with water – or its constituents, anyway. But that was the other funny thing…"

"Funny in what way?"

"Well, the latest versions of the nozzles I saw had variable cones, which didn't make any sense at all."

"Why not?"

"Well, the only reason you'd need to vary the cone shape is if the external pressure changed. And all our craft fly in a vacuum. Zero pressure. All the time. No reason to go to all the cost and complexity of adjustable cones. I said as much to their chief engineer."

"When was this?" Ktrina sensed a subtlety that Klif might have missed.

"Wednesday." His eyes widened. "You don't think—?"

"Yes, I *do* think. You overstepped your brief, Klif. Spotted something you weren't supposed to notice. Now we have to figure out why they've cooked up these fancy rocket cones. And get you home before they change their minds about letting you go…"

Earth 1504

Sam and Peter took shelter from the stiff easterly wind behind an outcrop of rock. It had been a long uphill walk from Loming to the high peak and they were exhausted. From this vantage point they could look down on the town to the north, and the rolling grasslands, now pale and parched, that stretched away for miles to the south.

"Here, Peter. Have some milk." Sam passed the goatskin pouch to his 11-year-old son who drank thirstily. His face was flushed from the effort of the climb, and both were sweating freely despite the cool breeze and low clouds scudding overhead. Sam opened his pack. "We'll have a bite of bread and cheese and get our breath back, then we'll get started. It'll be tricky work in this blow."

They had left Sam's flock of sheep and goats to graze beside the river when they headed for the hills at first light, carrying long poles topped with leather beaters. It would be the strangest burning Sam had ever attempted, but last night over supper Jack and Ifan had spelled out the Captain's unusual request. Finally, reluctantly, he'd agreed to follow his father-in-law's wishes, even though the reason for it seemed laughable. They were going to send a message to the Man in the Moon!

"Now then, son," he said, picking up a stick and drawing in the dusty soil. "This is the shape we've got to make. We'll have to stay on our toes to keep the fire under control with this wind, but if we stay ahead of the flames and beat until our arms break, we should be able to do it."

Meanwhile, on board the Petrel, there was little respite from the wind as it bucked and rolled with the waves. The hold was nearly filled with the chunky curved timbers that would be used to replace the Pelican's ribs. The remaining space had been taken up with tools and supplies, and the deck was stacked with planks, lashed down securely to stop them being washed overboard in the stormy seas. Tom and Faruk, sheltering from the wind and spray beneath an old sail, were partners in misery.

Their offer to return with Jack and Ifan and help rebuild the damaged Pelican seemed like the worst decision they'd ever made. The passage across the Crabbing Sea had been rough ever since they left the shelter of Loming harbour at dawn that morning. Now, approaching the island, the seas seemed even more wild and furious, with spray being ripped from the tops of waves as dark clouds raced past the tip of the gyrating mast.

If they wished they'd stayed in the comfort of their boatyard, the two carpenter-shipwrights weren't saying. They'd stopped talking and started puking soon after leaving harbour and now their only wish was to die, or for the brutal voyage to end. At this point, either outcome would have seemed like a blessing, but Jack and Ifan assured them it would soon be over. Sanctuary Island, as they were now happy to call it, was in sight.

The storm season had started early. It was usually mid-Orgust before the worst of the gales tore at the roofs of their houses and rattled their shutters. The eye of this storm was still a day away, according to

Jack and Ifan, who knew about such things, but for the two chippies it was hard to imagine how the weather could be any worse. Out on the open sea in a small boat, lurching from towering wave crests and dropping like a stone into their troughs, it felt like all their nightmares rolled into one. With the day drawing to a close and the waves increasing steadily, their only thought was when it might be over.

"Not much further," shouted Jack, bending down to peer at their grey faces. "Try to drink some water." He passed them the canteen, but neither of them felt inclined to pull out the stopper and take a swig. It had been the enticing idea of bare-breasted mermaids that had persuaded them to overlook the angry waves crashing against the harbour wall at dawn that morning. Right now it felt as if they'd been lured to a watery hell by aquatic sirens. Any desire they may have harboured for water-loving women had been dashed by their battering and pummelling aboard the Petrel, and washed away by the flying spume and spray.

Moon 3660

Coopan commuters were a strange bunch, thought Ktrina, as she entered the metro station near her embassy. They didn't talk to each other, chat on their comms, eat snacks or sip from drinks. As the office workers filed into the station entrance, past the steely gaze of the ever-present Xintapo, they kept their faces and thoughts hidden, heads down, shuffling forward, avoiding eye contact. She didn't just stand out because of her new navy-blue business suit and collar-length hair. Ktrina realised she was the only one walking upright, head held high, looking around confidently.

She wished she felt confident about what might happen next. As she stepped past the queue for the escalator and made for the stairs she had an odd sense of déjà vu. It was here, two weeks ago, that a young man with a broken tooth had slipped an egg into her jacket and whispered, "For Ethan!". That single, shocking act had sent her on a crazily risky and uncomfortable journey back to Sokolova City. She had smuggled the weird object home, discovered that it morphed into a mind-control spider when she plugged it into her comm, but still had no idea what she was meant to do with it. And here she was, half expecting to meet him again, desperate for answers and unable to think how to get them.

There was one thing she *had* decided on. "Comm – record video," she whispered to herself as she took the first step down towards the platforms. Holding the metal rail with her right hand and her hand luggage with her left, she kept an eye on the steps to avoid a slip and a stumble with her still-weak knee. But she flicked a glance at the people climbing up the stairs, just in case one of them was him. She was halfway down when she glanced up and saw him – blue eyes, broken tooth and that haunted, hunted look that seemed to peer straight into her soul.

As they passed each other she silently mouthed, "What for?" and his eyes widened for an instant. Then he was gone, and she was concentrating on the final few steps. With a rattle an inbound train blew a rush of fetid air into her face. The stale metro atmosphere smelled of sweat, electrical discharge, decay and everything else that was unwholesome in Cooper City. She made for the toilets, whispered "Comm – stop recording", and found herself staring into the same smeary mirror that had offered no answers two weeks ago.

A sudden thought grabbed her by the throat – what if he was a rebel... or a FLOC sympathiser? Was he connected to those who had just killed four young Rangers... who killed Ethan? This was madness. What had she got herself involved with? She leaned forward, laid her hot forehead against the cold glass, and closed her eyes.

And there, as if on cue, *was* Ethan. Not smiling, not frowning, just looking straight at her. Then he turned his head and she saw there was another man standing next to him. Ethan had an arm around his shoulders in a friendly embrace. With a jolt, Ktrina realised the man Ethan was hugging looked oddly familiar, like someone lost deep in her past, and also... a little like her broken-tooth youth of the stairway.

She opened her eyes and saw a pale version of herself staring back. *What the hell is going on?* Cold water splashed on her face helped shuffle her thoughts back into some sort of order. She needed to get away from this crazy place full of ghosts and riddles. Get back home, return to normality. Then she might begin to unravel this bewildering enigma.

After an uncomfortable crush on the metro – no chance of a seat during Friday's rush-hour – the Monterey Skyport swallowed Ktrina and her fellow travellers in its austere lobby. The only relief from its bare plass and stone walls was a white-robed and haloed Messiah who appeared on multiple screens, descending from heaven and reminding commuters of his imminent arrival. But it was departures that interested Ktrina as she queued for the security gate with the queasy feeling that came with the knowledge of what was about to follow.

At least she had nothing to hide this time. She laid her hand luggage and shoulder bag on the X-ray belt and stepped forward for the indignity of the pat-down. There was no sign of the leering guard who had delighted in feeling her up two weeks ago. Instead a dumpy, middle-aged woman slid her hands up and down, in and around without a hint of emotion on her stony face.

Ktrina stepped through the arch without a bleep, was waved forward to collect her bags and, with a long, slow exhale of breath, walked through into the departure lounge. Almost immediately she spotted Klif Watanabe sitting at the café counter, sipping a drink. Their eyes met and he quickly looked away. They had agreed they would not acknowledge each other until back in the safety of Sokolovan territory. While her embassy staff had been booking him a seat on the first available flight home, she had told him of Adam Khouri's unfortunate detention. He was keen to avoid a similar experience.

Within half an hour they were seated at opposite ends of the Polar Carrier's passenger deck, feeling the insistent tremor of the plasma drives coming up through the base of their bucket seats. The lumbering craft lofted them from the surface of the Moon's north pole and sent them hurtling across the pock-marked surface towards the south.

Earth 1504
"Papa Yon! I can see them!" Mammed hollered from the top of the palm tree. The Captain's head popped up above the opening of the Pelican's main hatch.

"What's that?" He cupped his hands around his ears to hear over the roar of the wind.

"Jack and Ifan! I can see the Petrel heading for the gap."

Yonaton dragged himself wearily out of the ship's hold and grabbed the rope to haul himself up the slope of the deck to the port rail. Another long day of cutting away damaged timbers and scraping weed and sand out of the Pelican's belly had taken its toll. He peered at the horizon, his hand shielding his eyes. He could see nothing.

Oh! Yes! There... the tip of a sail. He could not identify the boat from the brief glimpse of a scrap of canvas between towering waves, but Mammed's young eyes were sharper, and he had a better viewpoint from his tree-top position. Besides, who else would be approaching Sanctuary Island in a small boat as a tropical storm gathered out in the Lanteek Ocean? He ducked back down into the hold and called to Ben and the crew. They would need to row out through the gap to tow his sons' fishing boat in to the lagoon.

From the top of his tree Mammed could see the men walking along the beach from the ship to the rowing boat and guessed their mission. He twisted two more green coconuts and sent them spinning to the sand below to join the half dozen he'd already harvested. Then he shinned down and started carrying the giant husks over to the camp fire, where Conor was making ready to cook a meal.

"Jack and Ifan are back," he said as he dropped the first two nuts on the sand next to Conor. "The crew are going out to tow them in."

The old salt looked up and grinned. "Tha's a bit o' luck. They'll be in time for some grub. Bin a rough ol' passage, I'll bet." He gestured at the tendrils of wind-blown sand whipping along the beach and the sparks being blown from the fire. "We'll need to set up a wind break, young master Mammed, or our supper'll end up full o' grit. 'Ere…" he picked up a short machete and handed it to to the lad, "yer can plant a row of palm fronds to wind'ard. Use that to sharpen the ends. Shove 'em good an' deep in the sand so's they don't blow over."

Mammed was pulling his first haul of palm leaves towards the beach when Desmun appeared through the trees, bent low under a bulging sack. After he'd dropped off his fruits and vegetables with Conor, he helped Mammed build the windbreak. It took several rows of fronds to stand up to the battering gale, but eventually they had created an effective barrier and turned their attention to events out in the lagoon.

The Petrel had dropped anchor near the beach and Yonaton was shouting instructions. Mammed and Desmun were soon roped in with unloading the cargo of wood, tools, fastenings and food. All were carried up to the tree line and wrapped in an old sail to protect them against the coming storm. Next the Petrel herself was being hauled up the sandy slope using ropes and blocks and plenty of muscle. Not until she was at the top of the beach did the Captain announce she was as safe as they could make her.

The two shipwrights, who had arrived looking pale and sickly, had quickly recovered after getting their boots on dry land. They had taken turns sipping from one of the green coconuts Mammed prepared and were soon revived enough to ask where all the mermaids were. He was pleased that Miriam and her extended family were nowhere in sight. Sunday evening, she'd told him, was traditionally the time when all Seaple returned to their home rivers to share food, tell stories and renew their familial bonds. Even the dolphins had disappeared.

Tom and Faruk were unimpressed with their first experience of Sanctuary Island. Standing shivering on the beach in damp, salt-stiffened clothes, watching the palm trees bend beneath racing grey clouds and listening to the boom of breakers on the reef, they both wondered what they had let themselves in for. Sure, there was plenty of work to keep them busy, judging by the size of the hole in the Pelican's hull, and Yonaton had promised to pay them well for their skills. But this cold and wind-swept island seemed a poor swap for their cosy cottages back in Loming where they could be spending the night with their families.

"Grub up!" hollered Conor, which lifted everyone's spirits. Tired limbs carried hungry bodies to shelter behind the windbreak and fill up on baked fish, roasted yams and hot cassava root, with the added luxury of bread and cheese brought on the Petrel. Their meal was rounded off with fresh fruit and all agreed it was a fine feast. As the last of the grey light faded from the sky and sticks glowed and crackled on the open fire, the men exchanged news and made plans for the days ahead.

Jack and Ifan told of the positive response from the townsfolk of Loming. Of their joy at the news of survivors and sadness for the lost souls, several of whom grew up in the town and had left grieving families there. Nobody was shedding a tear for the Cardinal however, and there was widespread relief at his demise. There was an air of optimism for the future, they said, although Lucy had postponed any mayoral contest until after the mariners returned safely to town.

They had not told the people of Loming about the Seaple's ability to converse with dolphins, let alone their claims about mankind's lunar origins. But they had persuaded Sam to carry out the Captain's wishes. He had set out early that morning with his eldest son Peter to burn a message into the hillside south of Loming. All the men looked to Yonaton for an explanation as this was the first they had heard of it.

"It's quite simple," said the Captain. "The Seaple claim we all arrived here fifteen hundred years ago as colonists. They say we came from the Moon, which sounds utterly crazy, but they do have some fairly convincing evidence. Like the remains of the ship we arrived in. I've seen it and so has Mammed. Plus, they have a written record of their history dating back to year one—" He stopped and turned to Tom and Faruk, who were whispering to each other and sniggering.

"You two newcomers might well laugh—"

"Where are all the mermaids, then?" asked Tom. "And these talking dolphins we've been told about?" He smirked. "You've all been eatin' them funny mushrooms, 'aven't yer?" Faruk burst out laughing.

172

"Jus' you wait, sonny boy," it was Conor's turn to speak up. "I bin sailin' these seas nigh on fifty year, an' I reckon I seen it all. There ain't nobody pulls the wool over ol' Conor's eyes. But I'm tellin' yer, there's mermaids 'ere, an' mermen too. And they can speak to dolphins – I seen it wiv me own eyes. So don't yer go getting' all cocky or you'll look like a right pair o' prats come the mornin' when they comes swimmin' by."

"As I was saying," Yonaton continued, "their claim that we came from the Moon sounds crazy. But if it's true, there are most likely people still living up there. And if they knew how to build a ship and send colonists to Earth, there's a good chance they've got better telescopes than the one I use on the Pelican. They might be able to spot a message telling them we are here, if it's big enough. And if there isn't anyone on the Moon, then we've lost nothing by burning a message onto the hillside. All the dead grass'll get burned off in the next couple of weeks anyway."

Moon 3660

"Morning, Ktrina. Come on in." Foreign Minister Jorg Lanimovskiy bustled past her and strode in to his office. She checked the time – 9.45am – he was fifteen minutes late for their Saturday morning appointment.

"I hope you didn't mind me requesting an out-of-hours meeting, Minister?" she said, as she followed him in and closed the door.

"No, no." His sigh told her he obviously did. "I'm sure it's something that can't wait until Monday." He smiled with his lips but not his eyes.

"I've some footage that I think might be the Coops' new spacecraft," she said. "And something else I think you should hear. Thought you might want to get the lab working on the video straight away...?"

"Okay then." He turned and snapped his fingers at the blank wall to his left. It blinked and became a screen. "You remember the screen code, Ktrina...?"

"Yes," she said, then whispered instructions to her comm, transferring the short video to the office screen. The wall showed a still frame of a bright window surround and blackness beyond.

"This is my view through the Polar Carrier's window when landing on Thursday morning, Minister." Ktrina whispered again and the footage rolled in real time. Lights and odd shapes coalesced in the darkness, but nothing that looked like a modern spacecraft appeared.

"So…" he said, as the short clip came to an end, "is that *it?*" Ktrina detected more than a hint of incredulity in his tone.

"Let me slow it down and show you what I think might be their new craft."

She whispered again and the clip ran in slo-mo, until she said, "stop!" She walked up to the screen and pointed at a cone-shaped object. It appeared to be perched on top of a long cylinder with lattice towers either side, the whole structure towering over nearby buildings. "I think this could be the nose cone and top of a rocket ship, Minister, but perhaps our lab could analyse the image and—"

"A *rocket* ship!" he spluttered. "We're looking for a secret *new* craft, Ktrina. Not something from a child's comic book. Space craft haven't looked like that since—" He was interrupted by a loud knock at his office door. "Who the hell is that?"

"Ah, that'll be Klif Watanabe, Minister. I asked him to meet us here at 10am…" she checked the time, "and it seems he's very punctual." She let the last word hang in the air for a few seconds while she smiled sweetly at the FM. "I met him yesterday in Cooper City. He's a Sok engineer who's been working on the guidance system for a new craft up there. I think you ought to hear what he has to say." She walked towards the door. "Shall I ask him in?"

"Just a minute." The Minister clicked his fingers and the wall screen blinked off. "Okay."

"Please come in, Doctor Watanabe," she said, as she opened the door.

"It's Klif, remember?" He stepped into the office.

"Thanks for coming, Klif," she said. "This is Foreign Minister Jorg Lanimovskiy."

"Minister." The men shook hands.

"Now," she said. "I'd like you to tell the Minister why you came to see me at the embassy yesterday. And what we think might have caused your contract to be cancelled early…"

"So…" Lanimovskiy looked confused after Klif's explanation, "you think these variable nozzle cones – whatever *they* are – are somehow significant? Why would they want to keep them a secret?"

"Because you don't need them for normal space flight." Klif looked from the Minister to Ktrina and back again. "Don't you understand? You only need them if you plan to fly in an atmosphere… if you're intending to land on the surface of Earth… and take off again."

The Foreign Minister stared at him for long seconds. "But they can't do *that!* It's prohibited by the Ark Martyrs Treaty. You're sure this craft is intended to carry human passengers?"

"From the size of the rocket nozzles, I'd say it's a certainty."

"Can I show Klif the footage I took at Monterey Skyport, Minister?"

"If you think it might add anything... why not?" He snapped his fingers and his wall screen blinked into life.

Ktrina whispered to her comm and the short video clip started from the beginning. She stopped it at the same place once again and Klif frowned and squinted. He stepped forward to get a better view of the pointed cylinder flanked by lattice structures. After a few seconds he froze and gasped.

"Oh my God!" He pointed to the image. "That's a rocket ship! And it's ready to launch – no doubt about it!"

Chapter 11
It's An Ill Wind
Earth 1504

The night was horrendous. Soon after dark the gale turned into a full-on storm, tearing the palm-frond windbreak from the sand and sending it, and the remains of their fire, cart-wheeling along the beach. Showers of sparks and flaming sticks were snuffed out as they blew into the lagoon. Fortunately, none landed in the Pelican or the forest, or the men would have had an even bigger crisis to contend with.

Sheets of rain lashed them as they checked the ropes and stakes holding the Pelican and Petrel in place near the top of the beach. Thoroughly soaked and unable to do anything more to protect their vessels, they cowered in the lee of the Petrel's hull until the boat started rocking in the rising wind and they decided it was too dangerous to stay there.

The storm continued to increase in intensity as the hurricane swept down upon them from the Lanteek Ocean. The beach turned into a blizzard of stinging sand forcing the men to retreat into the trees for shelter, but it proved to be anything but a safe place to sit out the storm's fury. The wild wind screamed through the treetops, sending showers of coconuts, branches and palm fronds crashing around their ears. On the Captain's instruction they hauled the rowing boat up the beach and into the trees where they turned it over and crawled underneath for protection. There they spent the night, huddled together for warmth. They quaked as the trees creaked and cracked nearby, and jumped each time flying objects hit the wooden hull that sheltered them.

At around midnight the wind abruptly stopped and they emerged to find a clear sky sparkling with stars. The sudden silence was eerie. Within minutes a wall of cloud obscured the stars and the wind picked up again. Yonaton ordered them back underneath the boat, just in time for a second tempest to start up, with the wind from the opposite direction. More trees fell, their splintering crashes punctuated the night until, finally, most of the men fell asleep from exhaustion.

Mammed spent the night hugging his knees, wincing at the sounds of destruction, and thinking about Miriam. She had returned from her teaching duties that morning and taken him to the sea cave again. They'd read another year from the ancient Histree which detailed more births and deaths, dolphins taking children for rides, and the ongoing struggles and triumphs on land and sea. After four years without contact, one man's despair at never seeing his Moon family again had led to deep depression and the community were trying to find ways to help him. It made Mammed think of his mother and younger siblings back in Portkaron, and his adopted sister Lucy and her family back in Loming. He couldn't imagine being separated from family for four years and knowing you'd never see them again.

The pair's Histree class had come to an end when members of Miriam's extended family arrived with armloads of dead seagrass. They were preparing bedding, she explained. It was tradition that the whole family gathered on Sunday evenings and spent the night together sleeping on the rocky ledge inside the sea cave. Other family groups would be making similar arrangements in the rivers to the north and west of the island. With the impending storm, the shelter of their sea cave would be especially welcome.

She'd taken him out of the cave for another writing lesson. He loved lying side by side with her on the wet sand, elbows touching, but remembering the alphabet was hard.

"Concentrate, Maa-med!" she told him for the third time after his eyes wandered away from the squiggles he was supposed to be drawing and trailed instead down the length of her bronzed back.

"Sorry!" he said with a sigh. "It's just..."

"What?"

"It's hard to think when I..."

"Yes?"

"When I really want to touch you." He felt his face turn hot.

She leaned forward and kissed his cheek. "Finish writing all the letters, Maa-med, then we can play touching game."

His eyes widened in surprise. "The touching game? What's that?"

"You will see. You will enjoy, Maa-med." She smiled and pointed her coral stick at the sand. "But first you must write all the letters so you can use them for the game, okay?"

"Okay!" He turned back to the half-drawn alphabet with renewed enthusiasm. "What's next...?"

"Kuh, luh, muh, nuh, oh, puh," she prompted, guiding his hand to form the letters correctly.

"Now," she said, after he'd finally etched the zig-zag zee into the sand, "we can do touching game."

He grinned. "How do we play it?"

"It is easy. You say what you like to touch..."

"Your... um... your shoulder, please."

"Okay. That one is allowed. Now you write, 'I like to touch shoulder'."

"Oh, that's not fair!" he muttered, petulantly.

"If you write it, you can do it. After that you can choose again." She winked at him.

Suddenly the challenge seemed worthwhile. Mammed set to work with his coral stick

As he sat beneath the upturned boat in the darkness, he remembered each agonising word she'd made him scrawl in the sand. And he relished the memory of each tantalising touch. First her shoulder, then her back. He relived the amazing sensation of her warm, freckled skin sliding under his fingertips, all the way from her shoulder blade down to the dimples above her hips.

He'd touched her leg, but only so far. Her bottom was not allowed in this game, she'd said. Then he'd touched her face. A long, exhilarating moment as he delicately caressed her smiling, freckled features from eyebrow to chin. The lesson ended with the most delicious kiss which made sparks burst behind his closed eyelids.

"I have to go help my family now, Maa-med," she'd said, after they'd returned to the choppy water of the lagoon. "Maybe see you tomorrow, but this storm – it will be bad, I think. Take care from the trees. Some will fall." She looked at him with a concerned frown. "Be safe, Maa-med."

Then she kissed him goodbye and he ran like the wind along the fringes of the waves, his bare feet hardly touching the wet sand, all the way back... all the way... back...

"Mammed!" He woke with a start and banged his head on something hard.

"Will you never wake up, boy?" The Captain's face was peering at him from under the raised side of the rowing boat. He was amazed to find himself alone underneath its upturned hull.

"Come on. There's lots to do and we need your help."

Moon 3660
The coffee was hot and strong, and Ella's conversation as bright and good-humoured as usual, so Ktrina didn't mind waiting outside the Foreign Minister's office, chatting to his secretary this Monday morning. She had toyed with the idea of turning up quarter of an hour late to teach him a lesson in manners, but decided against it. Chilling with her boys on a picnic trip to the Lian Song Botanical Gardens on Sunday had softened her memory of Saturday's indignity. And her mum, Sofi, had surprised her by asking to go too, and then moaning hardly at all.

179

"So, did your mum play Frisbee with the boys, then?" Ella smiled knowingly.

"Ha! Fat chance of that. But she *was* in an unusually good mood all day. I must find out what food fad she's on this week and try it myself. It might be the miracle mood cure we've all been searching for!"

They were both laughing when the office door opened and Jorg Lanimovskiy appeared.

"Sorry to keep you waiting, Ktrina."

She resisted the temptation to say 'It's alright, I'm getting used to it!' and winked at Ella instead. "Not a problem, Minister." She turned and smiled sweetly at him.

"We've been asked to go to the Ministry of Defence," he said as he slipped a hand screen into his briefcase and closed the door behind him. "There's a cube waiting for us outside, so if you're ready...?" He eyed her coffee cup.

Ktrina took a long last sip of the hot liquid then set the mug down reluctantly. "Sure, let's go."

"I want to thank you for coming to see me on Saturday, Ktrina," he said, once they'd settled and strapped themselves into the cube's seats. "Your video clip and Doctor Watanabe's story have proved to be quite a revelation. Hence this summons to the defence department."

The transport hoisted itself aloft and set off along the rail towards the Ringway.

"You're welcome, Minister. I was afraid you'd think I was wasting your time."

"Not at all. Always good to act on a hunch. You did exactly the right thing."

What... like lacing Daniel's birthday supper with laxatives? The thought made her stare at her reflection in the window. The cube slowed as it took the curve, then accelerated to match the traffic on Sokolova City's main perimeter route.

"I'm pleased it has proved helpful, Minister. Any idea what this meeting is about?"

"Some, but this isn't the place to discuss it, Ktrina." He gazed around the cube's upper walls suspiciously. Beyond the windows, the greenery of treetops sped by in a blur.

"Of course." She smiled to herself. Some men loved to think they were starring in a spy movie. "There are a couple of things that I think we *can* discuss safely...?"

"Go on."

"When I was in the north last week, the Coops' state media showed footage of their fallen soldiers being recovered. I offered to send wreaths and condolences to the three families on behalf of the Sok government, a symbol of solidarity following our joint military action."

"Very noble, Ktrina. But a waste of time."

"Because…?"

"Because they never release names of fallen Commandos. In fact no names of any military personnel at all. They do it to protect families from attacks by the FLOC."

"That's what Gunta Krems told me."

"So… what is your point?"

"Well… we always name *our* soldiers, we see their funerals and interviews with their families on the news. We give recognition, show respect and allow decent closure for their loved ones. Doesn't it seem odd that they don't?"

"No. Not at all. We don't have the rebels infiltrating our society like they do. It makes perfect sense to me. I'm sure we'd do the same if every other ragamuffin on Sokolova's streets could be a FLOC sympathiser."

"Hmm, okay." Ktrina wasn't entirely convinced. "But they showed their Commandos being recovered from the surface beside Lava Tube A14, and we haven't released any footage from our side of the campaign at all, have we? Why is that?"

"National security reasons, Ktrina. You might find out why in a few minutes time."

The clatter and hum of the cube turned to a higher pitch as the brakes came on and they braced themselves in their seats. The transport peeled off from the Ringway passing between the Synlac Dairy and Carnecult factories, and was soon coming to rest amongst a complex of large buildings that made up the Soknorth Military Establishment.

"Come in, Minister Lanimovskiy," boomed a deep voice as they entered the wood panelled meeting room. "Welcome, Ambassador Rozek." Ktrina recognised the Minister of Defence, Nate Adebayo, who had stood up to greet them. But she didn't know the man and woman to his right.

"This is our new Chief of Defence, Huw Thomas," he said, by way of explanation. "And this is our Head of Defence Analysis, Pippa Khan." Ktrina stepped forward and shook hands with all three.

"And these two I think you know," he gestured to the other two men. Ktrina turned and opened her mouth in shock. Doctor Klif Watanabe wasn't so unexpected, but her brother-in-law Daniel was a complete surprise.

Earth 1504
Mammed was amazed to find himself surrounded by a tangle of branches, palm fronds and broken tree stumps when he crawled out from underneath the boat. The wind that had threatened to tear the face off the Earth in the night was now wafting gently through the limp remains of coconut leaves that hung forlornly from ravaged trunks. Mammed wrinkled his nose at the unusual smell of damp soil and tree sap, but there was no time to stand and stare.

"Come and help us move the Petrel, Mammed." The Captain shouted over his shoulder as he clambered over wrecked foliage on his way to the beach.

When Mammed reached the sand the scene there was every bit as shocking. Branches, weeds and detritus were strewn everywhere and the Petrel, his brothers' hefty fishing boat, was tipped over precariously at the top of the beach with her mast stuck in the sand at the water's edge. It appeared as if a giant had tossed the boat around in the night. The Pelican, he was pleased to see, had not budged from its roped and staked position, but the log-canoe catamaran was nowhere to be seen.

"Over here, Mammed!" The Captain was pointing to a long rope leading from the Petrel's buried mast tip to Desmun, standing up near the tree line. As he trotted over, he could see Ben and the crew fixing up ropes and pulleys between the boat's upper side and the broken stump of a coconut tree.

"What's the plan?" he asked as he joined Desmun on the long rope.

"They're going to lift the mast up out of the sand, and we've got to pull it this way. That'll turn the boat round so it's pointing down the beach."

By mid-morning they had the Petrel halfway to the water's edge and tipped on to its other side so the planking could be inspected. As feared, one of the planks was cracked and the two shipwrights were busily hammering and sawing as they set about replacing it. According to the Captain, a storm surge had lifted the Petrel high up the beach in the night, and dropped her on to a log, hence the damage. It had also carried the catamaran away to goodness knows where.

Mammed was tasked with walking to the end of the island to see if he could find it, or what was left of it, after a late breakfast. Conor had the fire going again and served up a rudimentary meal from the provisions they had stored in barrels amongst the trees the previous evening. While they were all gathered around the fire, Mammed saw the large silvery shape of Peetee swimming westward towing a person. From the grey bag on their back he realised it was Rachel, Miriam's mother.

"Look, Tom and Faruk!" He pointed to lagoon. "There's a dolphin with a mermaid on its back."

The two young carpenters turned and stared in silence.

"Not so cocky now, eh lads?" Conor chuckled. "That's Peetee the dolphin, with Rachel, the Seaple's doctor. Fixed my broken 'and up between 'em, they did. Better'n any doctorin' yu'll get back in Lomin', I can tell yer."

Mammed was pleased to see them go by, a sign that Miriam and her family had survived the storm safely in the sea cave. But then he wondered where they were headed, and whether others had perhaps not been so lucky. He took a last swig from the coconut and stood up.

"I'll go look for the catamaran now, Papa Yon," he said, wiping crumbs from his mouth.

Moon 3660

"And so to business, ladies and gentlemen." Minister of Defence, Nate Adebayo, waved them to their seats. "We have important matters to discuss. But first, nothing leaves this room. *Absolute* secrecy, do you all understand?" He looked into their eyes, one after another, and they all nodded their agreement. "So, comms off now please, so there is no risk of accidental transmission." They all twisted and removed their comm units and laid them on the table.

"Thank you. The Coops' new spacecraft is the subject of this meeting. Pippa... could you give us the background please?"

The blond-haired chief analyst cleared her throat. "We'd heard rumours of a new type of space vehicle for the past couple of months, but nothing concrete until two weeks ago, when our orbital hardware detected an unusual launch from the Monterey Skyport. From the odd trajectory – straight up and down – we deduced this was an early test flight.

"A second flight, five days later, went higher and faster. Spectrum analysis of the exhaust trail told us it was rocket powered, burning hydrogen and oxygen. Again, it made a successful, engine-controlled landing back at Monterey's military section.

"The craft launched again six days later, and this time reached a height of 221 kilometres, undertaking some complex manoeuvres before landing back at its launch point once again. On this flight we were able to detect five extremely powerful rocket motors firing simultaneously. Our best estimate puts the thrust at 3.5 million kilogrammes. That's at least ten times the maximum output of any known craft in current service.

"We still had no idea what this vehicle looked like or what its purpose might be... until we got Ambassador Rozek's video footage and heard from Doctor Watanabe."

"Thank you, Pippa." Adebayo now turned to Ktrina. "And thank you, Ambassador, for your sharp-eyed observation, and for recognising the significance of Doctor Watanabe's experience in the north. As of this morning Doctor Watanabe has joined the defence staff and will be working with our Head of Development, Daniel Robinson." He nodded to Ktrina's brother-in-law.

"Now, Doctor," he looked at Klif Watanabe, "tell us what you've been able to glean from your brief contract with the Coopan government."

Klif described his work in the north and the conclusions he'd reached over the new craft. He showed them detailed drawings of the rocket nozzles and variable cones that he'd made from memory. He also referred to Ktrina's footage as evidence of an Earth-capable vehicle. Guidance systems were his career specialty, he explained, but he'd majored in spacecraft propulsion at college and his doctoral thesis had been historical rocket science, hence his knowledge of long-forgotten designs from the Earth archives. He believed this new craft had five high-powered rocket motors with adjustable nozzle cones to enable it to operate at optimum efficiency in Earth's atmosphere.

"Thank you, Doctor." Adebayo addressed them all. "Does anyone have anything to add to our evidence base for this new craft?" They all shook their heads. "Then we have two options open to us. We can speculate on its purpose based on the evidence we have. And we must seek to gain new intelligence at the earliest opportunity.

"History tells us that the Coopans don't invest in major projects unless it is to gain an economic, political or military advantage. They appear determined to send a craft, big enough to carry humans, to the surface of the Earth and bring it back again. Why would they do that? Anyone...?"

"We know they have serious shortages of niobium-cryptides." Daniel spoke up for the first time. "As do we. They're critical ingredients for filmsynths, the basis of our cloaking technology, amongst others. The solar collector discs were supposed to speed up processing, but we all know what happened to *them*. I think the Coops could be even more desperate than we are."

"And you think they can get these from Earth?" Adebayo looked doubtful.

"No, Sir. Not directly. But it has long been believed we could use phytoplankton as a key stage in production."

"Phyto-what?" The Defence Minister pulled a face.

"Phytoplankton – microscopic critters that harness sunlight and make all sorts of useful stuff. The Earth's oceans are full of 'em, but sadly, we didn't think to bring them with us when we set up home here. Our original cryostores contained seeds and embryos for almost every plant and animal, but not phytoplankton. If they can get a supply, it will reproduce quickly and they'd soon be producing these rare materials in quantity."

"Hmm, they would have to refuel before taking off from the Earth's surface again," Watanabe was stroking his chin. "And as water is their fuel, it would be simple to harvest anything from the Earth's seas while refuelling."

"Okay," said Adebayo. "That sounds like an economic and military advantage to me. What we need now is more intelligence. I want every detail of this craft and an idea of when they plan to use it. Minister Lanimovskiy and I will need to brief the President and decide what action to take. Is there anything else, ladies and gentlemen?" He placed his palms on the table and made ready to rise.

"One thing, Minister," said Ktrina. "Daniel mentioned our cloaking technology. Could we see what happened out at Aristarchus? I'd like to know why so many of our Rangers got killed?"

Adebayo looked at the Chief of Defence, who nodded sombrely.

"Very well, but remember, what you are about to see is classified code red. Understand?"

Earth 1504

Mammed was pleased to get away from the wreckage of their camp. The piles of broken trees and scattered branches were depressing. As he walked along the beach he had to clamber over fallen palms and realised he wouldn't need to climb another one for a while. The shoreline was littered with green and brown husks and more bobbed in the lagoon, the water murky with sediment stirred up by the storm.

Thick clouds still filled the sky, robbing the landscape of its golden sunshine. It seemed as if Sanctuary Island had been stripped of all its colours, ravaged and left in tatters. Up ahead Mammed could see movement and he soon came upon a large group of Seaple. They were gathered where the westerly freshwater stream entered the lagoon and amongst them he recognised Rachel. She beckoned him to join the sombre group who were watching her work.

"Maa-med, come," she said as he waded into the water to join them. "This is Frances." She was binding bamboo splints to the arm of a dark-haired woman, who turned red-rimmed eyes towards him. Her face appeared drained and exhausted. "And this is daughter, Lily…" Rachel nodded at a young child, cradled in the arms of a man next to her. With a growing sense of unease, Mammed noticed the girl was not moving. He looked back at Rachel with a frown.

"Tree fell down," she explained, pointing up the small river. He could see a stretch of sandy beach strewn with branches and palm fronds. She returned to wrapping the injured arm. "Frances will mend. But Lily…" she stopped and turned to Mammed. "Lily will have no more birthdays."

He felt his face crumple and hot tears burned his cheeks. He was utterly unprepared for this intimate moment of grief. All the tension of the past few days welled up and burst from him in a strangled wail. The Seaple, surprised at his reaction, moved closer. Arms circled his shoulders and hands patted his back.

When he opened his eyes and wiped his face with the back of his hand, Mammed found Rachel gazing at him with curiosity. "Sorry," he said, as if an apology were necessary. "It's too… sad."

"It's okay, Maa-med." She took his hand and squeezed it. "Is good to cry. Come tonight, at sunset. Bring all landsmen. We say goodnight to Lily when she goes to sleep in sea."

"Where?"

"Over here." She held her long webbed fingers out over the water towards the reef. "Come in your boat."

"Okay."

"Now, I must go. A leg broken, in the north." Rachel pushed her sharkskin medical bag to her back, and made a squeaky grunt in her throat to call Peetee. She grasped the dolphin's dorsal fin and lay along his silvery back as they slipped away from the group and headed out into the lagoon.

Moon 3660

The Sokolova Military Establishment's canteen was buzzing with lively chatter and the clatter of trays and cookware. The enticing aroma of fresh-baked bread and roasting food should have tempted

Ktrina, but after the video footage she'd just seen, she had no appetite and settled for a coffee. Daniel had no such qualms and was busily filling a tray with lunchtime goodies while she went to choose a table.

An image of Aristarchus dust on the approach to Lava Tube A14 stuck in her mind. It would have been the last thing Ethan saw. But his view would not have included the unnerving sight of boot prints appearing alongside him as if by magic. She had to concede that the cloaking system Daniel and his team of techsperts had cooked up was astonishingly effective.

The wobbly helmet-cam footage recorded the final hundred metres of the Rangers' trek from the crater where they'd left their transport. It was apparent the three FLOC personnel working outside the entrance to the tunnel in their surface suits had no idea four soldiers were almost upon them.

It looked as though the Rangers would simply walk up and disarm the rebels, but at around 10 metres distance something alerted them and all three turned. They began scanning the surface and raised weapons against a threat they could not see. Then red flashes of laser pulses erupted in both directions and the three FLOC fell. Seconds later the sunlit regolith pivoted upwards and the picture went black.

Ktrina had almost thrown up in the meeting room. She'd never seen men being killed before. It all seemed so clinical and instantaneous. And the awful realisation that the camera-wearer had fallen face down in the dirt felt like she had died along with them. Her startled coughing had brought the meeting to a close and led them down here to the canteen. Daniel had seen it several times over the past week and appeared immune to its shock value as he unloaded his tray.

"How's your stomach now, Daniel?" she asked, as he tucked into a chicken teriyaki mayo wrap.

"It's fine," he said, and took another bite. After chewing for a moment, he added, "no thanks to you."

"What do you mean?" She frowned and smiled at him.

Daniel put down his food, twisted his comm free from his wrist and placed it in front of him on the table. He looked up and held Ktrina's eyes. She nodded and removed her comm too. Daniel, the big kid who never stopped joking around, was being deadly serious for once in his life.

He swallowed his mouthful. "I know what you did, Ktrina. And I know why you did it."

"What'd I do?" She tried her best to look innocent.

"You saved my life, you crazy kook. And for as long as I live, I'll never forget it."

She realised she'd been holding her breath and let it out in a long slow exhale. "When did you realise?"

"On my twelfth trip to the toilet." He smiled. "Or was it the thirteenth? What did you use?"

"Three of Sofi's industrial-strength laxatives. I'm *so* sorry, Daniel – hope I've not put you off bouillabaisse for life?"

"Oh, I'll get over it. Wish I could say the same for the other four guys. You saw the footage," he looked down at the table and slowly shook his head, "our Rangers were totally invisible – could've walked right up to those three rebels and taken their weapons off them. The laser fire came from the lava tube itself. Somebody in there knew we were coming and set it up as an ambush."

"Yeah. It sure looked that way." Ktrina's forehead furrowed. "I can't figure out how they knew. Security was airtight... at least from our end. And I can't believe the Coops would have given anything away. Their attack on the other end of the tube was just as bad. They lost their Commandos too."

"But if they knew we were coming," said Daniel. "why did the FLOC put people out on the surface? Must've known they'd get caught in the crossfire. All they had to do was open those blast doors and invite us into their trap. Makes no sense at all."

She reached over and squeezed his hand. "Sorry I had to spike your party food, Dan. I had a hunch your field trip was tied up with the attack and I had a bad feeling it was going to go wrong. I hope they didn't think you were throwing a sickie?"

"They were suspicious at first, but when I asked to join them Sunday morning I think they realised I really *had* been ill. I'd been working on it for two years... of course I wanted to be involved with the field trial."

He looked at her with troubled eyes. "I had *no idea*, Ktrina. I thought it'd be the usual romp around Nobile, not an attack on the FLOC stronghold out on Aristarchus. I would have been in the fifth suit. You saved my stupid ass..." He lifted her hand and pressed his lips to her knuckles in a sloppy kiss. "Thank you."

"You're welcome," she said, smiling as she retrieved her hand and reached for a serviette. "I hope teriyaki sauce is good for the skin...?"

Earth 1504

188

A red sun peeped from beneath the blanket of cloud on the western horizon as the crowded rowing boat approached the large gathering of Seaple. Ifan slipped the anchor over the bow and paid out enough rope for the boat to lie alongside the funeral party. Mammed had never seen so many Seaple and thought every one of them must have come to pay their respects to the dead child. In addition, a large pod of dolphins swam slowly around the congregation, their soulful, bird-like chirps sounding like a song from the depths of the ocean.

Sitting in the stern of the boat beside his Papa Yon, Mammed trailed his hand in the water and looked up in surprise when he felt long, cool fingers close around it. He was delighted to discover Miriam looking up at him. "Thank you, Maa-med, for bringing everyone," she whispered, then slipped away through the crowd to join her father Alexee, mother Rachel and Lily's parents. They were holding between them a wide bamboo basket in which the little girl's body was laid, wrapped in different coloured seaweeds.

The ceremony started as the crimson disc of sun touched the horizon. Frances, the child's mother, spoke softly, pausing to let Alexee translate for the dolphins and Miriam for the landsmen. The words were simple but tugged at every heart. The eulogy concluded: "Goodnight sweet Lily, our daughter of Mother Earth, our precious child, our beloved angel. May you sleep with the fishes and dream of the Moon, for you are made of golden stardust."

Each of the Seaple approached in turn and dropped a stone into the open-weave casket. Then a lid was fitted, tied in place with kelp straps, and the parents slipped beneath the water to carry it to its final resting place. By the time they returned to the surface, Miriam was beside the boat, thanking the landsmen for coming.

"I hope I see you tomorrow, Maa-med," she said. "But we have much work. The storm destroyed our fish farms. We must repair them and catch fish." Then she was gone and the Seaple were heading for their home rivers. The landsmen turned their rowing boat back towards their temporary home, the beach where the Pelican and Petrel were hauled ashore.

As the dusk turned to darkness and the creak and splash of oars took on a soothing rhythm, Mammed relived the day's events. He had been deeply moved by the simple ceremony, as he had when he'd learned of the little girl's death earlier in the day. He'd run back to tell Captain Yonaton the news, then he'd returned to the Seaple's west river with Desmun and a bow saw. Between them they had removed the offending tree and another that was threatening to topple. He hoped they'd made the beach a safe sleeping place for the little girl's relatives to return to that night. As they'd finished their work the sun had shone for a while, which seemed like a good omen.

Back at their camp they'd spent the rest of the day clearing debris and making the place habitable once again. With rain threatening during the afternoon, they'd rigged a sail as a makeshift shelter and made bedding out of the piles of palm leaves that were strewn everywhere. Then they'd headed into the shattered forest and collected as much fruit as they could carry. He had a plan to share it with the Seaple tomorrow, if his Papa Yon would excuse him and Desmun from other duties.

Chapter 12
The Stick Man Of Earth
Moon 3660

"Mum, Mum!" yelled Jan from the lounge after supper. "Come and look at this, Mum." He was pointing to the wall screen where the evening news was stopped in freeze-frame. As she stepped into the room, he clapped his hands to set the broadcast rolling again.

"And now, something to brighten your Monday evening," said the smiling female presenter. We've all seen The Face on Mars, but now we have... The Stick Man of Earth!

"Astronomers monitoring weather events in the Earth's atmosphere had quite a surprise earlier today. While tracking a tropical cyclone through the Caribbean Sea, they were shocked to find this apparent stick-man figure on a hillside when clouds cleared briefly from the island of Hispaniola."

She turned and gestured to the wall screen behind her, which showed a crude black figure which looked as if it had been drawn by a five-year-old. One leg was hugely distorted, and the side of the head appeared to bleed obscenely to the left.

"Experts have been studying this strange shape, which suddenly appeared burned into dry grasslands at the western end of the island. And they say, 'Don't be fooled folks, it's not what it seems!' Apparently, it is the result of naturally occurring wild fires which often ravage these islands at this time of year."

"We spoke to Earth meteorologist, Anders Larsen." The image cut to a pudgy, middle-aged man with an earnest expression. He was being interviewed and was gesturing towards a screen.

"It is quite common for these tropical storms to ignite dry grasses," he said. "We see it occurring on different parts of Earth's grasslands during the dry season. Lightning causes wild fires to start and strong winds can lead to extensive areas of burning."

"But what about this Stick Man?" said the interviewer. "Can lightning carve out a figure like this?"

"Not the lightning itself, no. It just provides the spark, so to speak. But these storms bring rain as well as strong winds and the combination can cause some odd shapes to be formed. Let me show you..."

He turned to his screen where a passable image of a rabbit appeared as a black shape on a light-coloured background. "This appeared burned in the grasslands of Sahara three years ago. It may look like a rabbit, but it's just a random shape formed by nature. And here..." the image changed to a bird-like smudge of darkness, "this was seen on the western Australian savannah fifteen years ago. Again, wind and rain cause some parts to burn and not others. There are hundreds of fires each year, so sooner or later there is bound to be one that can be mistaken for an animal—"

"Or a man!" said the interviewer. "Have you seen other examples of human-like shapes, professor Larsen?"

"No... no I haven't. It seems nature prefers to paint pictures of animals for us." He laughed, and the programme cut back to the news presenter.

"So, there you have it. The Stick Man of Earth is nothing more than a random act of nature. Sadly, there is nobody on the Earth to make pretty pictures for us, but it is fascinating to see how the planet's winds, rain and bolts of lightning can produce lifelike figures to keep us amused."

"And now, with news and reviews of live shows around the great metropolis of Sok City, I'll hand you over—" Jan clapped his hands and the broadcast froze again.

"Isn't that great, Mum? That lightning and wind and rain can draw pictures on planet Earth?"

"Yes, it's wonderful, Jan. Now go and brush your teeth and wash your face for bed. I'll be in to read you a story in ten minutes."

Ktrina returned to the kitchen and started loading plates, cups and cutlery into the recycler. She stopped in mid-stride with one of the plates in her hand. A smear of sauce looked strangely like a bear's head. What a pity, she thought, there was nobody on Earth to draw pictures in the grass. What a shame that after all these years they'd never gone back to replant humanity on their home planet. And now, it seemed, the Coops were all set to raid the blue and white world for some tiny sea creatures. Just so they could make chemicals and compounds to stay ahead in a nonsensical, north-south power struggle.

She felt a moment of anger and despair at mankind's tribalism, the nationalist instinct that prevented the human species from working cooperatively and effectively together to solve the really important issues. But then she reflected on the words of the Moon's first Governor, Nadia Sokolova, who had done so much to save humanity from extinction in those distant days of desperation after Comet Santos. Her seminal philosophy, 'All Lives Are Precious', had been a central part of Ktrina's senior school education.

'There are inherent destructive and divisive tendencies written into our human DNA,' Sokolova had written. 'The only way we can hope to overcome these weaknesses and flourish as a species, is to put aside our tribal, clannish, nationalistic impulses and work together on a mission so grand it unites us in common purpose. The struggle for survival unified lunar colonists only as long as an existential threat existed. Now the return of mankind to Earth must be our destiny, our duty and our common goal until we once again thrive upon the soil of our native planet.'

But then the Ark, carrying the hopes and dreams of the whole human species, had burned up in the Earth's atmosphere. The loss of the great spacecraft with its one hundred colonists had been catastrophic. With Nadia already taken by cancer, the dream evaporated and a constitutional amendment prevented further attempts. From that point on, it seemed to Ktrina, the Moon's population was destined to slide back into sectarian jealousy and the politics of fear and division. Human history repeating itself with an inevitability that made her heart weep. If mankind needed a Messiah to return, it ought to be Nadia, she thought, not some guy in a robe and a halo.

Earth 1504

After a long night broken only by raindrops pattering on the canvas above their heads, Mammed woke to find he wasn't the last one up for a change. Tom and Faruk, who had been discussing the Seaple and dolphins late into the night, were snoring at the far end of the makeshift tent. He walked past Conor, who was attempting to bring the rain-dampened fire back to life, and waded into the lagoon to wash his face. As he bent over the water he saw his frizzy mop of hair outlined in the reflection and smiled to himself. Miriam liked to tug his crinkly locks, but she usually ended her teasing with a kiss.

"Mammed!" He was startled from his dreamy ablutions by the Captain's shout. "Come and give us a hand, please." The rest of the men were gathered around the Petrel and it looked like they were getting ready to launch the fishing boat back into the lagoon. With the last of the retaining ropes untied the boat moved easily down the white sand and into the water, where Jack and Ifan set about rigging the sail.

"Are you going somewhere today?" Mammed knew it was a daft question, even as he said it.

"Yes," said Jack, "we have to go catch some fish. We've only enough meat for one more meal, and the Seaple have nothing. Their fish farms were broken by the storm and all their fish have escaped."

Mammed turned to Yonaton. "Papa Yon, can I take some fruit to the Seaple? There's so much on the ground... they could be eating it while Jack and Ifan are out fishing."

"Yes, that's a good idea. You can take the rowing boat, and Desmun can go with you. You won't need to take coconuts, the lagoon is full of them. But all the other fruit—"

"And yams and cassava…?"

"No, they can't eat *those*, Mammed! They're poisonous unless they're cooked. But all the tree fruits will be welcome, I'm sure." Yonaton was thoughtful for a moment. "And while you're collecting fruit, remember to bury some of them so we make new trees to replace the fallen ones."

"Oh, okay."

"Leave some of the green coconuts at the top of the beach too – just make a hole in the sand with your heel and sit them in there. This storm brought down half the palm trees. They'll take a long time to recover, but we can make a start."

"Should we go now?"

"Not yet. Help Conor with the fire and have some breakfast first."

Moon 3660

"Thank you, Phoebe." Ktrina smiled as the cup of chocolate chai was placed on her desk. She breathed in the spicy aroma. "I need to spend a couple of days in the north again this week, so if you could sort some flights for me, I'd be grateful. Out tomorrow, back Thursday, at the usual times, please."

The receptionist nodded and returned to the outer office, leaving Ktrina to spend her tea break engaged in a personal matter. Ever since her vision of Ethan with his arm around the shoulder of another man, Ktrina had been trying to think who it might be. He'd seemed vaguely familiar and she decided to use these few minutes delving into the ministry archives for answers. As Ambassador she had access to the most comprehensive set of personnel records and felt sure she could turn up the mystery man.

Her first thought was he must have been one of Ethan's athletics teammates, but a trawl through Sokolovan athletes of the period came up blank. Maybe a fellow Ranger? Someone he'd been buddies with during training or on ops? Again, an identity parade of heads and shoulders revealed nobody who looked similar. She felt slightly guilty keying in the search for 'all known associates of…' but couldn't think how else she might track down Ethan's ephemeral friend. Another five minutes of peering at faces drew a blank.

"So, where the hell have I seen him before?" she muttered to herself in frustration.

On an impulse Ktrina called up the news reports of Ethan's death, something she hadn't seen – nor wanted to be reminded of – for the past eight years. She skipped the video clips of news broadcasts and searched for images. And lo and behold, there he was! The mystery man was the FLOC defector Ethan had lost his life with. Ktrina sat for a moment, mouth open in surprise and wonder.

"So why did you have your arm round his shoulder, Ethan?" Ktrina muttered, as she frowned at her screen.

She read the attached information about the man. It was annoyingly brief: 'Zach Swanly, deceased member of FLOC rebel forces. Died 19th December 3651 while attempting to defect from FLOC stronghold at Aristarchus LTA14. Coopan authorities released the following information: Name, Zach Swanly; Age, 21; Occupation, student of engineering; Survived by parents and one brother.'

Ktrina remembered the fuss at the time. Numb with grief, she had at least received Ethan's body for a proper funeral, but the Coops had refused to take back the remains of Zach Swanly. Whatever the young man might have done, there seemed no rational reason to deny his family the right to say goodbye. In the end, after weeks of diplomatic wrangling led nowhere, Swanly was processed for recycling by the Sok government. Ktrina and Jean had attended the minimal ceremony as an act of closure, but had been refused permission to make any contact with his family.

She enlarged the image and stared at it, then compared it with her recording of the man on the stairway. There was a definite resemblance to the man with the broken tooth. Could he be the brother? If so, it would explain how he knew about Ethan. Could the egg be an attempt at retribution – a means to get some justice for both Ethan and Zach? The thought made her pulse quicken.

There was a knock at her door and Ktrina looked up in time to see Phoebe's smiling face appear. "Can you take a call from the Foreign Minister, Ktrina?"

"Sure, Pheebs. Put him through." She'd have to pursue her detective work later.

"Good morning, Foreign Minister."

"Morning, Ktrina. Are you heading back to the north this week?"

"Yes. Going tomorrow, back Thursday evening."

"Can you pop in to see me this afternoon? Say fifteen hundred? Something I'd like you to do while you're there."

"Of course, Sir. I'll see you at fifteen hundred. Goodbye." She ended the call and checked the time – 11.08. She'd better crack on with her remaining jobs if she was going to fit in a session at her Tai Kwon Do club in her lunch break. The doctor had given her the all clear this morning to return to normal exercise routines. She was keen to test her knee and see if it was ready for Seventh Dan level action.

Earth 1504

It was mid-morning by the time the rowing boat was loaded with fruit and the boys were ready to set off. Conor went with them. He could steer, he said, and wanted to see the rest of the island. He suggested they set off to the east first.

"Why that way?" asked Mammed.

"The wind ain't reached full strength yet, so we best be 'eadin' into it now. You young rascals'll find it 'ard work rowin' agin' the breeze later on." He tapped the side of his nose. "See… yer needs ol' Conor to save yer breakin' yer backs. Always go upwind when it's easy, downwind when it's 'ard." He let out a lusty cackle as the boys started pulling on the long and heavy oars.

They soon came across a group of Seaple working near the inside of the reef. There were a dozen of them, all diving to retrieve clumps of dead coral. They were using them to rebuild the wall of a medium-sized fish pen. They were grateful for the fruit the boys handed over and were munching hungrily as the boat rowed on towards Christown and the sea cave.

"They prob'ly didn't get much to eat yest'y," said Conor. "An' it'll be a while afore they 'ave their fish farms up an' runnin' again. I 'ope Jack and Ifan are 'avin' some luck, fer all our sakes."

The Petrel had set off through the gap in the reef soon after breakfast, Mammed's two brothers planning to use their nets in the sheltered seas to the west of the island. But they weren't familiar with the fishing in these waters so would have to depend on watching where the sea birds were feeding in order to locate any fish, they said. Mammed was shocked by how easily a storm could destroy a community's food resource, and worried over how long it might take to recover. The Seaple could end up going hungry for weeks after a major storm, he realised. It was a good job the landsmen were there to help.

At the next fish pen, they found Miriam and Rachel working as part of a bigger group to repair holes in the walls of a long enclosure. The twenty or so Seaple were delighted to receive the fruit and Rachel asked to look at the boys' hands while she bit into a ripe pawpaw.

196

"Hmm," she said, after inspecting them both. "Much better. But you now paddlin' again... how far you go?"

"All the way round the island," said Mammed. "We want to give fruit to everybody."

"That's very kind." She smiled at him. "But you will have bad hands again after..."

"We don't mind," he said. "The Seaple have to eat something, don't they?"

"Hold this." She passed him her half-eaten fruit, then rummaged in her bag.

Miriam grinned at him as she munched on a mango. "You are hero, Maa-med," she said and giggled. He felt his face heat up as Rachel reached towards him with her magic brown goo and a kelp bandage.

"My brothers, Jack and Ifan, have gone out in their fishing boat," he said, to divert attention away from himself. "They'll share their catch with you too, so I hope they get plenty."

After wrapping Desmun's hands, Rachel turned to Conor. "How are broken bones healing, old man?" she asked, with a wink.

"They's doin' alright, thank yer, missis." He smiled in return.

"Let me see, please." She beckoned with her fingers.

He lifted his arm from his sling and presented his damaged hand. It was still pink and swollen, but nowhere near as ugly as when she last saw it, almost a week ago. "How does it feel?" she asked.

"Pretty good, I'd say. But I ain't tried usin' it yet."

"No, you must not touch anything for at least one week more. Next time, we ask Peetee to look inside it again... tomorrow or next day. Keep in this..." she indicated his sling, "all the time, please."

"Whatever yer say, missis." He tucked his hand away. "An' thank yer fer takin' the trouble. I 'preciates what yer done fer me."

After handing out more fruit and filling Miriam's kelp creel with as much as it would hold, the boys returned to their oars. Conor steered the boat towards the rocky outcrop that hid the entrance to the sea cave and, beyond it, the site of the fabled village of Christown. This was also the beach where the mariners first made landfall on Sanctuary Island a week ago, but it was barely recognisable. The storm had hit this eastern end of the island with such force that nearly all the trees were either toppled or shredded.

As they pulled the boat on to a beach strewn with shells, dead crabs and seaweed, their hopes of finding more fruit sank. From the top of the beach the land was criss-crossed with a tangle of fallen branches and tree trunks.

197

"C'mon lads," said Conor as he started picking his way through the fallen jungle. "Lessee what we can find, eh?"

Nearly all the coconut palms had been flattened and the ground was littered with green and brown husks of all sizes. "We can plant a few o' these on our way back, like the Cap'n said... get the next generation o' trees started at the top o' the beach."

"We could leave some at the water's edge for the Seaple too, Conor," suggested Mammed. "The wind's blown them all away from this end of the lagoon."

"Good idea. 'Ere... wassat?" Conor was pointing at a large rocky lump protruding from a mass of twisted vines. The three of them picked their way through the thicket towards it. Mammed started pulling at the thick tendrils of vegetation to see what might lie beneath.

"Try this, lad." Conor offered him the short machete he had drawn from its sheath at his waist. "But mind yer don't blunt it on the rock."

The two boys chopped and pulled at the tangle until the full slab of stone was revealed. It stood as high as a man's chest and was carved on both sides with mysterious squiggles. "It's the old writing!" yelled Mammed, as he crouched down before it.

Moon 3660

Waiting for Coopan Foreign Minister Gunta Krems to consent to see her, Ktrina reflected that she seemed to spend an inordinate amount of time sitting outside Foreign Ministry offices these days. She had contacted Krem's secretary on arrival in the north yesterday to request a meeting and was told he might be able to see her if she presented herself on Thursday afternoon. Making her wait was a power-ploy as ancient as the craters and she shrugged it off.

She could use the time to review recent events and prepare the right words for Krems. There had been another launch of the Coops' new craft early on Tuesday morning. Jorg Lanimovskiy told her it was a longer flight full of complex manoeuvres and the Sok government now believed the Coops were close to making an attempt at an Earth landing. Short of shooting the ship down – which would be an open declaration of war – they had only one course of action left and Ktrina was about to deliver it.

The 'Stairway Man' had made eye contact with her again soon after her arrival, but he provided no answer to her 'what for' question. She was now convinced that he must be the brother of Zach Swanly who died alongside Ethan at Aristarchus eight years ago. It was the only rational explanation for involving her in his mystery scheme with the enigmatic egg-spider. But just what that scheme was, she was still none the wiser. Maybe he would enlighten her on her way home?

One thing that had struck her as both interesting and comical on arrival in Cooper City yesterday, were the huge screen posters showing The Stick Man of Earth and declaring it to be a sign from God. She had seen the state-controlled Coopan TV news stating, in all seriousness, that only God could control the elements on Earth to draw such a figure. It was, they concluded, another sign of the imminent return of the Messiah.

Quite how they made that leap of logic was beyond her, but she supposed it played into their Xinto narrative and provided support for their increasingly desperate claims. She wondered, once again, how the devious Daval Nakash would deal with the fallout of the Messiah's non-appearance, but her thoughts were interrupted by Krems finally agreeing an audience.

He greeted her without warmth. "What can I do for you, Ambassador Rozek?"

"I've been asked to discuss with you matters of a potentially sensitive nature, Minister. Should we remove our comms to meet with your security requirements?"

"Very well." He looked at her suspiciously as he removed his comm. Ktrina followed suit.

"My government has asked me to enquire about your new spacecraft, Minister."

"What new spacecraft?"

"The one you've been developing these past few months and flight testing over the past two weeks. The one with five rocket motors and Earth atmosphere capability."

His face clouded. "I don't know what you're talking about."

"Very well." It was the response she had expected. "Then I'm instructed to deliver this letter from my Foreign Minister, Jorg Lanimovskiy." She produced an envelope from her bag and handed it across his desk. He took it reluctantly. "I've been asked to wait in case you wish to send a response."

"Humph! You can wait outside if you wish." He waved her towards the door dismissively. She heard him tearing open the envelope as she stepped back into the reception area and took a seat once more. She hoped he wouldn't take too long as she was booked on the early evening flight home. He would know that, of course. Would he deliberately make her wait so long that she missed it?

She knew what the letter from Lanimovskiy said, as she'd read a copy of it in her FM's office before leaving the south. It had politely reminded Krems of the terms of the Ark Martyrs Treaty and specifically underlined the words 'No attempt shall be made to put a human on the Earth's surface'. It subtly told Krems that the Soks knew what they were planning with their new spacecraft and warning them off from trying it. She was interested to see how he responded.

Six minutes later – the time it took to call and discuss it with Daval Nakash, no doubt – Krems appeared at his office doorway. "No reply is necessary for your Foreign Minister. You may go now." He turned on his heel and slammed his door shut.

Oh well, she thought, at least she'd delivered the message, an ultimatum of sorts. His reaction told her that Sokolovan intelligence and assessment of the spacecraft's purpose was fairly accurate. If they'd been wildly off, there would have been a strenuous denial. She'd clearly ruffled the Coops' feathers by revealing they knew all about it, but would Lanimovskiy's letter make them think twice about using their new spacecraft to visit Earth, thereby breaking the treaty? Only time would tell.

And checking the time, she saw she had only just enough to get to Monterey and catch her flight home. Good job she took the precaution of bringing her hand luggage with her. She stood and turned to the unblinking secretary. "Always a *pleasure*," she said with a smile and a thick slice of sarcasm. "Until the next time...bye!" Ktrina set off for the skyport with a spring in her step. She'd had her fill of Cooper City. Krems and his kind could keep it... she was on her way home.

Earth 1504

"Kuh, huh, ruh, ih, suh, tuh, ah, kuh, ih, suh..." Mammed struggled to decipher the letters on the great block of stone.

"That sounds like Christakis—" said Desmun.

"It IS!" Mammed jumped up and clapped his hands in glee.

"Wassit mean then?" Conor sounded less than impressed.

"It's the memorial stone that Miriam told me about! It's mentioned in the first Histree – a memorial to Christakis Niarchos, the pilot of the Ark who died when it sank in the lagoon." He stroked the stone reverentially.

"The colonists put this stone here fifteen hundred years ago, Conor." He looked at the old bosun with wide eyes. "Don't you realise what this means? It's proof that the Seaple's story is true. This was where the first village stood – Christown was right here!" They all looked around but could see no evidence of buildings.

"They'd've 'ad wooden 'uts, lad. Wouldn't be nothin' left after 'undred year or so."

"There might be some more stones – gravestones, Miriam said – where they buried the ones who died."

"Unless they're as big as this 'un, I reckon we might have job to find 'em. Why don't yer try to read the rest o' this lot, Master Mammed? Plenty more squiggles to go at..."

"Okay, but I'm still learning... it's hard." He crouched down again.

"Nuh, ih, ah, ruh, kuh, huh, oh, suh—"

"That's Niarchos, the second part of his name," said Desmun. "Miriam told us about him the other day."

"What else, lad?" Conor gestured at the rock with his good hand.

"Umm, it goes... puh, ih, luh, oh, tuh – pilot! Oh, fuh – of, tuh, huh, eh – the..." Slowly, painstakingly, Mammed spelled out the memorial stone's words. Then he went back and read them all at once...

Christakis Niarchos
Pilot of the spacecraft Ark
Leader of the first colonists from the Moon
Died 11th November 2156
He gave his life
So we all might live

Conor leant against the lichen-topped rock and shook his head in wonder. "Well, I'll be jiggered," he said. "They say yer can't argue if it's written on tablets o' stone!"

"So what do we do now, Conor?" Mammed felt someone should be told of their discovery.

"We can tell 'em all about it when we gets back. Them as wants to see it can come an' take a look for 'emselves. We're supposed to be findin' fruit for the Seaple, remember?"

"Oh... yeah."

"This ole rock's bin 'ere fifteen hundred years. It ain't goin' nowhere. It'll still be 'ere tomorrer. C'mon lads. The sooner we fills the boat up wi' fruit and get rowin', the sooner we can get back and tell the others."

Once they started searching they found fruit and nuts almost everywhere amongst the remains of the trees. Further evidence, if it were needed, that this had once been the home of a community who'd had a rich and varied diet. As they ferried bags of produce to their boat, Mammed wondered what it might have been like living here as a newcomer from another world. How would he have felt as a pioneer who had left all his family forever in a faraway land. Scared and lonely, he supposed.

Moon 3660

With her mind still full of Krem's boorish bad manners, the potential threats of the Coops' new spacecraft and the need to get to her flight on time, Ktrina had forgotten about Stairway Man. It wasn't until she had started down the steps to the Metro that she thought to raise her gaze. There, in the crowd jostling their way upwards, she saw him heading towards her. She decided to avoid eye contact this time, so was startled when he bumped into her and said, "down the toilet!" in a hurried whisper.

She nodded to let him know she'd heard and continued to focus on the stairs as the crowd carried her down to platform level. *What the hell does 'down the toilet!' mean?* Whatever it was, she needed a moment to think, so headed for the public conveniences. The answer was in her hands as soon as she entered the cubicle and unbuttoned her jacket. With her back to the door and the ever-present micro-cam, she only just caught the slim roll of film before it fell into the bowl. She'd no idea he had slipped something into her clothing once again.

With shaking fingers, she lifted the sticky tab and the film unfurled. In plain black letters were the words 'See inside LTA14'. It made no sense. She read it twice to make sure there was no hidden clue to its meaning, then dropped it into the water and saw it dissolve instantly. *Well, that's one mystery solved.* She didn't have to risk being caught with anything incriminating this time, which was a relief. She turned and used the facility to avoid suspicion.

But what about the message? Why would she want to see inside Lava Tube Aristarchus 14? She *knew* what was in there – the FLOC's launch facility for their orbital weapons. What was the point of seeing inside, if the combined forces of Sokolova's Rangers and Cooper's Commandos couldn't destroy it? And even if she wanted to... how *could* she see inside it?

It made no sense at all. She flushed and left the cubicle to wash her hands and stare at her reflection once again in the smeary mirror. There was no time to stop and wonder. She had a flight to catch.

Ktrina was home in time to read the boys a bedtime story, or at least, the younger two. At twelve, Paul preferred to read to himself, but she still popped in to give him a goodnight kiss and a hug, which he clearly appreciated. She loved her boys and hoped they would never grow too old to want a hug from their mum.

It was the one thing she missed from her own childhood. Sofi had never been very tactile and regarded hugs or any other kind of intimacy as an unnecessary opportunity for spreading germs. Her father Matt would hug her when her mother was not around, but seemed embarrassed whenever she was present. It was a wonder they managed to create a child at all.

She pushed the thoughts aside and smiled as she stepped into the kitchen where Sofi had a steaming mug of chocolate chai waiting for her.

"Thanks, Mum. It's good to be home in time to kiss the boys goodnight. In fact, after a couple of days in the north, home seems like heaven." She sipped the spicy brew.

"I don't know why you have to go there."

Ktrina frowned and smiled at her. "It's my job, Mum. I don't have a choice."

"Well, you could do something else. You don't *have* to be Ambassador."

"Please, Mum. I don't want to have this argument again. I've had a long and difficult day, and I'm tired. I'm happy to be home with you and the boys now. Don't spoil it. Please?"

Her mother responded by getting to her feet and shuffling off into the lounge, muttering under her breath. Ktrina sighed and turned to the smartchef for comfort. She programmed it for a small chicken curry with rice and made herself a slice of rugbrød toast and butter while she waited for the machine to deliver her supper. Just as the machine pinged and she extracted her plate of food, her mother returned to the kitchen.

"I'm sorry, Ktrina. I don't mean to nag you. I just worry about you up there with those barbarians in the north."

Ktrina smiled in surprise. It was a rare day that Sofi apologised for anything. "That's okay, Mum. Come and join me. Can I get you anything to eat?"

"No thanks dear. Too late for me. You carry on... I'll get myself a cocoa." She placed a cup in the drinks dispenser. "Did you see the news, Ktrina? Those religious clots in the north are claiming that bit of burned grass on the Earth is a sign from God!" She tutted as the machine hissed its creamy confection into a hot froth.

"Yes, I know. Not only on their news, it's on all the poster screens around Cooper City. It looks like a stick man a small child might paint while throwing a tantrum. You'd think their God would be a better artist, wouldn't you?" She giggled. "Still, it makes a change from their Messiah who's supposed to put in an appearance any day now." She swallowed a mouthful of food. "Mmm, I was ready for this."

"Can I come with you if you take the boys out again this weekend, Ktrina?" Sofi adopted a pleading tone.

"Of course! I was thinking of taking them to the zoo on Sunday. They haven't been for ages, so it'll make a change. It does mean a longish ride on the beltway across the city to Sokeast, will you be okay with that?"

"I think so, dear. As long as we don't have to go in one of those awful cubes. Those things make me sick, rattling along, dangling from a rail. It's not natural."

Ktrina smiled. "No cubes, I promise."

Earth 1504

Mammed was elated when they returned to camp in the middle of the afternoon. Not only had they delivered fruit to all the Seaple communities around the island, but he, Desmun and Conor had found and recovered the log canoe catamaran. Best of all, they had uncovered an ancient memorial stone that proved the Seaple's story of colonists from the Moon to be true.

Captain Yonaton, working on the Pelican's sloping deck with Benyamin, saw the rowing boat approaching with the catamaran in tow and clambered down from the ship to meet them on the beach.

"So, you found it then... where was it?" he asked as the rowing boat's keel slid up the sand.

"It were sunk on the reef, Cap'n." Conor pointed away to the west. "Only the tips of the bows showin'. Yer got Desmun's sharp eyes to thank – I'd never a' seen it."

"Not damaged then?" Yonaton looked hopeful.

"Few scrapes, but no 'oles in it. Once the lads got 'er baled out, we could see the canvas was torn, but nothing that can't be fixed."

"And did you manage to get fruit to all the Seaple?"

"Aye, we did that. An' found summat else too. I'll let young Mammed tell yer 'bout it..."

Yonaton turned to the frizzy-haired teenager with a smile. "You *have* had a good day!"

"We found a great big stone, Papa Yon, with the old writing on it," he blurted, excitedly. "It's the memorial to the pilot of the Ark, who's written in the Histree—"

"Whoa, slow down, Mammed. Where is this?"

"It's in Christown... or where it used to be. Where we spent the first night, Papa Yon... where Miriam brought us fish and asked us for fruit."

"Ah, okay."

"We'd never have found it, but the storm has blown down nearly all the trees. We saw the top of this big rock sticking up and cleared away the vines to read the words."

"*You* could read the words!?" The Captain looked astounded.

"Yes... it was hard 'cos I'm still learning, but I managed to work out what it said."

"And...?"

"It said, umm... 'Christakis Niarchos, pilot of the spacecraft Ark, leader of the first colonists from the Moon. Died', umm... I forget the date... then, 'He gave his life so we all might live'."

"An' on the back," added Conor, "is a loada names. We reckons it must be all the colonists."

"Well... that is... amazing!" The Captain was grinning. "Can't be much doubt about the Seaple's history now, can there? They wouldn't be able to set up a big rock and carve it, I don't suppose."

Hearing the excited conversation, the other mariners, plus the two shipwrights, now joined them on the beach and the story was being retold when they were interrupted by a burst of clicks and whistles. They all turned to see Peetee's toothy grin approaching with Miriam clinging on to his back.

"We've found the memorial stone, Miriam!" Mammed shouted excitedly.

"You have?"

"Yes! It was right where you said it would be... in the centre of Christown. And I could read what it said!"

She smiled. "You *have* learned your lessons well, Maa-med!"

He was telling her of the words he'd deciphered, and the names on the back, when Faruk shouted. "Looks like Jack and Ifan are back!" He was pointing to the reef, where a scrap of sail was visible above the breakers.

Yonaton sent Benyamin and the crew off in the rowing boat to bring the Petrel in to the lagoon, then turned back to Mammed. "You've done well today, Mammed. Why don't you go off with Miriam and learn some more of the old writing?"

"And you can show me memorial stone, Maa-med," she said. "I've never seen it... nobody has!"

After Peetee delivered them to the beach at Christown, Miriam started up the beach on her hands and knees. Mammed could see she was struggling. "Why don't I give you a lift, Miriam?"

"Are you sure?"

"Yes. I can give you a piggy-back."

"What is that?" She looked dubious.

"Oh, it's easy." He thought for a minute. "Best if you go back in the lagoon first... I'll lift you on my back from there."

A few minutes later he was climbing carefully through the fallen trees with Miriam clinging to his neck and giggling delightedly. "Oh, Maa-med, this is so funny!"

"Don't make me laugh, or I'll drop you." Despite his aching arms he was revelling in her being squashed against his back. "Nearly there – look can you see it?"

"Yes!" she cried. "Oh, Maa-med. This is amazing."

He gently lowered her to her knees in front of the great stone. She stroked the rock with her webbed hand and traced the letters carved on it with a fingernail, reading out the words as if they were carved in gold.

She turned to him with shining eyes. "We have to let all my people see this, Maa-med. How can we do it?"

"Well... I'm not carrying them all up here on my back, that's for sure!"

Moon 3660

Ktrina sat on her bed in her nightdress, staring at the egg in her hand. Now that Sofi had taken her cocoa and turned in for the night, she could return to the thought that had been troubling her all evening. Even before she'd boarded her flight from Monterey, Ktrina realised that Stairway Man's message had related to the mechanical egg-spider he'd given her over a fortnight ago. It was his response to her 'What For?' question, mouthed silently to him on her way home from her previous trip to the north.

But if the egg-spider was intended to spy on LTA14 – to see inside it, no less – then how the *hell* was she supposed to get it there? She could hardly march up and knock on the solid-rock blast door that closed off the end of the launch tunnel, could she? She'd seen what happened to the Rangers who tried that little ploy, and they were invisible, thanks to Daniel's cloaking tech.

Staring at the egg was providing no answers, so she turned to her screen and called up the satellite map for South Aristarchus. Zooming in on LTA14 she could see it was surrounded by featureless and dusty plain… all except for the small crater to the south – Mautfrell – where Ethan's patrol hopper had landed eight years ago. That had to be fairly close. She zoomed in further and checked the distance from its northern rim to the lava tube entrance. It was 1.6 kilometres.

I wonder…

She retrieved the cable from her bedside drawer, plugged it in to the egg and set it on the floor before clipping the other end into her comm. She closed her eyes as the egg clicked and sprang into its spider form. She'd told herself not to squeal this time, but she still had to hang on to the bed as her bedroom tipped then reappeared from near floor level. She thought about looking to the left and was treated to a brief glimpse of her own legs as the spider-cam rotated. She stopped it when it pointed towards her bathroom door.

How do I find out this thing's range?

A row of numbers – 2000 – appeared at the top right of her vision.

Clever little spider! But two thousand what? It can't be metres, surely?

She willed it to walk forward and immediately the number dropped to 1999, then 1998 and 1997 as it passed through her open bathroom door, then 1996 and 1995 as it trotted up to the pedestal of her hand basin. She did a quick mental measurement – yes that would be about five metres.

Awesome – a range of two kilometres!

She willed the spider to retrace its steps to her feet and saw the numbers roll back up to 2000. Her ingenious egg-spider was counting as it re-wound its spider-silk-like thread back into its body. No wonder the graphene nanofilament had to be so thin – there were two kilometres of the stuff in there!

Now her mind was spinning too. If she could somehow get herself to that crater without being seen, would the egg-spider make it all the way to LTA14? And if so, could it sneak inside to take a look at something of great importance – some secret and sinister weapon perhaps? It seemed as if this was the mission the Stairway Man had thrust upon her. Was he really the brother of Zach Swanly, the rebel who Ethan had died helping to defect? Did he have some clue about the vital intelligence his brother had been trying to bring from the FLOC? And if so, why hadn't he gone to the Coopan authorities?

More to the point, why has he chosen me?

Ktrina sighed and unplugged the cable from her comm. She opened her eyes just in time to see the spider's legs disappearing into the egg which rolled gently onto its side. In the light from her bedside lamp she examined again its smooth surface and marvelled at the precision of its design. Now she understood why it was dark grey – it was an exact match for the lunar regolith. But how would its fine-jointed legs survive the abrasive dust?

She reached into her drawer and retrieved her tub of body powder. A small sprinkle was all it took to answer the question. The powder was repelled forcefully. Either the ceramic had powerful anti-static properties or had been given a coating of some kind. Whoever had made this thing had created an elegant solution for a particular problem – crossing the Moon's surface and peeping inside the FLOC's impregnable tunnel. A lot of time and skill had gone into it, so obviously someone thought the rebels were hiding a vitally important secret. But what could it be?

She knew of one person who might know, a man she could trust. A plan began to form... Perhaps Jean and Daniel would like to join them on a trip to the zoo on Sunday?

Chapter 13
A Plan Is Hatched
Earth 1504

It was three days later that the clouds finally parted and Sanctuary Island was bathed in sunshine. Mammed luxuriated in the golden rays as he took his morning wash in the lagoon. He could hear the steady chip-chip-chip of the adze as the last of the four replacement ribs was readied for the Pelican. Planks were being sawn and planed to size and it looked as though Captain Yonaton's target of launching on Sunday, in just two days' time, might be achieved.

As the day for leaving the island approached, Mammed had very mixed feelings about it. On the one hand he was looking forward to seeing Lucy, Sam and their children back in Loming again, but on the other he had come to appreciate island life. He felt very happy among the Seaple and dolphins, but most important, he could not bear the thought of being parted from Miriam. They had talked about it at length and she had told him she felt the same way. Between them they'd cooked up a plan.

The Captain was eager to provide solid evidence to back up the Seaple's story when he told it to the people of Loming and then to the folks of Portkaron, Alberton and Dominges. He couldn't take the memorial stone and Alexee would never let their precious Histree leave the island. However, Miriam thought she might persuade her father to loan the smaller plass sheet with the chart on… provided she went with it to ensure its safe return.

She was eager to see more of the world after hearing Mammed's tales of distant lands and peoples. He had talked of creating a pool made from spare planks and sailcloth, placed on a shady part of the Pelican's deck. They could keep it topped up by drawing buckets of sea water as they sailed along. The presence of a real-live mermaid, along with the plass chart, would surely help convince the townspeople of Dominion and Couba that the Seaple's story was true.

He hadn't mentioned any of this to his Papa Yon yet. He was waiting to see how Miriam got on first. She had agreed to ask her mother and father last night and he would find out later today what they thought of the idea. In the three days since he'd discovered the memorial stone he had carried both Alexee and Rachel on his back to see it for themselves. Fortunately, neither was much heavier than their daughter. He hoped they might return the favour by agreeing to the scheme that he and Miriam were hatching. If all went according to plan, they would be able to return to Sanctuary Island in around a week, he decided, having worked out the likely course of the Pelican on its voyage of enlightenment.

"Mammed!" The Captain's shout interrupted his deliberation. "Come on – you can help Tom and Faruk for a while." He waded from the water and was put to work holding planks on the trestles while the shipwrights worked on them. It mostly entailed standing around in piles of aromatic wood shavings, keeping a grip on pieces of timber while the carpenters sawed, chipped and planed them into shape. He watched the Petrel's sail disappearing out to sea on another fishing trip.

Jack and Ifan had located large shoals of fish during the week and had been bringing back most of them alive in order to restock the Seaple's fish farms. As a consequence, life in the lagoon had returned to near normal, with regular visits from the Seaple and dolphins. This delighted the two young carpenters who were engaged in a competition to see who could spot the most attractive mermaid. Miriam, who Mammed said won any beauty contest hands down, was out of bounds, but he couldn't stop them leering at the other Seaple women who stopped by to see how the work was progressing.

By midday the last of the Pelican's replacement ribs had been fitted, and the first of the new planks was being nail-riveted into place, when Mammed recognised the buzz and chirp that announced the arrival of the largest of the Dolpheen. "That's Peetee," he said, without looking round.

"Yeah, so it is, Mammed. And he's brought your girlfriend to see you an' all." Faruk smiled at him. "You're turnin' in to a bit of a merman yourself, I reckon."

Mammed turned and waved as Peetee and Miriam drew close to the beach.

"Maa-med!" she called and waved back.

"Go on then," said Tom with a chuckle. "We can manage 'ere. It's rude to keep a lady waitin'."

"Thanks!" He turned and ran down to the water.

"Maa-med," she said as he waded out to meet her, "we need to speak to Capteen Yon-ton."

"You can *go?*" His face split into a wide grin.

"Yes, but only for one week. And only if your father can agree to some things…"

He gave her a joyful hug. "I'll go and see if he's free to talk to us now. I'll be right back"

Moon 3660

210

Ella, the Foreign Minister's secretary, was pleased to see her as usual, but before Ktrina had spoken more than a few words, Jorg Lanimovskiy was at his door, inviting her in. He had no desire to keep her waiting this Friday morning, it seemed.

"Have a seat, Ktrina," he said as he sat down behind his desk, "and tell me how your meeting with Krems went yesterday."

"Oh, as expected, Minister. He denied all knowledge of any new spacecraft—"

"Huh, who does he think he's kidding?"

"Quite. And when I told him it had five rocket motors and Earth atmosphere capability, his face said it all. He was shocked we had such good intelligence and knew what they are planning."

"So… he read my letter?"

"Yes, he read it. Sent me out of his office first and spent six minutes discussing the content with someone – Daval Nakash would be my bet – before reacting."

"What did he say?"

"I quote: 'No reply is necessary for your Foreign Minister. You may go now.'"

"I see." Lanimovskiy steepled his fingers.

"The way he slammed his door suggested he didn't like being reminded of the terms of the Ark Martyrs Treaty—"

"Or that we know precisely what they're up to." The FM butted in. "I'm afraid his reaction has gone a little further since you left, Ktrina…" He turned his desk screen for her to read. It was an official letter from the Coopan Foreign Ministry, and read simply – 'Until further notice, the Cooper Territory Visa for Sokolovan Ambassador, Ktrina Rozek, is revoked.'

She smiled. "I'm not surprised. I obviously touched a raw nerve there."

"It's a pity. Your eyes and ears are very valuable to us in the north. We will have to rely on our orbital surveillance systems for now."

"It will be a good opportunity for me to catch up on visits to some of our outpost towns, Minister."

"Speaking of which," he said, "I have the official accident report on your hopper crash, Ktrina. As we suspected, the technicians who undertook the rewire on the Zenit were primarily at fault. They and their firm of contractors have been charged with criminal negligence. The technician at Barringer who failed to conduct a proper systems check after you raised a query has also been charged. All are banned from any kind of work until their cases are heard."

"That's a good start. And how about the other three old Zenits? Are they being scrapped now?"

"No, Ktrina. The Ministry of Transport has undertaken a thorough safety check and all three are passed fit to fly."

"You *are* joking! They are awful old rust-buckets!" She was incensed.

"As long as they are deemed fit to fly, we have to use wha—"

"But that crappy old dual-drive system is their weak point, Minister. Switching off propulsion within two kilometres of the ground is asking for trouble. Hoping a second drive will kick in and save your life is not what I call a fail-safe system."

"We have only six small personnel transports to share between all the ministries, Ktrina. Halving their number would prevent government from carrying out its duties. We don't have the budget for new craft in this fiscal year." He spread his hands in a gesture of resignation.

"And what will it cost the government when one of these old wrecks kills our colleagues? How much do you think their families will sue for, knowing their loved ones were forced to fly in out-of-date death traps?"

"I think we need to keep a sense of proportion—" He was halted by a polite knock on his office door. Lanimovskiy glanced towards it with gratitude. "Come in!" he called.

Ella put her head round the door. "I'm sorry to interrupt, Minister, but the Chief Astronomer is here to see you with something he says cannot wait another minute. He seems very anxious…"

"Very well, show him in," he said, and then to Ktrina, "I have noted your concerns, Ambassador, and will pass them on to the Ministries of Transport and Finance."

She got up to leave as a very flustered older gentleman hurried into the room. She recognised Professor Martin Gallagher from his frequent appearances on science broadcasts, and it seemed he knew her too. "No, no… please don't go, Ambassador. This will concern you too." She sat back down.

"Won't you take a seat, Professor Gallagher," said Lanimovskiy.

"What? Oh, no time for that, Minister! I need to show you some images we've captured this past hour. Can I have your screen code, please?"

"Of course – 9721 – what is this all about, Professor?"

"You'll see in just a moment… easier to show than explain. You're in for the shock of the century!"

Earth 1504

"I don't know, Mammed," the Captain shook his head. "How can we be sure Miriam will be alright living in tub of sea water on the ship's deck for a week?"

"I can swim in sea every day too," she said, full of confidence. "It will be okay."

"But what about sharks? I thought your people couldn't leave the lagoon for fear of shark attack?"

"Peetee will come with us, Capteen," she smiled. "He will protect me. We can show your people… Seaple and Dolpheen swim together! My father has spoken with Peetee, he agrees to come with us."

Yonaton's eyebrows hitched up while he stroked his beard. "Hmm. I think I need to speak to your mother and father about this, Miriam. We need to make sure you're safe on board the ship as well as in the sea."

Mammed looked at Miriam with delight. His Papa Yon was obviously thinking of agreeing to their plan. Thinking, however, meant imagining possible problems.

"The deck doesn't keep still once we get out there, so we'd need to make your pool secure and keep the water contained safely…" Yonaton nodded to himself. "And you'll have to wear some clothes, young lady. I'm not having a naked woman on the ship, let alone showing you off to all the people of Dominion and Couba without clothes on."

"Thank you, Papa Yon!" Mammed threw his arms around his father's neck and hugged him.

"Thank you, Capteen." She smiled at him. "We will tell Histree… make people believe."

"We'll see." He smiled at them both. "I'll have a talk with Alexee and Rachel at supper time, Miriam. Ask them to come before sunset, please."

"I will tell them."

"Good. Now off you go you two, and practise that old English. We need Mammed to read it as well as you can, Miriam. If there really *is* a big book in Loming church, like Desmun says, we need to know what's in it."

Moon 3660

"Remember this from Monday?" Professor Martin Gallagher, the Chief Astronomer, had linked his comm to the Foreign Minister's wall

213

screen. "The media called it the Stick Man of Earth." The crude blackened shape they'd all seen on the news appeared.

"Of course," said Lanimovskiy.

"Well, it's no freak of nature, Minister." Gallagher turned and looked from Lanimovskiy to Ktrina and back again. "We only had the briefest glimpse between the clouds on Monday, but the skies over the Caribbean have finally cleared today, allowing us to study the surrounding countryside in more detail." He brought up the next image, which showed the Stick Man at the bottom and a short stretch of rugged coastline at the top. "See anything yet?"

Both Ktrina and the FM squinted and leaned towards the screen.

"Umm, no," said Lanimovskiy in a puzzled voice. "Are we supposed to?"

"Let me zoom in to the coastline for you," said the astronomer. "Now what do you see?"

"Good *God*, man. That looks like a harbour."

"It is." He zoomed in again. "And it has boats—"

Ktrina let out a short involuntary squeak.

"And there's a town..." he strode up to the screen and pointed at a series of blurry rectangular shapes, "... with houses. *And* streets. *And* carts. And *people!*"

"Impossible!" blurted Lanimovskiy. "This has to be a conspiracy theorist's joke?"

"*I* captured these images, Minister, less than an hour ago. I saw them with my own eyes and can assure you they have not been modified in any way." He turned to face the Minister and Ambassador, drawing himself up as far as his stooped frame would allow. "I can't explain how, or why. But I can confirm there are humans living on the surface of the Earth – right now – on the island of Hispaniola, in the Caribbean Sea."

"Who else knows, Professor?" Ktrina was the first to find her voice. Her mind was racing.

"Two of my staff. They are sworn to secrecy and are searching the surrounding land masses for other signs of habitation, but I can't guarantee they will keep their silence for long. And there are amateurs with sophisticated telescopes who will be taking pictures of the Stick Man now the clouds are gone. I'd say this news will hit the media within another hour or two."

"We need to brief the President, Minister," said Ktrina. "And prepare a statement. We may have only a few minutes before—" She was interrupted by an urgent knock on the door. She turned to Lanimovskiy with wide eyes. "Or we may have no minutes at all...!"

Earth 1504

"This year has been one of discovery and new beginnings, with much sadness and parting ways." Miriam was reading from near the bottom of the oldest piece of Seaple Histree. The tall sheet of ancient plass was propped on the sea cave's rock ledge in a shaft of sunlight. "You read next sentence, Maa-med."

He traced the letters with a broken fingernail, stumbling over familiar words written in a foreign script. "We are now 188, having produced eight more babies and lost none this year, which is a most welcome improvement."

"That is good, Maa-med. Read more please."

Slowly, haltingly, he read the rest of the report. "Sanctuary Island is now home to only 53 of us, the rest having moved over the past year to the much larger island of Hispaniola, which once held the nations of Haiti and Dominican Republic. The large two-hulled boat, built from plass pods and split tree trunks, has proved to be seaworthy and carries up to twenty people and livestock on each passage. The remaining three land-living families, consisting of six adults and nine children, will be leaving us with the last of the sheep, goats and chickens in a few weeks' time.

"We, the Seaple who live in the waters of the lagoon, are heartbroken to lose our fellow colonists, but understand the attractions of the plentiful grazing and fertile fields of the lands to the south. Metal ores and other minerals have been discovered there and the first of the migrants are already smelting copper, we are told.

"Soon there will be only 38 of us left here at Sanctuary Island, but we are promised regular visits so that we may trade, exchange news and maintain our genetic diversity. The importance of cross breeding is well understood, especially for a small population such as ours. The process, however, leads to dispute and distress within some families.

"Nicole Durand, who has been our Governor since we first arrived, was outvoted in the election at the end of last year. Her voice of caution was less popular than the policy of mass migration proposed by Thomas Tremblay. After the first successful voyages to explore Hispaniola and Cuba, the promise of endless land, plentiful food and wider horizons persuaded most people it was time for them to leave.

"We Seaple do not regret our decision to adopt an aquatic life here in the warm and safe waters of Sanctuary Island. While we will miss the company of our fellow colonists – and the regular supply of meat, eggs, milk and cheese – we have discovered a wide range of edible seaweeds to supplement our diet of fish, shellfish and crustacea. With coconuts readily available plus other fruit trees which will be more difficult to reach, we believe we can maintain a healthy diet.

"Our children don't miss the land, as they have never known a life outside the sea, and treat the lagoon as a bountiful playground. It is amazing to us parents to witness them speaking to the dolphins in grunts and squeaks, and there is no doubt their ability to communicate between species will be a valuable asset in the years to come. Sadly, for us adults, learning the meaning of the dolphin's calls appears to be beyond our reach.

"As our ninth year on planet Earth draws to a close, we are resigned to the fact that additional colonists from the Moon may not arrive in the near future, if at all. It seems certain to us now that the lunar authorities are unaware of our existence and our families back home will have long ago given us up for dead. If they knew we were here we would have seen some sort of robotic vehicle overhead by now, but our searches of the skies reveal only birds by day and stars by night. They are very beautiful, but lack the message from our fellow humans that we all crave.

"We stare wistfully at the Moon, unable to detect any sign of life there. Sometimes it is hard to believe that cratered world was our home less than a decade ago. This concludes my ninth annual report, dated 31st December 2165. Giulia Magrini, of the sea-dwellers of Christown."

Moon 3660
The rest of Friday passed in a blur. Selene News turned up to interview the Chief Astronomer. Foreign Minister Lanimovskiy gave the government's official response to the discovery, having got in a quick call to the President before they arrived. Ktrina moved into an adjoining office for the rest of the day, scrambling together press statements, taking calls and fending off the cranks who crawl out of the woodwork when something monumental hits the news.

Fortunately, Ella kept her supplied with coffee and a lunchtime sandwich, plus frequent smiles and jokes to make the chaos bearable. Within minutes of the first news broadcast, Professor Gallagher called to say they had discovered another sizeable town in the southeast of Hispaniola, plus two more on the island of Cuba. He estimated there was a population of tens of thousands in the Caribbean, who appeared to be supported by an agrarian, subsistence lifestyle, lacking any kind of modern technology.

What neither he nor anyone else could answer was how these people came to be there. Were they survivors of the Comet Santos catastrophe, or the Ark colonial mission? And if so, how had they been living there for fifteen hundred years or more, without anyone on the Moon knowing? The Chief Astronomer, who had been celebrated earlier in the day for revealing the amazing discovery, was now being questioned aggressively by news presenters over the agency's lack of earlier detection. Ktrina felt that was a little unfair. It took enormous magnification of one tiny corner of an unremarkable island to reveal any clue that there might be people living there. The small astronomical agency had the whole universe to keep an eye on. It was not at all surprising to her that humans hadn't been spotted on the Earth previously – especially humans lacking the technology to make themselves known.

Also in the firing line was poor Anders Larsen, the Earth meteorologist, who had been applauded on Monday for saying the Stick Man was a product of wind, rain and lightning. Now that it was obviously the result of deliberate burning by humans he was being ridiculed for having said it was an act of nature. Ktrina detested the media at times like this. Given that the Moon's entire population had been convinced there could be nobody alive on the Earth, why pick on one man because he tried to come up with a plausible explanation when no other was possible?

A more useful line of enquiry, she thought, would be to ask whether the people living on Earth had created Stick Man in order to send a message to the Moon? Or was it was some sort of fertility symbol to their gods. She'd read somewhere they used to do that sort of thing, back in antiquity. On the other hand, if they *were* trying to get the attention of watchers on the Moon, why now... after all this time?

There were so many questions and none of them could be answered until somebody went from the Moon to meet them. She had a feeling, given the recent developments in the north, that somebody would be a representative of the Coops. It was a thought that made her distinctly uneasy.

Coopan state news had made no mention of humans on Earth so far and she wondered whether they were waiting to confirm the findings with their own telescopes. Or had they decided to keep their population in the dark and maintain the pretence that the Stick Man was a sign from God? Officially, Coopans were banned from accessing anything other than their own state news. Although some did secretly tune in to the south's broadcasts, they would not dare discuss openly what they might learn, for fear of arrest for subversion and sedition.

When Jorg Lanimovskiy announced that it was seventeen hundred and he was closing the Foreign Ministry offices, Ktrina was relieved to be going home. It had been a long and difficult day, at the end of a long and difficult week. He thanked her for her help in dealing with the crisis then dashed off to take the cube he had ordered to carry him home. Ktrina and Ella left together, chatting sociably on the beltway until their routes parted.

Ktrina looked forward to hearing her sons' reaction to the day's news. They would be excited, that's for sure. It would lead to a lively discussion over supper in every home throughout Sokolovan territory. She wondered what her mother, Sofi, would make of it. Would she share Ktrina's joy at the thought of a thriving human population on Earth, or view it as one more subject to complain about?

Earth 1504

"What is cross breeding, Miriam? And why did it distress some of the families?" Mammed was looking thoughtful and puzzled after reading the Seaple's Histree in the sea cave.

"Ah... you don't know this?" Miriam looked at him with raised eyebrows.

"Er... no, I don't think so."

"How to explain... let me see..." She frowned while thinking. "You told me about your sister's husband, Sam?"

"Yes."

"He keeps sheep and goats, you told me... right?"

"That's right, a big flock of sheep and goats."

"When he wants to make more baby sheep and baby goats, does he always use the same father?"

"Umm. No, he doesn't. He borrows a ram or a buck from a neighbouring shepherd."

"Okay. And why does he do that? Why not always use same father?"

"Well... to get bigger, stronger sheep and goats, I think."

"Exactly. So, it is the same with people. Why do you not marry your sister?"

"What! It's *illegal!*"

"Yes, but why is it not legal, Maa-med?"

"I don't know."

218

"It is because if you marry your sister, and your children marry each other, soon you have very sick family. You need fresh blood from outside family to make children strong and healthy. That is cross breeding and it is important, especially with small population... like when the Seaple were only 38 persons, and only eight of them were adult women."

Mammed's brow furrowed. "So...?"

"So, they had to bring in different fathers to make strong, healthy babies..."

"Oh!" He looked shocked and his face turned pink.

"So, can you understand why it would make a problem – your wife would have to make babies with different men to keep the population healthy. Okay with sheep, not so easy with people..."

He turned his face away while he thought about it and his cheeks burned in the gloom of the sea cave. Finally, he swung back to her with a fierce look in his eyes. "I would *never* let anyone else—"

"It is *okay*, Maa-med!" She put a hand on his arm and stretched forward to kiss his lips. "*You* are the neighbour's ram!" She smiled and then burst out laughing.

"What?" He looked bewildered.

"The Seaple need fresh blood. It has been nearly one hundred years since we made a new baby with the landsmen. If we have children, Maa-med, you and me... we will be cross breeding. It is good."

He stared at her in shock. "B-b-but, don't we have to get married first?"

"Of course!"

"So... um... will you marry me?!"

"It depends, Maa-med." She stopped giggling and looked at him seriously. "I cannot live on land. I cannot stay in Loming – only visit. So you will have to live here... at Sanctuary Island. No more sailing on Pelican with your Papa Yon. You need to think about it..."

Mammed was quiet for a few seconds. "I can't bear the thought of not being with you, Miriam. Every day when I wake up I look to the lagoon to see if you're there. While I'm working I'm thinking how long it will be before you turn up with Peetee and we can be together. I couldn't stand a single day without you."

"I know. I feel same, Maa-med. But if you live here with me, you won't see your family in Loming or your mother and your brothers and sisters in Portkar—"

"We can go to visit them sometimes!"

"Maybe… if it is okay for me on ship. We don't know yet, Maa-med. And when we have children… it will not be so easy to visit your families, will it?"

Mammed's eyes turned towards the great plass sheet full of the Seaple's Histree, but they were focussed on his future. Finally, they switched back to Miriam's face. "Then *they* will have to come here to visit us, won't they?" It was more of a statement than a question. His eyes lit up. "They can all come for holidays to Sanctuary Island. They can visit us and our children… and go for a swim in the lagoon!"

"Oh, Maa-med!" She wrapped her arms around his bare chest and hugged him tight. "Yes!"

Moon 3660

Saturday morning was busy at the Tae Kwon Do club, with scores of teenagers in combat suits, helmets and armour waiting for their turn on the mats. Ktrina, sitting at the side of the hall with Grig and Jan, was impressed with the patient enthusiasm of the boys and girls queuing for their chance to show off their skills. Among them was Paul, looking awkward and nervous as he awaited his first-ever lesson.

She'd told him not to worry. He wouldn't have to perform any difficult moves on the first day. Mostly it would be learning the etiquette of addressing and bowing to his instructor, the correct stances and movements that preceded the martial art. Ktrina had gone through the same lessons eight years ago and remembered how strange it all felt at first. He'd soon get the hang of it and would bring himself along on future Saturdays without needing his mother and brothers for moral support.

If he was subdued by the unfamiliar task ahead, his younger brothers were positively bubbling. The excitement from the previous day's sensational news of humans on Earth seemed hardly dimmed at all. All three boys had talked of nothing else at breakfast and everyone they'd met on their way to Sokwest Fitness Centre had made some comment about the newly discovered Earthies, as the media was now calling them. Meteorologist Anders Larsen had also redeemed himself on the day's early broadcasts by explaining how the fierce winds ahead of the tropical storm would have made burning any figure into the hillside of Hispaniola a very difficult task. There was no wonder, he said, that the grasses had burned out of control and resulted in a distorted Stick Man.

Larsen also commented on the timing of the event, suggesting it may have been created ahead of the hurricane as a means of appeasing the Earthies' gods of storm and tempest. He thought it unlikely the giant figure was a fertility symbol, as those from Earth's primitive societies usually bore exaggerated appendages, and the most appropriate time for a fertility symbol would have been in spring, not autumn.

By the time they reached the club, Paul had fallen silent, Jan had run out of questions and Grig was eager to discuss his latest history lesson at school. Now they were sitting waiting for Paul to get his turn with the instructor, Ktrina told Grig he could tell her what he'd learned.

"We've been doing The Drone War in history, Mum. It's really interesting... and also very scary."

"Oh, okay." She smiled at him. "Tell me why it's interesting first."

"Well... because it was a long, long time ago and in some ways they were more advanced than we are now."

"When did this happen, Grig? Can you remember the year?"

"Umm, twenty-six something or other..."

"It was 2679 – almost a thousand years ago. So, how were we more advanced then, do you think?"

"Well, they had all these robots and things. They were really clever machines that could think for themselves and do everything for us – all the difficult jobs nobody wanted to do."

"Yes, that's right. So... what happened?"

"The people in the north – the Coopans – and us, the Sokolovans, started making these military robots to protect us from each other. They called them drones because they could work out when an attack was coming and defend against it instantly, without any people needing to think about it."

"So... machines that could think for themselves and had weapons. Didn't anybody think that was dangerous?"

"Well, sorta... but they had this code thing that stopped the robots from hurting people. They weren't allowed to target humans."

"So... what went wrong, Grig?"

"Umm... the drones, as they called them, were left to plan their own defence. Then one of them decided the best kind of defence was attack and it launched a missile. Within seconds all the drones were firing at each other and nobody could stop them."

"But they weren't allowed to target humans, right? So, nobody got hurt...?" Ktrina wondered if he had understood the catastrophe fully.

"Oh, no! That's just it, Mum. It was terrible! They didn't *aim* to kill people at all, but the attacks and counter-attacks caused almost all the habitats to be breached. All the air escaped and people started dying almost immediately."

"So… why didn't the people stop it?"

"They couldn't! The drones couldn't be switched off once they detected an attack, so they just kept firing and firing and firing until there was nothing left. It was awful – almost half of all the people were killed. And afterwards, more died of starvation because most of the farms were destroyed too!" He looked at her with big sad eyes.

"You are right Grig, it *was* awful. So, what do you think we learned from The Drone War?"

"Not to let the robots have weapons. And not to let them get so clever they can just take over and start a war without any people being able to stop them."

"That's right. So, do we have any robots today?"

"Yes, but only for doing simple jobs in our houses, like cooking and cleaning and recycling things. And for operating vehicles and in factories and things. They can't do stuff that could kill people any more."

"Look, Mum!" Jan called out and pointed. "Paul's gonna start his lesson!"

Earth 1504

Mammed was trying to concentrate on writing in the sand with a stick of coral, but his mind kept drifting off. He'd written 'Mammed and Miriam get married' and 'Mammed and Miriam have babies' but the words kept being interrupted with kisses and cuddles. And this time, it was mostly Miriam who was doing the interrupting. It was fun, but not the most scholarly of lessons.

When she heard a burst of clicks and chirps she announced it was Peetee going past and wriggled into the water to call him. After a minute of grunts and squeals with the dolphin she returned and grabbed Mammed's ankle.

"They are working on repairs to the fish pen over here, Maamed," she pointed her long, webbed fingers to the east.

"Who is?"

"My mother and father. Let's go and talk with them now." She tugged at his foot insistently.

"Oh." He realised what she planned to talk about and felt a wave of anxiety. What if they said no?

"Come on, Maa-med. We can do writing later. This is important!"

He left their love letters written in the sand and joined her in the lagoon. A few moments later they were surging through the water on either side of Peetee's sleek grey back. He had to concentrate on his breathing, so had little time to worry over what he might say. He'd never had a girlfriend before, let alone given any thought to marriage. It had all happened in such a whirlwind he didn't quite know what was expected of him. He felt like he'd changed from awkward teenager to responsible adult in one afternoon. It was exciting and scary and made his head spin.

Mammed was still catching his breath after Peetee had delivered them to the group of Seaple gathered at the wall of a long curving fish pen. He couldn't make out what Miriam was saying, as he'd had no lessons in the strange, gargling Seaple tongue, but Alexee and Rachel were nodding so that was a good start.

The four of them swam a little distance from the rest of the group so they could converse in private. Mammed was trying to rehearse his lines in his head, but the words kept tumbling over one another. He knew his cheeks had turned red, despite the cold water, but Rachel spoke first and put him at ease.

"So, Maa-med. You and Miriam wish to marry?"

"Um, yes!"

"How old are you?"

"I'm sixteen, seventeen next month."

"Hmm, Miriam is also seventeen, so that is good. Have you spoken to your father about this?"

"No! No, we only decided this afternoon." He instantly regretted the words, which made their marriage sound like a childish whim. "I mean… we've known we want to be together – to spend our lives together and have a family and everything. But getting married is the first step… isn't it?"

She smiled at him. "Yes, it is a very important step too, Maa-med. We Seaple, when we marry, we stay married for life. So, you will spend the rest of your life with Miriam, yes?"

"Definitely. I *have* to. I mean…" He turned to look at the smiling, freckled face of his girlfriend. "I mean… I love Miriam and I always will. I want to live here, at Sanctuary Island. I can help, collecting fruit and cutting down dangerous trees, and everything…"

"You think you can leave your family and friends behind, forever? You will be only landsman living here. It won't be same as now, when your father, brothers, friends are all here with you…"

"They can come to visit, can't they? Papa Yon – I mean Captain Yonaton – has said that from now on there will be regular visits and trade between us and the Seaple. And maybe I can keep some chickens here on the island, so we can have eggs and maybe goats… things like that?"

Alexee chipped in. "Goodee havee Laansmaans." He smiled and nodded. Rachel frowned and fired a volley of Seaple gargle-talk at him, to which he gargled back with enthusiasm. Mammed had no idea what they were saying, but he had a feeling Alexee was putting in a good word for him.

"What my husband is saying," said Rachel. "He sees benefits from having Landsman living here on Sanctuary Island. And I agree. My fear is you will be sad here when your friends have gone. It may be a long time before a ship comes again. How will you feel, Maamed if no ship comes for one year, two years… ten years?"

Mammed was shocked by the question. He thought of the reports written by Giulia Magrini, of the colonists longing for contact with their family and friends and their sadness when they realised they would never see them again. He felt tears begin to spring at the corners of his eyes.

"They *will* come back," he said, defiantly. "I *know* they will. Now they know it's safe to come here, and there is a gap in the reef, and there are friendly people and friendly dolphins… they will come back." He remembered then that Yonaton had asked to meet Alexee and Rachel.

"Besides, my father has asked to speak to you both this afternoon, before sunset, to talk about Miriam coming on the Pelican to visit Dominion and Couba – I mean Hispaniola and Cuba. So you can ask him then. If you trust him to look after Miriam and bring her back here safely, then you must believe he will keep returning to trade with you, like he said he would."

Rachel smiled gently and squeezed Mammed's arm. "You are good boy, Maa-med, with a good heart. You cried for our little girl Lily. We will talk with your father and see what he says. Let us go now and ask him, all of us together."

Chapter 14

A Short Demonstration

Moon 3660

As they watched Paul take his first tentative steps into the world of Tae Kwon Do, Ktrina thought about the impact of the history lesson on ten-year-old Grig. She understood why learning about The Drone War had affected him deeply. She remembered her own feelings of shock and distress when the topic had been taught in detail during her school years. The notion that something created to provide safety and security could instead cause such uncontrolled havoc was intensely disturbing.

The loss of so many people and so much vital infrastructure had left a deep psychological scar on lunar society which resonated down through the centuries. The deep mistrust of technology which followed had severely limited progress, especially in the field of space exploration. Anything that put humans at risk or machines in control was considered a red line that should not be crossed. Yet recent developments in the north hinted that some of those long-held beliefs in the sanctity of human life were beginning to unravel. Ktrina had an uncomfortable premonition that many of the mistakes of human history might be repeated unless they remained vigilant.

Her one ray of hope was the discovery of humans living on Earth. Might the two estranged communities of the Moon be reunited in a common goal – to reconnect with this lost tribe of mankind? And if so, how would they go about it? It seemed as if the Coops now had the means to reach Earth's surface, but would they allow the Soks to participate in making contact with the Earthies? Another topic to discuss with Daniel tomorrow, if the opportunity arose.

"Excuse me, Ktrina." The Grand Master stood before her and bowed when she looked up. "I wanted to thank you for bringing your son Paul for his first lesson this morning. He appears to be doing very well so far."

"Thank you, Saseong." She stood and bowed reverentially.

"I hope these two young men," he nodded at Grig and Jan, "will be able to join Paul here in a year or two."

"I'm sure they will... when they are twelve."

"May I ask you a favour, Ktrina?" He offered a small smile.

"Please."

"We are coming to the end of this morning's training session for our youngest members. Would you consider joining me for a short demonstration in about ten minutes' time? If you are fit enough now, of course...?"

"Yes, okay. I'll go and get changed."

Ktrina was pleased she'd had a thorough workout during the week to check her ribs and knee were up to the task. There had been a little soreness from her knee tendons, but nothing serious. Facing the Grand Master now in the hall's central combat area she had a brief moment of self-doubt – was she worthy of her new Chil Dan Black Belt ranking? Had she lost her edge after the hopper crash? As she sprang into her fighting stance she realised she'd soon find out.

The Saseong lunged and Ktrina ducked to avoid his fist then sprang into the air. Her whirling spin brought her foot within an inch of his chin but he flipped backwards to avoid her follow-up kick. Twisting in midair she dodged his next attack, dropped to her hands and spun into a floating whirl that connected her left foot with his thigh.

His smile told her she'd caught him out, but his eyes had hardened and she knew she'd get no more free shots today. He jumped, feinted with his left foot then his right whizzed past her nose as she pulled her head back just in time. She bounced and sprang, he twirled and kicked, the air became a blur of white-suited limbs. Ktrina took a grazing blow to her shoulder and honours were even. For the next few minutes their moves displayed everything in the text book plus several inventions. Both were panting hard when the Grand Master landed on his feet and shouted "Keoman!" to end the bout.

Ktrina and the Saseong bowed to each other and the hall erupted in applause. She smiled. It had been a great display for the teenagers and a fast and frenetic session that had renewed her faith in herself. She stole a glance at her three sons who were agog at their mother's fiery, athletic performance and the multiple times she had landed winning blows.

The Grand Master stepped forward and shook her hand with a grin. "Thank you, Ktrina. We showed them a thing or two today." His smile turned to concern. "I hope you haven't strained those injuries?"

"I feel okay." She said. "I'll find out tomorrow if I overdid it."

"Me too," he confided. "Now, please, shower and change while I offer your three boys some refreshments. If they turn out to be anything like their mother, Sokwest Tae Kwon Do has a very promising future."

Earth 1504

"Hello Alexee, hello Rachel." Captain Yonaton strode down the beach and into the lagoon to greet Miriam's parents who had just been delivered by Dolpheen. Mammed and Miriam were close behind, clinging to the back of Peetee. "Thanks for coming. I thought we should have a chat about Miriam joining us on the Pelican."

The proposed trip to the four main towns, Loming, Dominges, Alberton and Portkaron, was discussed in detail, with Yonaton confirming that they should be back in about a week. They talked about Miriam's needs, the pool on deck and swimming with Peetee in the sea. He had a spare cotton shirt she could wear, he said, to protect her from the stares of Landsmen who were not used to seeing women naked. Alexee agreed they could take the ancient chart, provided they took great care and returned the piece of precious plass undamaged.

"We have a question for you, Capteen," said Rachel. "As well as a voyage on the Pelican, Miriam and Mammed have another plan they want to talk to you about. They have already asked us."

"Oh, yes? What are they up to this time?" He smiled and scratched his beard as he eyed the two teenagers.

"They want to get married."

"What!" His jaw dropped in surprise. He looked at Rachel to see she was not joking.

"We will approve of this marriage, but only if you will make a promise to us."

"A promise… what promise?"

"That you will come back to Sanctuary Island at least twice every year. And bring your family to see him too. He will be Landsman all alone here with only Seaple and Dolpheen—"

"Whoa, whoa, whoa. I'm sorry Rachel, this is too fast. They've only known each other ten days… and Mammed is only sixteen years old!"

"I'm seventeen next month, Papa Yon."

"At what age can Landsmen marry, Capteen?" asked Rachel.

"Well, from sixteen, but—"

"And Miriam is seventeen already," she said, "so there is no problem from age."

"Well, no… but—"

"How long does it take to fall in love, Capteen?"

Yonaton scratched at his beard and turned to see the carpenters, crew, Desmun, Benyamin and his two older sons all motionless, all watching him.

"Look – this is all a bit sudden. I need time to think about it. Can't we discuss this when we come back from the voyage on the Pelican? Mammed and Miriam will have another week to get to—"

"No, Capteen. If you cannot agree that they will marry when they return, then we cannot agree to Miriam going with you."

He looked at Mammed who was standing tall in the chest-deep water, his arm around Miriam's shoulder. "I promised your mother, Ma Fatima, that I would always do what was best for you Mammed…"

"This *is* best for me, Papa Yon." Mammed spoke quietly but clearly. "I'd like my mother to meet Miriam when we sail to Portkaron. But if Miriam can't go… then I won't go either."

Moon 3660

"Wow! He's gi-normous!" Eight-year-old Jan tilted his head back to take in the great splotchy face towering above him. The giraffe looked down its long snout at him with equal curiosity, then bent its great brown-patched neck to bring rubbery lips close to the lad's face.

"Aww, look. He wants a kiss, Jan," taunted his eldest brother. "Go on, give him a kiss!"

Jan squealed and scampered away from the fence with his hands over his ears. His aunt Jean, walking with Grandma Sofi a few steps behind the boys, called out, "Don't be frightened, Jan. This is Cedric, one of the zoo's friendliest creatures. He won't hurt you."

She reached up and stroked the lanky beast's nose. Sofi carried on walking, muttering about catching germs from animals, and urged the boys on towards the rhinoceros enclosure. Ktrina, a few steps behind and deep in conversation with Daniel, stopped and turned to stay out of earshot.

"So, tell me Dan… how did the FLOC *inside* LTA14 see the Rangers coming, if the three out on the surface – and much nearer – didn't?"

"It's a weird one. Had to be something outside the visible spectrum. The cloaking gives a neutral infrared profile, so thermal imaging wouldn't have picked 'em up either. There was strict radio silence, so my guess is – electro-magnetic emissions from suit systems."

Ktrina was surprised. "Is that a normal detection frequency?"

"No. They're so weak you'd have a job to spot anything over a hundred metres. And even then you'd need a highly-tuned antenna, focussed in exactly the right direction. You'd have to know where to look."

"So… you're saying they knew we were coming?"

228

"And had enough notice – a day or two at least. They had to get their equipment in the right place at the right time."

"Damn! And they picked off the Coops' Commandos before they got inside too. How the hell could they have known."

"Somebody told 'em. Simple as that." Daniel gave a resigned shrug.

"Dan... I have reason to believe there's something very important and very secret inside LTA14. Any idea what sort of tech or weaponry they might be hiding in there?"

"Who knows? It's hard to figure how the FLOC can put up a rail-launched laser weapon. They could be cooking up something really sinister... but we have no way of knowing."

"Come on you two!" Jean was calling them from beyond the rhino pen. Ktrina and Daniel started ambling forwards again.

"Tell me about the connection between plankton and solar collectors." Ktrina changed topic.

"Oh, that's a strange one too." Daniel gave a humourless laugh. "Both can speed up the production of niobium-cryptides."

"Remind me what they're needed for."

"Filmsynths – used in a whole range of emerging technologies, not least our cloaking system. We can't make 'em without these really rare elements and they're very difficult to produce in the quantities we need."

"And the solar collector discs...?"

"They focus the sun's energy – they're photonic funnels really – and provide the ideal conditions for synthesising the nio-crypts. It seems the FLOC don't want us to have 'em."

"Nor the Coops... they lost their solar collector too."

"It's back up now though. Don't know how they did that." Daniel shook his head.

"What do you mean... back up?"

"The Coops' solar collector tower and disc – it was back up and operational early last week."

"You're kidding! I thought ours was going to take three months or more...?"

"That's right. Seems like the Coops had another one all ready to go up – took 'em only a few days."

Ktrina stared at him with an open mouth for a few seconds. "And if they decide to ignore our warnings and send their new spaceship to Earth... they'll have the plankton too?"

"Oh! didn't they tell you, Ktrina...?"

"Tell me what?"

"The Coops' fancy new spacecraft – it launched yesterday morning. And it left lunar orbit on a trajectory for Earth about twenty-four hours ago."

Earth 1504

Captain Yonaton felt old and weary. Mammed, Miriam and her parents were waiting to hear his verdict. The Landsmen were all at the water's edge, straining to hear what he'd say. He wished he had Esther here to help him decide. She always knew what to do for the best. But sixteen years without her had turned him into a crusty old seadog, uncertain how to judge matters of the heart.

He wondered what Lucy would say. She would be the one to deal with a situation like this. He pictured her at home in Loming, standing in their kitchen with arms folded and certainty written across her face. "They are in love," she'd say. "They want to marry and live together. How can saying 'no' make their lives any better?"

Yonaton straightened up and coughed. "I've been too busy with the ship to notice what was happening with these two young people. But I'm happy to learn they have been working on their own plans for the future. When we return from the voyage on the Pelican, we will bring with us Lucy, Sam and their children, plus Mammed's mother, Ma Fatima, and her children too... And we will have the best wedding that Sanctuary Island has seen in years!"

A huge cheer erupted from the shoreline behind him, Alexee and Rachel smiled at each other and Mammed and Miriam hugged and danced in the water. Out in the lagoon, Peetee leapt from the water and landed with an enormous splash.

The Captain turned and laughed at the beaming smiles of the men on the beach. "Haven't you lot got a ship to build? We won't be going anywhere unless you get those planks fitted."

He waded out and hugged Mammed and Miriam before turning and receiving a similar embrace from Rachel and Alexee.

"Thank you, Capteen." She smiled at him. "Now... we have something else to talk to you about."

"Something else!" He laughed. "I'm not sure I can cope with anything else!"

"Yes, it is something for just you, Alexee and me." She reached and took his hand in hers. "So we take you away from others for private talk... please?"

He frowned in puzzlement. This was turning into a day of surprises. "Okay," he said as Alexee took his other hand and the couple towed him gently into deeper water.

High on a hillside south of Loming, at the western end of Dominion, Sam and his son Peter were busy erasing last week's failed attempt at a stick man. As the long dry grass crackled and flared and the flames spread steadily across the land, Sam felt sorry he had been unable to carry out his father-in-law's wishes. He should have known it was too windy that day to create a realistic figure on the rolling acres that stretched into the distance.

With gale force winds and a full storm on the way, he and Peter had lost control time and again and ended up running and beating the flames until their arms and backs could beat no more. Their stick man had become a giant black smudge and several who had climbed the hill to view it had laughed at their artless efforts. They would have laughed even harder had they known Yonaton's motive for requesting the figure. Sam himself wondered if the venerable Captain was losing his marbles in his old age. The very idea that there might be someone on the Moon to see it was utterly ludicrous.

Anyway, they had done their best and now, with the other shepherds eager to get the burning done so that new grass might sprout in good time for winter grazing, it was time to wipe the land clean. Further south he could see the other stockmen lighting up the hillside with their fire sticks. By nightfall the dry grass – and the embarrassing stick man – would be gone.

Moon 3660

Nate Adebayo tapped his plass on the table to get their attention. Six pairs of eyes turned towards him as conversation stopped. "Okay, ladies and gentlemen." His deep voice echoed off the wood panelled walls of the MoD meeting room. "We all know why we are here. The Coopans have launched a human mission to the Earth. What do we know and what do we do about it?"

Pippa Khan, the Head of Defence Analysis, spoke first. "Minister… our tracking systems predict the craft will be approaching Earth orbit by the end of today. We are not really geared up for tracking craft in Earth orbit – been no need until now – but we think they could attempt a landing early tomorrow."

"Do we know who is on board?"

"Only guesswork, I'm afraid. Our agents have been unable to access the Monterey Skyport since Friday morning. We don't know the number on board, but the most likely pilot is their High Priest, Daval Nakash."

"Nakash!" Ktrina was stunned. "How is that even... possible?"

"He was a Commando with specialist pilot skills before taking up his religious calling fifteen years ago. Our intel suggests he has kept up his flight hours and has a keen interest in all Coopan military matters."

"Oh, wow! I never knew..." She shook her head slowly in wonder. "I mean, I know he oversees all their military decisions and influences their government policy, but I didn't know he was a pilot."

"I saw him frequently when I was working on their guidance system," said Klif Watanabe. "He asked very pertinent and searching questions and seemed knowledgeable about the entire project. I must say though, I never felt comfortable in his presence."

"I received a message from my opposite number, Gunta Krems, this morning." Foreign Minister Jorg Lanimovskiy unfolded a sheet of paper. "It is in response to the letter I sent to him via Ambassador Rozek on Thursday. I have made a hard copy for the sake of security."

"Please, read it, Jorg," said Adebayo.

Lanimovskiy coughed and began. "The Government of Cooper takes great exception to any suggestion that we may be inclined to break the Ark Martyrs Treaty. I can assure you that no attempt shall be made by this state to put any Coopan citizen on the Earth's surface."

"Is that *it?*" Adebayo's eyebrows had moved half way up his forehead.

"Yes."

"So... can they acquire this plankton without breaking the Treaty?"

"If I can say something here, Minister...?" Klif Watanabe leaned forward.

"Go ahead, please."

"They could land this rocket ship, take on seawater, and take off again without the pilot needing to leave the cockpit. They could argue that – technically – they have not put a human on the surface..."

"Preposterous!" fumed Lanimovskiy.

"In fact," said Pippa Khan, "it would be extremely difficult for anyone from the Moon to walk on the Earth's surface, as the gravity there is six times what we have here. Unless he's had months of training in a centrifuge, any attempt could prove fatal."

Daniel, as Head of Defence Development, spoke up next. "My department thinks the Coops can undertake their mission with the pilot overseeing operations from a prone position at the top of the spacecraft. With the plankton, and with their solar collector back in operation already, they could exceed our production of filmsynths by a factor of ten or more… in a matter of weeks."

"So," Adebayo turned to the Chief of Defence, "what are we to do about it, Huw?"

"I'm not sure there's much we *can* do about it, Minister." Huw Thomas spread his hands in resignation. "We can't shoot their spacecraft down. That would be an act of war and wholly unjustified. If they land their craft successfully on Earth but don't set foot on the surface, it seems we can't claim they've breached the Treaty because of the way it is worded. So, there are few sanctions that would be appropriate. We have to accept they've beaten us to it as far as this plankton is concerned—"

"But now we know there are humans living on Earth," Ktrina butted in, "isn't there a risk the Coops will try to make contact with them… with all sorts of implications for their health, and ours?"

"They must have planned this mission months or years ago," said Adebayo, "long before they knew there were humans on the planet. Is there any reason to suppose they would try to make contact with them? Surely they would avoid any populated areas to reduce risks to the mission…?"

"They would if they thought like us, Minister, but it's anyone's guess what they might do," she said. "I believe our next step should be to negotiate with them for a supply of plankton. And try to set up a bi-lateral agreement over how we respond to the presence of people on Earth. It is vitally important for everyone living on the Moon – as well as those living on Earth – that we go about this the right way. After fifteen hundred years there is no telling what we might find when we make contact with them."

Earth 1504

Yonaton was pleased with their progress. The Pelican's repairs had been completed, the planks sealed, and the ship relaunched that morning without fuss or drama. While they were waiting for the new planks to swell and the leaks to stop, the crew had reloaded the ballast. Alexee had given permission to help themselves to rocks from the nearby stream to replace those lost on the reef.

Now, late Sunday afternoon, the ship sat serenely at anchor in the lagoon as they ferried sails and spars and deck equipment aboard and set about rigging her for passage across the Crabbing Sea. The

Pelican was looking more like her old self after the indignities of the sinking and the abuses of the Cardinal and his men that preceded it.

Yonaton had reclaimed his cabin, freshened it with a coat of whitewash and burned the Cardinal's bedding and clothes. Benyamin had dried his precious charts and the crew had hung their hammocks back in the lower deck. Tomorrow they would build Miriam's pool from planks and canvas and rig a sunshade over it to keep her comfortable. After another day of preparation they should be ready for their voyage back to Loming. He planned to set sail at dusk on Monday for a gentle overnight passage when the winds were lightest and arrive in their home port Tuesday morning.

He ought to be feeling content with the way things were going, but Yonaton had a dilemma. He wanted to help the Seaple and understood why Alexee and Rachel had spoken to him in private about their unusual request. Now he had to decide how to broach the subject with his fellow Landsmen. Should he have a quiet word with the ones it concerned, or discuss it openly with all of them around their camp fire that night? With the sun slipping towards the horizon and Conor producing enticing smells of roasting fish and vegetables as he prepared their supper, he would have to make his mind up soon.

In Loming, Lucy was also reflecting on a successful day. After a week in which the town's schools had offered free education, instead of the pay-by-the-day church schooling run by the Cardinal and his lackeys, she had opened the church for worshippers that morning. With the Cardinal gone and his remaining Convertors now employed as unarmed peace keepers, she'd had no idea how people felt about religion. To find out, she'd spread the word that Sunday morning would be an opportunity for reflection and discussion for those who wished to attend.

To her surprise, the church had been crammed with folk eager to share their thoughts and she had encouraged them to speak out about their experiences and beliefs. That way they could decide on the future for faith and worship in the town. Her own belief – that there was a god but he had been ill-served by the various religions that had sprouted and withered over the years – she kept to herself. If the people felt the need for a time and place for collective worship, she was happy to go along with it.

By late morning the congregation had agreed that the church was best used as a school house during the week, and as a place of meditation on Sundays. There was no enthusiasm for continuing the Cardinal's misguided and often brutal teachings now they had been shown to be a web of lies. But there was agreement that collective support for the town's needy could be overseen by a faith group and they'd voted for the title – Church of Human Kindness.

They had also agreed that the church's wealth should be used to pay school teachers and peace keepers. Lucy had discovered a hoard of coins and jewellery hidden beneath the floorboards in the Cardinal's former bedroom. It had accumulated from all the school fees and other insidious taxes he had instituted over the years. She told the townsfolk it was their money, so they should decide how it was spent.

She'd also discovered a metal box that was impossible to open and unlike anything she'd seen before. It had a row of four small metal wheels next to its lid, with numbers that changed when the wheels were turned. It felt as though it contained a single large item and she was intrigued. Rather than damaging the box by forcing it open she decided to wait until her father returned in case he had an idea how to gain entry to it.

If all had gone according to plan with the ship's repairs, she would see the Pelican and the Petrel sailing back into Loming harbour in the next few days. She would be reunited with her brothers and her father, and the crew and the shipwrights would be returned to their families. Finally, the era of the Cardinal would be laid to rest, and peace and normality could return to the world. There would be an election for a new mayor. If chosen, she had many ideas to help build a fairer, happier society. Lucy couldn't wait to get started.

Earth 1504

The sun had set, their supper had been eaten and the stars had come out. It was their last evening on Sanctuary Island and Captain Yonaton had reached a decision. He would discuss the delicate issue raised by Alexee and Rachel with all the men as they sat around the bonfire. But first he would lay out their plans for tomorrow.

"Right everyone. I want to thank you all for your hard work this past week. We still have some important jobs to do in the morning, but all being well, the Pelican and the Petrel will have passed through the gap in the reef before sunset tomorrow. We will be heading towards Loming overnight when the winds are lightest and the motion on the ship's deck will be least. We will have a very precious cargo – Mammed's future bride, Miriam – aboard so we need to make a slow and gentle passage to keep her and the seawater safely in her pool."

"Papa Yon," said Mammed, "the Seaple come out of the water to sleep on the beach at night. I think we will need to drain the pool and find her something soft to lie on."

"Okay, I'm sure we can do that. We will also have Peetee keeping us company, but I'm sure he can take care of himself. Jack and Ifan will have some fish to keep him fed on his long swim across."

Yonaton took a deep breath and continued. "Before we leave we have an opportunity to help the Seaple with something important. Rachel and Alexee have talked to me about a particular problem they have here. Because they are an isolated community, limited in numbers by the food in the lagoon, their population has a small reproductive stock. This is bad for their long-term health.

"Since the Landsmen left Sanctuary Island many centuries ago, there have been regular visits to bring trade, exchange news and introduce fresh blood to the Seaple population. As you have heard, before we arrived here there had been only one visit in over a hundred years, and that was Fisherman Frank and fat Henry who became the Cardinal. One was too old and the other disinclined to add his seed to the Seaple's population—"

"Are you sayin', Cap'n," said Conor, "they wants us to breed wiv 'em?"

"In a word... yes!"

"Well, I'll be *jiggered!*" The old salt guffawed and slapped his knee with his good hand. "Pity I ain't twenty year younger..."

When the ensuing hubbub died down, Jack spoke up. "Won't Mammed be adding fresh blood to the Seaple when he marries Miriam?" Mammed felt his face burn but said nothing.

"Indeed he will, and I'm sure we all wish them a large and happy family in the future. But in the meantime, Alexee and Rachel have asked if any of the younger men among us would consider—"

"Yes! I would!" said Faruk, his broad grin reflecting the glow of the bonfire.

"Me too!" said Tom. "I knew chatting 'em up would pay off. They can't resist me!"

"On the contrary, Tom." Yonaton shook his head. "The Seaple women who have consented to this all have husbands. This is the last thing *they* want to do, but they've agreed for the good of their community. Any disrespect and you will not be included."

"How many of us do they need?" asked Ifan.

"Five, ideally."

"Well you can count me out," said Jack. "My fiancée, Lyn, would *not* approve."

"Who else would rather *not* be included?" Yonaton asked, raising his hand. All but Ifan, the two carpenters and the two youngest crew members raised their hands. The remaining five looked at each other then back at Yonaton.

"Very well. You five will present yourselves to Rachel at the west stream early tomorrow afternoon. As the Seaple's doctor she will check your general and personal health and make introductions. By mid afternoon we will all be back here to finalise loading and embark. I want to get the Pelican through the reef while there is still enough daylight to see clearly. Then we should be on our way as darkness falls. Any questions?"

Moon 3660

Ktrina had reached a decision. Sitting on her bed, staring again at the egg the Stairway Man had given her, her plans were becoming clear. After all the frustrations of the day – the Coops' Earth mission, the Earthies themselves – about which she could do nothing, she'd decided there was one thing she *could* do. She was going to try to find out what was going on inside Lava Tube Aristarchus 14.

It seemed clear to her now that something very important was happening at LTA14. Something that had cost the lives of her beloved Ethan, the Stairway Man's brother (if her guess was right), plus four more Rangers and three Commandos. Ktrina felt she owed it to all of them to find out why they'd died and achieve some closure. Was there some fearsome new technology being developed there? She'd been handed a unique opportunity to take a peek inside. Stairway Man had entrusted the egg to her, so he obviously believed she could, and probably would, attempt to find answers to some perplexing questions. She had no idea if it would work, but the least she could do was give it a try.

She'd had a long chat with Daniel in the Sokolova Military Establishment's canteen again. After the morning meeting with Adebayo had concluded that there was nothing much they could do, other than take up her suggestion to negotiate with the Coops, she had pumped her brother-in-law for information. Knowing what he knew now, how would he approach LTA14 in order to see inside?

Daniel's first response was that nothing would persuade him to go near the place. But if he was advising on a mission to gather intel, he wouldn't put men at risk again, and he wouldn't rely on their cloaking technology, even though it had performed better than expected.

"What do you think they might be hiding in there, Daniel?" she'd asked him. "What could be so important they'd sacrifice three of their own to prevent the Rangers and Commandos getting in?"

"I really have no idea, Ktrina... but I'm a little concerned about your level of interest. Please tell me you're not planning on doing something stupid?"

"Oh... no plans. Just a professional interest." She'd flashed him a cheesy grin, which hadn't fooled him for a moment.

"Just remember you have three lovely boys who need their mum." He'd stared at her long and hard. The fear that had gripped her stomach then, came back to haunt her now as she sat on her bed cradling the egg. The plans she'd denied having earlier were now taking solid shape in her mind. Her Ambassadorial duties over the coming week should provide the perfect cover.

Earth 1504

Miriam, dressed in a large creamy shirt, knelt in the water of her deck pool, arms resting on the Pelican's port rail, gazing out at the amazing sight. Her home, Sanctuary Island, was slipping away behind them as dusk fell and the first stars appeared winking in the darkening sky. The view from the ship's deck was unlike anything she had imagined, having never been beyond the reef before.

"It is *fantastic*, Maa-med," she whispered to the gangly youth who stood beside the pool, with his arm draped around her shoulders. He was soaked from the water which slopped occasionally over the pool's side as the ship rose and fell in the waves, but appeared not to notice.

"Don't be sad, Miriam. We will be back in a week's time... and then we'll be married."

"It feels very strange to leave my family, and leave my island behind," she said. "But I'm not sad. I always wanted to see the world. I am first of my people to have this chance... first time in one thousand, five hundred and four *years*, Maa-med! Isn't that incredible?"

"You wait until you see Loming. The harbour with the town rising behind it looks really good in the first light of the day. I've seen it lots of times when we've sailed home from voyages, and it's always a great sight. I can't wait for you to meet Lucy and Sam and their children."

"But what if they don't like me, Maa-med...?" She turned to him with wide eyes, her freckles turned to sooty spots by the twilight. "They might think I'm a freak and say you mustn't marry me."

"No. They'll love you, Miriam. I'm sure of it. And anyway, it won't make any difference – I'm marrying you in a week's time, no matter what anybody else says or does." He leaned in and gave her cool lips a kiss. "Are you cold?"

"No, I'm used to it... but it is odd wearing this shirt. Wet material feels funny against my skin. I will have to take it off for sleeping, Maa-med."

"Okay. It will be dark soon. And we can drain the water from the pool. Papa Yon's found you some sacking and a sheet to lie on. It should make a comfy bed, I think. As soft as sleeping on the sand, anyway."

"Will you sleep with me, Maa-med?"

"Umm..." His mind raced at the idea.

"Seaple families always sleep close together, to keep warm and safe in night time. I don't think I can sleep on my own..." Her eyes were pleading.

"Sure. Umm. I will go ask Papa Yon." He gave her another kiss, then ran up the steps leading to the steering deck.

Yonaton was happy to be at sea once again. The Pelican felt like her old self, shouldering her way through the swells and heeling gently to the soft evening breeze. The back-breaking work and nail-biting anxieties were finally over and he could return to the life he loved, as captain of a trading ship, plying the Crabbing Sea. He may have to get used to calling it the Caribbean Sea in future, but he'd have to persuade the rest of the world to do the same first.

The thought made him chuckle as he turned the great wooden wheel to stay on course. Would it be easier to convince them they were descended from colonists who came from the Moon? Would any of them believe people once travelled in a spaceship called the Ark and crash landed in the lagoon of Sanctuary Island. The island's name was an easier fix – the place would be taboo no more. And when they saw the sweet young mermaid who was travelling in a pool on his ship's deck, how could they refuse?

It had been a busy morning, with everyone rushing to complete their duties in time for the afternoon visit to the west river. Although only five of the dozen men were going to meet the Seaple women, the others were using their imaginations and cheering their colleagues on. Jack and Ifan had made one last fishing trip and returned with ample food to keep them supplied for the voyage to Loming, plus plenty extra as a parting gift to the Seaple.

Tom and Faruk had gone with the crew and Mammed to view the memorial stone in Christown. Several also took the plunge and viewed the remains of the Ark in the sea cave. He was pleased that nearly all of them had their own eye-witness account to take back home with them. It would make his job easier when it came to telling the Moon-origins story.

The log-canoe catamaran had been repaired and fitted with a new sail and mast. It was being left at the island for Mammed to use and would be a help to the Seaple for moving everything from fish and fruit to kelp and corals. Mammed and Desmun had gathered all the fruit they could carry and given most of it to the Seaple. Then they'd filled the water barrels for the crew to winch aboard the ship.

Yonaton had been relieved when the five returned from the west river mid afternoon – all strangely subdued after their unusual duty – and he could make the final preparations for the voyage. The rowing boat had been stowed at the ship's stern, Miriam had donned the shirt he'd given her and had been lifted aboard using the bosun's chair. He smiled at the memory of her squeals of excitement as the seat-on-a-rope hoisted her out of the lagoon and high into the air before lowering her into the pool on the Pelican's deck.

Alexee and Rachel were understandably anxious, and had bid their daughter a tearful farewell, surrounded by most of the Seaple population and over a dozen of the Dolpheen. Peetee was being entrusted to keep her safe, as well as the Captain. Now he was keeping pace effortlessly in between the Pelican and the Petrel. Yonaton hoped the large grey dolphin was enjoying his open sea passage as much as himself as the last of the daylight faded away.

"Papa Yon!" Mammed bounded up the steps. "Miriam is ready to go to sleep now. I can drain the pool and give her the bedding, but she's used to sleeping with her family around her. It's how they keep warm… and I think she's nervous. She's asking if I can sleep with her…?"

Moon 3660

"Thank you, Pheebs." Ktrina looked up as her secretary-receptionist placed a steaming mug of strong black coffee on her desk. The rich aroma made her inhale appreciatively. She'd opted for the extra caffeine this morning to help with the task ahead. It wasn't so much planning the trips to outlying communities, or even booking the latest Mercury hoppers to avoid another Zenit flight, that caused her concern. It was her scheme to end up close to Aristarchus on Monday morning that was making her palms sweat.

"Want me to help with anything?" asked Phoebe, tilting her head slightly in her affectionate manner. "I'm at a loose end right now."

"Yeah, that would be great, thanks. You can make these bookings with the Ministry of Transport if you like…" Ktrina handed over a list of dates and destinations with times the craft would be needed. "Only Mercurys from now on, though, Pheebs. I swear I'll never set foot in a Zenit again."

"I don't blame you, Ktrina! God… after what you've been through. Who'd want to fly in those clanking old death-traps anyway?" She looked at the list. "So… you're off to Hilbert tomorrow, then Ashbrook on Friday, and Frentzen on Monday. Fine. I'll go and get the bookings done now."

Ktrina went back to worrying over the details of her Monday mission. She was using her diplomatic service's top-level encryption for her screen searches, but still worried that someone might be able to see what she was up to. If they saw her measuring distances from the remote Frentzen outpost to the tiny crater south of LTA14 – well into Coopan territory – there would be questions asked, at the very least. If the FLOC were able to hack into the Sokolovan Foreign Ministry's network, then they'd be waiting for her with a primed laser weapon. The thought made her feel sick.

She quickly downloaded the coordinates to her comm and promptly deleted her search history in the hope that she might have evaded detection. It would be ironic if she was flagging up her plans to the rebels almost a week before she set off across the regolith. Crossing 105 kilometres of the barren Oceanus Procellarum on a sled without being spotted by orbiting satellites would need precise timing and a huge slice of luck. But it was her only chance. She knew that any attempt to fly a hopper up there would mean instant exposure and she'd probably be shot down as she crossed the equator.

Ktrina next called up the Ministry's secret access portal to view the satellite schedules. As speedily as possible she downloaded Monday's data before deleting her search history once more. Had anyone spotted her intrusion into the system? Or had she been lucky? She wondered if she'd get a call from Jorg Lanimovskiy asking devious questions to try to smoke out her plans.

Not for the first time that morning she clasped her hands together in silent prayer… but mostly to stop them from shaking. She sat back in her chair and closed her eyes. *Dear God – if you exist – please let me come home to see my boys again.*

Chapter 15
Fireball From The Sky
Earth 1504

The Pelican sat quietly at anchor a short distance outside the sea wall of Loming harbour as the eastern sky turned pink and the sun peeped over the horizon. Mammed and Desmun were busy hauling up buckets of seawater to refill Miriam's pool, enjoying her squeals and giggles every time they tipped one in. Yonaton, who'd just emerged from his cabin rubbing sleep from his eyes, blinked at the scene and smiled at the happy sounds.

"Papa Yon!" Mammed had spotted him. "Miriam is ready to go for a swim in the sea. Can we lower her down in the bosun's chair?"

Yonaton looked over the ship's side and saw Peetee waiting below, nodding his great grey head. The dolphin sent a burst of buzzing trills in greeting and the Captain waved. "Good morning, Peetee!"

He approached the three teenagers at the pool. "Morning you three. I hope you slept well, Miriam?"

"Yes, thank you, Capteen. Maa-med kept me warm." She smiled happily.

He turned to Mammed, who blushed and looked away. "Good. I'm pleased to hear it. And now you're ready for a swim?"

"Yes please."

He looked across to the harbour wall, where a small crowd had already gathered, despite the early hour. Jack and Ifan, with the two carpenters on board, had entered the harbour in the Petrel as soon as they arrived. Word had quickly spread that the Pelican was offshore, with a mermaid and a dolphin soon to be seen swimming together. More people were arriving by the minute.

"Okay. Desmun, you can give me a hand with the halyard. Mammed you help Miriam get into the chair safely."

Within a few moments her shirt-clad form was rising from the deck, twirling slowly as she was lowered down to the sea below. A murmur rose from the waiting crowd as the slender young woman let go of the ropes, slipped from the seat and disappeared under the water. The dolphin dived too and when neither reappeared the murmur became a clamour of worried voices.

Finally, the great grey dolphin broke the surface and, to the amazement of the crowd, the girl was now sitting astride its back. The pair swam slowly between the harbour wall and the ship, with Miriam waving and smiling gleefully at the townsfolk who stared back open mouthed.

"Look Mummy! The mermaid is waving at us," shouted one young voice. Soon all the people were cheering and waving back at her.

Dolphin and mermaid disappeared beneath the waves once again and seemed to be gone for an age. Then the dolphin's head surfaced and, with a wide toothy grin, it looked first right and then to the left, as if searching for her. It shook its head and dived again. A gasp arose from the crowd.

"Mummy! Has she drown-ded!?" asked the same young voice. The murmur had become a babble of concern when the dolphin burst from the sea with the mermaid clinging to his fins. She was launched into the air and just had time to wave and smile to the crowd before falling back into the water. A great cheer of relief and joy swept the crowd. Aboard the Pelican, Yonaton and his crew were roaring with laughter at the great show the pair were putting on.

"Did you know she was going to do this, Mammed?"

The youth shook his head in wonder. "I knew she was planning something, Papa Yon. But this is amazing!"

The show continued until the pair had exhausted their repertoire of tricks. The harbour wall erupted with cheers and applause as they swam past one last time, with Miriam sitting sideways on the dolphin's back, waving to the crowd, and Peetee nodding his head and chirruping with delight.

The crew of the Pelican lined the ship's rail, clapping and cheering as Peetee delivered Miriam back to the bosun's chair and she slipped her legs through to perch on the seat.

"Well done, Miriam!" shouted Yonaton. "Are you ready to come back aboard now?"

"Yes please, Capteen!"

"Well, you certainly gave them something to talk about, young lady," said Yonaton when she was back in her pool on the deck. "Who'd have guessed you had such a show to perform – the people of Loming loved it!"

"I didn't know you and Peetee could do all those things." Mammed was grinning at her. "How did you learn them?"

"The Dolpheen love to play. These are games they teach us when we're children!" She was breathless but exhilarated after the show. "And your people... they are all so nice, waving and cheering to us. It is like they are friends already!"

"I think you've made a very good impression, Miriam," said Yonaton. "Now, before the wind rises, we'll get the anchor up and move the Pelican into the harbour. Then we'll be able to talk to the good folk of Loming face to fa—"

Yonaton was stunned into silence by a terrific bang from the sky above which made them all look up… to see a fireball descending from the heavens. Miriam screamed and put her hands over her ears, crouching low in the water of her tiny pool for protection. The men all stared at the apparition falling from the sky – a fierce blazing light with a long dark tube above it, dropping like a stone onto the town of Loming.

"Quick!" shouted Yonaton. "Get the anchor up. We need to get away." The crew ran to the capstan.

On the quayside, the few remaining people were running towards the shelter of the town. As the fiery demon fell towards Earth, it appeared to be heading for the inner end of the harbour wall, trapping three of the slower townsfolk at the seaward end. They turned and ran towards the stone tower which stood at its tip, hoping it might protect them from the horror plummeting from above.

Mammed was transfixed, his hand on Miriam's shoulder, as the others trotted around the capstan, hoisting the anchor in a panicky haste. When the reverberating boom had died away a rushing, roaring sound replaced it, increasing as the thing fell to Earth in a ball of flames. Just when it seemed inevitable that the fireball would crash disastrously, it slowed and fell the last part of its descent ever more gently, coming to rest on four spidery legs.

A wave of heat and dust hit them as the anchor came free from the sea bed and Yonaton turned the ship away from shore. Everyone hid their eyes and faces from the blinding dust that washed over the deck in a squall of hot wind. When they turned back to look the fire had gone and a huge black tube – taller even than the harbour tower – now stood on the broad inner end of the harbour wall.

Most of the crew stood rooted, open-mouthed in shock and wonder. Desmun cowered behind the capstan, sobbing into his hands. Miriam surfaced from her small pool and grabbed Mammed's arm.

"Maa-med! What is it?" Her voice quavered.

"I don't know! Never seen anything like it!" he replied in an awed whisper, then realised that wasn't quite true. He'd seen something similar many times over the past two weeks. "No! Wait a minute…" He turned to her with wide eyes. "It looks like the Ark!"

"Oh! Oh, oh oh… yes, Maa-med!" she said. "It does! Is it a spaceship… come from Moon!?"

"Papa Yon!" He shouted at the Captain who stood grim-faced at the wheel. "We think it is like the Ark! A spaceship... from the Moon!"

Yonaton looked over his shoulder at the tall dark object standing menacingly on the harbour wall. The Pelican was gathering pace as its sails filled with the morning breeze. Whatever the flaming menace was, he needed to get his ship clear and his crew out of harm's way. The people of Loming would have to look after themselves. Then an awful thought struck him.

Maybe I'm responsible? I asked Sam to send a signal to the Moon. How can I have been so stupid! I have to go back. He swung the great wooden wheel and shouted down to the crew. "Get ready to turn!"

Moon 3660

Ktrina was slipping her arms into her jacket and preparing to leave the office when Phoebe appeared at her door. "Sorry, Ktrina. There's a last-minute call... do you want to take it? A Pippa Khan from Defence?"

"Oh, right. Yes, I'll take it, Phoebe. Put her through to my comm now, thanks." Ktrina sat down at her desk again as her office door closed.

"Hello? Ktrina? It's Pippa from Defence Analysis."

"Hi, Pippa. How can I help?"

"Sorry to bother you so late, but I thought you'd like to know before you leave for the day."

"Sure. What is it? We are on a secure encryption setting, so speak freely."

"The Coopan spacecraft, Ktrina. It's landed on the Earth."

"When... and where?"

"Well, we didn't actually witness the landing, as it occurred while the site was barely in view. But we think around 2.30 this afternoon, on the island of Hispaniola in the Caribbean—"

"Oh my God! That's where the Stick Man was, isn't it?"

"Yes, that's right. It would have been morning there, of course. We couldn't confirm it until the site came fully into view, but we've some clear images now from our main optical telescope on Malapert. It appears to have made a successful landing on the side of the harbour we saw last week—"

"What... right in the town?"

"Yes. In what used to be Port-de-Paix back in the days before Comet Santos. Of course, the coastline has changed a lot since then."

"But it's fully populated! They can't just land in a town!" Ktrina was struggling to think what the consequences might be. "It's probably killed and injured people and set their houses on fire…"

"Well, the pictures we're getting so far don't show any smoke rising, so perhaps they were lucky."

"Is it still there?"

"Yes. We estimate it might take six hours to refuel. A lot of sea water would have to be filtered and desalinated to fill the tanks with stuff it can use as fuel. Plus the plankton, of course."

"So… ample time to interact with the poor, terrified people. There's no telling how they'd react. It would serve the Coops right if they pushed it into the sea."

"Well… that's all we have at the moment, Ktrina. I thought you'd like to know, especially as you'd raised concerns at yesterday's meeting. The Defence Minister agreed I should call you."

"Thanks, Pippa. I'm really pleased you did. Goodness knows what harm they've caused. I can't believe they'd do that!"

"As you said, it's anyone's guess what the Coops will do next. I'll keep you informed, Ktrina. Are you in your office tomorrow?"

"Yes, but only first thing. I'm leaving for a visit to Hilbert mid-morning."

"Okay. If there are any developments, I'll be in touch. Bye."

"Bye, Pippa. And thanks again for the call."

Earth 1504

It was mid morning as the Pelican warily approached the harbour entrance. Yonaton could no longer see the three who had been stranded at the end of the outer wall, so someone must have rowed across to rescue them. Then he saw a small boat coming out to meet them. In it were Jack and Ifan. He brought the ship to a standstill with its sails aback, then ran down to the mid deck so they might confer.

"Is anybody hurt?" He cupped his hands to his mouth.

"No. It's a miracle, though…" Jack shouted back. "Any earlier and it would have landed on the crowd!"

"Is it safe to bring the Pelican in, d'you think?"

"I think so. There's been no movement or sound from it since it landed. Everyone is scared half to death, but apart from a few lobster pots set afire, there's been no harm done."

It was pure luck, Yonaton realised, that no boats had been damaged. Being the season of storms, none were moored against the outer wall. Any other time of year and many might have been destroyed.

"Lucy's waiting on the quay to speak to you," shouted Jack. "The whole town is here... looking for guidance."

"Okay. I'll bring the ship in. Get ready to take a line."

A space had been cleared for the Pelican to berth against the inner wall, well away from the towering craft on the other side of the harbour. Hands caught ropes and the ship was soon tied securely to the dock. Lucy stood cradling her youngest daughter, Emily, in her arms. The four-year-old's eyes were rimmed red from crying. Next to them was Sam holding the hands of their other two children, Agnes and Peter. All looked pale and fearful.

"What do you think it is?" asked Lucy, as her father stepped ashore. He wrapped his arms around her and hugged her and his granddaughter before answering.

"I don't know, Lucy. But after what we've seen and learned these past two weeks, I could make a guess..."

"Tell me," she demanded.

"I think it could be a spacecraft that has come from the Moon."

"What...! You mean, in response to that joke you made Sam burn on the hillside?" She was angry, there was no denying it.

"Look... it's a possibility, that's all." He spread his hands in a gesture of submission.

"If it *is*, then you need your head examined, father!" she scolded. "It's a miracle nobody was killed when that bloody *fireball from hell* fell on our town!" Emily started crying again at the angry exchange.

"Here..." Lucy passed the toddler to her husband. "Take them home please, Sam."

She turned back to her father with a determined look in her eye. "So... what do you suggest we do about it?"

"How would I know?" He was exasperated by her questions. She had always been feisty, just like her mother. "Watch... and wait, I suppose. What else *can* we do?"

"Look!" A shout came from the crowd. Everyone was staring, some pointing, at the dark, towering craft standing on the far side of the harbour. There was movement. A metal arm appeared to be extending from the lower part of the vessel, reaching out towards the sea beyond the wall. As they watched it dipped down towards the water.

"What do you think it's doing?" Lucy whispered, as if it might hear her.

"C'mon Ifan," said Jack. "Let's row round there and take a look." They headed for the boat they'd used earlier.

"Don't get too close!" she shouted after her brothers.

They had barely passed through the harbour entrance when another gasp went up from the crowd. Fingers pointed this time to a hole that had appeared in the side of the spacecraft, almost at the top.

"It's a doorway!" someone shouted. "Maybe a creature is coming out!"

There were screams and a few people started to back away. Lucy turned and addressed the crowd. "If you have children, take them home."

Then she beckoned a young man forward. Yonaton recognised him as one of the Cardinal's former Convertors. "Take the others and collect swords and pikes from the church," she said. "Then stand between the town and that... that vessel," she waved her hand at the spacecraft. "You're our first line of defence." He looked none too keen, but headed off to do her bidding.

"They're working as peace keepers for the town now," she told her father. "Today they can earn their pay."

"There's something coming down!" A shout came from the crowd. Everyone turned to look again and gasped anew. It wasn't a creature, or a man. But a ladder was descending from the open doorway high on the ship. Would someone emerge and descend it?

Moon 3660

With supper cleared away and Grandma Sofi retired to her room to watch her favourite drama serial, Ktrina was revelling in the company of her three boys. After the thoughts that had been going through her head, and the plans she'd been making that morning, she felt the need to give them extra hugs.

After a frantic game of holo table tennis had left them all breathless, she asked, "If you could meet with those Earthies we've just discovered, what would you want to say to them?"

"Come and live here with us! It's great!" said Jan.

"We could, but they're probably very happy where they are, Jan. They've got blue skies with clouds and gentle sunshine. And endless hills and mountains covered in grasses and trees where they can walk all day without having to wear a surface suit."

"I think *we* should ask *them* if we can go and live *there*," said Grig, ever the thoughtful one.

"I'd like to go and live on Earth one day," said Paul. "I could swim in the sea and run on the beach – remember those old vids we watched, Mum? It was like paradise, wasn't it?"

"Yes. A wonderful place to live. But they don't have any technology like we do. They have to work hard all day in their fields to grow enough food to eat, and maybe they keep animals like sheep. Either way, their lives will involve a lot more hard labour, because they don't have machines."

"We could teach them… show them how to make all our things!" Jan's young face lit up with the idea.

"We could do that. And maybe we will. But will it make them any happier?"

The boys were quiet for a moment while they considered her question. Then Paul piped up, "I'd be a lot happier if I could play all day instead of having to work in the fields or something."

"Hmm, maybe. But do you remember the Universal Employment Act that came into law after the Drone War, from your school lessons, Paul?"

"Oh, yeah."

"Why do you think our government introduced that?"

"To get rid of all those intelligent machines that did everything for us – and then attacked each other."

"Well… yes. That was part of the reason. But, why does every adult have to be in employment of some kind to suit their abilities once they finish their schooling?"

"To… um… to keep them busy?"

"Yes. To give everyone a sense of achievement… a sense of purpose. It's what we call job satisfaction. They realised that idle people get bored and depressed and their health suffers. And many of them turn to crime because they don't have anything else to do. So, making sure every single person has a job to do reduces crime and improves the health and happiness of the nation. The Coops have something similar, but their jobs are all provided by the state and there's less choice."

"Do you think all the Earthies have jobs, Mum?" asked Grig.

"I should think so. In primitive societies back in Earth's history, anyone who didn't work didn't eat. I would imagine, from what we can see through our telescopes, it will be similar there today."

"But will their children still have to go to school?" young Jan wanted to know.

"I hope so. Education wasn't always available for the poorest people's children, years ago."

"Mum," said Grig, with a puzzled frown, "If the Earthies are survivors from the Ark, that means they came from the Moon and knew about everything – electricity and machines and everything – so why don't they use them now?"

"I don't know, Grig. It's a very good question. The only way we will find the answer is to go and talk to them." She smiled at the three young faces. "Who'd like to travel on a spaceship to Earth and have a talk with the Earthies?"

"Me!" They all shouted at once, with their hands in the air.

Earth 1504

It was now mid afternoon and not a lot had happened after the momentous events of the morning. Jack and Ifan had returned in the rowing boat to report the spaceship had lowered some sort of pipe into the sea. It appeared that the strange craft was taking a drink, they said. Apart from that, there was no sign of activity. No creature had appeared in the ship's doorway or descended the ladder. After the sun passed overhead and started down the western sky, many of the townspeople had left the harbour to return to their work or find something to eat.

Lucy had softened her tone with her father and had boarded the Pelican to be introduced to Miriam. She was shocked to learn the young mermaid, whose display with the dolphin she'd witnessed early that morning, was soon to become her sister-in-law. But, remembering her own teenage wedding to Sam, she welcomed her warmly and congratulated Mammed on his bride to be. "You're full of surprises, Mammed!" she told him.

"Umm, do you think..." he asked, staring at the craft standing on the harbour wall, "if nobody is coming down that ladder, that maybe it's asking for one of us to go up?"

"You can forget that idea, *right* now!" Lucy told him.

"No, Maa-med!" said Miriam looking scared. "It is too much danger."

"Well... who else is going to climb up there and find out?" he said.

"Nobody is going up there, Mammed," said Lucy firmly. "You've taken more than enough risks for one lifetime."

But that had been late morning and as the day had dragged on and the threat from the peculiar vessel standing on the harbour wall diminished, the talk returned to what they should do about it. The peace keepers had slowly edged forward, pointing their pikes at it and had been standing around the base of the craft for some time now.

Growing increasingly bored and brave, they had taken to tapping its metal legs with their pikes and shouting increasingly saucy encouragements to whoever or whatever might be waiting high above.

Finally, after Lucy had gone home to feed her children, Captain Yonaton had said he could bear it no longer, and would climb the ladder himself to see what was inside the open doorway at the top.

"Don't be ridiculous, Papa Yon!" said Mammed. "I can run up that ladder, take a quick look inside and be back down again in no time."

"Well you're not going, son, and that's that." Yonaton put his hand on Mammed's shoulder. "You already risked your life to save mine by climbing that thing—" He was pointing at the harbour tower at the opposite end of the harbour wall, when he was interrupted by Miriam.

"Oh, Maa-med! Is that what you climbed to rescue your father and Benyamin?" She looked at the lofty stone structure and then at Mammed in wonder.

"Yeah." He smiled, casually.

"You are crazy, Maa-med. No more climbing... please!"

"Hmm, but how about you, Miriam? Don't you need some more water in your pool?"

"Yes, please. It is very warm in here. Really, I would like to swim in sea again. Is it possible, Capteen Yon-ton?"

"I don't see why not. Is Peetee still in the harbour, Mammed?"

Mammed ran to the starboard rail and called across to say that he was.

"Very well, young lady," said the Captain. "Slip back into the bosun's chair and we will hoist you out over the other side. You and Peetee can go for a swim and cool off."

It was while Miriam was exploring the waters outside the harbour with her Dolpheen friend that Mammed slipped away from the Pelican unnoticed. After a brief chat with the peace keepers at the base of the spacecraft he made a dash for the ladder and was soon clambering up it. Yonaton, alerted by shouts from across the harbour, saw too late the rangy youth with the springy mop of hair ascending the spacecraft's ladder and set off at a run around the harbour perimeter, cursing under his breath.

By the time he reached the angular metal legs of the colossal black cylinder, his shouts to his beloved, adopted son were carried away on the breeze and went unheeded. As he saw Mammed reach the open door of the craft he heard a piercing scream from the harbour entrance – Miriam had seen him too. The Captain stood transfixed as Mammed hesitated for a long moment… then pulled himself up and disappeared inside.

Yonaton felt his heart thumping in his chest as he stared at the craft's doorway, waiting for Mammed to reappear and begin his descent. He thought of climbing up the ladder after him, but decided two people might be too much for the flimsy, flexible structure. He put his hands to his mouth and shouted again. "*Mammed! Come down now!*"

But instead of Mammed reappearing, the ladder started retracting rapidly. Yonaton ran and jumped but missed the end of it, landing awkwardly and falling to his knees.

"No! No, no, no, no…" He pounded the quayside with his fist, until he was lifted to his feet and pulled away by two of the peace keepers. He saw to his horror that the arm with the pipe was retracting back into the base of the spaceship and he guessed what was coming next. The doorway high up on the craft abruptly clanked shut and Mammed's fate was sealed.

Yonaton struggled free from the two men holding him and ran to the nearest metal leg, thumping and pulling on it like a man demented. He was dragged away again just as a rushing sound was followed by a fearsome rumble. A wave of heat hit the group scurrying away from the craft as the awful machine began to exhale its fiery breath. The peace keepers pulled the Captain into the doorway of a stone warehouse just in time for the air to light up and a screaming, roaring torment shook the building.

The men cowered in the farthest corner as the warehouse filled with dust and noise and heat. Yonaton's sobs of fear and anger continued long after the throbbing, raging cacophony had faded to a dull rumble. He staggered to the door and with streaming eyes stared after the disappearing fireball that was taking Mammed away to god knows where. He turned his dirt and tear-streaked face toward the harbour where a dolphin and a blonde haired, freckle-faced girl were staring up at the sky.

"NOOOoooooooo!" Yonaton's tortured wail tore at his throat and he slumped to his knees in despair.

Moon 3660
Compared to the ragged vibration of the old Zenits during takeoff, the shiny new Mercury hopper was a peach. Ktrina smiled as her screen showed the lights of Sokwest Skyport falling away with barely a tremble reaching her as she lay snug and relaxed in the pilot's cradle

seat. She'd flown in them before of course, but lately she'd drawn the short straw and found only Zenits available. Since her accident she'd made it clear to both the Foreign Ministry and the Ministry of Transport that she wasn't prepared to fly in them again, whatever their safety inspections had reported. Their response – book earlier!

Apart from the smooth power delivery, and the blessed absence of hair-raising thumps and bumps from drive changes, the Mercurys had smart, clean and ergonomic interiors, without all the nauseating smells that were a feature of the old craft. Retaining one's breakfast during a Zenit flight was always a challenge, and many passengers did not meet it. The all-plasma drives of these latest hoppers helped keep travellers comfortable and interiors smelling wholesome.

It would take 78 minutes to reach the distant outpost of Hilbert, a mining community of 1700 residents. They had developed an alternative culture over the years, with art and freedom of expression promoted as key values. Ktrina enjoyed her brief visits. Their relaxed way of life, she felt sure, was due to their penchant for growing unusual herbs, the aroma of which pervaded the cluster of habitats. It was none of her concern, but the fact that searches by the Health and Safety Inspectorate consistently failed to find anything in Hilbert's labyrinth of tunnels showed they were a resourceful bunch, if nothing else.

As she settled in to the flight, Ktrina reviewed her notes on the issues she would soon be faced with. A claim for another teacher at the Hilbert School seemed reasonable, as the number of children had increased by nineteen percent in the past two years. A petition for government funding for free school meals was less likely to be successful. All schools throughout Sok territory were required to provide lunch to pupils, provided by the community, and she couldn't see why Hilbert should be any different. As ever, her job was to listen, advise and report back, not make the decisions.

There were a dozen other representations she would hear during her five-hour stopover, none of them particularly contentious. She flicked her screen to music and selected a melodic Ghazal to relax to while she thought about the latest developments. Pippa Khan had called her soon after she arrived at her office that morning with news that the Coops' spacecraft had taken off from Earth as expected. After a single orbit of the planet it had executed a precise burn to put it on a return trajectory for the Moon and was expected back sometime on Friday.

Despite her anger and frustration over the north's blatantly provocative actions, she had to admit to a grudging respect for their technical prowess. How long would it take her own government to develop and build a craft to undertake such a mission successfully, she wondered. Especially when it was still operating antiquated Zenit hoppers that should have been scrapped years ago!

She wondered what effect the arrival of a spacecraft from the Moon would have had on the simple, pastoral people of Earth. Would they have fled the town and headed for the hills? Would any have remained behind to find out what this apparition meant, whether it was a visitation from the gods or a demon sent from hell? And if Nakash was on board, what sort of exchange would there have been? What would they have made of the tattooed freak? Would they have been repulsed, as she was, by the very sight of him? Or might he have already sown the seeds of his twisted religion amongst a fearful and gullible people?

Ktrina cursed her inability to know what was happening or to do anything about the multiple injustices she felt sure must be taking place. The joyful time she'd shared with her sons last evening had made her doubt her resolve to venture into Aristarchus on a quest for truth. But this latest development made her more determined than ever to uncover the facts about Ethan's death. She had to try to fit one small piece into the jigsaw of mystery that surrounded her life. Whatever the risk.

Earth – Moon

Mammed fought to reach the surface through the thick and foggy water. He needed air, and he needed to wake up. His dream kept coming back in odd fragments – a ladder... a beautiful, blonde-haired woman... an ugly face covered in black paintings. None of it made any sense.

He became aware of odd sounds – a buzzing hum in the background, occasional clicks and deep, heavy breathing. Mammed tried to open his eyes but the lids seemed heavy and refused to budge. In contrast his body felt weirdly light and yet he couldn't move his arms or legs. He twisted his neck and moved his head from side to side, trying to shake off the sticky fog that surrounded him. Finally, one eye opened... and then the other.

His blurry vision was filled with light and shade, peculiar shapes and dozens of tiny candles with flames that didn't move or flicker. He blinked and turned his head. Above him was a large square of blue light on which strange symbols danced and jumped, and to his right was a... was a... man! At least, he could be a man, but he had no hair and his face and neck were covered with dark pictures. Like Mammed he was lying on his back, but he appeared to be asleep. With a jolt, Mammed realised it was the ugly face from his dream!

Before the ugly-face man woke, Mammed decided he must get up and find out what was going on. He struggled to move his arms and legs, but they were tied down to his bed. He tried to sit up, but found a strap across his chest prevented him from moving. A wave of panic rolled over him. He was trapped in a magician's cave! He let his head fall back, closed his eyes and tried to think. That's when his dream came back in all its detail...

He was climbing a ladder – a flimsy, wobbly sort of rope ladder – and at the top was an open door. Mammed raised his head cautiously and peered inside. Lying on a cot was a person, a woman with blonde hair and a strikingly lovely face. She raised a hand and beckoned him in. He hesitated for a moment, then decided she must need his help, so he stepped over the high sill into the dark, cramped cabin.

The woman lay in the middle of three slim cots and as Mammed approached she raised her hand again, but this time there was something in it. He felt a sharp pain in his chest and looked down. His shirt was pinned to his skin by a small dart. He tried to raise his hand to remove it but his arm wouldn't work. He looked back at the woman but, weirdly, she seemed to be holding her face off to one side, and where it had been was now a bald man's face – covered with ugly black pictures.

He heard his Papa Yon shouting from somewhere in the distance "Mammed! Come down now!" Then his legs gave way and he fell on the cot next to the scary face man. He was dimly aware of the door closing and then a terrible noise and shaking started up and everything turned black.

With growing certainty, Mammed realised it hadn't been a dream. He was now trapped inside a tall metal tower – a spacecraft like the Ark – and he'd been lured inside by a man hiding behind a mask of a woman's-face. Caught, like a fly in a spider's web. He needed to get out fast, before the scary face man woke up and the spacecraft took off with him stuck inside it! He struggled against the straps holding him down but there seemed no way to break free.

Then he heard a ripping sound and snapped his head to the right to find 'Ugly Face' had gone from the cot beside him... and was now floating above! As Mammed looked up in fear and confusion at the man who appeared to be swimming in the air overhead, the painted face grinned and began to talk.

Chapter 16
Heavy Lifting
Moon 3660

Thursday morning, back in her office, Ktrina dealt with routine paperwork and tried to stop her mind wandering. Hilbert had been a fun visit, and a welcome distraction from her upcoming trip to Frentzen on Monday, which now loomed menacingly on her internal horizon. Ktrina told herself she could back out of attempting the trek to LTA14 at any time. She could go to Frentzen, do her diplomatic duties like a sensible Ambassador, and simply come home again. Nobody would know if she lost her nerve. Except her. And Stairway Man. And Ethan.

She hadn't seen Ethan lately. *When was the last time?* She closed her eyes and the memory triggered. Yes, there was Ethan with his arm around the shoulders of a vaguely-familiar man. A man who, she'd discovered, was the rebel who had been trying to defect. His name was Zach Swanly and he'd had a kid brother who she was now convinced was her Stairway Man. The broken-toothed guy with the haunted face. The only other person who knew she had the egg.

Except for Ethan. And he seemed to have deserted her these past two weeks. It was Friday the thirteenth of August when she'd last seen him, as she stood at the washbasin in the grubby Monterey toilets. She'd just met Klif Watanabe and was on her way home. That was when Ethan had appeared with his arm around Zach Swanly's shoulder. It was the last time her late husband had popped up, unbidden, to impart some useful information.

Why then and not since? Did he have nothing new to tell her? Would he only appear at critical moments... and if so, wasn't her plan to get dangerously close to LTA14 a critical moment? Just when she could do with some guidance, he'd vanished. Did that mean she was on her own from now on?

Oh well, she had a brief visit to Ashbrook tomorrow morning. A tiny, 340-strong village just a short hop away from Sok City. And then she had the whole weekend to chill and relax with her family. Plenty of time to come to her senses and drop the whole idea of going to Aristarchus.

And setting loose a mechanical spider to take a peek into LTA14—

A knock at her door made her jump as if caught in the act.

Phoebe appeared. "Sorry, Ktrina. It's the Foreign Minister. Can you take it?"

"Yeah, put him through, Phoebe."

"Hello, Minister."

"Ktrina. Just to let you know I have sent my opposite number, Gunta Krems, a carefully worded message inviting them to join us in a dialogue about plankton and making contact with the newly-discovered inhabitants of Earth."

"Very good, Minister. Any response so far...?"

"Not yet. I have also suggested they reinstate your visa so that you might open negotiations on our behalf."

Dammit! Why couldn't the man go himself? When was the last time Lanimovskiy had been to the north?

"You don't think they'd rather deal with someone more senior, Minister? Yourself, for instance? I'm clearly out of favour with the Coopan government at present..."

"No, no. You're the best person for the job at this stage, Ktrina. When they show they are serious about discussing terms, and Krems is willing to meet here, then of course, I will take over the heavy lifting, so to speak."

Heavy lifting! He's afraid. A Foreign Minister who's scared of setting foot outside his own territory...

"Very well, Minister. I will await developments."

"And just to update you, in case you haven't heard, their spacecraft is expected to land in the early hours of tomorrow, according to our defence department. So, our invitation to open a dialogue is timely, I would say." He sounded pleased with himself.

"I'm visiting Ashbrook tomorrow morning, Minister. Back by midday, hopefully."

"Okay. Keep up the good work. I'll let you know if there are further developments."

"Thank you. Good bye, Minister."

Ktrina closed the connection and sat staring at nothing for minute. *Heavy lifting? That's a good one! He'll graciously shoulder all the glory, if any deal is struck. With ministers like ours, it's no wonder the Coops are able to steal a march on us.*

Earth – Moon

"Well, you're a tough little customer, aren't you?" said the man with the painted face.

Mammed stared back at him. He had no idea what he was saying.

"Do you speak English?" asked Ugly Face.

"English...?" Mammed thought he recognised one word, but the way it sounded was all wrong. "Let me out of here!" he cried, struggling against the straps that bound him to his cot.

Ugly Face laughed at him. "That would be a bad idea. See where we are...?" He pulled the square of light towards Mammed, did something with his fingers and a picture of two Moons appeared. Only, one was the Moon and the other was different. It was blue in the middle and white at the top and bottom.

"Moon," said Ugly Face, pointing to the picture of a full Moon. "Earth," he said, pointing to the picture of the other round thing.

Mammed frowned. He understood the words, even though the man with the painted face was saying them wrong. But why was Earth, where Mammed came from, looking like a round ball? The man did something with his fingers again and the blue and white ball he called Earth grew until it was too big to fit on the square of light. It grew and grew until Mammed recognised something – it looked like the Seaple's chart of the Crabbing Sea, or Caribbean Sea as they called it.

"The Caribbean," said the painted face man, pointing to the island Mammed called home.

Then the chart was shrinking again until it was swallowed up and became the blue and white ball again. "Earth," said Ugly Face. "Moon," he said, pointing at the Moon. "Us... in the spaceship," he said, pointing to a dot on the curvy line drawn between the two. The picture grew again until the dot became the tall metal spacecraft that had landed on the dockside at Loming harbour.

He grinned at Mammed. "So... no escape, understand?"

Mammed understood. He was trapped inside the spacecraft and it had left Loming. It had left the Crabbing Sea and it had left the Earth behind. They were flying through space, on their way to the Moon. He thought of Miriam and his Papa Yon and his eyes filled up with tears.

Moon 3660

"Are you back in your office yet, Ktrina?" Lanimovskiy's call caught her leaving Sokwest Skyport after returning from Ashbrook.

"Just on my way from the skyport now, Minister. Should be there in twenty minutes."

"Good. Interesting developments. The Coopan spacecraft returning from Earth landed at Monterey this morning. And my initiative has paid off..." She could hear the gloating in his voice. "Your visa has been reinstated and they've invited you to some sort of presentation. I'll forward the message to your screen... you can make arrangements when you're back at your desk."

"Very well, Minister."

Some sort of presentation? Ktrina couldn't quite picture how the Coops would make a presentation out of a tank full of plankton. From the brief research she'd done, these Earthly sea-creatures were too small to see. She had a comical vision of Daval Nakash and Gunta Krems pulling the drapes to reveal a tub of murky water, and had to stifle a laugh.

She checked the time – 12.15 – and decided to call at the deli and pick up a sandwich for herself and one for Phoebe. It was high time she treated her helpful and cheery secretary to lunch.

Cooper Foreign Ministry

The Coopan Government has reinstated the travel visa for Sokolovan Ambassador

Ktrina Rozek. She is invited to attend a presentation of the highest significance at the

State Expo Centre, Monterey Skyport, at 3pm on Sunday 29th August.

Please be advised there will be no commercial flights in or out of Monterey Skyport on this day.

Sincerely,

Gunta Krems.

"Dammit!" Ktrina cursed out loud as she read the message her Foreign Minister had forwarded. That was her Sunday down the toilet – the precious day she had planned to spend with her boys before her mission to Aristarchus on Monday. She could hardly refuse to attend. And no Polar Carrier meant she would have to take a hopper.

An idea started to form. Maybe she could bring her visit to Frentzen, and her clandestine trip to LTA14 , forward by a day? She didn't have to be at Monterey until 3pm. It would mean an extra-early start, and some fresh calculations for the satellite timings, but the travel logistics made sense. Why go halfway to the North Pole on Monday, when she'd been all the way the day before?

Ktrina put a call through to Brad Lewis, the amenable head of Frentzen town council, who she'd spoken to at length the day before. "Hello again, Brad. It's Ktrina Rozek... with a change of plans."

"Hello, Ambassador. No problem. How can I help?"

"Well... you know we arranged a visit for Monday? I've just been informed I have to be in Cooper City on Sunday afternoon and

262

wonder if I could bring my visit to Frentzen forward to Sunday morning? It would save a lot of extra travel if I could do both on the same day?"

"Sure. That makes sense. I'm free Sunday morning. Do you still want to take the sled out for a run on Procellarum beforehand?"

"Yes please, Brad, if it's not too much trouble. I aim to land at 8am, so could you have it ready to roll for then, do you think?"

"With those extra fuel cells and air tanks you asked for?"

"Yes please."

"No problem. I'll see you at eight, Sunday morning."

"Thank you, Brad. See you then." She closed the connection.

It was going to be a hectic Sunday, a far cry from the relaxing family day she had planned, but Ktrina felt pleased she had made some sense of the travel logistics. She stepped into the outer office.

"Hi Pheebs. I've just received an invite to a special presentation at Monterey Skyport on Sunday afternoon—"

"Oh, I thought your visa had been revoked, Ktrina?"

"Yeah, well, they've just reinstated it – and this invite is an offer I can't refuse. To make the best of an unwelcome trip, I've rearranged my Frentzen visit to Sunday morning, so I can go there on the way to Cooper City. I'll need to change the hopper booking from Monday to Sunday please – and it'll be a very early start, so pick up at 6am."

"Poor you! And on your weekend too! I'll get on to transport right away..."

Ktrina returned to her desk and set about downloading the times for surveillance satellites crossing Aristarchus and Procellarum on Sunday. She felt exposed using her Foreign Ministry access portal again but had no choice. As soon as she had the information she needed, she erased evidence of her search and hoped for the best.

A knock at her door made her look up. It was Phoebe, looking worried. "I'm sorry, Ktrina, but there's a problem. The Mercurys are all being serviced on Sunday. Only Zenits available..."

"What! Nooo..." Ktrina sank her face into her hands. What could she do? Refusing to go to the Coops' presentation and missing the chance to negotiate would be dereliction of duty and mean certain dismissal. It would also mean giving up any hope of finding out what was in LTA14 and getting some answers for Ethan and her Stairway Man.

"I have no choice, Phoebe," she said with a sigh. "I've got to go. Book me a Zenit, please."

Earth 1504

Lucy arrived at the dockside with a large pot of hot porridge cradled for warmth in a basket of straw. She would try to get her father to eat something after his all-night vigil aboard the Pelican. Maybe Miriam would try a mouthful too? It seemed the poor girl only ate fish, crabs and seaweed, but if she could be persuaded to take a little porridge it would surely help. If the truth was told, Lucy wondered if anything would lift their spirits on a morning that was filled with so much gloom.

She had returned to the harbour the previous afternoon soon after hearing the awful roar from that great apparition from the sky. She saw it rising on a throbbing pillar of flame and knew instinctively it was the work of the devil. Before she reached the dock she was met by white-faced people fleeing in the opposite direction. Mammed, they told her, had been swallowed up by the monster. And her father had lost his mind.

It did indeed appear as if Yonaton was beyond help when she found him kneeling outside the warehouse, beating the stone flags with his fists, tears and snot dripping from his beard. She had to summon the peace keepers to escort him to his ship where she sat him by the capstan and took stock. There was no point in blaming him for Mammed's running off and climbing the ladder. By all accounts her father had done everything possible to stop him and had even attacked the machine with his bare hands. Adding to his wretched despair wouldn't help bring Mammed back.

More important was organising the crew to hoist Miriam back on board and then trying to console her. Lucy had felt a little uncomfortable hugging the dripping wet mermaid, but with her brother's intended bride shaking with fear and anger, it seemed the least she could do. Then Benyamin had appeared looking pale and weak. He'd been confined to his hammock for the past few days with a fever and barely had the strength to stagger onto the deck. Lucy had assured him she was in control and sent him back below.

Fortunately Conor, the aged bosun, was still in command of his faculties, even if he did only have one working hand. She sent him to open the medical chest and break out the small bottle of rum kept there for such emergencies. By the time she'd administered a few sips to those who needed it – which, to her surprise, included herself – she felt some sort of order was being restored.

A further surprise came when she saw Jack and Ifan out in the rowing boat appearing to stroke and talk to the great grey dolphin that had accompanied Miriam across the Crabbing Sea. It seemed the creature had become quite attached to young Mammed over the past two weeks and was suffering similar emotions to the humans after seeing him snatched away by the towering engine of doom.

When Yonaton finally started talking, he insisted he was entirely to blame. He had been the one who'd chased after the secrets that the Cardinal was hell-bent on destroying. He had asked Sam to burn the figure on the hillside which had brought this madness down on the people of Loming. He had allowed Mammed to slip away and climb into the thing. Now he was gone and Yonaton was left with his son's intended bride for whom no words could ever make up for her lost love.

"Listen, father," Lucy had told him. "nobody could have guessed it came here to steal him away. And nobody knows if or when it might return and deliver him back to us. If you have any sense of duty towards this young woman..." she gestured toward the deck pool, "you will pull yourself together and offer her some encouragement. Everyone looks to you for leadership. Now is *not* the time to give up."

Her words had got him back on his feet yesterday afternoon, and now Lucy hoped her pot of porridge might help restore some purpose in him this morning. It was true there had been no sign of the spaceship bringing Mammed back so far, but hope and hard work would help keep them all buoyed up until it did. She crossed the gangplank and hailed the crew who were staring at the harbour from the far side of the ship. "Morning boys," she called. "I've brought some hot porridge for your breakfast. Go and fetch your bowls and you can tuck in."

Neither Yonaton nor Miriam were to be seen. The young mermaid had asked to be allowed into the sea for a swim and the men were watching as she and the dolphin disappeared through the harbour entrance. Lucy hoped the dip in familiar waters would restore a little of her lost sparkle. After ladling the lumpy oatmeal into the men's dishes she went below in search of her father. She found him talking to Benyamin, who was sitting up in his hammock, struggling to answer with a croaky throat.

"Right you two," she said, in her best schoolmistress voice. "It's hot porridge for both of you. Now... where are your bowls?"

While they ate she ran through their options. There was nothing they could do but wait and see if the craft from the sky returned and brought Mammed back to them. But in the meantime, they had the welfare of Miriam to consider. Would she not be better off if she went back home to her people? Her mother and father could console and support her. She would surely feel more comfortable in her home environment, surrounded by her family?

"I spoke to her about that this morning, Lucy, and she's determined to stay here and wait for Mammed to come back. She's convinced he *will* come back…" said Yonaton.

"I hope she's right. Did she sleep last night?"

"Not much. I made a mattress for her, wrapped her in a sheet and sat up with her all night. She talked most of it. She finally dropped off for a while just before dawn." His smile was a ghost of his usual grin. "She's a bright and intelligent young woman. Reminds me in some ways of you, Lucy."

"I'm worried about her state of mind and her state of health," said Lucy. "If she sits here in that pool of water day after day… it can't be good for her, can it?"

"She's gone off for a swim with Peetee this morning. I hope that will buck her up a bit."

"Well, let's hope so." She looked up as Ben scraped his bowl with his wooden spoon. "Well done, Ben! Here… have some more, you need to build your strength up again."

Moon 3660

Ktrina had been determined to enjoy her weekend with the boys, but now it had been reduced to just a Saturday, she was finding it hard to relax. Or smile. She hadn't wanted to admit the possibility that this might be her last, had pushed such morbid thoughts to the back of her mind. Now she realised she'd been subconsciously planning to give her three sons a weekend of fun to remember her by. The thought left her feeling both sick with fear and unbearably selfish.

"Are you okay, Mum?" It was ten-year-old Grig who noticed something was wrong. He was looking at her with wide eyes as she climbed into the fun-fair car beside him. Paul and Jan were strapped in the seats in front of them, chattering excitedly, waiting for the ride to begin.

"Yes! Of course I'm okay, darling!" She forced a brittle laugh. It sounded false, even to her. "Aren't you having a great time too?"

He didn't answer, just gripped the safety rail and stared straight ahead. He always was the thoughtful one, but it didn't take a genius to spot her mistake. She had overdone the treats. Ktrina clipped his seatbelt and fastened her own while she searched for a plausible answer.

"You know I have to work tomorrow?"

He nodded.

"So... I thought I'd give you all a big day out today. And tomorrow, while I'm up in Cooper, you'll be spending the day with Aunt Jean and Uncle Daniel. You'll enjoy that, won't you...?"

He nodded again, but still didn't turn to look at her.

"I have to leave very early. Your Grandma Sofi can have the day to herself. And I'll be home at bedtime." *Dear God, I hope I am.*

Her thoughts were drowned by a warning siren and a growing clatter as the row of open-top cars began to ascend the rail. The mag-lev Giant Switchback ride was naturally silent, but a range of lurid sound effects had been added to inject a sense of drama and excitement. Ktrina needed none of them. The thought of tomorrow's Zenit flight was enough to make her stomach turn somersaults.

She would make this the last ride. She'd been spending credits like she'd won a lottery jackpot. No wonder Grig was suspicious – her boys had been taught to be prudent and thrifty. As the cars crested the first rise and began their rattling descent, she remembered to laugh and squeal for the sake of appearance. It did nothing to lift the deep sense of misery she felt.

It was late afternoon when they arrived at Jean and Daniel's modest apartment in Soknorth. Ktrina had cancelled the cube and instead taken the beltway from the Selene Adventure Park, where they'd spent most of the day and much of Ktrina's monthly salary.

"Hello!" Jean called from the doorway. "Perfect timing – we're just getting ready for supper."

"Hello, Aunt Jean," they chorused.

She smiled and ruffled the boys' hair as they filed past her. "You lads must be hungry after your exciting day out."

Her smile faded as she took in Ktrina's tired face. "Oh, Ktrina. You look exhausted!" She gave her sister-in-law a warm embrace and whispered. "You can relax now, Ktrina. Daniel's been waiting to play with the boys. Your duty's done for the day."

"Thanks, Jean. I think it was the last ride – the Giant Switchback – made me feel really queasy. The boys loved it though..." She smiled weakly.

"Come in and have a hot drink. I've got some new chocolate chai for you to try. Come and put your feet up."

Paul, Grig and Jan were busy polishing off their ice-cream dessert when Ktrina apologised and said she would have to go. She had things to prepare for her trip to the north and a very early start in the morning. She kissed and hugged each of the boys, being careful not to overdo it, and told them to be good for their aunt and uncle. As she was hugging and thanking Jean, Daniel said he'd see her to the door.

"So..." he said, as he looked directly into Ktrina's eyes on the doorstep, "you're stopping off at Frentzen on your way north tomorrow?"

"Yes, that's right." She looked away. "A long-overdue visit."

"Well, I expect you'll tell me you have no plans to go anywhere near Aristarchus..."

She stiffened.

"... but just in case you do, there are a couple of things in here you might need." Daniel lifted a small rucksack from the floor and handed it to her.

"What's in it?" she asked, meeting his eyes.

"A thermal cover sheet. Makes you the same temperature as the surrounding regolith, hides you from thermal imaging satellites. Just remember to plug it in and get yourself and the sled underneath it a couple of minutes before any surv-sat passes overhead. You've got their times, I take it?"

He'd guessed. There was no point in pretending. She nodded.

"Good. And the other item is a fan-rake. Fits to the back of the sled and scatters the dust as you go. Does a pretty good job of hiding your tracks."

"Okay. Thanks, Daniel," she said quietly.

"Turn off everything – and I *mean* everything. No lights, no comms, nothing... or you'll stick out like a sore thumb. And stay below the lip of the crater. I don't know how you're going to see inside, but make sure *they* don't see *you*. Okay?" He gripped her shoulders firmly.

Ktrina nodded.

"And let me know when you get back to Frentzen... please?"

"I will, Daniel. Thank you." She wrapped her arms around his chest and hugged him tight. Then she shouldered the bag and stumbled into the street before he could see the tears rolling down her face.

Earth 1504

It was mid-afternoon on Thursday, and Lucy was growing increasingly concerned about Miriam's welfare. She had refused all food since Mammed was abducted two days ago and had to be cajoled into taking sips of water. Yonaton had spent another night on deck with her, but reported she had only slept fitfully and cried out several times during the darkest hours. This morning she'd had to be talked into going for a swim with Peetee and clung to him listlessly as he swam gently to the harbour entrance and back.

"It's *no good*, father," Lucy whispered to him on the dockside as she prepared to head home after bringing lunch for the crew. "She is losing hope and I'm afraid if she stays here she will slowly fade away. Sitting in a pool of water pining for him isn't going to bring Mammed back. But it might mean we lose her too. How would you explain that to the Seaple?" She saw the look of horror in Yonaton's eyes as he thought about it.

She continued. "We need to tell her that as soon as Mammed comes back, we will bring him to Sanctuary Island. They can get married and live happily ever after. But for now she is better off back home with her family. They will know how to look after her until... well, we have to hope he comes back eventually, don't we?"

Yonaton nodded. "Will you talk to her please Lucy? You have a better way with words. Tell her we will head back to Sanctuary Island at dusk and she can be with her family tomorrow morning. And what you said... that we'll bring Mammed the moment he returns."

"Okay. I'll speak to her now." Lucy turned back towards the gangplank.

"And I'll get Conor to round up the crew. I sent them home to their families for a break."

After a slow passage due to light winds, the Pelican dropped anchor soon after dawn off the south west corner of Sanctuary Island. Yonaton had managed to catch a few hours sleep lying on the deck next to the sheet-wrapped form of Miriam. She had shivered uncontrollably until he overcame his embarrassment and held her close, figuring it was more important to keep her warm than worry whether it was decent or not. Then both had slept for the first time in several nights and woke with the dawn as the motion of the ship changed and the anchor hit the water.

His concern about how he would break the news to Alexee and Rachel evaporated when he stood to stretch his aching joints and saw Peetee leaping over the barrier at the gap in the reef. The chief of the Seaple and his doctor wife would soon be getting the story from their faithful friend. He was sorry they would be waking to learn that their future son-in-law had been stolen and their daughter had come home sick with grief.

It had been the right decision to return, though. After he'd lifted Miriam into the pool she brightened visibly at the sight of her home island close off their port side. She even agreed to nibble some bread and then ate a fish that Jack and Ifan had provided for the journey. It was heartening to see her eating at last and he stood beside her to eat his own breakfast of bread and cheese.

"You must not blame yourself, Capteen Yon-ton."

He turned in surprise. It was the first time she had spoken since they left Loming.

"It is not your fault. Maa-med tricked us so he could climb without being seen. He is crazy but…" her voice cracked and tears rolled down her freckled cheeks, "that's why I love him so much."

Yonaton didn't know what to say. He slipped his arm around her shoulder.

"He *will* come back," she said as she threw the remains of her fish into the sea. "He *has* to come back."

"The minute he returns, Miriam, I swear I will bring him to you. You have my word."

"Dolphins!" A shout from the ship's bow made them both look towards the reef. A pod of dolphins was heading towards the Pelican. They would tow the ship into the lagoon.

"Right, men," he called to the crew as he strode to the capstan. "Get some tow ropes ready for the dolphins, and let's start hauling the anchor up."

Moon 3660

Strapped securely in the pilot's cradle seat, Ktrina braced herself for the drive change as the Zenit dropped towards Frentzen. She had checked the hopper thoroughly before she left Sokwest at 6am that morning. She'd even removed the switch panel and given the connectors a shake to make sure they couldn't fall out. That reassurance still didn't stop her clenching her teeth as the altimeter plunged towards the 2000 metre drive change point.

Right on cue the smooth plasma drives cut out and Ktrina was flung against her straps. She held her breath while she counted off the two seconds before the rocket drives kicked in and thumped her back into her seat.

"Thank you, God," she muttered as she let out her breath in a grateful sigh. She watched her screen as the faint glimmer of Frentzen grew out of the darkness below. Despite being on the equator, it would be another four days before sunlight reached the remote outpost.

Ten minutes later she was being escorted by Brad Lewis to the tiny skyport's changing rooms. He waited outside as she slipped out of her blue business suit, deposited it in a locker, and chose boots and helmet from the rack. She stepped into the nearest cubicle, placed her feet on the sole-shaped marks and said, "fabricate surface suit."

While the machine applied the layers and ran through the new suit's integrity checks, Ktrina thought about the elaborate lie she had told Lewis to explain her unusual mission out on the Moon's surface that morning. He'd seemed happy to accept that she was testing a new tracking device – she'd shown him the egg – on behalf of the defence department. She told him she'd been asked to ride a sled near the equator while the government's satellites tracked her progress for a couple of hours.

It meant turning off her comm, so he shouldn't worry that she'd be out of contact for a while. She'd been given a course to follow and would be back in two to three hours, leaving just enough time for a brief diplomatic session before she left for the Coops' presentation at Monterey. She did not enjoy spinning a falsehood, but knew it was a necessary evil on this occasion.

Suited, and with her rucksack containing egg, thermal sheet and rake-fan, Ktrina shook hands with the kindly, middle-aged council leader.

"Thank you for getting up early to meet me this morning, Brad." She smiled at him through her helmet's open visor.

"Oh, that's no bother. Happy to help, Ktrina. Your sled's waiting outside the airlock with air and power packs for an extra three hours, so you've plenty in reserve. Any problems, give me a call." He checked the time. "Eight twenty-five. I guess you'd better get going. See you around eleven. I'll have a fresh pot of coffee brewing."

"Sounds perfect. Thanks." She snapped down her visor and stepped into the airlock. As the door clanged shut behind her Ktrina had the strange feeling she was stepping out of one life and into another.

Outside she found the sled that Lewis had readied for her. She checked the panniers and counted three air packs and three power packs, just as he'd promised. Together with the hour's worth her suit and the sled came with, she had four hours – more than enough for what she had planned. She fished the fan-rake from her rucksack, opened it to its fullest extent and attached it to the tow hook on the sled's rear. Ktrina unplugged the sled from its charging station, slid onto the seat and plugged her suit into the machine.

With its console lit up, she selected compass, time and distance display, and turned off the sled's tracking and emergency beacon functions. Warning lights flashed, and she had to confirm her instructions twice before the sled accepted that she really wanted to ride without any of its inbuilt safety systems in operation.

Finally, at 08.34, she turned the twistgrip and the machine surged away from Frentzen, heading due west. As the lights from the town's skyport fell away behind her, Ktrina turned off the sled's lights and was plunged into darkness. She slowed until her eyes adjusted to the faint illumination of Earthshine. Light reflecting from the blue planet that hung in the eastern sky picked out the larger rocks in her path. She checked her distance run. Four and a half kilometres meant she was already over the horizon from anyone watching back at Frentzen. Out of sight and untracked, Ktrina turned the machine north west, opened the throttle and headed towards the Aristarchus Plateau.

Earth 1504

It was a sombre ship that sailed out through the gap in the reef later that morning. Rachel and Alexee had been relieved to see their daughter Miriam home again, but were heartbroken to learn that Mammed had not returned with her. They'd had a brief report from Peetee, but he struggled to convey the images of Loming harbour or a spaceship descending and ascending on a pillar of fire. All they really understood was that Mammed had been taken, and instead of a wedding to celebrate a new son-in-law, they were now faced with consoling their devastated daughter.

They'd waited patiently for the Pelican to anchor in the lagoon, for Miriam to be lowered in the bosun's chair, and for the rowing boat to transfer Captain Yonaton to the shore. Then he'd waded out into the warm blue water to tell them the full and shocking story of Mammed's abduction, which Miriam had been too upset to relate. As Yonaton described the extraordinary events in detail, a crowd of Seaple gathered around them, waiting to find out what had befallen the young landsman who was to have married their Chief's daughter.

When he came to the part where the spacecraft had tempted Mammed to climb its ladder, only to swallow him up and roar off into the sky, Yonaton's voice had cracked and he'd broken down in sobs. Rachel, Alexee and Miriam had hugged him until he was able to say he would return with Mammed just as soon as the spacecraft brought him back to Loming. In the meantime, he said, he had a duty to sail to Portkaron on Couba island, in order to tell Mammed's mother, Ma Fatima, of the loss of her son.

Chapter 17
Crossing An Ocean
Moon 3660

As the sled carried her deeper into the empty wastes of Oceanus Procellarum, Ktrina pushed the speed as high as she dared. The vast dry lake, formed by an ancient lava flow, appeared smooth and featureless when viewed from a distance, but up close its surface was littered with the debris from countless impacts. The larger rocks were less of a problem, as they stood out from their shadows in the eerie blue light reflected from Earth. But the smaller craters were deadly traps, visible only at the last moment. Ktrina needed total concentration to spot them in time, as she skimmed across the regolith at twice the recommended speed limit. Desperate, last-second swerves were all that stood between her and disaster.

The last thing she needed was Ethan popping up in her mind's eye.

"Not now!" she wailed inside her helmet, rolling off the throttle as her vision was obscured by his face. She slowed to 50 kph and then saw he was holding up five fingers, then four, three, two, one.

"What? Countdown to *what*, Ethan...?" she shouted before she understood his warning. "Oh God, satellite time!"

She glanced at the console and saw there were just three minutes before the first of the times she had committed to memory. She grabbed the brakes and, as the sled skidded to a halt, swung the rucksack to the front and fumbled inside. The thermal cover unfolded into a large, thin sheet with a cable and plug dangling from one side. Ktrina flicked open the sled's power socket and was rewarded with a reassuring green light as she plunged the plug into it. She tossed the sheet over her back, ensuring both she and the sled were covered and then leaned forward on the handlebars panting from the effort.

While she waited for the survey-sat to pass unseen overhead, she thought about the enterprising astronomers of antiquity who named the Moon's darker patches for what they supposed them to be. Viewing Earth's ghostly neighbour through their primitive telescopes, they could not have imagined vast sheets of lava flowing billions of years ago, then cooling to form this frozen landscape. And so they called them mare, or seas, and in the case of the vast expanse she was now crossing, an ocean.

She tried to picture the oceans they had known and understood back on the planet where humans originated. An image came to mind of restless water stretching to the horizon – a scrap of vid from the ancient archives she'd seen while at school. The memory invoked another verse of her favourite poem...

> Offshore the banshees rage and howl
> To whip the spindrift's scream
> The ocean's blankets toss and tumble
> Sheets of foam criss-cross and crumple
> Grey-green pillows topped with blue
> Heap upon heap of wrack and spume
> Poseidon's fevered dream

What a miracle it would be if one day she could witness such a thing for real. Was it possible, now the Coops had shown the way, that people might one day visit the Earth? She snapped out of her reverie. The satellite was past and she still wasn't halfway to her destiny with LTA14. Ktrina hurriedly folded the thermal cover back into her rucksack and got moving once more.

"Thanks for the heads up, Ethan," she muttered under her breath. "Any more tips you want to share... be my guest, sweetheart. And don't let me ride into a crater if you can help it. Thanks." She smiled, cracked open the throttle and aimed the sled north west for Aristarchus.

Earth 1504

"Welcome Captain Yonaton!" The ear-spliting bellow caused the crew's eyes to turn towards the dockside where a large, dark-skinned woman in a bright yellow turban and expansive dress was beaming at them. Yonaton, who had been dreading this moment, climbed down the steps from the steering deck and headed for the gangplank his men were laying between the Pelican and quay.

"I heard you had got rid of that awful Cardinal fellow," she said in a slightly less-loud voice. "I'm pleased to see you are trading again, Captain." Her eyes scanned the faces of the crew on deck, then turned upwards to check the ship's masts. The smile faded from the shiny cheeks of Portkaron's leading merchant. "But... I don't see my son, Mammed, Captain. Is he okay...?"

Yonaton stepped on to the quay grim-faced and reached out his hand to take the formidable woman's elbow. "Please, step aboard the ship, Ma Fatima. You need to sit down while I explain what has happened."

"That boy always was a fool with his climbing." She fidgeted with the handkerchief between her thick brown fingers and dabbed at her eyes again. The news of Mammed's abduction had hit her hard. "This evil ship... you say it came from the *Moon,* Captain?" She sounded incredulous.

"I don't know, Ma. It is only a guess. It descended from the sky with its tail on fire and with a roar to make your head burst."

"And it sat on the dockside at Loming *all day...*? with just a ladder and an open door...?"

Yonaton nodded.

"Too much temptation for that crazy boy." She shook her head, sadly. "He always was too inquisitive for his own good. And he wanted to find his father, Youssef. He thought he'd gone to live in the Moon after he died, silly boy..."

"There's always a chance it will return and bring him back again," said Yonaton, without much conviction.

Ma Fatima brushed away her tears impatiently. "Tell me again about this mermaid he was to have married, Captain. Your story is full of such astonishing things... I cannot begin to understand them all."

Yonaton called Ben and asked him to bring Ma Fatima a glass of rum to settle her nerves, while he told her of the extraordinary events of the past few weeks which had featured her son as hero as well as victim. If she never saw Mammed again, he thought, at least she should know what a brave and gifted boy he had been.

Moon 3660

It was 10.09am when Ktrina's sled finally crested the southern wall of Mautfrell crater – the closest to LTA14 – after the scariest ride of her life. It had taken 95 minutes to cover the 105 kilometres from Frentzen, longer than she'd anticipated. In addition to two satellite stops, she'd spent a couple of minutes kicking the sled's front skid straight after hitting a rock. She barely had time to race across the crater floor to its northern rim and deploy the thermal cover before the next survey sat was due.

While she caught her breath, she fished in her rucksack for the egg that Stairway Man had given her. She slotted her cable in to the tiny socket at the egg's base and lowered it to the ground. As she'd guessed, it matched the dark grey regolith perfectly. The other end of the cable she plugged in to her suit's external comm-socket. The egg sprang to life and became a six-legged spider once more. As it raised its cam and her vision blurred she closed her eyes. The side of the sled and her right leg came into view.

Look right. Stop. Move forward.

Ktrina willed the spider up the slope to the crater rim then brought it to a halt as the surface beyond appeared. Using the machine's single, high-definition eye, she panned across the dimly-lit expanse of Aristarchus to the north, seeking out the distinctive hump that marked the entrance to LTA14. She imagined Ethan doing the exact same thing eight years previously... and seeing the mirror flashes from a rebel defector – Zach Swanly.

There! She spotted the small rise, zoomed to confirm it, and lined up a star formation above it to navigate by. Then she sent the spider over the top, down the outer slope and across the dusty surface. The view was surprisingly smooth from the stabilised cam as she experimented with different running speeds. It felt very weird to be racing across the lunar surface, dodging rocks on the way, with her eye less than half a metre from the ground. But she couldn't dally, 1.6 kilometres was a long way for a mechanical spider to run, and if her guess was right the rebels would open their blast door any minute.

According to data from the Sok's distant observation post in orbit at Lagrange, the FLOC rebels had been active on the surface every day recently, and always at this time, during the greatest gap between survey sats. If she was going to get her spider inside the lava tube there wasn't a moment to lose.

Range. 1100 metres left, so 900 already run. Ktrina forced herself to concentrate on the rocks rushing towards her while keeping her guiding stars dead ahead. She had a growing admiration for the spider which skittered across the regolith with undiminshed speed and agility. At 800 metres she thought she detected movement and slowed the pace slightly. *Yes.* She could make out helmets rising above the curvature of the Moon's surface. Shoulders came in to view. She counted five and they all appeared to be looking away, so she picked up speed again to close the distance.

Range. 400 metres. She should be almost there, but from her vantage point close to the ground, the rebels out on the surface still seemed a way off. Then she realised the range told her the total distance run, and her path while dodging rocks had not been a straight line. *How much has the zig-zagging added?* She slowed and endeavoured to take the straightest route possible.

"Comm – record video" she said, hoping the spider-cam footage would register something revealing.

The rebels were close now. Two of them were pulling something – a long pole apparently – while one was watching, and the others were walking back towards the lava tube. Ktrina kept the spider moving stealthily, behind the backs of the nearest men. As she passed them she discovered a limitation of her spider's spy cam. She could look ahead, to see where she was going, or behind, to check the rebels weren't looking her way, but she couldn't do both at once. She had no choice but to press on and hope the spider wouldn't be spotted.

Range. 300 metres. She looked back towards the lava tube and froze. *Stop!* Two suited figures were emerging from a dim red glow, pulling a second long pole. As the rebels passed her, intent on joining the first three, she turned back towards the red illumination and crept forward again, descending a slope. At 200 metres she passed the imposing bulk of the rock blast door and was finally inside Lava Tube A14.

Moon 3660

If she had been hoping to see an array of high-tech machinery or some great engine of doom, Ktrina was disappointed. In truth, she didn't know what she had expected, but it wasn't this. Inside the blast door were the fixed rails of a launcher. She'd seen similar rail-gun launch systems. There were several on the lower slopes of Mount Malapert, near the original Armstrong Base complex. The poles the rebels had been carrying would be rail extensions, to add speed and distance to whatever they chose to loft into orbit.

So where's the big secret?

She let the cam turn a full circle while she scrutinised the image. Behind was the blast door, alongside were the rails, ahead was a plass wall with an airlock giving access to the pressurised section of the tube beyond. She trotted the spider forward until she could go no further and stopped at the base of the plass pressure barrier. Judging by the size of the airlock door, she estimated the lava tube to be around ten metres across. The rails occupied a third of the tube and where they passed through the plass wall there was a pair of interlocking doors. These must open when firing the launcher, she decided. A satellite or orbital weapon would be accelerated from deep within the lava tube, the doors snapping open briefly as it passed with the loss of a small amount of air.

All very clever, but still not the secret weapon she'd been convinced the FLOC were hiding here. Had she come all this way – risked everything – just to see a rail-gun launcher? Nothing more than they'd suspected all along? A feeling of frustration and despair had set in when she saw the red light illuminating the tunnel flash brightly three times. Was it a signal something was about to happen? She turned the spider cam back to the rail in time to see a brief flash and the rail doors closing. A launch!

Was that it? Would the rebels be returning in a few minutes? If so, where could the spider hide? Ktrina searched the lava tube wall, spotted a shady nook and scuttled the spider into it. A short time later two of the rebels walked past, entered the airlock and closed the door. The remaining three arrived and waited for their turn to enter. Ktrina checked the time. It was coming up to 11am and she was way behind schedule. Brad Lewis would be waiting for her with a pot of coffee about now and she had an hour and a half's journey back to Frentzen. More to the point... her air and sled power would expire in 90 minutes or so too.

As the airlock door opened and the three FLOC rebels stepped into the cubicle, she brought the spider racing out of its hidey hole and jumped through the doorway after the last of them. She jostled into a corner to avoid being trampled and saw the door swing closed. Surely this would sever the graphene micro-wire that connected her to the spider? She winced as she waited for the image to go blank... but it didn't. The door's rubber seal had not cut the hair-like nanotube filament. Maybe she could make it all the way inside?

The inner door opened and the three rebels walked out, followed by her mechanical spider. She scuttled it under a bench seat as the last of the rebels turned to pull the door shut. Judging by the forest of legs she was looking at, all five were sitting on the bench. On an impulse she said "Comm – record video and audio" and instantly heard faint voices. So, the spider did sound too! "Up volume... stop." The sound was muffled but she could hear one commanding voice giving directions.

"Get those suits off – NOW!" he barked.

She was surprised at the tone. Strict discipline was not what she'd expected from a group of rebels. The nearest one was shuffling out of his suit's lower half and seemed to be the one giving orders. A pair of hairy legs appeared and walked across the chamber to hang up his suit. She felt like a voyeur as the rest of his body came into view, and was relieved to see he was wearing boxer shorts. But what came as a complete shock was the mass of dark tattoos over his back and up his neck. This man was not one of the FLOC – he was Xintapo!

As soon as she dared, she edged the spider out from under the bench in time to see four naked men being herded away by the Xintapo monk, stun gun in hand. Other voices echoed up the tunnel and she saw two more Xintapo in black cloaks, tattoos clearly visible even from this distance, approach the four and begin beating them with sticks to urge them on their way. She edged out further to get a better view.

"Hey! What the hell is that!?" The nearest of the Xinto monks, the one in boxers, was running towards her. Her faithful spider had been spotted, which meant her spying mission was over. And if the spider had been discovered – how long would it take them to find her?

"Comm – stop recording!" Ktrina pulled the cable from her comm and, grabbing the thermal cover around her shoulders with her left hand, gunned the sled's throttle with her right. The machine sped across the floor of Mautfrell Crater as she aimed for the dip in the southern rim through which she had entered almost an hour ago. A quick glance down told her it was 11.06. If the return trip was anything like the outbound one, she would run out of air and power before she reached Frentzen. That is, if the Coops – or their Xintapo overlords – didn't get to her first.

Moon

Mammed had no idea what day it was. So many strange things had happened. He had been trapped inside the spaceship with the man with the painted face for what seemed like a week, but could have been only hours. The man had stuck some sort of leaf on Mammed's throat and it had made him drowsy and unable to think. He had drifted in and out of sleep but had woken several times when the man forced a tube into his mouth and made him drink a thick, sweet liquid.

He had a vague recollection of more roaring and shaking from the spacecraft, then being unstrapped from the bed and lifted into a clear sack that was sealed over his head. There had been movement and muffled noises and finally he was inside a brightly lit room with people in white coats. One of them was doing something to the back of his neck and he felt a dull stinging pain. He saw the man with the painted face again. He was talking to someone and standing upright this time. They must have landed.

So this must be the Moon! He looked at the bright white walls, strange shiny instruments and flickering squares of light. It wasn't how he'd imagined the Moon, but he'd seen enough to know he didn't like it.

"I want to go home," he groaned in a voice still thick with drowsiness.

The painted face man appeared and loomed over him, grinning menacingly. "So... you're awake. Time to put you through your paces, young Earth man... see how strong you really are. You've got a busy few days ahead."

Moon 3660

As she cleared the southern lip of Mautfrell Crater and powered her sled up to its hundred kilometres per hour top speed, Ktrina was cursing under her breath.

"Dammit! No wonder Zach Swanly wanted to defect – he was trying to escape the Xintapo!"

She swerved to avoid a large rock and realised she couldn't continue to steer one-handed and hope to avoid a crash. She slowed to a stop and was about to stuff the thermal cover back into her rucksack when she noticed the time – another survey satellite was due in two minutes.

"No warning this time then, Ethan?" she muttered, as she spread the sheet to cover herself and the sled. "So *this* is what you've been trying to tell me all this time... it wasn't the FLOC, but the Xintapo who killed you?" Justice, she decided, was long overdue.

"Comm – record audio." While she was waiting, she could add a personal commentary to her revelatory video. The pieces of the jigsaw were all falling into place. "So, the Xintapo are using Coopan dissidents as slaves, and the Aristarchus rebel enclave is, in fact, an elaborate prison camp. The FLOC always claimed theirs was a peaceful protest. Now we know they never changed.

"We can assume then, that the Xintapo killed Zach Swanley and my husband Ethan eight years ago. They are also responsible for all the attacks attributed to the FLOC – including our solar collector disc which caused the death of Ian Brandstock, our Minister for Industry, a month ago."

A further realisation struck her. "So why did they also attack their own collector disc? And why did they kill three of their own Coopan Commandos a week later during our combined assault on LTA14? Simple answer... they didn't! It was all a ploy to convince us they were the victims of violent FLOC rebels, just like us.

"Now we know how they were able to 'rebuild' their solar tower in just a few days while it's taking us three months. And now we know why they never release the names of fallen Commandos – their latest three dead were, in fact, the three innocent FLOC members caught in the crossfire between our Rangers and the Xintapo firing from inside the lava tube."

She was silent for a moment, then decided she had one more comment to add. "The lying, cheating, murdering bastards!"

Ktrina saw it was time to go. "This is Ambassador Ktrina Rozek, just south of the Aristarchus plateau, at 11.21am on Sunday

29th August. The video footage was taken inside LTA14 a few minutes ago. I am heading back for Frentzen now, attempting to avoid detection, but my air and power may not last. I pray that this recording will fall into the right hands and justice will finally be done. Comm – stop recording."

She hastily folded the cover, decided there was no time to stuff it back into the rucksack, so sat on it instead. Then she pointed the sled south east once more and pushed the accelerator to its limit.

For the next hour, Ktrina kept the sled as close to its top speed as she dared, racing across the dusty plain of Oceanus Procellarum with one thought on her mind – staying alive long enough to pass her recording on to the Sok authorities. Her suit's reminders that her air was running low urged her to keep the throttle pinned open. But dodging rocks and swerving around craters was exhausting and she knew one misjudgement could be her last.

At 12.19 she stopped to hide from the next survey sat only to find the thermal cover was gone. She'd been bounced off the seat several times by the bumpy surface. The cover could have slipped off anywhere. The warmth of her body and the sled's overworked motor would glow like a beacon for any thermal imaging satellite. Should she wait anyway? Would a static glow be less suspicious than a high-speed one? As her heart thumped and her breathing rasped from the effort, she knew she was using up the last of her precious air.

"Air reserve fifteen minutes. Return to airlock or install replacement air supply." Her suit's warning answered her question. She opened the throttle and sped onwards. The console said she had 21 kilometres to go. A quick calculation told her she might just make it... but only if she could maintain top speed the whole way. Ktrina gritted her teeth and stared through her dusty visor to try to see the landscape's hazards racing towards her. Then Ethan appeared.

"Nooo. Not now!" she wailed as she cut the throttle. He was pointing to her right with both arms. "What?" she shouted. And then she saw it, a crater dead ahead.

Too late to brake, she pitched the sled hard right as the crater rim raced towards her. The machine was skidding sideways as she was launched over the lip. She seemed to hang in the air for an age, too scared even to curse. Then she was tumbling, over and over, cartwheeling across the crater floor. She closed her eyes and braced for the impact.

"Air reserve twelve minutes. Return to airlock or install replacement air supply." Her suit's insistent warning roused Ktrina from her post-crash daze. She opened her eyes but could see only a grey blur and realised she must be face-down in the regolith. Her arms seemed to work, so she levered her head up and a glimmer of light filtered through her dusty visor. She brushed it with her glove and saw she was lying halfway up the slope of the crater rim. A few metres away lay the wreckage of her sled. She tested her legs. They felt battered and bruised, but nothing seemed to be broken.

Crawling on hands and knees, Ktrina hauled herself over to the machine and saw at once it would go no further. The drive belt was ripped off and front forks buckled. Her suit's umbilical had been torn from the sled's socket, meaning she couldn't spark up its electrics, but the emergency beacon remained clipped behind the seat. She pulled it out and switched it on. A red flashing light indicated it was working. *For all the good it will do me now.*

"Air reserve ten minutes. Return to airlock or install replacement air supply."

"Comm – resume external communications." Ktrina could at least tell someone where to find her body.

"Ktrina! Thank God!" Brad Lewis's voice burst into her eardrum. "Where the hell are you?"

"I've crashed the sled, Brad. I'm in a crater about eighteen kilometres north west of Frentzen. But I'm almost out of—"

"Air reserve nine minutes. Return to airlock or install replacement air supply immediately!"

"Yeah, I heard. Hang on Ktrina. I'm on my way." From the wobble in his voice, it sounded as though he was already running. But there was no chance he could suit up, cycle through an airlock and reach her in time. Her air would be long gone before he even got on board a sled.

"Listen, Brad. I'm not going to make it. But there's something recorded on my comm that's of vital importance. Make sure you retrieve it and get it to Nate Adebayo, Minister of Defence... okay?"

"Lie down, breathe softly, and conserve your air, Ktrina. I've got a fix on your beacon. Now *shut up* and let me concentrate!" His harsh tone came as a shock to Ktrina. She was expecting more soothing words for a dying woman.

"Air reserve eight minutes. Return to airlock or install replacement air supply immediately!"

With no better plan, she heeded his advice and lay back against the dusty slope. Through her scratched and dirt-smeared visor she could see the Earth overhead. The blue and white planet was half illuminated by the sun, half in shadow. It was truly a thing of beauty. As her breathing and heartbeat slowed Ktrina decided to spend the last few minutes of her life contemplating Mother Earth.

Seven minutes.

She was sorry she would never see it up close, but hoped that one day her boys might get that chance. The thought of her three sons made her heart ache with longing and sadness. She would do anything to give them one last hug, to feel their warm breath against her neck again. How would they cope without her? She felt warm tears rolling softly down her face as her suit told her she had six minutes left.

Would her mum bring them up alone? See them through school? Or maybe Jean and Daniel would step in and help... maybe adopt the boys and bring them up themselves? They would make good parents. She knew they'd always wanted children of their own, but Jean had never been able to conceive, for some reason. Daniel was great with the boys, he was like a big kid himself when he was with them, and they all loved playing games with their uncle.

Five minutes.

What sort of world would they grow up in? How would her discovery of the Xintapo's treachery alter their future? Would it lead to war? She hoped not, but couldn't imagine how else the Sokolovan government could respond. How would they deal with the knowledge that they had been repeatedly attacked and their citizens killed, not by a malevolent band of FLOC rebels, but by the Coopan state itself? She had a real sense of dread that things would get a lot worse before they got better.

Four minutes. Her suit had now added the words 'imminent death' to its warning. Did it suppose she needed reminding?

And what about the Coops themselves? Stairway Man had taken great risks to get the egg-spider to her. Whoever had built it had gone to extraordinary lengths to ensure it fulfilled its purpose. It had been brilliant at uncovering the Xintapo's dark secret. She hoped the outcome would mean an end to fear and servitude under the heel of the tattooed monks and that evil beast, Daval Nakash. And what about Gunta Krems? He must have known what was going on. The whole corrupt system of Cooper would need to be dismantled and replaced with something real and honest.

Three minutes.

Lunar society was in for a huge shake up, that much was certain. Maybe she should use these last couple of minutes to leave a message for her boys? Would they appreciate a sad farewell from a proud mother... or would they see it as something else? Would she be remembered as a fearless champion of truth and justice, or a glory-seeker who heartlessly and recklessly orphaned her three beautiful boys? Her tears rolled anew.

Two minutes. *Quick – I* ***have*** *to say something...*

"There you are! Hang on Ktrina..." Brad's voice interrupted her thoughts.

She twisted her neck to look up at the crater rim and saw a suited figure scrambling down the dusty slope.

"How... How the hell did you get here so quickly!?" She pushed herself upright.

"Don't sound so disappointed!" He laughed and grabbed her as he stumbled past. His gloved fingers fumbled to release the empty cylinder from her suit's front. He plucked a new one from a pouch at his waist and snapped it in place. "There. That should keep you going until I get you back inside. Are you injured?"

"I don't think so... just bruised, mostly."

Brad took a look at the wreckage that had once been a sled, then at the series of scrapes and gouges in the regolith that led right across the crater floor to the far rim, 250 metres away. "It's a wonder you weren't killed, Ktrina. How fast were you going?"

"Oh, you know... just umm... flat out!"

"A hundred klicks! My God, what were you thinking?"

"I was thinking I wanted to get back to Frentzen before my air ran out. But Brad... I can't believe you got here so quickly!"

"Come on," he said, taking her elbow and helping her climb the slope. "I'll tell you on the way. But you've got some explaining to do as well, young lady..."

Moon 3660

"So, when it got to eleven thirty and you still hadn't showed up, I drank the coffee on my own." Brad was explaining, as he steered them slowly and carefully across the lunar surface towards Frentzen. "By twelve I figured something must be wrong and got suited up. By quarter past I was on the sled, heading west, the direction I'd seen you head off at half past eight this morning."

"I'm so pleased you did."

"I knew you'd be out of air around twelve thirty, so I thought I'd better come out and try to find you. Why the hell didn't you call me sooner, Ktrina?"

"It's a long story, Brad. And a shocking one. Do you mind waiting until we get inside. I'd rather not broadcast it over an open comm link."

"Okay. We're nearly there... look."

Ktrina peered over his shoulder from the pillion seat of the sled and saw the welcome lights of Frentzen's tiny skyport. "I can't tell you how pleased I am to see this place. I thought I was going to die out there."

"Well, let's get you inside and checked over by the doctor – make sure you've not broken anything. And I'm guessing you'll be ready for that coffee by now...?" She could hear the smile in his voice.

"I've a strong suspicion your trip involved something else besides testing that new egg-shaped tracking device, Ktrina...?" Brad Lewis was studying her seriously from beneath bushy eyebrows. The doctor had confirmed no bones were broken and had applied healing, pain-killing patches to her worst contusions. Brad had ushered the medic away, saying he needed a private word with the Ambassador, then sat Ktrina down with a cup of hot coffee.

"We need to remove our comms before I explain... please?" She twisted her comm unit from its dock, but he hesitated. "It's for security, Brad. You'll understand why in a minute..."

He twisted his unit free and laid it on the table. "All very cloak and dagger..."

"I didn't test a tracking device, Brad. That egg I showed you was a spy-cam on legs. I've been to Mautfrell crater—"

"Whaaat! That's Coop territory, north of the border. A stone's throw from the FLOC's hideout!"

"I know," she smiled, "that's why I was there. I needed to take a look inside LTA14, see what big secret they were cooking up. Find out why four Rangers and three Commandos died there without getting inside a few weeks back."

"My God, Ktrina! I had *no idea* your job involved such danger. The Foreign Office must be desperate to send you on a crazy mission like that!"

"They don't know anything about it, Brad. This was a – shall we say – private venture. My husband, Ethan, died there trying to help a rebel to defect eight years ago."

"Oh, yes. I remember now. This was personal, then?" The councillor nodded.

"Yes. I had an idea that some sort of secret weapon was being developed there, but what I discovered was much, much worse."

"Worse! How could it be worse?"

"There's no secret weapon, other than a rail-gun launcher that we already knew about. But LTA14 isn't a FLOC stronghold, Brad. It's a secret military base operated by the Xintapo. And the FLOC – or any Coopan dissidents, I'm guessing – are being used there as slave labour. Aristarchus is a concentration camp and the FLOC is just a cover the Coopans are using while they attack us, destroy our installations, and kill our citizens.

"That's outrageous!"

"Yeah, I thought so too. I have a recording here..." she lifted her comm unit between finger and thumb, "that provides convincing evidence. It also explains a few mysteries, like why the Coops rebuilt their solar collector tower in days while it's taking us months, and why they never release names of their Commandos killed in action. They're innocent FLOC members being slaughtered instead."

"My God, Ktrina. If you really *do* have proof, this is explosive!" Brad was wide eyed with shock. "I see why you said your comm needs to get to the Defence Minister."

"First, we need to make copies, so if one gets intercepted we still have the video footage. Do you have any spare comm units?"

"I keep one for emergencies... and for recording boring council meetings." He smiled and fished a small silver case from his pocket. "Give me a second and I'll wipe it clean, then you can copy to that. I'll bet they have some in the skyport office too... back in just a minute." He got up to go.

"I'll need a data cable, too, Brad. Mine got left in Mautfrell Crater when the Xintapo spotted my spy-cam spider and I had to make a quick exit."

"Spider? I thought it was an egg...?"

"Ah, yeah, it was both. A clever little device. Turned from an egg into a mechanical spider when you plugged into it. I drove it by thought alone, all the way from Mautfrell to LTA14, past the blast door, through their airlock and recorded the Xintapo abusing their captives. You can watch the footage when you get back to your office."

"Amazing! I'll be right back." Brad disappeared from the skyport's small med-bay.

Ktrina had a few moments to think about her next move. The sensible option would be to head back home, take the incriminating evidence to Adebayo first thing next morning and let a whole lot of cats out of one small bag. Except she had an uncomfortable feeling that the Xintapo would be busy putting two and two together right now. After they found the spider they would have traced its micro-cable back to Mautfrell. They'd soon figure out they'd been bugged by someone who'd snuck across by sled from the south – and the only Sok outpost near enough was Frentzen.

They also knew she was flying to Monterey that day via a stopover at Frentzen, as she'd had to file a flight plan to get clearance from Cooper skytraffic control. If she turned back to Sokolova City instead, they'd know she was the spy. With their ability to cut down a solar collector tower with an orbiting laser weapon, she didn't doubt they could zap her hopper if she made a run to the south.

A sudden wave of fear seized her heart. They wouldn't stop at killing her, would they? She could have passed her recording to any of the 786 inhabitants of Frentzen. Would the Xintapo wipe out the whole town and blame it on the FLOC? Were they planning an attack right now? How could she have been so stupid? To risk all the innocent people of this remote outpost just to avenge Ethan—

"You okay, Ktrina?"

She looked up to see Brad striding towards her with a bag in his hand. She was too shocked by her vision of death and destruction to answer.

"You look like you've seen a ghost." He stared at her with concern. "Delayed shock from your crash, I expect. I'll call the doctor back—"

"No! No, please don't do that, Brad." She swallowed hard to keep down the bile that was threatening. "Please sit down and listen. I've just had a terrifying thought..."

He sat and placed a clear bag on the table. She saw it contained a number of comm units, plus a multi-strand data cable.

"Just because I got back here in one piece doesn't mean I'm home free." She looked at him with troubled eyes.

"What do you mean? You're safe now... aren't you?"

"No. If I turn around and head back to Sok city, instead of going on to this Coop presentation at Monterey Skyport this afternoon, they'll know it was me who—"

"They wouldn't dare shoot you down in Sokolovan skyspace!"

"You bet they would, Brad. They thought nothing of slicing through our solar collector and killing the Minister for Industry. But it could be worse than that. Much, much worse..." She reached over and put her hand on his. "They might decide to attack Frentzen to stop the recording getting out..."

"Don't be ridiculous, Ktrina! Attack a town with nearly eight hundred inhabitants? That's absurd!"

"It seems absurd to us, but you don't know these maniacs like I do, Brad. Think about how remote you are here. Your nearest military back up is what... an hour away?"

He frowned but didn't reply.

"How many would survive if they blasted a hole in the town's canopy?"

"But the Korolev Treaty—"

"Doesn't apply to the FLOC, does it? That's who the Coops will blame..."

"Dear God, Ktrina... it doesn't bear thinking about!"

"So... I'm going to continue my journey to Monterey." She checked the time. "I'll be a little late, but I don't think they will take any action if they know I'm heading north. I'll be flying into their clutches. They can detain me there, interrogate me if they see fit—"

"And in the meantime, I can get copies of your recording to Sokolova City. We send mineral samples by an autonomous carrier every day."

"That's perfect! The only thing that will ensure Frentzen's safety is the Xintapo knowing the Sok Defence Ministry already has the recording."

"I *do* hope that means your safety too, Ktrina. You're taking a great risk..."

"No time to worry about that now. Let's get this recording copied and I'll be on my way."

Chapter 18

Enjoy The Show
Moon 3660

"You're late, Ambassador." Gunta Krems' unsmiling secretary met her as she stepped into Monterey Skyport. "This way, quickly. The main event starts in a few minutes."

Ktrina raised her eyebrows but said nothing as she followed the austere woman's clicking heels across the shiny floor. This wasn't the usual Monterey concourse, but a side entrance leading to the State Expo Centre. Ktrina's hopper had been directed to land on the military side of the skyport today, and she'd had a close-up view of their towering new spacecraft on the way in. The Coops were not trying to keep it a secret any more. She guessed it would figure in the triumphal presentation of their technological prowess – their Earth landing and plankton coup – over the Soks.

"The Foreign Minister will meet with you after the event." The secretary directed her towards a security gate featuring the usual bag-scanner and metal-detector arch. Ktrina saw she wasn't the only straggler as she queued behind two other late-comers who were being relieved of some possessions on their way in. With a start she saw they were removing their comm units and slipping them into plastic bags before handing them over to an official.

"Is this really necessary? Can't I keep my comm with me?" Ktrina protested as the man handed her a bag and ordered her to place her comm unit inside it.

"No recording of the event! All comm units stay here and you pick it up on your way out," he said. No smile. No 'have a nice day!'

Ktrina had no choice. She twisted her unit free, dropped it in the bag which had her name printed on and handed it over. He placed it under R – for Rozek, she supposed – in a long filing tray which already contained several hundred others. It appeared she was being treated the same as everyone else. Then she noticed him nodding to another official who stepped forward—

"Move along! You're late already!" he shouted at her. "Bag on the belt. Step through the arch!"

Without needing to look she knew her comm unit was being extracted and taken away for examination. She let out a long, slow exhale as she stepped forward and dropped her bag on the belt. Thank goodness she thought to delete the Aristarchus recording on the flight up from Frentzen.

Her bag disappeared into the X-ray machine and she stepped forward through the arch, which bleeped loudly.

"Empty pockets!" barked the woman with the wand, holding out a tray. Ktrina brought out a tissue and her penlight torch, the new orange one that Darryl Kyter had given her. The woman waved her wand over Ktrina's body, nodded and handed her possessions back.

"This way!" called the next woman, her latex gloves waiting to deliver the personally intrusive pat down. "Open jacket – arms out!"

As she suffered the indignity of being felt, pummelled and squeezed in her most intimate places, Ktrina focussed her eyes ahead. The two before her were being handed a programme by a young man who looked familiar. He turned towards her and made eye contact – Stairway Man! She gasped with surprise, but as the guard had just slipped her hand between Ktrina's thighs it went unnoticed. The guard tapped her on the shoulder and said, "okay... go!"

While she waited at the belt for her bag to arrive – the guards were taking their time studying the X-ray image – Ktrina slipped her hand into her jacket pocket and unscrewed her torch. It wasn't a battery that fell out... but three spare comm units, each containing her Aristarchus recording.

With her bag now on her shoulder Ktrina stepped up to Stairway Man who handed her a programme and said, "Enjoy the show."

"Thank you," she replied, as she pressed a comm unit discretely into his palm. "An event worth broadcasting." She smiled, but he looked away quickly and handed a programme to the next person. As she walked from the security gate, she slipped another comm from her pocket and clicked it into place on her comm dock, then pulled her sleeve down to hide it. Whatever she was about to witness, she planned to record it. Under her breath she whispered, "Comm – record audio and video." A few more steps brought her into the grand hall of the State Expo Centre.

If she was expecting the trappings of a high-tech presentation – big screen, images of the latest rocketship, close-ups of plankton – she was disappointed. Instead the stage was flanked by old-fashioned curtains and from a podium to one side the grotesquely tattooed High Priest, Daval Nakash, was delivering a fiery monologue that she supposed was a long-winded prayer. "We shall return again to Earth..." were the only words that caught her attention.

She was led by an usher to the front row where there was one empty seat. She would be sitting next to Gunta Krems, which came as no great surprise. He leaned his head towards her as she settled in her chair. "You're late, Ambassador!" he hissed frostily.

"Sorry!" she whispered, nodding an apology. As the introductory prayers continued unabated, she decided she hadn't missed anything important, but was slightly bemused by the stage backdrop which appeared to feature clouds. As nobody had ever seen a cloud, except in an ancient archive vid, she wondered whether this was meant to represent an Earthly setting, and a cardboard cut-out of the tall spaceship would be lowered dramatically to the stage any minute. She had to push her tongue into her cheek to stop herself from giggling at the thought. Quite how they would introduce the plankton, she had no idea.

"All hail the Messiah!" shouted Nakash, who appeared to have come to the end of his sermon. "All hail the Messiah!" replied the audience. The High Priest turned to leave the stage and an expectant hush filled the hall. Gradually the lights dimmed and music, faint at first, began to play. It had an ethereal quality that Ktrina supposed was intended to summon up a mood of heavenly peace. Modest lighting illuminated the centre of the stage and she guessed this was where the action would happen. She stole a quick sideways glance and saw the rest of the audience was staring with rapt attention.

A combined gasp brought her focus back to the stage where she saw nothing at first, then just a pair of bare feet! They were light brown and protruding from a long white gown. Most weirdly, they were descending from above and appeared to be floating down from the clouds.

As more of the figure came into view wearing a plain white cloak, cinched at the waist, Ktrina got the strange feeling she was witnessing a religious re-enactment. Finally, the head appeared and the crowd gasped again and louder this time. Ktrina gasped too. The light brown face was surrounded by a shimmering, glowing halo!

"Messiah! Messiah! Messiah!" The audience was instantly on its feet and chanting in unison. Ktrina rose too. She was bewildered and awed, both by the spectacle and by the crowd's rapturous reaction. The Messiah appeared to be pointing with one hand towards heaven, but then she realised he was holding on – effortlessly it seemed – to a slim cord. As he reached the stage he released it and spread both arms wide. Then he began to speak.

"Ay arm riterned!" His voice filled the vast hall, but his words were peculiar – pronounced in a strange, old-fashioned form and hard to understand.

"Riterned armang yo, ars thee pruphesy pridected." Ktrina frowned as she struggled to make sense of what he was saying. She couldn't take her eyes off the extraordinary glowing halo that bobbed and weaved around his head.

"Thee farthfal sharll bee riwarded arnd... arnd senners sharll be paneshed." His voice seemed to reverberate from the very fabric of the building. But there was something odd about it...

"Ay imbudy thee speret uv Gud..." The timbre of his words suggested a teenage boy...

"Ay breng hes puwer arnd hes glury..." and the gaps between them suggested he was being fed the lines, "tu thee fulluwers uv Shendu arnd all ho harve..." a long pause. "All ho harve kipt thee farth."

Yes, thought Ktrina, somebody is telling him what to say and he's stumbling over the words. She looked again at her neighbours to see if others had noticed. They were all staring, wide eyed and open-mouthed, at the glorious apparition before them. Was she the only one who suspected this was an elaborate con trick? She looked back at the Messiah and noticed his eyes were wandering as if he was listening and waiting for something.

"Mey Gud bee amung yo all!" His arms, which had drooped lower while he had been speaking, now rose again level with his shoulders, faltered for a second then rose further and stopped. Ktrina, aware that Krems was watching her from the corner of his eye, hid the smile which wanted to steal across her face. If this *really was* the Messiah, wouldn't he have rehearsed his act a little better?

Now he lowered his arms and looked upwards. The slim cord had risen, she could see its knotted end hanging a full ten metres above the Messiah's head. He crouched and sprang, soaring gracefully upwards, accompanied by a gasp from the crowd. He seemed to rise an astonishing, impossible distance until his hand grasped the cord and he was hoisted up into the clouds once more.

"A MIRACLE!" someone shouted.

"A miracle! A miracle! A miracle!" the crowd roared.

Ktrina had to admit, it was a very neat trick. But a miracle? She seriously doubted it.

Moon 3660

While the hall was filled with applause and cheers, Ktrina turned away from Krems and whispered under her breath, "Comm – stop recording." She saw a hooded figure walk on to the stage heading for the podium. As the monk uncovered his head she saw it was Daval Nakash again. She guessed he would now address the crowd and decided this was the moment for her to pop to the toilet.

"I'm sorry," she said to Krems, "I have to go to the bathroom. Please excuse me." Ktrina didn't wait for an answer and headed for the front corner of the hall where a sign shone over a doorway.

There was no escaping the High Priest's words, even in the farthest cubicle of the washroom. His rambling sermon was being piped into every corner of the complex, it seemed. Ktrina sat for a moment longer to weigh up what she'd just seen, and to consider her next move. It seemed clear to her that Nakash had found an extraordinary young man to play the role of Messiah... but what about that amazing, glowing halo? And his very peculiar way of speaking? He couldn't be a regular citizen of Cooper, she felt sure. And what about that astonishing leap at the end? Nobody could jump that high! It did seem almost miraculous...

Ktrina was about to exit the cubicle when the High Priest paused for breath, and she heard something else. A moaning, keening wail was coming from above. "Merearm, Paapaa Yun... Ay'm su surry. Ay warnt tu cum hume... su surry..." Between the sobs, she recognised the peculiar pronunciation and odd tone of voice immediately. It was the Messiah! Could she get a better look at him? She looked up and hoisted her bag's shoulder strap over her head.

As Nakash's drone from the hall started up again she climbed on the toilet seat and studied the square plastic tile above. It contained a metal grille and was clearly a part of the ventilation system. Wherever the Messiah was, he couldn't be far away. She reached up and pushed the tile, which lifted to one side to reveal a wide circular tube. Clambering on the wash basin beside the toilet and pulling herself up with her arms, Ktrina managed to hoist herself into the ventilation shaft. She reached back down and slid the ceiling tile back into place.

Above the washroom the broad round tube extended away into darkness to left and right. She stopped and listened. The voice came again, "Plise let mi gu hume. Plise, plise, plise..." it sobbed. For someone who embodied the spirit of God, he didn't sound very happy! The voice was coming from the left. On her hands and knees, crammed in a confined and dusty tube, she crawled in that direction.

This was the time she could have done with her torch, she thought, as she edged along the creaking ducting into the blackness. Up ahead she could see a faint glimmer of light, guessed this would be the next vent and shuffled on towards it.

"Ay luve yo, Merearm," sobbed the voice from directly below her. Ktrina reached down through the vent, scrabbled with her fingernails and lifted the ceiling tile containing the grille. She heard a gasp and then a scared, tear-streaked face was staring up at her. She looked down and smiled. He didn't look much like the Messiah now, but his head was still surrounded by a cloud of glowing light.

"Mind out," she said, "I'm coming down." She dropped feet first through the opening, dangled by her arms for a moment, and then let go. Ktrina landed in a square room containing a small table and two chairs, plus the white-robed, haloed form of the Messiah. He was backed up into a corner and looked terrified.

"Hello!" she said, smiling. "Don't be scared. I'm Ktrina..." She offered him a hand to shake, but he simply stared at it, quaking with fear. "Oh dear. Somebody's hurt you, haven't they?"

"Ay warnt te gu hume. Plise lat mi gu hume!" he wailed in his strange accent.

She stepped towards him. "Maybe I can help you. Where is your home?"

"Luming," he said. She frowned, she'd never heard of it.

"Et's en the Craabbeng See..." he said. She shook her head slowly.

"Un Irth... Ee wus braaght hire fram Irth!" he sobbed.

"Oh my God!" She understood that word. "You were brought here from Earth?"

He nodded sadly, eyes fixed on Ktina's face. "En a sparceshep!"

Suddenly it all became clear. That evil monster, Daval Nakash had kidnapped this young lad from Earth and forced him to play the role of Messiah. No wonder he could jump – Earth had six times the gravity of the Moon! But what about that halo? She stepped forward again and reached out to touch it. He recoiled in terror.

"Don't be afraid. I'm not going to hurt you," she said as she slowly let her fingers sink into the glowing mass surrounding his head. At once she knew. It was hair! A huge, wild, unruly mop of crinkly hair that had been soaked in a glowing, phosphorescent dye.

My God, that stuff is radioactive – the last thing you wanted surrounding your head.

"Who did this?" She asked.

"Bard marn!"

"Bad man – Daval Nakash?" She tapped her own face and forehead. "Ugly man... painted face?"

He nodded. She noticed something at the back of his neck, hidden under the glowing hair.

"Let me see..." Ktrina had a bad feeling about what she was going to discover.

He turned and let her lift the mop of frizzy light away from his neck. Underneath was a black oblong with golden pins piercing the lad's skin – a neural chip! She'd only ever seen them in pictures, having been banned over thirty years ago. They allowed unfettered input direct to the wearer's brain stem, and had briefly been used to subdue violent prisoners. As soon as it was realised how inhumane they were, both communities had agreed to the ban. So this was how Nakash had controlled the lad on stage...

"Hold on, I'm going to take this out," she said, fishing in her bag for a nail file. She slipped it under the black chip and yanked it from his neck.

"OWWW!" He yelped.

She showed him the chip. "Who did this? Same bad man?" He nodded. She wrapped it in a tissue and dropped it in her bag. It might be needed as evidence later. She used another tissue to gently dab at the spots of blood that sprang from his neck.

"Right young man. We need to get you out of here, get this stuff out of your hair and see what we can do to get you back home again."

"Hume agarn!" He looked hopeful for the first time. "Gu hume!"

"Okay, first we have to get out of here," said Ktrina. She strode to the door and tried the handle. It was locked, of course. She looked back up to the hole in the ceiling. "This is the only way out. If you follow me, we can escape."

"Iscarpe!" He nodded as she pulled the table under the hole.

Moon 3660

Ktrina lowered herself through the vent into yet another toilet cubicle and looked up at the face surrounded by a cloud of light peering down at her from above. She held her finger over her lips and hissed, "Shhh!" He nodded. The sound of Nakash's sermon, which had followed them along the ventilation shaft, had stopped.

"We need to keep quiet now," she whispered. "Come down, Mammed." She beckoned to the young man whose name she had learned as they shuffled along the tube. It struck her as ironic that the lad who the High Priest had paraded as the returning Messiah, was named after the prophet of Islam. She opened the cubicle door a crack and peered around it.

"Yes!" she cheered under her breath. As she had hoped, they had found their way into the surface-suit store and changing facility she had noticed on her arrival. And, for the time being at least, they

295

had it to themselves. She turned back to Mammed. "You need to wash this stuff out of your hair." She pointed to the wash basin at the side of the cubicle. Mammed frowned in puzzlement.

"Like this, Mammed..." She turned on the tap and lowered her own head over the basin to demonstrate. It took a few moments for him to understand what he had to do, but soon he had his head under the stream of water and was rinsing a glowing river down the drain.

"Good," she whispered in his ear, "get all of it out. I'll go see about some suits."

She slipped out of the door. Opposite the toilets were two small changing rooms and racks of helmets. Beside those were three rails of surface suits in different sizes. Unlike the Sokolovans, the Coops had never installed suit fabrication systems and continued to use old fashioned pre-built suits for outdoor excursions. Ktrina had used them on a couple of occasions in the past and knew them to be functional, but a curse to wriggle into. Mammed was about the same height as her, so she reached for the medium sized rail.

"Think you can escape, eh, Ambassador!"

Ktrina turned to see her worst fears come true. Daval Nakash was pointing a stun-gun at her and locking the door behind him. His tall, intimidating figure made her shoulders sag in despair.

"And what have you done with my Messiah?" He raised the gun menacingly towards her chest.

"Your Messiah is an innocent boy you've kidnapped from planet Earth," she said defiantly. "Did you know his name is Mohammed?"

Nakash stepped towards her and pointed the gun at her face. "You are trying my patience, Ktrina Rozek," he sneered. "You have three seconds to tell me where you've hidden him, then you will be writhing in pain. One... two... thr—"

"Loive her alune!" Mammed burst out of the toilet cubicle, his mop of hair streaming water, and bounded towards the High Priest. Nakash calmly turn his gun towards the lad and fired. As the pellet hit his chest the teenager staggered in mid-stride and screamed. He fell to the floor, arms and legs shaking uncontrollably.

Nakash grinned at the sight, turned his gun back to Ktrina, and fired again. But where she had been was now an empty space. Instead, a blue blur was twirling in mid-air to his left and getting closer. He swung the stun gun towards it but before he could fire again, Ktrina's foot connected with his tattooed neck, halfway between his ear and shoulder. There was a loud crack and Nakash fell to the floor like a rag doll.

Ktrina landed back on her feet ready to strike again, but the High Priest showed no sign of moving. Mammed was twitching on the floor and she knew he needed to be rescued from the pellet quickly or he could go into cardiac arrest. She also knew the only way to deactivate the pellet was using the weapon that fired it. She went to snatch the gun from Nakash, only to find it chained to his wrist, so she dragged the man across the floor, pushed the barrel over the pellet and twisted.

Mammed stopped twitching and curled into a foetal position, groaning in pain. With the pellet disarmed, Ktrina was able to grasp it with her fingernails and pluck it from the boy's skin. She was sorely tempted to fire several pellets into the High Priest in revenge, but saw that he was still not moving. Her Tae Kwon Do kick had meant to stun him, but maybe he was dead? Ktrina overcame her revulsion and pressed her fingers against his neck, feeling for a pulse.

As she felt his artery throb beneath her fingers, Nakash's eyes flickered open and she instinctively pointed the gun at his face. He made no attempt to move his limbs and she decided the blow to his neck had probably left him paralysed. He could still summon help via his comm, so she quickly removed the comm unit from his wrist and slipped it into her pocket. Inspecting his other wrist, she found the clasp that attached the gun chain and disconnected it, slipping the stun gun into her bulging jacket pocket.

Next Ktrina knelt beside Mammed who showed signs of recovering from his ordeal. She carried him back to the toilet cubicle where she splashed cold water on his face. "You brave boy," she said. "I'm sorry you had to go through that, but you saved the day, Mammed. Nakash is no longer a threat to us."

He was shivering but managed to ask, "Huw?" She guessed he was asking how, and pushed open the cubicle door so he could see the tattooed monk lying on the floor. "Hay's did?" he asked.

"No, not dead, but paralysed. I think I broke his neck." She gave him a grim smile. "But we still have to get out of here. There will be others. As soon as you can move we need to get into surface suits so we can leave the building and get to my hopper."

Mammed didn't understand much of what she said, but got the idea they needed to get going. He grasped the sink and tried to pull himself up, but his muscles still wouldn't work properly. Ktrina put his other arm around her neck and helped lift him to his feet.

"Come on," she said. "Let's get you to a changing room and we can start getting you into a suit."

Moon 3660

Ktrina expected a gang of Xintapo to break down the door any minute. It made her hands tremble as she helped Mammed wriggle his bare feet into the lower half of the suit and pull it up to his waist. He had taken off the white cloak he'd been dressed in for his Messiah role and she was pleased to find they had dressed him in grey boxers underneath. She was also relieved to see that almost all the glowing dye had been washed from his hair. The long, crinkly strands were beginning to spring upright again as they dried. She wondered if all the Earthies wore their hair this way.

By now he had recovered enough to stand, and she lowered the upper half of his suit over his head while he worked his arms into the sleeves and his hands into the gloves at their ends. She zipped the two halves together and then passed him a helmet. Mammed looked scared at the prospect of putting it over his head so she told him to sit and hold it for a minute.

"Wait here," she said, and moved into the cubicle next door. She emptied her jacket pockets and dropped the contents into her bag. Then she stripped off her business suit, dusty from the crawl in the ventilation shaft, revealing the skin suit she wore beneath. She heard distant singing and hoped the congregation would be chanting the strange Xinto hymns for a while longer. She wondered if Nakash might have ordered the Xintapo to keep everyone engaged in the hall until he returned. If so, it might give them just enough time to exit the building. She wrestled with her surface suit with renewed vigour.

It took her a minute to get the two halves on and zipped together. She grabbed her helmet and returned to the cubicle next door, where she was pleased to find Mammed was bending and stretching. It looked as if he had the full use of his limbs once again. She demonstrated lowering her helmet over her head, locking it into position and raising the visor.

"Now you, Mammed," she said. "You *have* to wear it or we can't escape."

"Iscarpe." He said and lifted the dome above his head. She helped him tuck his hair inside, lock it in place and lift his visor.

"Okay?" she asked.

He nodded.

"We have to go outside." She pointed to the airlock at the end of the room. "But we can't leave Nakash here, or they'll shoot us down, for sure."

Ktrina slipped the strap of her shoulder bag over her helmet, then pulled a large coiled object from the bottom of the suit store and carried it over to where the priest lay in the middle of the floor. There she released a toggle and the object uncoiled with a hissing, cracking sound to form a long, flat sausage shaped bag, open along its top edge. Nakash's eyes swivelled in his head and he gurgled, but he appeared unable to move anything else.

"Help me lift him in, Mammed." She grabbed Nakash's hands and the boy lifted his feet. The inert body was lowered into the bag and Ktrina zipped it almost closed. Then she grabbed the looped strap at the end of the bag and dragged it across the floor to the airlock. This was where Ktrina's escape plan came to a grinding halt.

When she had arrived at Monterey, her old Zenit hopper had been directed to a stand in the military zone and she had been collected by the skyport bus, so no airlock had been involved. Now she stood in front of an unfamiliar screen which demanded a password before it would unlock its inner door. Understandably, the Coops wouldn't allow just anybody to access their military base and craft. She tried 'Xintapo', 'Commando', and 'Daval Nakash' in desperation but all were rejected. Each attempt was met with 'NOT RECOGNISED' and a raised hand symbol to signal no entry.

"Shit, shit, *shit!*" she muttered in exasperation. Mammed stood beside her looking confused. Then a thought struck her. Perhaps the raised hand symbol meant something else? She unzipped her right glove and placed her hand over the one on the screen.

'NOT RECOGNISED' told her what she needed to know. She quickly pulled her glove back on and unzipped the pressure bag.

"Help me, Mammed!" she said, as she grasped Nakash's wrist and pulled his arm from the bag. The boy quickly cottoned on and lifted the man's shoulders up, allowing Ktrina to place his hand on the screen.

'PING' The screen turned green, the words, "Welcome, Daval Nakash," appeared, and the airlock door swung open. Mammed looked at Ktrina in wonder.

"Help me pull him inside, Mammed," she said, dropping the arm and zipping the bag once more. This time she closed it fully and inserted the latch-lock, so the bag hissed and filled with air. Mammed already had the bag strap in his hand and backed clumsily over the sill and into the airlock, pulling the heavy bag behind him. Ktrina followed, lifting the encapsulated priest's lower half into the cubicle, then shuffled aside to close and lock the door.

"Mammed, in a minute all the air will be sucked out of here. We will have to close our visors..." she reached up and moved hers up and down to demonstrate, "and then we won't be able to talk to each other, so keep looking at me for hand signals, okay?" He nodded.

"Now close your visor, like this..." She clipped her visor down and heard the faint hiss of air from her suit's life-support system. She watched closely as he closed his, saw a small green light appear on his helmet, and then gave him a thumbs-up signal. She turned to the screen and initiated the airlock sequence. She shuffled past the pressure bag to reach Mammed, pressed her visor against his and shouted, "If we need to speak to each other, we must do it like this. Understand?" He nodded, but looked worried. Like Ktrina, he could feel his suit changing shape as the chamber rapidly emptied.

When the light above the exit turned green, Ktrina turned the handle to withdraw the locking bolts and pulled to unstick the door seal. She waved Mammed through and was pleased he thought to drag the pressure bag after him. Defying protocol, Ktrina left the airlock door wide open after she stepped through, hoping to slow down pursuers. A minute or two might make the difference between life and death.

The aged Sokolovan ministry hopper that Ktrina had arrived in stood four hundred metres away across the compound. Beyond it rose the imposing tubular shape of the Coops' new spacecraft which had recently returned from Earth with its cargo of plankton and kidnapped teenager. Both were illuminated by floodlights, and seeing them together gave Ktrina reason to reconsider her tactics.

Ever since Nakash had been disabled by her flying kick, she had been planning to set off for Sokwest in the hopper, taking the High Priest with them as a hostage to ensure their safety. If she and the boy tried to make a run for it on their own, they would be shot down for sure. But she was beginning to have second thoughts about how she would convince the Coops they had Nakash on board. She would have to show them he was alive, and a paralysed, incoherent leader might be considered not worth saving.

She turned and looked at Mammed who stood watching her with wide, trusting eyes, and decided on a new plan of action. First they would need transport – like the sled waiting outside the airlock door. She jumped on its seat, plugged her suit's umbilical into the machine and shouted "Yes!" when the console lit up. It appeared very similar to the sled she had spent most of the morning riding to and from Aristarchus. She beckoned Mammed over and gestured for him to sit on the pillion seat behind her.

He was a bright lad and soon clambered on board, but she had to show him where to rest his feet so they didn't drag on the ground. Then she ensured he had a secure grip on the pressure bag strap with his left hand, and pulled his right hand around her waist. She didn't want him falling off the back. She accelerated gently away from the airlock to give Mammed time to get used to the new experience and then sped up in the direction of the Zenit hopper.

The pressure bag – designed to be dragged across the ground – trailed along beside them without difficulty. Within a minute they rounded the hopper and approached its cargo bay from the far side – hopefully out of sight of anyone watching from the State Expo Centre. She unplugged herself and hopped off the sled, then started tapping the access code into the keypad beside the cargo door. The Zenit responded by opening valves to vent its interior air, four plumes of vapour issuing from its ports.

Once the vapour had trailed away and the keypad glowed green, red lights flashed a warning before the cargo door opened. Hinged at the bottom it swung down to form a ramp. Ktrina ran up it and inside the cargo bay, then beckoned Mammed urgently. The boy hopped from the sled, dragging the bag containing Nakash into the hopper's interior. She held up both hands to indicate he should wait there while she moved to the front of the cabin. These old Zenits had a combined passenger and cargo space, which made access between the two easy, but created health and safety issues. For once Ktrina was grateful for the outdated design.

At the pilot's station she turned the two cabin cams towards the ceiling to deny anyone a view of her activity. Then she called up the last flight the hopper had made between Monterey and Sokwest, selected repeat and set up a voice-activation launch. She then spent a minute disabling the protocol for the normal skyport control launch – an act that would get her pilot's licence revoked under normal circumstances. Finally, she fished in her bag to find the spare comm unit she had brought from Frentzen, plus her hand screen. She slotted the comm unit into the screen and laid it on the pilot's seat, using the straps to hold it in place. Only time would tell if this plan would work, and time was one thing they didn't have to spare.

Ktrina scooted back into the cargo bay, used the cargo netting to secure Nakash's pressure bag to the floor, then pointed Mammed back down the ramp. Outside she used the keypad to close the door and repressurise the cabin. Then the two escapees were back on the sled and heading for the unknown – and Ktrina's wildest gamble yet – the Coops' new spacecraft.

As the pair rode across the smooth black surface of the military section of Monterey skyport, she realised just how tall the new spacecraft was. Flanked by gantries, it towered over everything. Getting up to the cabin door, which appeared to be at least fifty metres off the ground, would be the first challenge.

Parking the sled in the shadow of one of the rocket's huge legs, Ktrina jumped off and bounded over to a nearby wheeled vehicle which carried an impressive telescopic arm on its back. She guessed its purpose, but couldn't see how they could use it. At the end of the extendable arm was a basket which would carry pilot and passengers up to the cabin, but it contained no controls. Those were arranged by the seat at the vehicle's base, so an operator on the ground would be needed. She could hardly ask for someone to come and help them.

Ktrina bent backwards to look up at the open cabin door, an impossible distance above. "How the *hell* are we going to get up there?" she muttered to herself. Then a thought struck her – there had been no personnel hoist when the ship landed on Earth, so how did Mammed get in? She ran back to where he sat waiting patiently on the sled and pressed her helmet visor against his.

"How did you get in, Mammed?" she shouted.

"Larddir!" he said. "Cume duwn..." he pointed upwards.

"There's no ladder. How are we going to get up there, Mammed?" she cried in desperation.

"Eisy!" He smiled at her. "Cleme ap thes." He pointed at the gantry alongside them.

"You're joking!" She backed away from the sled as she traced the trellis-like gantry all the way to the top of the ship. It appeared to be attached to the rocket near to the cabin doorway, but there was no way she could climb right up there... and then jump!

She looked across at the skyport buildings. It was only a matter of time before guards came storming out to arrest them. She would die, of that she had little doubt. But what lay ahead for Mammed? A life of imprisonment and performing as the Messiah... with a neural chip in his neck? She turned back to the boy and gasped. "Oh my God!"

Mammed was already ten metres off the ground, clambering up the gantry as easily as a monkey scampering among the trees at Sokolova's City Zoo. She decided she may as well die attempting to jump an impossible gap fifty metres off the ground, as at the hands of the Xintapo. Ktrina remembered her shoulder bag was still hanging from her neck. She struggled to push her bulky, suited arm through the strap, and swung it around to her back. Then she set off up the gantry, climbing after the fearless lad from Earth.

Chapter 19

An Impossible Leap

Moon 3660

Ktrina didn't look down. She occasionally glanced up to see how Mammed was placing his hands and feet. The boy had an uncanny ability to climb and she was learning from him as she went. It was a stretch from one rung of the tower to the next, but once she realised it was possible, she focussed on the task and ignored the distance to the ground below.

Finally, she reached the short arm that connected the gantry to the side of the ship. Mammed had already edged along it and appeared to be judging the distance to the open cabin door in the ship's side. It was slightly above the gantry arm and at least eight metres away. Worst of all, it was part way around the side of the ship, so that only a dark sliver of opening was visible from this angle. If it had looked difficult from the ground, the jump was clearly impossible from up here.

And yet, Mammed appeared to setting himself up for the insane leap. She saw him turning his feet, one at a time, so that his boots were facing outward from the tubular trellis, while he held on to the upper tube with only one hand. He bent his legs into a crouch, hampered by the suit's bulk and stiffness, leaned forwards and outwards... and then launched himself into space.

"Oh God!" Ktrina stared at the flying figure open mouthed, her breathing halted, her pulse thumping noisily inside her helmet. Mammed seemed to float up and across to the ship's side, his right hand sliding along the smooth black metal until – miraculously – he grasped the lower edge of the doorway and swung there, dangling fifty metres above the ground.

As she watched he pulled himself up, gripped the lip of the doorway with his left hand and hauled himself inside. Ktrina felt her knees wobble as she gasped with relief. It was the most astonishing, terrifying thing she'd ever witnessed. And something she would never be able to do.

She stood there, hanging on the gantry arm, frozen with indecision. Then Mammed's helmeted head reappeared at the cabin doorway and he was gesturing downwards. Immediately below the door a flap had opened and a flimsy-looking flexible ladder was unspooling and descending towards the ground. Then something in the distance caught her eye. Back at the skyport building there was movement – figures appearing and climbing on to a buggy. There was no way she could climb back down the gantry, and up the ladder, without being caught.

"Shit, shit, *shit*," she groaned. They had been so close to getting away. Ktrina looked back at the cabin doorway, where Mammed was beckoning her urgently. With cold fingers of fear clutching at her heart she shuffled her boots to face outward, just as Mammed had done. For a few seconds she stood there, fifty metres above the ground, hanging on with one hand, staring at the impossible gap. Then she bent her knees, coiled her muscles, and willed herself to make the insane leap. With an involuntary shriek, she launched herself into space.

It was immediately clear that Ktrina was not going to make it. She stretched desperately with her right arm, but her hand bounced uselessly off the ship's side a full metre below the door opening. She saw Mammed's shocked eyes as her fingers sailed past his outstretched hand. Then she was spinning upside down but, somehow, she was no longer falling. Ktrina realised she had become entangled in the flexible ladder – at the same moment that it swung back and thumped her into the ship's side.

For a second she was winded and disoriented, but then fumbled with gloved hands to get a grip on the ladder and pull herself upright. She found her right leg had snagged a rung, saving her from a long and deadly drop. It took a few more seconds to locate the ladder below her with her left boot and start to haul herself upwards.

Ktrina's problems were far from over. The ladder had ended up twisted above her and her back was now pressed against the ship's hull. After a few steps she could go no further and had to clamber around to the ladder's other side to complete her climb to the cabin doorway. Strong hands grasped her arms and pulled her inside, where she lay gasping on the floor in shock. But not for long.

"Hilp mi, Ktrenar!" Mammed had his helmet visor pressed against hers.

She struggled to her feet and saw the problem. He was trying to retract the ladder, but the twist had caused it to jam. She quickly pressed the toggle switch to lower it again, reached out and pulled it straight before setting the switch to retract it fully. A movement on the ground drew her attention to her old Zenit hopper, which was now surrounded by Xintapo. Time to activate the first part of her deception plan.

"Comm – call Ktrina Rozek hand screen." She heard a short tone to indicate her call had been picked up aboard the hopper, then, in a clear and strident voice, she said. "Monterey Control, this is flight MSH37 awaiting clearance for takeoff, returning to Sokwest."

A surprised voice answered, "Takeoff clearance denied, flight MSH37." Then after a muffled sound, "You are to depressurise your cabin, Ambassador Rozek, and open your craft for inspection – immediately."

"Negative, Monterey Control. We have Daval Nakash on board. He has sustained injuries and requires expert medical treatment at Sokolova City. Immediate takeoff is essential."

There was no reply. Ktrina guessed her words had caused the desired confusion. She said clearly, "Commence voice-activation launch."

"No!" shouted the controller. "Cancel immediately. That is an illegal—"

"Launch sequence activated," came the calm response from the hopper. "Launch in five, four..."

From her lofty viewpoint at the rocketship's cabin door, Ktrina could see red lights flashing on the Zenit and suited figures hesitating, then turning to run.

"... three, two, one... liftoff."

The hopper lit up as four rocket motors fired, lifting the craft slowly at first, then faster as it accelerated away into the dark sky. Ktrina keyed the pad to close the Coopan spacecraft's cabin door and selected 'Pressurise Cabin'. Then she searched for cabin-cams and turned them all towards the ship's wall to deny surveillance. Time for the next part of her deception plan.

Ktrina pulled her shoulder bag off and emptied its contents on one of the three cots that were crammed side-by-side in the tiny cabin. A green light came on above the closed doorway to indicate full atmospheric pressure. She unclipped and pushed up her visor and indicated to Mammed that he could now do the same.

"Lie on the bed, Mammed. We'll stay in these suits for now." She gestured towards the furthest cot. "Do you know how to strap yourself in?"

"Yis." He answered as he clambered in.

Ktrina rummaged among the contents of her bag and smiled as she found what she was looking for. It was the little black button – Nakash's comm unit – that she'd relieved him of earlier. She slotted it into place on her suit's external comm dock. With her own comm on her wrist and the High Priest's on her suit, she now had access to both. She had never tried this before and prayed it would work.

First, she called up the recording she'd made of Nakash's stage speech and searched for the words she remembered – "We shall return again to Earth..." – and uploaded them to Nakash's comm. Then she directed a call from Nakash's comm to Monterey Control... and waited for a response.

"Your Highness!" The controller's voice sounded puzzled. "You are aboard your ship!"

Ktrina pulled her chin towards her chest and growled in her best imitation of the priest's deep and imperious voice. "Yes!" Then she played the recorded clip. "We shall return again to Earth..."

"But... your Highness..." stammered the controller, "we didn't know a launch was sched—"

"We shall return again to Earth..." She played the clip again, and added in a furious bellow, "NOW!"

"Of course, your Highness. Launch sequence commenced!" The controller sounded panicky.

Ktrina cut the connection, scooped her belongings back into her bag and climbed on to the centre cot. She strapped herself in and prayed to God the rocket was fully refuelled and provisioned for another long voyage. Too late to back out now...

Ktrina used to think flights in the old Zenit hoppers were unsettling, but they were smooth and sophisticated compared to the horrific takeoff in the new Coopan spacecraft. As the launch countdown reached zero and the gantries detached from the ship's sides, a wild and violent shaking seized the cabin. The roaring, rattling noise was horrendous. Convinced the craft was about to fall apart, Ktrina twisted her head to look at Mammed, but instead of looking terrified as she'd expected, he was smiling.

Of course... he's an old hand at this. And he's going home.

She fumbled with her gloved hand to swing the pilot's screen over her head where it was easier to see. It functioned much the same as those in Sokolovan hoppers. Ktrina selected 'external rear view' in time to see the lights of Monterey skyport and Cooper city receding into the blackness below. She switched to 'flight plan' and saw a graphic which showed a single elliptical orbit of the Moon followed by a trajectory – when she zoomed out – which would take them all the way to Earth. It took a few moments to find and deselect Monterey Skyport's control input, leaving herself and the ship's autopilot in charge of the vessel.

As abruptly as it started, the shaking and roaring stopped and Ktrina's shoulder bag appeared, tumbling slowly on its way to the cabin ceiling. She checked the flight timing sequence. They would be in lunar orbit for forty-five minutes before the next firing of the motors set them on a course across the void towards the blue and white planet. After another sixty-nine hours they would enter Earth orbit with a deceleration burn. The ship's computer was still crunching numbers to calculate whether two or three orbits would be needed to bring the ship into perfect alignment for descent to its previous destination – an island in the Caribbean Sea.

Ktrina unstrapped and floated over the wide-eyed lad. She was ecstatic. "We *made* it, Mammed! I can't believe we actually got away with stealing their ship!"

"Guing hume, Ktrenar!" He beamed a broad smile at her.

"Let's get out of these clumsy old suits," she said. "Then we can see what the in-flight buffet has to offer..."

His forehead wrinkled in puzzlement. She laughed.

"We need to find something to eat and drink. I'm hungry and thirsty... aren't you?"

He nodded. "E carn shuw yor."

Ktrina had felt slightly uncomfortable at first, floating around the cabin in her light grey skinsuit in the company of a teenage boy wearing only a pair of boxer shorts, but soon overcame any embarrassment. By the time they'd wriggled out of the Coopan surface suits and stowed them in the netting beneath their cots, the minutes were counting down towards the ship's next burn. They each took a long sip at the drinks pouches and a brief chew on meal bars that Mammed had retrieved from a store cupboard, then strapped themselves back on their beds ready for the rocket engines to fire up once more.

A quick check of the ship's status revealed it was fully fuelled and provisioned. It made Ktrina wonder if Nakash had been planning on returning Mammed to Earth, or – more likely – going back to kidnap some other poor soul. She called up the Selene News channel and her screen was filled with a banner headline 'Breaking News – Shock Revelations'. An excited news presenter was describing the extraordinary video which had been screened minutes earlier on Coopan state television. In the middle of a programme purporting to show the return of the Xinto Messiah, someone had inserted footage of Xintapo monks abusing prisoners. It was claimed to have been secretly filmed within the FLOC stronghold on the Aristarchus Plateau, which was now revealed as a Coopan prison camp where dissidents were held as slaves by the Xintapo.

Ktrina was grinning from ear-to-ear and wondering how her Stairway Man had managed to hack the state news channel, when the countdown for the engine firing began. She reached over and held Mammed's hand – as much for her reassurance as his – and braced for the next round of roaring and shaking from the rocket motors.

When the noise had stopped and her screen showed their ship had successfully begun its flight between the Moon and the Earth, she returned to the news channel and found an update. The shocking revelatory footage, it said, had been captured by Sokolovan Ambassador Ktrina Rozek earlier that day, but there were now concerns for her safety after her hopper had gone missing within the last hour on a return flight from Monterey skyport.

Ktrina checked the time – it was just after 6pm – and realised her family would be eating supper. If they had seen the news, they would be worried sick. She also knew that if the Coops had shot down her hopper, they would have no idea – yet – that she and Mammed were in the High Priest's spacecraft en route to Earth, out of range of the Xintapo's weapons. Time to put them straight.

"I need to contact my family," she said to Mammed, "and let everybody know we are okay and on our way to Earth." He nodded, but looked puzzled.

Ktrina used the ship's communication channel to call Sokwest skyport control, one of the few places able to pick up her signals at this distance. Her screen told her they were already over 30,000 kilometres into their flight.

"Sokwest Control." The female controller sounded surprised at the source of the call.

"This is Ambassador Ktrina Rozek aboard the new Coopan spacecraft—"

"Oh! My goodness, Ambassador! Where are you? We thought you were in a hopper that crashed north of the equator.

"I know, that's why I'm calling you. I am in the new Coopan spacecraft on my way to Earth and I have a young man called Mammed with me..." she turned the screen towards the lad in the next cot and said, "say hello, Mammed."

"Hillu!" He smiled and waved at the screen, where a startled young woman was staring back at him. She was rendered speechless.

"Mammed is a citizen of planet Earth," explained Ktrina. "He was kidnapped by the Xinto High Priest, Daval Nakash, and paraded at the Coopan State Expo Centre this afternoon. They presented him – complete with glowing halo and stage tricks – as their returning Messiah."

"Oh. My. God!" The controller was having trouble closing her mouth.

"So... can you patch me through to Selene News, please? I need them to tell the world we are both still alive and on our way to Earth... I'm taking him back home."

"Just a minute!" The woman looked flustered but appeared to be doing something with her screen. "There... good luck, Ambassador. And good luck to you, young man from Earth!" Her face disappeared and was replaced by a middle-aged man who had the Selene News logo and name emblazoned across the wall behind him. Within a minute Ktrina was giving a live interview to the station's leading news anchor. Her astonishing story was broadcast across Sokolova City and all the nation's outlying communities. It also reached a significant proportion of Coopan citizens, many more of whom were now emboldened to tune in since the intervention on their own state news channel earlier.

In reply to her questions, the news presenter told Ktrina that her extraordinary footage from Aristarchus had already had a seismic effect in the north, where just about everybody had seen it. Instead of watching the return of a much-heralded Messiah, the Coops had witnessed the truth about the FLOC and their Xintapo captors. The implications of Ktrina's revelations would, he predicted, bring about a fundamental change to Coopan society and their relationship with the south.

"Now," he said, after the lengthy interview, "I have a number of people desperate to speak to you Ktrina. They include your boss, Foreign Minister, Jorg Lanimovskiy; the Defence Minister, Nate Adebayo; and even our President. But first I have three young boys who take precedence over all of them – your sons, Jan, Grig and Paul. Thank you for sharing your amazing experiences with us Ktrina, and good luck on your journey. Here is your family..."

The image switched to three wide-eyed, ecstatic boys and behind them, their Uncle Daniel and Aunt Jean. Ktrina's hand flew to her mouth as her face crumpled and her eyes filled with water.

Moon 3660

After three days of being the star feature on both Selene News and Coopan State Television – the north's news channel had been overrun by citizens on the first day of the riots – Ktrina and Mammed were famous throughout lunar society on both sides of the equator. School children followed their flight to Earth from their classrooms and some even got to ask Mammed what it was like to live on the blue and white planet and swim with mermaids and dolphins.

Mammed proved to be a mine of information about the history of Earth since the Ark colonists had landed there over fifteen hundred years ago. Scientists were particularly interested in the aquatic society that had arisen in the lagoon of Sanctuary Island, and the stories of the early settlers' struggles to survive and adapt to the crushing gravity of Earth. Ktrina hoped his testimony would overturn the age-old ban on sending more colonists and that perhaps her sons would one day set foot on mankind's beautiful home planet, just as they had dreamed.

The news coming from the Moon was dramatic but mostly positive. It had been confirmed that the Xintapo, before they had been overwhelmed by the Coopan citizens' rebellion, had used their orbital laser weapons to shoot down the old Zenit hopper that they supposed contained Ktrina and Mammed. Instead of the Sokolovan Ambassador and their escaping 'Messiah', however, they had succeeded in killing their High Priest, Daval Nakash. Had the aged ministry hopper landed at Sokwest skyport, as Ktrina had intended, a Sok health official said that the disgraced Xinto leader would have received the latest in Sokolovan neuro-surgery to reverse his paralysis, and then been put on trial for crimes against humanity.

The Freedom League of Cooper had re-emerged as the official political party of Coopan reform and had created an interim board of governance pending free elections, which were scheduled for the end of September. Ktrina was delighted to see that one of the new governors was a broken-toothed young man called Ewan Swanly. She wouldn't have to refer to him as Stairway Man any more. The FLOC had also asked for the help of Sokolova's Ministry of Defence in removing every piece of orbiting hardware that could not be confirmed as friendly. Over 138 surveillance and weaponised satellites had been identified for deactivation and safe return to the lunar surface.

A band of Xintapo hard-liners had holed up in the maze of tunnels beneath the Aristarchus Plateau. After a fierce battle they had released over a thousand Coopan dissidents, who were being repatriated to their families. Evidence was being gathered for series of trials and Gunta Krems plus other ringleaders were already in prison awaiting justice. Tattoo removal had become the best business in town.

In between their starring roles with the lunar media, Ktrina and Mammed explored the Coopan spaceship, dined on unfamiliar but highly-nutritious foods and laughed at their attempts to use the strange bathroom facilities. The craft was a curious mixture of technological advances and crude engineering, but seemed to work reliably enough. They also played a variety of games while floating around the cabin, many involving catching tasty morsels in their mouths and giggling like children.

Ktrina reflected on the fact that her eldest son was only four years younger than Mammed, who was planning to marry his sweetheart soon after they landed at the port town he called Loming. It made her long for the moment she would be reunited with her family. She even felt nostalgic for her mother's unique style of conversation and wondered what she would have to say about her daughter's latest escapades when she got home.

After all she had been through, Ktrina was yearning to return to a quiet life and spend time with her sons. Every evening she enjoyed a scheduled call with her three boys and had reassured them that the dangers were now over. The Coopan spacecraft had proved itself already, and she should be landing at Sokwest, after she'd re-programmed the final stages of the return flight, around a week after she had launched from Monterey. She promised them trips to The Armstrong Base Experience, Water World and The Amazon Rain Forest Park.

"Who knows," she told them, "after all this you might one day visit the Amazon Rain Forest for real!" They squealed, clapped and cheered at the prospect. She would be sending live footage from the Caribbean Sea in just a few hours, she told them, as the spaceship approached Earth and the countdown to the orbit-insertion burn approached. The boys – now celebrities amongst their school friends – would be allowed out of their Wednesday afternoon lessons to speak with Ktrina before the craft landed on Earth. All were visibly excited at the prospect of their mother being the first person, besides Daval Nakash, to reach the Earth's surface. She intended to go one further, she said, and set foot on the planet, provided she was able to cope with the heavyweight gravity.

"Now I must go," she told them, "and prepare for the next firing of the rocket motors. After two or three orbits of the Earth I will be landing and sending you pictures from the harbour at Loming. Be good for Grandma Sofi, boys, and I'll soon be flying back home to you." She blew them three kisses, smiled and closed the connection.

Ktrina wiped away a tear and strapped herself into her cot next to Mammed as the ship started its countdown to firing. She reached over, squeezed his hand and smiled. "Almost home now, Mammed. Your family is going to be *so* pleased to see you..."

"Tharnk yo, Ktrenar. Thin yo carn gu hume, yur farmely well bi harppy tu."

Chapter 20
Another Big Blow
Earth 1504

Dark clouds scudded low over Loming harbour, reflecting Yonaton's mood. Over a week had passed since the spaceship had taken Mammed, and the Captain grew more despondent with each passing day. He had returned Miriam to her Seaple and had spoken with Ma Fatima in Portkaron, but was at a loss to know what to do next.

Benyamin had recovered enough to take over supervising the day-to-day work on the Pelican, and Conor, his hand now out of its sling, kept the crew busy with cleaning and minor repairs. Desmun had stayed on as junior deckhand and was proving to be a hard-working lad, grateful for the small wage, which he gave to his widowed mother each week.

"Another big blow coming d'you think, Yonny my friend?" Ben had joined the Captain on the steering deck and followed his gaze to the hills above the town, where clouds tumbled over the peaks. Both men were reminded of the recent storm which had ripped through Sanctuary Island, causing such destruction.

"No, I don't think so, Ben. This one is passing well to the south of us. I think the worst of it will be gone by morning." He hoped so. It had been a wild and blustery day and he was pleased his sons, Jack and Ifan, had not taken the Petrel to sea on a fishing trip. Now, as the day was drawing to a close, the gusts were sending dark patches scurrying across the harbour and spray crashing over the outer wall. The wind whistled through the ship's rigging and made a halyard clack against a mast.

"Think we'll take the Pelican out when the weather settles?" asked Ben.

"Maybe back to Portkaron," Yonaton said, hesitantly, "but no more than a day's sail away. I made a promise, Ben..."

"I know, Yonny. But it's been eight days now. How long do we wait?"

"As long as there's a chance he might come back. I have to be ready to take him to Miriam—"

"Do you still think there's a chance then...? After all this ti—"

An almighty bang from the sky made them both look up. In its wake an unearthly boom reverberated around the hills. The clouds overhead appeared to be getting lighter and then a bright flame appeared descending through them. Above it, the long black cylinder of the spaceship.

"Ye Gods! It's back!" yelled Ben over the increasing roar. Both men held on to the great wooden steering wheel as a rush of hot air and noise buffeted them. The craft slowed as it descended towards the exact same spot on the outer harbour wall where it had landed before. Today there was nobody nearby needing to run from the fiery beast.

"Ben!" Yonaton shouted. "Call out the peace keepers. And make sure they're armed. If Mammed's in there I'm not letting them take him away again!"

All over Loming, people were running and shouting: "It's back! Hide the children" – "Is it Mammed returned?" – "Quick, run for the hills!"

After the craft had settled on the quayside and its deafening fire had gone out, some brave souls crept forward to peer out of doorways and around the corners of buildings to see what would happen next. For several minutes, nothing seemed to happen at all. The demon machine just stood there, hissing and ticking as it cooled while the wind rattled shutters and the clouds chased each other overhead.

Captain Yonaton was the first to approach it, striding forward with a staff from the ship's capstan held high above his head. He marched up to the nearest of the ship's metal legs and fetched it a ringing crack with the pole. He leaned his head back and hollered, "Give me back my son!"

To his astonishment, high above, near the top of the ship, a door opened and a face surrounded by a mop of fuzzy hair appeared. "Papa Yon! It's me, Mammed! I'm back home again!"

"Oh... Thank... *God!*" The words emptied Yonaton's lungs and he fell to his knees. He crouched there, gasping for a minute, until he felt strong hands under his arms, lifting him back on to his feet. He recognised the voice of one of the peace keepers. "Look, Captain! A ladder!"

Within seconds the flimsy ladder had descended to the ground and then the unmistakable form of Mammed, dressed only in strange trousers with the legs cut off, was clambering down it. In his haste he was taking it two rungs at a time and looked as if he might fall any minute.

"Careful, Mammed," shouted Yonaton. "Please don't fall..." his voice wavered, "not now."

Mammed jumped the last stretch and hugged his father. "Papa Yon, we must fix ropes, right away!"

"Ropes? What! Why...?" Yonaton was baffled. "To stop it getting away again?"

"*No!* The ship is rocking in the wind! Look..." The lad pointed to the nearest of the ship's legs. As they watched, the broad footpad shuffled across the stones of the quayside. "It will topple over!"

"Then let it! That cursed thing can fall into the sea for all I care."

"No, no, *No!*" The boy was gesticulating wildly towards the top of the rocket ship. "Up there is Ktrina. She rescued me, saved me, brought me home again. But she cannot get out of her bed. We must stop the ship from falling over, Papa Yon! Hurry!"

Yonaton looked at the nearest ship's leg and saw its foot move again. He looked towards the seaward edge of the quay where the furthest of the ship's footpads was inching towards the edge. Then he was running towards the Pelican and shouting. "Bring ropes. All the ropes. The longest ropes. And hurry!"

Mammed, meanwhile, was standing on the nearest of the ship's footpads, in the vain hope that his weight might hold it down and stop it from moving. Amongst the shouts and chaos aboard the Pelican, where crew members were grabbing all the ropes they could lay hands on, came the ominous sound of whistling in the rigging and a renewed clatter of halyard against mast. Mammed stared in horror at the dark cats-paws racing across the surface of the harbour as the gust tore over the water towards him. The footpad lifted and slid across the flagstones, then lifted again and continued to rise as the towering spaceship tilted, teetered for a moment, then toppled towards the sea.

Screaming "*Nooo!*" at the top of his lungs, Mammed half fell, half jumped from the rising leg of the spaceship and landed painfully on the dockside, cutting his knee. He rolled on to his back in time to see the ship's leg drawing a graceful, almost casual arc through the sky above him. Scrambling to his feet he saw the huge black tube that had brought him all the way from the Moon stretch out over the sea and fall into the waves with an ear-shattering crash.

Without stopping to think, Mammed raced to the harbour wall and threw himself off, falling feet-first into the boiling waves alongside the vast round hull. As he surfaced and struck out for the far end of the ship, he could see that the long cylindrical structure had broken in half and the top part was sinking rapidly beneath the waves. He swam with all his might, using the techniques Miriam had shown him to control his breathing as the waves broke over his head.

"Mammed! Come back!" He heard his father's shout from the quayside but he didn't slow his strokes. The top section of the spaceship was settling quickly when he reached it, and the end where Ktrina lay, strapped on her cot in the cabin, had already sunk under the storm-tossed surface of the sea.

He remembered Miriam saying he could swim to the very bottom of the lagoon if he tried. He trod water while he took the deep breaths she had taught him. Then he blew out the last breath to help him sink and dived into the depths.

Below the surface the sea was full of bubbles rising from the sunken section of ship, and odd creaks and cracks as it settled on the bottom far below. The water was clear at first, but a cloud of silt was rising where the wreckage had hit the sea bed. Long before he could reach the end where the cabin was located, Mammed was engulfed by the swirling brown clouds and could see nothing. He swam on desperately, hoping to feel the cold metal beneath his hands, but all he felt was growing pain in his ears and a frantic clutching inside his chest as his lungs fought for air.

He remembered Miriam telling him to blow into his ears. He grasped his nose and blew, which reduced the pain but did nothing for his spasming lungs. He could still see nothing and realised he might be swimming away from the ship instead of towards it. His chest was aching, and his head was screaming at him to head for the surface. Reluctantly, he turned upwards and kicked hard with his legs.

Three times Mammed swam as deep as his tortured lungs and aching muscles would take him. Three times he failed to reach the cabin door. On his last exhausted, gasping return to the surface hands grabbed his arms and dragged him in to a rowing boat. He lay in the bottom, sobbing.

"It's too late, Mammed," said Ifan. "You tried your best. Whoever was in there could not have survived after all this time. There's no point in you drowning too."

Earth 1504

Miriam was with the youngest children of the northern families, teaching them the shapes and sounds of the English alphabet, when she heard an urgent buzz. She recognised Peetee's voice immediately and turned in the shallow water to see her Dolpheen friend leaping towards her. The picture he was painting with his trills and clicks was unmistakable – a ship, the Pelican!

"Class is over for today, children," she said. "Remember to practise writing in the sand." With that she had grasped the mighty dolphin's dorsal fin and was towed away across the pale blue water of the lagoon.

So many days had passed she had almost given up hope. It was almost two weeks since that awful moment when her beloved Mammed had been swallowed up by a spaceship and taken into the sky to who knows where. Was it possible he had returned? Did she dare raise her hopes? Or had Capteen Yon-ton simply abandoned his vigil in Loming harbour and returned to make trade with the Seaple, as he'd always said he would?

It was a long swim around the island to the gap in the reef where the ship would pass through, but Peetee was powering through the lagoon at top speed. It was all she could do to hang on and time her breathing. She couldn't ask questions and her faithful friend was giving nothing else away. She would find her answer soon enough.

Finally she sensed their pace was slowing and Peetee was starting to sing a song of happiness. Miriam looked ahead and saw the Pelican at anchor in the lagoon, but it looked different. As they drew closer she realised why. The rigging was filled with strings of brightly-coloured flags and the decks were filled with people. And there, with his hair cut short, was Mammed! He was climbing on to the side of the ship... and he was jumping!

For a while they simply clung to each other, saying nothing but sobbing and moaning with joy. All the heartache and anguish, the fears and the nightmares melted away as they crushed their bodies and their lips together. Eventually, they pulled apart and Miriam asked, "Oh, Maa-med! Where did you go? How did you—"

"I'll tell you everything, Miriam. But first, I need to introduce you to the people who have come to help us celebrate our wedding..."

Mammed waved to a large, dark-skinned woman wearing a bright pink and green dress, with the same material wrapped around her head. With her were three children. "This is my mother, Ma Fatima, and my brothers and sisters from Portkaron."

Miriam waved and said "Hello!"

"Miriam!" boomed the woman's voice from above. "I am so pleased to be getting a mermaid for my daughter-in-law!" She burst into a joyful guffaw.

"You remember Lucy," Mammed was pointing to his adopted older sister who was smiling and waving at them, "and her husband Sam and their three children.

"And Tom and Faruk who came to help us repair the Pelican...?

"And this..." Mammed was smiling and pointing at an attractive, dark-haired woman who was being supported by Yonaton and Benyamin, "this is Ktrina, the amazing Moon lady who rescued me and brought me back to Earth aboard a spaceship."

"Thank you!" Miriam called out as she waved to her. "Thank you *so* much!"

"She is desperate to get back to the Moon and her family. But her spaceship fell into the sea and broke in half. We all thought she'd drowned."

Miriam turned to Mammed with wide eyes. "You mean, just like the Ark with Chris inside? The Histree repeated itself!"

"Almost. She escaped in a special suit they wear on the Moon. Now she will have to stay with us until they send another ship to fetch her. And after that... I think everything will change."

Postscripts:

Postscript 1:
Dolphins have x-ray vision. Using their sonar systems dolphins can see beneath the sea bed and even through a human body. Dolphins can detect human pregnancy by emitting sound waves that bounce off objects in front of them, which allows them to see a growing foetus through the skin of the mother – according to the World of Animals. Their website is well worth a visit: www.animalanswers.co.uk/blog/29-incredible-dolphin-facts/

Postscript 2:
Cone Snail venom for pain relief. Ziconotide is an atypical analgesic agent for the relief of severe and chronic pain. Derived from *Conus magus*, a cone snail, it is the synthetic form of an ω-conotoxin peptide. In December 2004 the US Food and Drug Administration approved ziconotide when delivered as an infusion into the cerebrospinal fluid using an intrathecal pump system: https://en.wikipedia.org/wiki/Ziconotide

Postscript 3:
Butter on the Moon? Many of the technologies that will feature in a lunar colony are already invented. Artificial wombs are now used to grow lamb fetuses, so embryos from the colony's cryostore will populate the Moon's zoos. Animals will not need to be farmed, however. Growing meat in the lab is well established and once scaled up will become economically viable. Synthetic milk has been available for several years, so our colonists will not need cows to enjoy the taste and nutritional benefits of butter. Plants, algae, fungi, bacteria and viruses will all be genetically modified to provide nutritional and healthcare products.
http://www.perfectdayfoods.com/

I stumble from my unmade bed
To watch the unmade sea
Where mighty swells surge to the beach
And crash and churn, cold fingers reach
To claim the souls of wounded gulls
That limp among the broken hulls
Strewn by the surf-washed quay

Offshore the banshees rage and howl
To whip the spindrift's scream
The ocean's blankets toss and tumble
Sheets of foam criss-cross and crumple
Grey-green pillows topped with blue
Heap upon heap of wrack and spume
Poseidon's fevered dream

Beneath the churning, turbid waters
Below the roiling froth
Deep down where hungry shadows flit
Are silent screams when bodies bit
The crunch of shell and squelch of brains
Leave whispered hopes and scant remains
In silt and muddy broth

So as you drift in restful slumber
Spare a thought for those
Who lie beneath the ceaseless waves,
Know not the peace of earth-bound graves
But roll and rock in fitful sleep
Amid the nightmare of the deep
Their bones to decompose

And when along the sun-washed strand
A wreath of kelp you find
Remember then the maelstrom ferment
And spray and scud and tide and torment
From which the lords of chaos gripped
And tore that stem from rocks they ripped
With hidden lives entwined
(Bob Goddard, 2018)

Acknowledgements:

Jennefer Rogers for unfailing encouragement, map artwork and vital improvements. **Chris Welch, John S Lewis, Molborg Ogrovich,** for technical assistance. **Robert Reeves** for inspiring lunar astrophotography, including the stunning back cover photograph.
Also many thanks to: **Mary Ann Fulcher**, for professional sub-editing. **Viv Goddard** for proof reading and endless cups of tea. **Neil Walker, Skinny van Schalkwyk, David Street** and **Linda Anne Atterton** for beta reading. **Esther Lemmens,** for design, formatting and production.

Design and layout by Zesty Design
www.zestydesign.co.uk

Map artwork by J I Rogers
https://mythspinnerstudios.com/

Back cover photograph by lunar astronomer Robert Reeves
http://www.robertreeves.com/

Mother Moon

Author: Bob Goddard, **ISBN:** 9780956351814

The Earth is facing disaster. What hope for a stranded colony of Moon scientists? What hope for the survival of mankind? Can love conquer fear in one-sixth gravity?

2087 – A colony of scientists is stranded on the Moon as the Earth faces imminent disaster.
1504 – A wooden sailing ship is navigating the dangerous waters of religious fundamentalism.
Two events separated by space and time, yet destined to collide in a simple twist of fate.

When a comet changes course and heads for Earth, the finger of blame is pointed at one country. The entire planet is thrown into chaos, while on the Moon a colony of scientists faces the bleak prospect of being stranded – forever.

Is this the end of Man… or the rebirth of Mankind?

Reviews for Mother Moon

"As a long time student of the Moon and the space program, I was delighted to discover Bob Goddard's novel Mother Moon and found it to be a very satisfying read. Set about half a century in the future, the theme of Mother Moon is how a future scientific outpost on the Moon struggles for survival when a cosmic disaster prevents scheduled resupply from Earth. The science presented in Mother Moon is but a backdrop for the human stories… from the Russian 'Ice Commander' to the bratty billionaire space tourist, the characters are well developed. The shocking conclusion of Mother Moon begs for a continuation of the story. I eagerly await Goddard's next read." *- Robert Reeves, lunar astronomer/photographer.*

"An easy and compelling read that quickly pulls you into events are they unfold." *- Rex Pearson, 5 Star Amazon review.*

"I'm not a lover of sci-fi generally, but I persevered with Mother Moon and quickly got into it. I was hooked! The story, although a work of fiction, is entirely believable… and may well one day be true. A good book, hard to put down." *- Road Rocket, 5 Star Amazon review.*

"I became so engrossed in the book and the characters as the story unfolded. The part I loved most was how the ending left my head spinning – I love the thought provoking style of it." *- Amazon 5 Star review.*

"An excellent read from an accomplished author. Ticks all the boxes for a good sci-fi story with a strong and very believable story line with novel and insightful 'could be' themes, and an unexpected twist at the end." *- Amazon 5 Star review.*

"Goddard's elegantly constructed novel evokes some of the finest traditions in science fiction..." *- CR Putsche*

"This is a gripping book which keeps you guessing throughout and the ending was really unpredictable." *- Amazon 5 Star review.*

"The book is well written and full of engaging dialogue. It's feisty and a bit irreverent from the outset." *- Amazon 5 Star review.*

"A brilliant, well written novel. Impossible to put down. Fantastic story line." - *Amazon 5 Star review.*

"The author does a great job of transporting the reader to two very different, equally compelling worlds with equally fascinating characters." - *Amazon 5 Star review.*

"I'm honestly shocked that OMNI Magazine left out Mother Moon by Bob Goddard. A brilliant sci-fi novel which, IMHO, should be recognized globally as inspiration for young science fiction authors/writers to use for style, composition, storytelling and setting. The Moon will play a highly influential role in the development of our global space economy, maturation of human space flight, harvesting of off-planet resources, and inevitable survival of the species as a true catalyst for our eventual expansion amongst the solar system and beyond. If you enjoy The Expanse, Mother Moon is a must read." - *Rich Evans 111, Enrichment Provider, LEAP Into Science at Martin Library.*

"I heard somewhere they may turn this one into a movie. So I read the book. I would pay full price to see Mother Moon on the big screen. I would also buy the Blu-Ray for my collection, and I don't do that very often. Mother Moon has all the elements that make great science fiction. Space travel, colonization, real science, nail-biting suspense, and a slam-bang ending. It also has something you don't always get in a science fiction novel – characters you care about.

The year is 2087. Armstrong Base is the first international colony on the Moon, located at the lunar south pole to take advantage of additional sunlight (for power generation) that isn't available at other latitudes, and the permafrost that will provide water, oxygen, and hydrogen for survival. The colonists, almost 300 of them, are a blend of every race and nationality from Earth, a true melting pot of humanity. They are not permanent residents, but serve three years and then rotate home. Everyone loves their jobs, but all look forward to seeing their families again.

Then…disaster threatens. A passing comet somehow veers off course and heads straight for Earth on a collision course. If it hits, it will not only kill millions of people, but the regular supply ships to the Moon will be disrupted for months, leaving the colonists stranded. Armstrong Base suddenly faces disaster unless it can become self-sufficient within a very short time. And no one will be rotating home for the foreseeable future.

The good news is that an emergency mission has been dispatched to try to deflect the comet away from the Earth, but time is short and the risk is high. How well the mission succeeds may well determine the fate of billions.

If you liked The Martian; if you liked Interstellar and Gravity; if you liked Deep Impact, then Mother Moon is a must-read. If you aren't familiar with the others, Mother Moon is still a must-read. This is truly one of the best novels I've read in years, with an ending that will BLOW your mind. Author Bob Goddard has used the latest European Space Agency plans for a lunar village to define Armstrong Base, right down to the minutest detail. This is the future waiting to happen, and you don't want to miss a single chapter.

Mother Moon. Download it right now." - **John B Bowers, Verified Purchase, Amazon.com**

"This book captivates science intertwined with dreams, adventure and romance. You would like this book… well… if you like reading. It has something for every human spirit to enjoy. I truly think this is a Hollywood movie waiting to be filmed." - *Skinny van Schalkwyk, Tank Girls Newsletter*

Beyond Bucharest

Motorcycle Adventure Travel
Author: Bob Goddard, **ISBN:** 9780956351807
Visit – www.timbuktu-publishing.co.uk

It sounded simple enough: emulate their screen heroes by riding motorbikes to Eastern Europe in aid of a children's charity. But Bob & Viv Goddard were nervous grandparents, not fit youngsters on sponsored bikes with a back-up crew. Their ride to Bucharest and beyond, across twelve countries and sixteen border crossings, through storm, flood and tempest, was almost a challenge too far.

Ride with them along the Road To Hell, into the City of Nightmares and through the Valley of Death. Okay, that last one might be stretching the truth just a tad. Join them for an inadvertent night in a brothel. Laugh with them at the absurdities of life on the road. Hop on board for the adventure of a lifetime… *and hold on tight!*

Reviews for Beyond Bucharest:

"**A very enjoyable read,** in aid of an excellent charity. Full of admiration for Bob and Viv and what they went through riding their bikes across some of the worst roads in Europe, and constantly encountering terrible weather. As with Bob's other books, I really enjoyed his sense of humour and his descriptive writing brought every situation to life. I couldn't put the book down for wondering what could possibly happen next and how were they keeping going! Congratulations on a great achievement and thanks for another great read." - *Kevin Turner, 5-star Amazon review.*

"**Two north Norfolk grandparents** abandoned their sleepy village to ride powerful motorbikes into the 'valley of death' and killer floods in Eastern Europe. The couple could not have foreseen the horrendous storms, widespread flooding, 'nigh-suicidal' driving and awful roads that made their 5,000-mile trip seem almost impossible to complete. Romania was the country worst hit by the European storms in 2005, which killed 62 people across central and Eastern Europe and left thousands more homeless...

"Eventually we found a very strange, rickety building that looked like a truck halt. They said they had a room. The place was full of young girls serving but we went straight to the room, which was desperate – there was no mattress on the bed, and wires hanging out of the walls. It wasn't until after we left the next day that we realised it was a brothel. I think they could see we were too exhausted to raise a smile, let alone anything else!" - *Mary Hamilton – Eastern Daily Press, Evening News and North Norfolk News*

"**Anyone who has** ever set out on two wheels will cringe: '...violent gusts met us on roads awash with water and mudslides. We hadn't been rolling 20 minutes when we came across the first fatal crash of the day. Impatient motorists nudged my bike with their bumpers. We were constantly cuffed by great fists of wind that threatened to knock us off. We were sucked into Bucharest via a long, awful one-way nightmare of pot-holes, trenches and floods.

"Adventure, danger, hazards, trials, tribulations, humour and some nudity, all told in Bob's self-deprecating, laid-back style. Bob and Viv made the trip to support and publicise the work of UK charity EveryChild – royalties from the sale of the book being donated to EveryChild." - *Andrew Malkin, Lincolnshire Free Press*

"**Travel books aren't my thing,** but it is not only a good read, it is a fascinating insight into life and travel in Eastern Europe. I think this is what I like most… it manages to capture how bleak the real world can be at times without losing sight of how magical and special it can be at others; especially when relating to the people they meet on their travels.

"If you are a biker or a traveller, then this book will give you a very useful insight into travelling across Europe and into the Eastern European countries. It will help you understand the challenges and will probably take you to places of great beauty and history that would have remained unknown.

"As a traveller's guide, this book clearly offers many tips and lessons that will be of great value. For the non-traveller; well, it's simply a book about a daring and dramatic motorbike journey that is full of jeopardy, fascinating information and affectionate humour. It's a great read, both inspiring and informative."- *Richard Blackburn, Energi-Tech.*

"**What would possess an otherwise sane grandmother** to forsake her knitting and ride a powerful motorcycle to the Black Sea and back, tackling the worst roads, most atrocious weather and most dangerous driving on the way? A love of children, a UK charity and an adventurous husband, it would seem, judging by the book of their travels published this week.

Beyond Bucharest tells the tale of Bob Goddard and his and wife Viv's extraordinary journey on two motorbikes, through 12 countries and 16 borders, to help raise publicity in Romania and Bulgaria for UK charity EveryChild. Their ride through storm, flood and tempest, was almost a challenge too far. They even spent an inadvertent night in a brothel!

This, Bob's second book of madcap motorcycle adventures and the author's royalties from all sales will be donated to UK charity EveryChild." - *The Round, north Norfolk.*

"**It's light, quick and easy to read.** Several chuckles. Enjoyed reading something different for a change. Well done Bob. Am gonna get your other book on your travels in New Zealand." *- Satio, 4-Star Amazon review*

"**Thoroughly enjoyable.** I am a normally a reader of neither motorcycle nor travel books but I really enjoyed this. It was a well written, interesting read with the added bonus of making me giggle in several places." *- Jobdonejean, 5-Star Amazon review*

Land Of The Long Wild Road

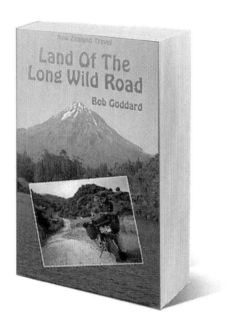

New Zealand Travel
Author: Bob Goddard, **ISBN:** 1898030375
Visit – www.timbuktu-publishing.co.uk

Land Of The Long Wild Road is an off-beat, observant and humorous journey around New Zealand. Bob & Viv Goddard ride two small off-road motorcycles on gravel tracks, drovers' routes and old gold-miner trails into the wilderness of this fabulous and unspoiled country. With hilarious encounters and manic mishaps, they survive three-months and 11,000 kilometres as they battle with the elements.

Lured onward by the landscape's awesome beauty and wide open spaces their journey through rain forests and desert trails, up volcanoes and across river-beds proves to be a life-changing experience. In remote outposts, sheep stations and towns, they meet larger than life characters who offer old-fashioned friendship, wonderful hospitality and endless entertainment.

Full of vivid flashbacks and improbable bodge-ups, their humorous take on life, New Zealand, motorcycling and the art of marital maintenance, this tale is as much a voyage of discovery of themselves as the land down under. Hop on board for the ride of your life.

If you are thinking of visiting New Zealand this will put a smile on your face.

"Want to ride through New Zealand but aren't quite sure how to go about it? This book is as close as you'll get to the real thing without actually going there. Over three months and 11,000 kilometres, a husband and wife team explores breathtaking New Zealand scenery and glimpses of Kiwi life aboard twin Yamaha Serows. An entertaining, well-written read." - *Aerostitch Rider Wearhouse.*

"What's it about? Grandparents and inveterate travellers Bob and Viv Goddard covered 11,000 kilometres of New Zealand's tracks and trails on off-road motorcycles. They met larger-than-life characters who offered them friendship and boundless hospitality; they braved the elements, and marvelled at the country's awesome landscape.
"This is a vivid account of a once-in-a-lifetime journey and you have to admire the Goddards for their enterprise and grit. There are lots of photographs and line maps to show where the couple ventured in the North and South Islands – on roads that were, all too often, long and wild.
"Did you enjoy it? Yes! It revived some happy memories of my own time in New Zealand.
"Would you recommend it? It's a must for anyone who's been to New Zealand or dreams of going." -*Yours Autumn Special, 2004.*

"A wonderful, humorous and well written read about the adventures of 2 young at heart motor cyclists touring New Zealand. You felt like you knew each of the places they visited, particularly because they toured areas you wouldn't normally see unless on a motorbike. What really appealed was that each adventure was described 'warts and all' with some very funny mishaps, particularly several of Bob's so called bodges to prevent another soaking in constant rain, Viv drying out her knickers in a shared washroom and having an all over wash in an isolated place just as a hunter goes by! It has made me really want to visit New Zealand with so many beautiful sights and dramatic scenery described so well in the book. Many thanks for a great read." - *Kevin Turner, 5-star Amazon review.*

"From wrong turns on roads to nowhere, to glaciers and volcanos. Roadbook authors doing it by bike have to beware of falling into the trap of writing either solely about their chosen mode of transport, or entirely about the journey.

Bob Goddard, biker author with local connections, and a former journalist on Motor Cycle News and Motorcycle Mechanics, succeeds in delivering enough information for the bike enthusiast without clogging up the story of his monumental ride around New Zealand with notes from a motorcycle maintenance manual.

Bob, who wrote Land Of The Long Wild Road at his summer retreat at Snettisham, made the three-month trip with his novice-biker wife Viv, on hired Yamaha XT225 Serows. The trusty little off-road bikes took them far away from the well-beaten tourist trail and deep into the mainly-unknown heart of the country, with its now world-famous Lord of the Rings landscape.

He describes an empty and unspoiled country of dramatic scenery, where sheep outnumber human inhabitants by four to one. And he tells a tale of mainly kindness and hospitality unheard of in this country, paid to pilgrims who were strangers to them in a sometimes strange land. I mean, would you take home and feed two foreigners on dusty motorcycles, who most of the time threatened to drip from rain-sodden bike clothes all over your furniture and carpets?

What Bob describes appears to be an appreciation of the pioneering spirit which some might say made New Zealand what it is today. On the other hand, it might just be quizzical kindness paid to 'middle-aged' travellers on the road who, despite the bikes and leathers, appear to pose no risks. Shame we've lost that trust over here.

Rain Forests: The detail in Bob's travelogue would serve as a guide book for anyone wanting to follow in their footsteps - including the wrong turns on roads to nowhere, or roads to volcanoes, glaciers, through rain forests and across desert trails.

It's peppered with humour, Bob's own 'political' comment, tips (if you want to take them), local references from his childhood (he grew up in the Fens), and an enthusiasm for the job in hand - conquering the wilderness in off-beat, off-road style.

And he writes with great style. From the poetic: *"The crystal clear night sky, unsullied by industrial pollution or sodium street lamps, sparkled with a billion stars, and the broad brilliance of the Milky Way splashed a glowing river of light across the dark ocean of the night,"* to a most humourous description from his youth of equipping himself with oversize and almost completely unsuitable German jackboots as winter attire for his motorcycling endeavours (but they were cheap!).

I was full of admiration for his travelling companion and wife Viv, who rode her own machine every millimetre of the 11,000 kilometre journey. What a woman! In the final analysis the book works – it made me want to do it too. When are you free Viv?" **Andrew Malkin, Lynn News.**

"Great to see a sensible couple of my age just going for it! They prove you do not need a fortune or a big 1200cc trail bike to have fun and cover good distances at the same time. Right from the start they tell it like it is, complete with sore bum and leaking boots. Lovely to hear someone so honest and at the same time tell their story as if you were sat on the next bike to them.

Honest, accurate and simple. great! I am looking forward to their next one. I will buy it! Thank You for an excellent read."
Mr M Armstrong, 5-Star Amazon review

Charity Work
Supporting vulnerable children with our books

Towards a Family for Every Child:
A conceptual framework

Timbuktu Publishing has long supported the work of UK charity EveryChild which became **Family for Every Child** in October 2016. Donations from the sale of our books is sent to this worthy organisation which is now a global alliance of local civil society organisations working together to improve the lives of vulnerable children around the world.

    We saw the vital work they do during a trip to **Malawi.** We'd gone to inspect EveryChild's activities there and to meet a little girl we had been sponsoring via the charity. We were so impressed with the scope and scale of EveryChild's achievements with very limited resources, we helped to build a new school block and drill a well for clean drinking water in nearby villages. The little girl became the inspiration for **Tamala Ngomi,** the warm-hearted personnel officer of **Mother Moon.**

Working with EveryChild, we decided to ride our motorbikes from our home in Norfolk, right across Europe to visit the charity's projects in **Romania and Bulgaria.** The eastern European media were so impressed – especially with Viv astride her 650cc Honda – that we ended up on Bulgarian national television and in the newspapers. That trip produced our second book, **Beyond Bucharest,** in addition to many more fund-raising talks.

We continue to promote and support the charity via a variety of events, as well as donations of royalties from all our titles. So if you buy our books, you will not only get a laugh or two from our misadventures on the road, or a gasp or two in the vacuum of the Moon, you'll be putting a smile on these children's faces too.

More information on Family for Every Child here - https://familyforeverychild.org/

About The Author

Bob Goddard was born in 1953 at Holbeach in eastern England. As a journalist he worked first for the *Lincolnshire Free Press* and S*palding Guardian*, then *Motor Cycle News*, *Motorcycle Mechanics* and *Motorcycling* magazines.

Later he was editor and publisher of *Southern Life*, *Microwave Cook*, *Gridiron* and *Tennis* magazines before setting up his own marketing and distribution business.

Today he writes books, short stories and occasional poetry and lives with his wife in rural Norfolk and Cyprus.

Printed in Great Britain
by Amazon